IN SEARCH OF AUTUMN

IN SEARCH OF AUTUMN

BOOK TWO IN THE EBONDALE COLLECTION

MICHELLE DAVIS-NEWELL

SCRIBERITE
PUBLISHING LLC

First Edition 2025

ISBN: 979-8-9930871-1-5 (Print)
ISBN: 979-8-9930871-0-8 (E-book)
ISBN: 979-8-9913474-2-6 (Hardback)
ISBN: 979-8-9930871-3-9 (Audio)

For my Lake Park Family in North Kenwood/Oakland, the community that welcomed me, raised me, and showed me I could be anything I aspired to be. Your strength, resilience, and sense of community are unmatched.
To the people who lived in the buildings: The Horseshoe Buildings (1130, 4120, and 1132), 4040, and Lake Park Place (3983 and 3939):
You are EBONDALE.

THE SISTA CODE

Autumn Gardener sat in the executive chair, facing the Vice-President of Marketing, her posture a rigid, forced performance of calm. Her manicured fingers were a tangled, nervous knot in her lap.

Clammy, restless.

The faint elbow prints on the cool leather armrest betrayed how long she'd been bracing herself.

The last time the thirty-two-year-old sat in this office with nerves this frayed was ten years ago, when she was being interviewed for an entry-level marketing role at Titan & Lewis Media Group. She'd been green at the time, an ambitious and hopeful college grad whose degree hadn't even been framed yet.

Now, a decade later, she was back in the hot seat.

The room hadn't changed much, still lined with large-paned windows that caught the morning sun. The air was saturated with the scent of vanilla incense that her boss swore boosted creative energy.

But the warmth of the atmosphere did nothing to stop the ice from coiling in Autumn's gut.

Across the desk was Kendra Lawson, the first Black VP at the company who had defied every expectation and set new standards of excellence.

As she sat silently, she clasped her hands tightly on the desk, the gold

Apple Watch glinting in the warm light. She looked as composed as she always did. Her emerald wrap dress was crisp. Her caramel skin was glowing; oversized, gold-rimmed glasses perched perfectly on her nose. Her box braids were pinned up into a twist, shiny and unfazed, much like her expression.

But her eyes betrayed her, holding a weight that her polished veneer couldn't mask.

This was not simply an executive.

This was Autumn's professional mentor.

Her "work bestie."

The only other Black woman in leadership who had taken her under her wing, shown her the ropes, and made her laugh over high-priced lattes on crazy, stressful days.

Now Kendra couldn't look her in the eye.

"Kendra?" Autumn's voice was calm. Too calm, betraying none of the panic dancing under her skin. "What's going on?"

Kendra sighed and leaned back in her chair, her lips painted a deep plum and pressed into a tight line. "Autumn..." she started, her voice low but steady, "as your friend and mentor, I wanted to be the one to tell you."

She cleared her throat.

"This is not an easy conversation to have."

Autumn forced a dry swallow past the lump in her own throat. Beads of sweat peppered her forehead as she watched this normally poised and ultra-professional woman struggle to speak.

Kendra's brows crinkled above her lenses. "I want to preface this by saying this has absolutely nothing to do with your performance. You are, without a doubt, one of the most brilliant minds we've ever had in this firm."

She straightened, her tone shifting into executive mode.

Practiced, almost sterile.

"We've been forced to make some difficult restructuring decisions. Effective immediately, the Brand and Communications Strategy division is being dissolved."

Autumn caught her breath.

Dissolved.

The word hit with surgical precision.

Cold, clinical, irreversible.

A decade of relentless climbing wiped out in a single word.

It all made sense now.

The whispers in the hallway.

The sudden shift in the executive team's demeanor.

The way her last two client proposals were left untouched: "on hold until further notice."

The layoffs that had already sliced through other departments like a silent axe.

The firm-wide pivot toward AI-driven branding.

She'd believed… no, she'd hoped that her team would be spared. After all, they were the firm's rainmakers. And until this moment, she was being groomed to lead them.

"And me?" she asked, her voice sharp with quiet fury.

Kendra adjusted her glasses, then clamped her hands tighter. "All roles, current and future, are being eliminated."

Autumn remained stoic, her facade holding, as a cold weight plunged through her torso, sinking like a stone in water.

Her role. Gone.

The promotion she'd been promised: Director of Brand and Communications Strategy. Gone.

"I want to be clear," Kendra continued, her voice softening, "this has nothing to do with your performance. You've always exceeded expectations. You've—"

"Just… don't." Autumn's tone was biting.

She let the sting settle in.

Then she exhaled, slow and measured, through her nose.

"How long do I have?"

"Two weeks," Kendra announced. "Because of your seniority, you'll receive a generous package, including six months of severance, full benefits until—"

Autumn let out a brittle, humorless laugh that made Kendra wince. "Six months. That's what ten years of blood, sweat, and loyalty is worth?"

"Autumn… "

"No, really." Her tone was fueled by a bitterness she couldn't temper. "I gave this place my weekends, holidays, and my daughter's first dance recital. I turned down jobs for this place. I loved being here."

Kendra closed her eyes briefly, tapping long red nails on the desk. "You think I don't know that? I was right here with you."

"Then tell me," Autumn seethed, leaning forward and locking eyes. "Did you fight for me?"

Kendra froze.

Autumn watched her boss, her *mentor*, wrestle between the instinct to protect and the impulse to preserve her position. That hesitation, those silent seconds, said more than any words could.

Kendra's eyes lowered. "I advocated where I could. But I have bosses, too."

Autumn's stomach flipped. "So, no."

"I made as much noise as I could without putting both of us at risk," Kendra defended, her voice cracking beneath its practiced control. "You know how this works, Autumn. You've seen it."

"Yeah." Autumn's jaw was tight. "I've seen it. Didn't think I'd be on the receiving end of it. Not from you."

Kendra removed her glasses, placing them gently on the desk as she met Autumn's glare.

"Listen to me."

She leaned in, no longer the executive behind the layoff script; now, she was just a woman.

"This company doesn't get to define you. You've got more talent in your pinky finger than most execs in this damn building. You are smart, strategic, and a natural leader. I know what you're capable of. This? This job was a detour, not your destination."

Autumn looked away. The words rang with conviction. But right now, it felt like HR gaslighting.

She stood, her movements smooth despite the churning in her gut. "I'll get you my transition plan by next Friday."

Kendra stood as well, her mouth opening and then closing, as if she wanted to say something more. But Autumn was already exiting the door with her head high and her heart breaking.

Outside the office, the world buzzed on.

Phones rang, keyboards clicked, and assistants scurried as if nothing had changed. But for Autumn, everything had shifted.

Once at her desk, she sat zombie-like. Her eyes drifted over the markers of the world she'd built since she had arrived in Atlanta.

A photo of Jordan and Layla, her eight-year-old son and nine-year-old daughter, smiling on their first day of school.

Her framed Spelman degree.

Then she looked at the shelf lined with annotated branding books, including a glossy hardback with Kendra on the cover: *Leading As A Black Woman in Corporate America: A Creative Executive's Playbook.*

Autumn picked up the photo of her children, her thumb brushing across their faces.

Her babies. The reason she kept pushing.

She inhaled, then slowly released the breath.

In two weeks, she would have no job.

But she had them. And thanks to years of being smarter with her money than she'd ever been with her heart, she had a portfolio that would buy her time.

And that meant she'd figure it out.

Somehow.

* * *

THE LOW MURMUR of conversation and the clink of ice in tumblers filled the intimate space of Nine to Five, one of Midtown Atlanta's more refined after-work happy hour hangouts.

Dark wood paneling, dim lighting, and a long marble bar gave the venue a sleek, grown-folks-only vibe.

It was the kind of place where executives made million-dollar deals over bourbon and interns lingered, hoping to be noticed by someone who could open a door.

At 5:37 on a warm May evening, golden sunlight spilled through the front windows, casting long shadows across the floor as Jagged Edge's *I Promise* hummed low through the speakers.

Autumn slid onto a high stool at the far end of the bar; close enough to feel part of the energy, far enough to be left alone. The edge of her blazer brushed the counter as she shrugged it off and draped it across the back of her seat.

She gave a subtle nod to her favorite bartender.

Before she could get comfortable, a man with a loosened tie and overbearing cologne sat down next to her.

"Hey, sexy," he drawled with a smug grin, leaning into her space. "You look like you're waiting for a man like me to—"

Her hand shot up abruptly. "Bruh," she snapped, not bothering to look at him. "Not even right now."

He blinked, startled. "Damn. I was only trying to—"

She tilted her head just enough for him to see the menacing glint in her eyes, instantly shutting him down. He raised his hands in surrender and slid out of the seat, muttering "bitch" under his breath as he walked away.

The bartender approached with a look of amused sympathy. "What can I get you, Ms. Autumn?"

"Whiskey Sour," she answered, trying but failing to muster a smile.

Her voice stayed steady, but her fingers gave her away, tapping softly on the bar, curling, then flattening again.

As the bartender moved off, she caught her reflection in the mirror behind the shelves: deep brown eyes rimmed in black eyeliner, expressive even in exhaustion; cocoa-brown skin bathed in soft light; full lips pressed into a line that once curved into easy laughter.

Her natural curls, usually tucked into a tight bun, had started to fray, rebelling like they knew the day had unraveled her.

At five-feet-seven, with a body that once leaned more sharply athletic, Autumn now lived in the soft space between toned and gently padded.

A hint of pudge had settled at her midsection, the kind that came from skipped workouts and stress-laced snacking. But her curvy size twelve still held its power.

Normally, she moved in this place like a woman in control. But tonight, she looked like she was trying not to crack in public.

Her thumb instinctively went to the inside of her left wrist, tracing the name inked in delicate script there: *Asia.*

A promise made in grief before she'd fled Chicago for a new life. A tether to the girl she used to be. A reminder that she had survived loss before.

Her phone buzzed as the bartender returned with her drink. She pulled it from her purse and saw the message light up:

KENDRA

I know where you are. Stay put.

I need a drink too.

Autumn smirked. Of course, she would need a drink.

Ten minutes later, Kendra strode into the bar, her black-and-gold pumps clicking confidently against the polished floor. Her dress was still pristine, not a wrinkle in sight, and her braids held their polish. She looked every bit the powerhouse one would expect to see gracing the cover of Forbes Women.

But when her eyes locked with Autumn's, something vulnerable flickered behind those gold-rimmed glasses.

She slid onto the barstool next to her. "You kicked it off without me?"

"I needed a head start," Autumn said flatly, lifting her glass. "This is round two."

The bartender approached, and Kendra ordered without looking up. "Old Fashioned, heavy on the bourbon. Thanks."

They sat in a pocket of silence as the music changed. Lauryn Hill's *Killing Me Softly* floated through the speakers, sounding like a confessional.

Kendra shifted. "You okay?"

Autumn looked straight ahead. "I will be."

"I figured you'd be pissed."

"You figured right."

"I didn't want it to go down like this."

"And yet," Autumn bit, her voice laced with sarcasm, "here we are."

Lauryn's voice carried the chorus between them, mirroring the thick tension.

Autumn waved for a refill.

"Chris must be getting the kids this weekend," Kendra assessed.

"You know," Autumn side-eyed her, "you could've gone home. I don't need a babysitter."

"I didn't come as your boss," Kendra replied. "I came because I know what it's like to walk out of that building, wondering who the hell you are without the job you poured your heart and soul into for years."

Autumn's head tilted. "Is that supposed to make me feel better?"

"No," Kendra retorted. "It's supposed to make you feel less alone."

The bartender placed their drinks in front of them.

Kendra took a slow sip before speaking again.

"I've been at that company for fifteen years. Mentored interns who now outrank me. Smiled through being labeled 'aggressive.' Was called 'intimidating' for speaking plainly. You think I don't know what it's like to give a place your soul and get your spine stepped on in return?"

Autumn stared into her glass. "You could've said something. You could've warned me."

"I wanted to," Kendra confessed quietly. "But I was fighting to keep my seat at the table. I thought if I could hold on long enough, I could pull you into the room with me."

Autumn turned to her. "So did you fight for me... or just for your seat?"

Kendra's gaze held steady. "I fought for both." She drained her drink slowly. "And I lost one."

The words landed like a slap and a balm all at once.

Autumn closed her eyes, trying not to let the emotion overtake her. She lifted her drink and stared down at the amber swirl. "You know, I thought I had made it. I really believed if I kept my head down, worked my ass off, didn't ruffle too many feathers—"

"You'd be safe," Kendra finished.

Autumn nodded. "I played the game. I followed the blueprint you gave me."

"We always follow the rules. And then they move the goalposts."

"That part," Autumn echoed dryly, sipping from her glass. "I gave them everything." Her voice cracked. "I missed so many firsts with my daughter. Fired off emails from the ER while my son was getting a breathing treatment after a damn asthma attack. Led pitches while my marriage was falling apart." She shook her head slowly. "All for what?"

"I know." Kendra turned to face her fully. "You gave them brilliance. Strategy. Loyalty. But they were never going to return it the way you deserved. You were exceptional, but you would never be exempt."

Autumn took another long sip, willing the tightness in her chest to dissolve with the liquor. She let the syrupy sweetness and the burn of the bourbon coat her tongue, a liquid haze attempting to numb the sharp edges of her day.

"So, what about the rest of the team? Are they all gone?"

Kendra stared into her glass, her lips pursing.

Autumn's head shook with a rueful grimace. "So, who did they keep?"

"Walter Schumaker." The name flowed from Kendra's lips with bitterness.

"Oh, that's fucking rich!" Autumn exploded. "He hasn't been there half as long as me, and he's mediocre even on his best day."

"You think I don't know this?"

A few seconds of tense silence followed before Kendra leaned in slightly, her voice lowered. "You think it didn't kill me to sit there, brag about your numbers, your portfolio, only to watch them nod and choose the white dude with half your talent? I went toe to toe in those meetings. But the game is rigged. They made a business decision. And I had to protect my seat so I could keep fighting from the inside."

Autumn grunted and threw her hands in the air. "Why the hell did I give them so much?"

"The same reason I did," Kendra answered. "Because we thought if we were twice as good, we'd be okay."

Autumn's laugh was rueful. "That lie again." She cocked her head. "You want to know the real kicker? I was so close. So damn close to that promotion. You told me I was next."

"You were."

The cloud of silence loomed over them, testing their professional friendship.

Kendra broke it with a sigh. "I will not pretend that keeping this from you wasn't a betrayal of the sister code. And I'm not asking you to forgive me."

"Good," Autumn said, half joking. "Because I don't."

Kendra cracked a muted smile. "But I hope someday you'll understand. That, sometimes, we do what we have to so that at least one of us makes it to the other side."

Autumn drained the last of her drink, feeling it burn all the way down.

She set the glass down and reached for her purse. Pulling out a hundred-dollar bill, she stood.

"I gotta get home," she said, feeling the subtle effects of the alcohol.

Kendra nodded. "I figured. And it's on me."

Autumn didn't protest as she put the cash back in her purse.

"Promise me one thing," Kendra added.

Autumn raised an eyebrow. "What's that?"

"Don't shrink from this. Never let them make you feel like you were less than."

Autumn's eyes welled. "You taught me to advocate for myself in that place. Don't be surprised when I finally start doing it."

Kendra offered a faint, bittersweet smile. "That's my girl."

Autumn didn't respond. Instead, she walked out into the night, her shoulders squared.

2

SAME LIE ON REPEAT

The opening chords of Jazmine Sullivan's *Bust Your Windows* screamed from Autumn's phone, waking her from a deep sleep.

That ringtone was reserved for one person, and she'd set it with deliberate, unapologetic intention.

Petty? Absolutely. A necessary reminder? Without a doubt.

It wasn't about feelings. It was about remembering who the hell he was and making sure she never forgot.

Chris Wallace.

The man she'd given fifteen years, two children, and the entirety of her nervous system to.

He was the smooth-talking Howard sophomore she'd fallen for in her freshman year at Spelman; the one she'd married months after graduation, convinced his promises were a foundation she could build a life on.

She divorced him a year ago after realizing the foundation was cracked beyond repair.

She stared at the ceiling, the haze of Sunday morning coming sharper into focus as the buzzing stopped and started again. She looked over and grabbed the phone off her pillow.

Why was he calling so early? It was 9:07. He shouldn't be bringing the kids home until at least late afternoon.

A short chime signaled that he'd texted after she didn't answer. Because, of course, he couldn't send a voicemail like a normal adult.

CHRIS

Dropping the kids off after their cousin's b-day thing. Should be back from the party around 5. I'll pick up another inhaler for Jordan on the way. He told me he's running low.

That she'd have extra time to sulk was surprisingly refreshing. She tapped a quick "*OK*," then buried her face in the pillow.

Moments later, the phone buzzed again. She held it above her head, squinting to read.

CHRIS

Jordan can't wait to show you his new crossover. Prepare to be impressed. He gets it from his daddy.

He ended the text with a smile emoji.

She exhaled through her nose, a bitter laugh bubbling in her throat.

That man still acts like we're cool, she thought.

Like he hadn't turned her world inside out with more than a decade and a half of dishonesty, half-truths, and hollow apologies.

She swiped out a reply with low energy—

Can't wait to see my lil man 🤍🤍🤍

—and dropped the phone on the mattress.

Sunlight filtered in through sheer curtains, painting soft lines across her comforter. This was indeed a late start for her.

Normally, she would've been halfway through a face mask, coffee in hand, with her personalized Spotify "Sunday Zen" playlist floating through the house while she worked on a pitch deck for the coming week.

But this morning, she'd barely made it out of her dreams.

And even those had felt heavy.

She inhaled slowly, eyes closed, tracing her Asia tattoo.

Her fingers lingered on the ink, a ritual that usually grounded her.

Today, it only reminded her that loss had become a pattern she couldn't outrun.

Autumn had told no one about the layoff yet.

Not her best friend and godfather to her children, Amir.

Not her sister, Mia.

Not her kids.

Not even Chris, who would probably smirk his way through some self-righteous monologue about how much she'd invested in that job, even to the detriment of missing out on things at home.

It wasn't lost on her that they hadn't let her go immediately. She was expected to show up on Monday morning as if nothing had changed.

Like her ten years of loyalty weren't being boxed and archived.

That two-week notice wasn't a courtesy; it was a leash.

Their way of ensuring the completion of her final, most pivotal project with grace before disappearing quietly. Because that's who she'd been.

The ever-diligent corporate diehard.

The project was her baby: the Jefferson and Johnson account. It wasn't just the firm's biggest client; it was a massive, Black-owned multimedia company Autumn had championed from day one.

For over a year, she had poured herself into building the strategy for Jefferson and Johnson's historic expansion into the African market.

The Ghana launch was her brainchild, a bridge she was building between Black audiences across the diaspora.

It was legacy work.

And now, she was expected to pass her soul to the next person in line quietly.

But the thought of opening her work laptop, which was usually a Pavlovian response, felt like lifting lead today.

She sat up slowly, adjusted her bonnet, threw on a pair of boxers and the oversized Chicago Bulls sweatshirt Amir had given her last Christmas, and walked to the kitchen barefoot.

The house was still.

Too still, without the usual clatter of the kids arguing over mundane stuff, or the typical smell of bacon and waffles.

Now, the silence amplified the ache.

She poured herself a cup of coffee from the pot she'd set to auto-brew every morning, dolling it up with a mixture of French vanilla and caramel creamers. She sipped and reclined against the porcelain counter, staring at nothing.

The coffee tasted like cardboard. Her shoulders sagged like they belonged to someone twice her age. Even standing upright felt like an effort.

The cell phone rang. This time, the fun, playful energy of *Hey Ya* by Outkast belted out. A look of joy spread over her face as she answered.

"You must be sensing this funk," Autumn joked and walked back to her bedroom, coffee mug in hand.

"It's so loud," Amir returned on cue, "I could smell it all the way in Chicago."

Amir Jackson was Autumn's first true friend. Before Atlanta, before Chris, before the life she built and the one that fell apart, there was the easy, unconditional acceptance of her best friend.

They met as nine-year-olds in the fourth grade, two kids from the same block navigating the same world in the urban community of Ebondale.

It was Asia, however, that braided their friendship together a year later. She named them the legendary "Triple A" squad, turning their duo into a sacred trio with an unbreakable bond, a loyalty Autumn felt deep in her bones even now.

She laughed heartily, a deep guffaw that almost made her spill her coffee.

"Please. It's called aromatherapy."

"Yeah, okay." His laugh was rich. "All I'm getting is coffee and that pink and black silk bonnet. Tell me I'm wrong."

She snatched the bonnet from her head and flung it across the room. "You're wrong," she lied as she plopped on the bed.

"That bonnet been through some things," he joked. "If it could talk..."

"It would tell you to mind your ashy business and put some lotion on those crusty ankles."

"See, that's why we can't have nice moments," he muttered in jest.

Autumn could hear him moving. Bags shifting, keys jangling.

"For your nosy and nappy info, I just bought shea butter. Are you still in bed?"

"I'm bed adjacent."

He laughed. "So, yes."

She sipped her coffee and stared out the window, her demeanor shifting.

"I'm tired, Amir."

"I figured. Your texts been giving 'bare minimum, don't ask me nothing' vibes."

A smile crept in, but it faded fast. "Yeah."

He didn't push to try to fill the silence that followed. He waited.

She took another sip. "Chris has the kids. The house is too quiet. That's all."

"Mmhmm." Autumn could hear his car start. "I know that's not all, but I'm gonna let'chu cook."

She rolled her eyes with an airy chuckle.

"You ever think about moving back home?" he asked casually.

"To Ebondale?" Her brow arched. "Is that a real question, or are you bored in traffic?"

"Nah, just thinking."

She put her cup on the nightstand and leaned back into the bed. "You know I'm not built for Chicago winters anymore."

"Woman, it's snow. Nature's dandruff. Calm down."

"I'm serious," she laughed. "I've been gone a long time. But, I've heard how different things are now."

"Yeah, it is. Ebondale has completely changed. The youth center's growing. We got a garden now. Real lettuce and everything."

The pride rang in his voice.

"Look at you. Homestead Zaddy."

"Wow," he deadpanned.

"What?"

"Don't ever say that again."

They both laughed, and it opened something up in her. It was enough to break through the funk.

"You good though, for real?" he asked. "Like... really good?"

Autumn hesitated, the words *I lost my job* pressing against the back of her teeth. For a second, it almost tumbled out, but she swallowed it back, the truth catching like gravel in her throat.

Then she sighed.

"I got laid off."

Silence.

"Damn," he finally said, his voice softer now. "When?"

"Friday. I still have to work the next two weeks. Like it's business as usual."

"And you haven't told anybody?"

"Not yet. You're the first."

More silence.

"I'm sorry, Aut. They don't even know what they're losing."

A knot formed in her throat, but she quickly swallowed it down. "They know. That's why they waited til after I built that campaign. And why they're giving me time to finalize it. I know the game."

"Still. You deserve better."

She didn't argue.

"Do you need anything?"

Her heart smiled. That was Amir.

"No. Financially, I'll be okay for a while."

"Right. And emotionally?"

"Same." The single word was like dust in her mouth.

That may have been the biggest lie yet.

* * *

At 12:39 in the afternoon, Autumn was back in bed, mug refilled, streaming season three of *Living Single.*

Still in the same sweatshirt.

Still not ready to face the rest of the day.

Her phone lit up again. Her sister Mia was FaceTiming her.

Mia Samuels was Autumn's half-sister, but that word didn't even begin to cover the tea.

Their father, a man with messy timing and wandering loyalties, had gotten both their mothers pregnant at damn near the same time. The result was two girls, born six months apart, growing up in the same Ebondale zip code but in two different worlds.

Mia was from the projects known as The Bricks.

Autumn was a few blocks away, in the house she shared with her mother and their father. He'd kept them separate on purpose, a cold, unspoken rule with no "why" attached.

When they were adults, Mia had been the one to reach out, the one to build the bridge their father had always refused to. And that first "hello" was the best thing that ever happened to Autumn.

But "best" also meant she knew her too damn well.

Mia had a Ph.D. in spotting her sister's bullshit. Autumn was not in the mood to be dragged right now.

She sighed before pressing accept. She placed the phone below her chin to avoid showing her face. "What?" she answered, her tone dry.

Mia squinted at the screen. "Why am I looking into your nasty nose? Where's your face? Pull the camera up. I need to see if I should call an ambulance or just roast you."

"You got jokes," Autumn muttered, but obliged and faked a smile, her face now fully visible.

"Damn." Mia took a sip from a green smoothie. "That's your pamper-me Sunday look?"

"It's my leave-me-alone look."

"Oh. That's cute. It's giving 'midlife crisis, while I'm in my thirties.'"

Autumn rolled her eyes. "What do you want, Mia?"

"I wanted to see if you were still alive. I ain't heard from you all weekend. You didn't even post your 'Sunday reset' story on the 'gram."

"I'm just a lil tired."

Mia narrowed her eyes. "You're never 'just tired.' You're exhausted, overwhelmed, but never 'just tired.' So... what's really up?"

Autumn paused. For half a second, she considered blurting it out.

After confessing to Amir, her emotional energy was spent. She didn't have it in her to tell the story again, to see the pity in her sister's eyes.

"Work's been a lot," she said instead.

Mia leaned back in her chair. "So, lying to your big sis, huh?"

"You're only six months older than me."

"Don't matter. That's still older."

Autumn sighed and changed the subject. "How are my nephews?"

"The twins are doing what four-year-olds do. Being messy and loud as usual. Malcolm is getting disrespectful with the mouth, so I've had to check him a couple of times."

"He's a teenager, sis. You know how it is."

"Yeah, well, you'll be on this side of mommy-hood in a few years," Mia retorted.

"Tell them Auntie Aut said *hey*."

"You can tell 'em yourself." Mia leaned closer to the screen. "You gonna tell me what's really going on, or do I need to call Amir to get the tea?"

She looked down at her chipped nail polish and let the silence stretch out until even the air seemed heavy.

"I got laid off," she admitted finally.

Mia blinked. "Wait, what the hell? They laid you off? After everything you've accomplished there? All the awards you won?"

Autumn nodded slowly. "Ten years. Gone in thirty minutes. Kendra couldn't even look me in the eye."

Mia was silent for a moment. "Have you told the kids?"

She shook her head. "Not yet. I just... I need a minute to breathe first. And figure out what the hell I'm gonna do."

Mia softened. "You don't have to figure it all out today. And you don't have to do it alone either."

"I know," Autumn acknowledged, her voice barely above a whisper.

"Look..." Mia continued, "You can come here. Bring the kids. Stay with us for a while until you sort things out. The boys will be hyped to have Layla and Jordan around."

Autumn's smile was small and tired. "That sounds good. A nice summer getaway. You sure, though? Seems like you've got your hands full."

"I'm built for chaos," Mia said, grinning. "Come on home, sis. It'll be fun. The kids can see their godfather, Amir, and you can relax for once."

Mia's offer floated in the air, like a tempting lifeline. Autumn chewed on her lower lip, her thoughts racing. "Let me think about it, okay?"

"Don't think too long." Mia's voice was warm. "'Cause you'll think yourself out of it. Just come home, even if only for a visit."

"I'll call you back," Autumn promised. A few minutes later, she said goodbye to her sister and let the silence of her home rush back in.

At 4:57 p.m., she was still in the same sweatshirt but threw on yoga pants in anticipation of Chris arriving with the kids. Her hair was pulled into a curly ponytail on top of her head, her skin barefaced.

The bell rang at 5:02.

When the door opened, Jordan was bouncing on the balls of his feet, all energy and smiles.

"Hey, Ma!"

He was a miniature echo of his father; the same soft, caramel-colored skin, the same wide grin, with a wild halo of curls that defied gravity. Looking at him was sometimes like seeing a ghost of the man she'd married before she knew the full story.

"Watch this!" He spun past her into the living room and immediately started practicing his crossover on the hardwood floor.

And then there was Layla, with the attitude of someone much older than her nine years.

"He is so annoying." She trailed behind Jordan, glitter shimmering on her cheeks, a half-eaten cupcake held carefully in a plastic bag. She reached up and kissed her mother on the cheek. "Hey, Mama."

A perfect fusion of both her parents, her skin was a shade deeper than her brother's, and her thick, curly hair brushed her shoulders, a reminder of Autumn's own. But it was her eyes, observant, knowing, and already wise, that were uniquely hers.

Chris followed them inside, and Autumn took him in for a second as he engaged with the kids.

The Howard sophomore was gone. Now standing before her was a man who embodied thirty-three years with an almost frustrating ease. That chinstrap beard was new, an attempt at a more mature look, she guessed, carved with surgical precision into his low-cut fade.

But the eyes were the same: a deep, intelligent brown that could make you believe any story he was selling. He still had the power to command a room just by standing in it, a fact she knew he was well aware of.

As Jordan continued his dribble and Layla removed her shoes, Chris gave Autumn a once-over and raised an eyebrow. "You alright?"

"I'm fine," came the fast quip, moving to close the door behind him.

"You sure?" he quizzed. "When I talked to you Friday... you didn't sound like you."

She forced a smile. "I'm just tired. There's been a lot going on at work lately."

The same lie on repeat.

Funny how he'd finally learned to ask if she was okay, now that it was too damn late.

He crossed his arms and leaned against the wall. "Maybe you need to take some time off. Get a chance to breathe."

Autumn gave a dry chuckle and shook her head. "Yeah. Something like that."

He tilted his head, like he wanted to say more, but Jordan called out from the next room, and the moment passed.

They watched him leave a few minutes later, the kids saying their casual goodbyes. It was as if everything were normal.

And she smiled, like her world wasn't quietly falling apart.

As the door clicked shut and the kids ran upstairs, Autumn leaned back against the solid wood, her smile slipping.

No one knew yet that she was unraveling.

And for now, that's precisely how it needed to stay.

3

LIPSTICK ON WHITE SILK

*a*utumn rarely got the kind of sleep that left her mouth open and a little drool on the pillow. A sleep so deep it felt almost criminal. Courtesy of those strawberry melatonin gummies Kendra recommended. So, when her phone buzzed like it had beef, she cracked one eye open and glared at it.

6:01 a.m.

Her eyes adjusted to the red digits glowing on her alarm clock. Her "*mom*" instincts kicked in, but her gut said: *Don't answer it.*

The kids were safe.

And nothing good ever came from a phone call before sunrise.

She let it roll to voicemail. But when it buzzed again like it had something to prove, she groaned, snatched it up, and swiped.

"Hello?" she rasped.

"Good morning, Autumn."

The smug, nasal voice sent a jolt of irritation straight down her spine. Walter Schumaker.

Autumn should've trusted her first instinct to ignore the call. His early-morning ego trip was not on the bingo card, especially not on her last day.

"Walter? Why are you calling me before the sun is fully up?" Her voice was flat, already bracing for the nonsense.

"Oh, nothing too urgent," he said breezily. "I wanted to wish you the best on your next chapter. I imagine you'll land somewhere great. Somewhere... more aligned with your creative style."

Autumn narrowed her eyes at the ceiling.

Style.

He always found a way to reduce her strategy to a vibe.

"Well, thanks, I guess—"

"I mean," he interrupted, voice smooth as a boardroom pitch, "we didn't always see eye to eye creatively, but there was always mutual respect. I admired how passionate you were about authenticity."

Her teeth clenched.

Passionate. Another coded word.

She waited.

"Anyway," he continued, "I'm taking over the Jefferson and Johnson campaign, and I need the editable files for the creative. I'm meeting with them this morning to discuss some strategic pivots."

"Pivots?" Autumn sat up straighter, fully awake now. "That campaign strategy was approved by the client and the senior team weeks ago. The Ghana launch is locked."

"Yes, but..." he hesitated, a practiced pause for dramatic effect, "I'd like to make some light adjustments."

"What adjustments, Walter?"

"Only a few tweaks," he said airily. "The feedback was strong with the core demo, but leadership has some top-level concerns about broad relatability. We think the current visuals might limit global appeal."

Autumn closed her eyes for a second to quell the rising tide of anger. Then, she spoke with a calmness that belied the fire in her stomach. "What are you talking about? The goal was to connect with their core audience."

"Of course," he drew the word out with condescending patience, as if soothing a trivial concern. "But to ensure this has a truly global reach, the creative needs to feel more aspirational, with a more international flavor. Less specific to the Chicago, Atlanta, and DC experience.

The current ad, while powerful, might resonate with the audience in Accra, but what about an even broader appeal? We're limiting our client's expansion potential."

There it was. The oldest trick in the global marketing book: diluting a specific identity in favor of a generic, "palatable" one.

Her voice was dangerously calm.

"Walter, the entire point of the 'legacy work' we sold them on was showing the real, successful African American faces behind this brand to create a genuine connection with the Ghana demographic."

"I hear your passion, Autumn," he said, the dismissal clear in his tone, "but we need to think about the broader optics. A more polished, international cast would garner more appeal."

"The people in the ad campaign are the actual employees of the firm. The executive team *they* gave us to feature."

"And we can supplement them with some professional international models," he countered easily. "Just to elevate the concept."

"Walter." Her voice sliced through his corporate jargon, sharp and final. "Today is my last day. All project files were turned over to Kendra yesterday. If you want to pitch a new, sanitized campaign that waters down the client's identity, you can talk to her."

Autumn ended the call and tossed the phone onto the bed like it was contaminated.

For a minute, she sat.

Breathing.

Still.

Then she moved.

Her joints popped as she leaned into a stretch, the slow crackle of her body protesting the day before it had even begun. Usually, positive affirmations guided her morning routine. Today, there was only the residual sting of that conversation.

She dropped into her first squat, arms reaching forward. "They always say it's about optics," she muttered under her breath. "But it's never their image that has to shift."

Her torso twisted, arms reaching side to side, sweat already beading along her brow.

"Global appeal," she echoed mockingly, rolling her eyes toward the ceiling. "Like Black people don't exist around the globe."

The frustration simmered beneath her skin, seeping through each movement. She was irritated—and tired.

Tired of dancing around coded language.

Tired of watching authenticity get diluted in the name of "reach."

Tired of having to translate her culture into something palatable.

Autumn reached overhead and pulled into a side bend, letting the stretch open her ribs. Then a deep lunge followed, and with it came release —physical, emotional. She breathed through the burn, willing her pulse to steady.

By the end, her body was damp, her limbs loose.

But it wasn't peace she felt.

It was resolve.

Walter didn't get to color her last day in pettiness and veiled digs.

Not today, Satan.

She showered quickly and threw on her robe, determined to find a sliver of peace in getting the kids ready for school. But the universe was not in a giving mood. "Oh, you wanted peace?" Chaos seemed to mock. "Not today, Autumn."

From the moment her feet stepped out of the bedroom, pandemonium greeted her like a petty ex.

"Jordan, where are my doggone socks?!" Layla shouted from her doorway.

"I don't know... Why you asking me?" he hollered back from his room.

Hands on her hips, neck rolling like a nine-year-old auntie, Layla snapped, "Because you were wearing them. Leave my stuff alone, ole crusty head boy!"

"I don't gotta do nothing! Find your own stupid stuff!"

The shouting from the kids grated on nerves already shredded by Walter's call. A vein pulsed at Autumn's temple as she appeared in the center of the hallway like a referee entering the ring. "Both of you. Out here. Now!"

They stomped out of their rooms, faces scrunched, arms folded.

"Layla, grab another pair of socks, it ain't that serious. Jordan, stop touching your sister's stuff, and you're finding her socks when we get home." She pointed her well-practiced mom finger. "Act like y'all got some sense. I'm not doing this today. Move like you got somewhere to be or you'll be walking to school."

They mumbled under their breath and turned to retreat.

"What was that?" she snapped.

"Nothing," they murmured in unison.

Autumn whipped around and returned to her room, not giving a damn about whose side of justice was right. All she wanted was to breathe in peace for five minutes.

But once again, peace would elude her today. Ten minutes later...

"Mamaaaa!" Jordan screeched. "Layla won't let me eat the cereal I want!"

Autumn flew down the stairs, one arm in her shirt, hair barely pinned. "What the hell is going on in this house today?!"

Jordan, on the verge of tears, pointed accusingly. "I wanted *Froot Loops*! She's making me eat *Cheerios*!"

Autumn, now in full survival mode, grabbed the box of Cheerios, dumped them in a bowl, stirred in some sugar, and placed it in front of him like a prison warden slamming a tray on a cafeteria table.

"Eat that damn cereal and don't make another sound. Am I clear?"

"Yes, ma'am." He grabbed his spoon like it was a lifeline.

She locked eyes with Layla, whose grin was teed up to taunt. "Don't even think about it."

With that fire momentarily extinguished, she bolted upstairs like a woman on borrowed time, determined to salvage what was left of her morning.

She flipped open her makeup case and snatched her favorite weapon of confidence—Fenty Icon Velvet in "The MVP."

One slow, practiced drag across her bottom lip.

Then the top.

And as she leaned in to admire the rich, defiant red... *smear.*

A slip of her hand sent the open tube dragging across the collar of the white silk shirt.

Her favorite one.

The crimson streak bled across the fabric like a betrayal.

Autumn froze.

The hiss caught in her throat.

And just like that, the weight of every emotion that had been held back by sheer will pressed down, hot and heavy.

She clutched the sink, blinking back tears, the stain glaring proof of how nothing, not even a damn tube of lipstick, was safe from the chaos.

"Dammit!" she shouted, louder than intended.

The sound cracked through the house like thunder.

Layla peeked her head into the room, wide-eyed. "You okay, Mama?"

"No." Autumn's voice broke on the word. "I ruined my favorite shirt."

Tears stung as the familiar knot in her shoulders tightened again.

She closed her eyes and inhaled.

One... Two... Three.

Without a word, Layla gently pulled Jordan back and softly closed the door.

Alone now, Autumn sat on the bed, the silk shirt clinging to her damp back.

The room was quiet, save for the sound of her breath trying to calm the storm.

She didn't do church. Hadn't set foot in one since Asia's funeral.

But today?

She prayed.

"God... Big Guy... I need you to hold my tongue and my peace today, because my spirit is about three seconds from telling Walter Schumaker about his entire bloodline. Don't let me walk in there with this energy. I won't give them that satisfaction."

She stayed like that, suspended in the stillness, letting the silence be a sanctuary.

Minutes passed.

Slowly, her shoulders dropped. Her breath evened. The pressure in her chest loosened enough for her to stand again.

Autumn moved through the bedroom, the chaos of the morning and the sour taste of Walter's phone call still clinging to her. The simple act of changing her shirt felt like a deliberate shedding of the negative energy.

She paused in front of the mirror, peering at the woman staring back; at the eyes that held the shadow of a pointless corporate battle.

For a moment, she let herself feel the sting of being undermined. Then, with a slow, intentional breath, it was all pushed away.

The negativity receded, replaced by a surge of the quiet strength she was learning to call her own.

* * *

THE KIDS TOSSED their book bags into the mid-size SUV. Today started out rocky, but Autumn was determined to send them to school with positive vibes.

"So, I got some news for you guys," she started, tossing a quick smile at them through the rearview while driving.

Their faces lit up.

"Aunt Mia invited us to spend the summer with them in Chicago. How does that sound?"

The excitement was palpable as they squealed with delight.

"Can we go to Navy Pier again?" Layla boomed.

"We can. What else do you want to do?"

"Ooh, can we get our favorite pizza?" Jordan almost popped out of his seat.

"Absolutely, baby."

The rest of the ride was filled with excitement at eating good ole Chicago food and having an amazing time in Autumn's childhood city. By the time they were dropped off, their mood was light and carefree. Her job, at least in that moment, was done.

But the fragile peace shattered the moment the car merged onto I-285.

The interstate was a red-lit cemetery of brake lights.

A full-on parking lot.

Atlanta traffic wasn't just inconvenient; it was a spiritual test. And this morning, she was fresh out of armor.

The anxiety crept in like a thief, stealing her reclaimed joy. The silence inside the SUV grew thick, making her thoughts louder.

The day's weight came rushing back, flooding every corner of her mind. Today, at 5:00 p.m., she would officially be unemployed.

Two weeks of pretending.

Smiling for the kids.

Laughing at texts.

Acting like everything was fine when she was barely holding on.

Amir's check-ins helped. Mia's encouragement meant everything. But this storm, she had to ride out on her own.

Atlanta had once been her refuge from grief and trauma. Now it felt like an emotional prison with a luxury townhouse and overpriced coffee.

Her mind started replaying the tape.

The slow death of her marriage to Chris.

The exhausting battles for recognition at work.

The thousand tiny cuts of microaggressions she smiled through every single day.

And now, the greatest achievement of her career, which was built from the ground up, was being snatched away and handed over to a man whose arrogance was only matched by his mediocrity.

The weight of it all pressed in until breathing felt like work. She let the window down, her free hand tightening on the steering wheel. A dangerous, seductive thought whispered from a part of her she hadn't heard from in years: *What if we just go?*

Then—

BAM!

Autumn slammed the brakes, but it was too late. The car in front of her had already clipped the one ahead of it, and she became part of the chain reaction. Her body jolted slightly, and lukewarm coffee splashed across her chest and lap. Her heart rate spiked.

For a moment, she didn't move, still gripping the wheel, staring ahead as if trying to see through time itself.

Horns blared. A weary "C'mon, man!" came from the car she'd hit. With a groan, she pulled onto the shoulder with the other two drivers.

Twenty agonizing minutes later, after exchanging insurance info and confirming no one was hurt, she was finally back in her car, hands shaking, blouse stained, and her last nerve completely fried.

It wasn't a major accident.

But to Autumn, it felt cosmic.

Like the universe had thrown down a challenge.

She sat on the shoulder for a while and exhaled hard.

Engines hummed past. Brake lights blinked like warning signs.

The whisper came back. This time louder.

Go.

Just. Fucking. Go.

The cosmos wasn't challenging her anymore. It was shoving her out the goddamn door.

When she finally made it to work, Autumn moved through the front doors like a ghost.

Her steps were slow. Her face was unreadable. Not from sadness, but exhaustion, the kind that lived deep in the bones.

There was no farewell party. No catered lunch. A sagging, "Good Luck" balloon was tied to the back of her chair, and an HR packet was already waiting on her desk.

She didn't want fanfare, anyway.

This was how they'd sent others off: quiet, transactional, and efficient.

Now it was her turn.

Autumn logged in. Ran her final reports.

Cleared her inbox.

No tears. No lingering nostalgia.

Ten years poured into it now seemed like water down a drain.

And still, she wasn't leaving empty-handed.

She had her peace. Her integrity. Her professional reputation intact.

And a damn good severance package.

At 3 p.m., Kendra buzzed her line.

"Can you step into my office before you head out?"

Autumn smoothed her coffee-stained blouse and headed down the hall. Kendra's door was cracked open like a quiet invitation. The door blinds were tilted enough for privacy.

Inside, the energy was soft. Just what Autumn needed.

A matte black box with a satin bow sat on the desk next to a white orchid in a glass vase. Kendra stood, gestured to the chair across from hers, and waited until Autumn sat before speaking.

"Before anything else, congratulations."

Autumn blinked. "For what?"

"For finishing the Jefferson & Johnson campaign with integrity. And for not letting that egotistical clown rattle you this morning."

A twitch of a smile tugged at Autumn's lips. "You heard about that?"

"Walter called me right after he hung up with you. He wanted your files. I told him he was out of luck." Kendra folded her hands neatly. "I met with the client this afternoon. They signed off. Full approval. No edits. No feedback. You, Autumn, will get the credit. Not him."

Relief warmed her chest, but it didn't bloom into joy. It was quieter, like the faint drone of a battle won long after the war was lost.

"Thank you," she breathed.

"You earned it."

They sat in silence for a moment, the churn of the office outside faint behind the closed door.

"I know I didn't get to fight for you the way either of us wanted," Kendra said, her voice low. "And I'll probably regret that for a while."

Autumn nodded, but her gaze was steady. "You don't owe me any regrets. I appreciated your honesty."

Kendra exhaled. "Then here is more of that: This place didn't deserve you. But you still left it better than you found it. That campaign—that win —that's yours."

She slid the matte box across the desk. "Open it when you're ready."

Autumn accepted it, her fingers brushing the ribbon.

As she stood to leave, Kendra added, "Promise me one more thing?"

"What's that?"

"Whatever you do next... make sure you're doing it for you. Not for them. Not for some title. For you."

Autumn nodded, offering a small smile.

One that finally reached her eyes.

She wasn't walking away with a job title.

She was walking away with her dignity—and that felt like enough.

* * *

WHEN THEY ARRIVED HOME, the sky was tinted rose gold.

The kids, thrilled it was Friday, had already kicked off their shoes by the door and run to their room to shed their school clothes.

Autumn changed out of her blouse, pulled her hair up, and prepared a fun dinner.

Spaghetti with giant meatballs.

Garlic bread.

Baby carrots.

They ate in near silence at first. Even Layla, the queen of fourth-grade gossip, was unusually muted.

Autumn crunched a carrot and glanced up. "Y'all okay?"

Layla looked at her brother, then back at her mom. "Is everything okay with you?"

Autumn's chest tightened.

She swallowed. "Why do you ask?"

"We saw your box," Layla said quietly. "In the trunk. From your office. And you've been... kinda sad."

Autumn put her fork down.

There was no sidestepping this.

It was time to tell them the truth.

"I don't work at the company anymore." Her tone was steady. "Today was my last day."

Layla tilted her head. "Did you quit?"

"No, sweetheart. They let me go. But I'm okay. We're okay."

Jordan's face scrunched. "So... we gonna be poor?"

"No, baby," she murmured, her smile tender and reassuring, giving his small hand a comforting squeeze. "I saved money. They gave me a really nice check before I left. We're safe. And, I have time to figure things out."

Relief washed over the kids' faces as they nodded, their eyes shining with renewed energy.

Shortly after, the clatter of forks against plates and happy murmurs filled the air, sounding like a symphony of satisfied hunger. Their energetic vibe had returned.

But inside, Autumn still felt the chill. Not from fear or regret. It was the weight of uncertainty, of an unplanned future.

Not knowing what came next and carrying that weight alone while still showing up with a smile was heavier than any job loss.

4

DON'T FORGET WHERE
YOU CAME FROM

*A*utumn had always believed in plans. Not just shopping to-do lists or weekend itineraries, but color-coded calendars, three-year projections, and backup plans for her backup plans.

She was the woman people called when their lives got messy.

But this, sitting still, not knowing what came next? The limbo was gnawing at her in ways that couldn't be explained.

It had been three weeks since she sat the kids down and told them the truth about losing her job. They took to the new reality better than expected.

She didn't.

Each morning, she made coffee like she was headed somewhere. Dressed in a silk blouse and slacks with nowhere to go, she'd sit at her dining room table, click open her laptop, and refresh job boards.

And the offers came... kind of.

One company asked her to consider an entry-level position. "You're overqualified," the recruiter had said, her smile audible even through the phone. "But if you get your foot in the door, there's room to grow. We fast-track talent like yours."

Autumn nibbled the inside of her cheek, her pulse ticking up. Fast-track? She'd led teams, mentored whole departments, juggled million-dollar campaigns. Now they wanted her to run someone else's calendar? It wasn't just offensive; it was disorienting.

She wasn't hard up for cash, so it wasn't about the salary, though God, that was insulting, too. It was about the ten years of her life she'd poured into her craft.

It was about principle. It was about pride.

She clicked through another job listing that didn't deserve her résumé. Her hand hovered over the mouse, then dropped into her lap.

The sigh that escaped fogged her screen and tightened her chest.

Her fingers pressed into her temples, chasing a calm that wouldn't come.

Leaning back in her chair, she rubbed the back of her neck as her thoughts drifted, past the stress, past Atlanta, all the way back to a bedroom in Ebondale that smelled like electric hair curlers and cocoa butter.

* * *

AUGUST 2010.

Autumn had barely turned eighteen, packing up everything that could fit in a suitcase and two duffel bags, surrounded by everything that had shaped her—and everything she was trying to escape.

The box fan buzzed in the window, dragging in warm air mixed with the faint smell of fried food from the neighbors downstairs.

Outside, the block hummed with its usual soundtrack: barking dogs, car engines idling too long, and somebody's uncle blasting *Happy Feelin's* by Frankie Beverly and Maze from a front porch while barbecuing.

In her tiny bedroom, her walls were a living scrapbook: cutouts from *ELLE*, *Teen Vogue*, her various academic awards, and a vision board she and Asia had crafted during their junior year. Words like Spelman, empowerment, and success were glued next to images of Black women in fitted suits, expensive cars, and brownstone-lined blocks.

There were dried rose petals still pinned to the top corner, from the bouquet Asia gave her after they got their Spelman acceptance letters.

The suitcase lay open on the floor, halfway filled with hope and summer clothes.

Amir sat on her bed, tall even then, his fresh twist-out haloing his head like a soft crown. His dark skin was smooth after overcoming the worst acne breakout last year. His legs dangled off the side, socked feet tapping the bed-frame to some internal rhythm only he could hear.

Head tilted slightly, he picked at a loose thread in the comforter, his expression calm but focused, like he was trying to memorize this version of his friend before she left.

"You really leaving," he said, not as a question but like a truth he'd been trying not to say out loud.

"Yep," Autumn replied, folding another tank top.

She smoothed it carefully and set it in the suitcase, her movements precise. "Orientation's next week. I'm tryna get in early and settled before all the chaos."

"Man, you officially breaking up the band, Yoko!" he joked, though his face stayed serious. "I wish you weren't going so far."

She looked up, a small smile tugging at the corners of her mouth. "I wish you were coming to Atlanta with me. That was the plan, remember? It was supposed to be the Triple A crew, taking over the A."

"Nah. I'm staying right here. NEIU's Center for Inner City Studies— that's where I'm supposed to be."

She scrunched her nose and threw a tank top at him. "What are you gonna do with a degree in Inner City Studies?"

He caught the shirt and twisted it in his hands. "I'on know. Try to make a difference in Ebondale, I guess. Somebody has to. I wanna understand this place... help change it."

He leaned back against her headboard, one arm behind his head like he was at ease, but she could see the tension in his jaw.

"I just feel like," he continued, "if everybody leaves, who's left to fix the problems?"

Autumn wanted to scream that surviving was fixing the problem. That leaving wasn't abandoning; it was breathing.

Instead, she paused mid-fold. Her fingers stilled over the soft cotton of a yellow sundress.

"I can't," she said, her voice quieter now. "I can't stay here, Amir. Me and Asia used to dream about getting out. About Spelman or Howard, hanging out at brunch spots, getting internships."

She looked at him. "We all said we'd do it together."

"Asia said she was dragging me along," he teased, his smile a little sad.

"Yeah, and you said you'd come. Morehouse accepted you and everything."

He nodded slowly, tossing the tank top into her suitcase like a three-point shot. "I know. But that was before …"

His voice faded.

The silence swelled, thick with everything that they didn't say.

That they still hadn't grieved properly. That Autumn hadn't been able to walk past the spot where Asia's body fell a year ago. That every time she heard gunshots now, she froze.

She swallowed. "Well. Now I'm doing it for both of us."

Amir's lips parted like he might respond, but he simply nodded.

They sat in the stillness for a moment as the fan blew soft air across their skin.

She glanced at the vision board again. At Asia's laughing face tucked into the corner, her eyes still bright, forever seventeen, forever planning a future that had Amir at its center.

Autumn remembered the afternoon they'd glued his Morehouse acceptance letter to the board right next to Asia's Spelman one. "Future Mr. and Mrs. Jackson," she had declared, her voice full of certainty.

Ebondale had taken too much. Staying felt like being trapped in an endless cycle of despair.

"I get it," Amir said finally, as if reading her thoughts. "Just promise me you won't forget where you came from."

Autumn met his eyes. She wanted to say, *of course not*, but the truth was murkier than that.

Part of her wanted to forget.

She wanted to build a new story that had no footnotes of grief, no underlines of survival.

She nodded and turned back to her suitcase, folding another shirt like it was armor.

The silence stretched, comfortable and uncomfortable all at once.

Amir didn't say he'd miss his best friend.

Autumn didn't say she was scared.

But both knew those things were true.

Outside, a car horn honked three times. It was her mother's signal that it was time to go.

She zipped the suitcase with shaky hands. Amir jumped up to grab the heavy luggage, walking out the door with it and two of her other bags.

By the time she made it down the stairs, her transformation was complete. A trick she'd mastered at thirteen, right after her father died. It was the art of performing strength. Her eyes were dry, her shoulders squared, and she fixed a steady smile on her face; an act she'd perfected so well she barely remembered herself any other way.

This was simply another scene.

The Spelman campus hit her like a blast of heat. Not only from the Atlanta sun, though it was doing the most with its humidity and high-noon glare, but from the energy of it all.

The confidence.

The sisterhood.

The ambition.

Black girls with Senegalese twists and big hoops scurried past with duffel bags and parents trailing behind. Laughter echoed across the quad like a chorus. The air smelled like coconut oil and pride.

Autumn stood in front of the apartment building for a moment, suitcase and bags piled beside her, phone in hand, trying to catch her breath.

She was here. Finally.

But "here" didn't feel like escape. Not yet. It felt like disorientation in a cuter zip code.

She'd gotten in on a full-ride scholarship for academics, which included housing in an exclusive on-campus apartment. She and Asia had been giddy about the possibility of living on campus together.

"Autumn, right?" a voice called from her left, startling her.

She turned around. Her new roommate, Kiara, stood at the curb surrounded by boxes and shouted instructions to her older brother, who was lifting a microwave out of the trunk as if it weighed nothing.

Kiara was tall, brown-skinned, with bright acrylics and a voice that didn't believe in whispering. "You from Chicago, right? Oh girl, you gon' love it here. We got a stove and fridge that work and everything."

Autumn laughed despite herself, tickled by the distinct Atlanta accent. "So, I've heard."

Kiara pointed to the guy who was now hauling three large suitcases toward the building.

"Chris, come meet Autumn! That's my brother. He's a finance major at Howard, so he think he better than everybody."

Chris approached, lifting the bottom of his T-shirt to mop the sweat from his brow. The move was casual, unthinking, but the effect was electric.

For a split second, a landscape of perfectly defined abs was revealed, his skin the color of warm, light caramel.

Oh. Okay.

The thought was immediate and uninvited, and Autumn had to force herself not to stare.

He grinned, seemingly unaware of the momentary short-circuit he'd caused in her brain. "Don't believe her. I'm the humble one in the family."

He had a wide, easy smile that was intentionally disarming. His shoulders filled out the fabric of his t-shirt perfectly. A clean fade. A Howard key lanyard dangling from his pocket like a statement.

And a way of looking at her like he already knew her.

Something fluttered low in her belly as he took her extended hand, and his thumb skimmed her knuckles. The touch was brief, subtle, but unapologetically sure of itself.

"Nice to meet you, Autumn," he smiled, the cleft in his chin deepening as he held her hand and her gaze. "So, you're the one stuck with my loud-mouthed sister this year." He shot a playful look back at Kiara. "Don't worry, I'll make sure to check in on you. See if you need rescuing."

Autumn laughed, a genuine, flustered sound. "I think I can handle her."

"I'm sure you can." His smile broadened, his eyes still holding hers.

He winked as he walked away to finish moving his sister's things. "Until next time, Autumn."

The rest of that day blurred into frantic movement: check-in, campus tours, Kiara's constant talking, sweaty students running all over the place.

But it was seeing Chris in motion that stuck.

He was different from the guys in Ebondale, carrying an easy, magnetic confidence that drew her in before she could even put up a defense.

The way he held the door open for them with his foot while balancing three boxes.

The way he looked at her when he thought she wasn't paying attention.

The way he said her name. It all hit different.

They swapped numbers before he left.

By that weekend, they were texting. By the next month, they were video chatting.

It was fun. It was new.

And Autumn needed *new*.

Their first few months as a long-distance couple were golden.

Chris made her laugh when she forgot how. He sent random playlists of his favorite music, late-night memes that said everything he didn't verbalize, and voice notes that made her cheeks hurt from smiling. On weekends, he'd catch the Megabus or bum a ride from a friend to visit.

When he walked onto campus, heads turned. He was that guy. Cool, polished, with just enough edge to make her friends whisper, "Girl, don't drop the ball on that one."

She didn't plan to.

Aside from the ambition he wore like a custom-made sweater, he knew how to hold her hand in public and her waist in private. Knew how to say all the right things; "you're different... you're the one... I'm trying to build something with you."

Autumn was still mourning Asia, though she didn't talk about it much. But when Chris held her, the ache didn't scream so loud.

He was her peace and her distraction.

Her connection to a new future.

The first time she found out he'd cheated came through someone else's mouth.

One of Kiara's friends slipped up at a party, casually mentioning Chris and some girl at Howard. The words hit like ice water, but Autumn played it cool, smiled, nodded, and excused herself before the tears could betray her.

That night, the call was inevitable. She answered on the second ring.

"I messed up," he said before she even spoke. "It didn't mean anything. I was drunk, she was drunk..."

His voice sounded shaken, almost childlike. "I don't want to lose you."

For a long minute, nothing was said.

"Baby?"

"I heard you."

"I love you, Autumn."

That was the first time he'd said it. And that was all it took.

The constant forgiveness didn't make sense. But because her heart ached louder than her pride, Autumn told herself all couples went through rough patches.

Over the years, it became a pattern, with Chris doing just enough to keep her, never quite enough to deserve her. But Autumn, disciplined, focused, raised to make things work, stayed committed to the plan.

Her father was a man who kept two families two blocks apart and called it normal. Her mother stayed. This was not new to her.

She told herself she wasn't a quitter. That a relationship was work. That Black love was worth fighting for.

By graduation, she had an internship with Titan & Lewis and a fiancé already climbing the ranks at a mid-sized investment firm.

On paper, she had it all.

And for a while, that's how it felt.

Her career took off fast. She was good; sharp, strategic, always two moves ahead.

Two beautiful babies followed. She had a beautiful home in Buckhead. A husband who became VP before thirty-three.

From the outside, her life was perfect.

Until it wasn't.

* * *

Now, Autumn sat in a quiet townhouse with a life she had mastered... but no longer recognized.

The screen saver on her computer had kicked in.

Her untouched coffee had turned cold.

She wandered into the hallway, not looking for anything in particular, just avoiding the laptop. Avoiding another rejection email or worse, one that offered condescension.

Pausing in front of the closet, her hand rested on the doorknob. She wasn't sure what pulled her there.

She reached for a bin on the top shelf. The lid resisted slightly before popping free.

Inside there were baby blankets, Layla's baby shoes, Jordan's superhero onesie, and beneath it all... a small, worn teddy bear.

It was dusty. Ragged. One plastic eye missing, the fabric around its neck thinned from being hugged too tight for too many years.

It was Asia's bear. She remembered the day Amir gave it to her friend. It was their first Valentine's Day as a couple. Asia had treasured that thing, sleeping with it every night. "He keeps the nightmares away," she'd once admitted to Autumn in a giddy whisper. It was the same conversation where she'd finally confessed that she and Amir had lost their virginity together.

Autumn never asked what the nightmares were about.

The night before Autumn left for Spelman, Amir had tucked it into her suitcase with a sticky note that said, "Don't forget where you came from, nerd."

Autumn had kept it on her dresser in the college apartment until Chris teased her about it.

Now it was buried in a bin with the rest of her past.

She sat cross-legged on the hallway floor, the warmth of the memories flooding her. She brought the bear to her face, the worn fabric smelling faintly of dust and time and a life she'd almost forgotten.

Her thumb traced the outline of the missing eye. "I should've let myself remember," she whispered, not referring to the bear.

That was the thing about grief. It didn't shout, nor did it rush.

It waited. Quiet, patient.

And today, it had come to sit beside her.

Not to punish her.

To remind her.

Of Asia. Of Ebondale.

Of the person she used to be before trading memory for momentum.

The house creaked with afternoon weight, but Autumn didn't move.

She sat in the quiet, holding a ragged bear and her own unraveling peace.

And for once, she didn't rush to fix it.

She let the grief breathe.

5

THANKS TO YOUR EGO

The unexpected blare of the doorbell at 7 a.m. on a Saturday cut through the kitchen, where Autumn stood stirring oatmeal, the aroma of brown sugar and cinnamon still warm in the air.

Thinking it was too early for the Witnesses, Autumn shuffled to the door in fuzzy pink slippers, wiping the sleep from her eyes and peeking through the blinds.

Her stomach dropped.

What the hell is he doing here?

Chris stood casually on the front porch, hands buried deep in the pockets of a black Howard hoodie. His matching joggers hung effortlessly, damn near perfect.

The morning sun covered his honey-brown skin like a filter, highlighting the deep cut of his jawline, the fullness of his lips, and the glint of the diamond stud in his left ear. The same kind he used to wear when they first met.

Bold, cocky, and still just as irresistible.

Why does he have to look like a walking commercial for freshly divorced Black dads, she thought, sighing aloud.

It's definitely too early.

Autumn opened the door. "Did you forget this was my weekend?"

His eyes locked onto hers. "Nah. Nothing like that." He offered that gleaming, polite smile that still disarmed.

She moved aside, mostly to give herself a reason to look away.

He stepped inside, bringing the chilly morning air in with him. He reached back and locked the door after she closed it, a smooth, thoughtless motion from a time when it was his place to do so. The soft click of the deadbolt echoed in the entryway, a sound that felt both familiar and deeply out of place.

A hint of his body butter followed him; sandalwood and vanilla, the one she used to steal for herself when they were together. It snuck into her senses like an unwanted memory.

"Can we talk?" he asked.

Autumn ran a hand up to her head, then froze mid-motion when her fingers brushed her silk bonnet. She hadn't washed her face, hadn't brushed her teeth, hadn't even looked in the mirror yet. She was standing there in a cropped tank and pink satin shorts with old polish on her toes, and sleep still in her eyes.

A sudden, sharp awareness rolled through her, followed by heat rising in places she didn't invite it to when his eyes roamed over her with a glint of appreciation.

Don't you dare.

She checked herself instantly.

This was lust, based on history. A flash of familiarity, nothing more.

Still, the knowing curl of his lips told her he'd noticed.

"About what?" she snapped, trying to regain ground.

Chris rubbed a hand over his chin, a gesture she remembered from a hundred arguments and even more apologies.

"Wait, can I just say this first?" he murmured, eyes sliding over her again like a man who was still entitled. "Damn. You still look good."

Autumn blinked.

Then she straightened, putting distance between them.

She knew where this game could take her. She'd fallen victim to it many times since their divorce.

"What do you want, Chris? It's seven in the morning; the kids aren't even up yet."

He hesitated. "Jordan texted me last night. He said you lost your job a few weeks ago?"

Her spine stiffened. "So, you popped up uninvited... To do what exactly?"

"I was worried."

"No, you weren't," she said flatly. "You were nosy."

His response was a typical Chris move: a small, disarming chuckle and a shake of his head. "There's that attitude."

He held up his hands in feigned innocence when she bristled. "Okay, listen. I didn't come here to fight. I think we should talk. For the kids."

She paused at the sound of bubbling oatmeal; a reminder this morning was hers before he showed up.

"You've got five minutes," she quipped over her shoulder, halfway to the kitchen.

He followed, settling into a chair and straddling it backward like he still belonged there.

That irritated her more than it should have.

He looked around, taking in the space. Not like a guest, but like a man silently evaluating his ex's life.

"So," he looked at her squarely. "What's the plan now?"

Her eyes narrowed to slits as she turned to face him. "Excuse me?"

"You're out of work. I wish you'd told me sooner, but we're here now. I know unemployment will not sustain you and the kids. You can't do this alone, Autumn."

"I've been doing this alone," she snapped.

Chris's eyes darkened, his voice raising a notch. "First of all, that's bullshit. I take good care of my kids. The only thing you do alone is live here. And that was your choice."

Autumn's fists flew to her hips. "It sounds like you really came here to throw shade about me losing my job."

"No, I came here to offer a solution. I think it would be good if we moved in together again. I can help with finances, and we co-parent for real."

She stared at him like he'd grown a second head. "So let me get this straight. I build a life on my own... and because that life has shifted, you really think I'm gonna fold back into yours?"

"I think you need help," he countered, his voice cool. "And, as usual, you're too damn headstrong to admit it."

A tense second passed.

Autumn turned to stir the oatmeal, her movements steady even as a storm raged inside her.

She was not mulling over his words; she was actively building a wall against them. Each swirl of the spoon was a brick. Each sprinkle of cinnamon for the kids was mortar. She was constructing a fortress of calm, trying desperately to keep him and her own fury from crossing over.

"So... I ask again," he continued. "What's the plan?"

She set the wooden spoon down with a deliberate clink against the counter. She turned, leaning one hip against the stove, and flashed him a look that was slow and unbothered. It was a false front, but he didn't need to know that. "Survive. Like I always do."

"Come on," he drawled, his voice tightening. "Let me help. Sell the townhouse, and you and the kids move in with me. I'll take care of things until you're back on your feet."

Autumn laughed. A low, dry chuckle. "Chris, I'm not sinking. You think because I'm not clocking into a job right now, I'm suddenly helpless?"

She filled two bowls with steaming oatmeal, setting them on the table.

"I don't see how you do it by yourself. This community is expensive as hell; the mortgage alone would eat your unemployment check whole. Child support can cover it, sure, but the other expenses—"

"Look, I know you don't understand this." She moved effortlessly through the kitchen, trying to keep her expression cool as she grabbed juice from the fridge. "You were too busy trying to prove I didn't need to work by paying every bill when we were married. You didn't even notice I'd been stacking most of my paychecks for years. So, while you insisted on being 'the man,' I was building my savings. I'll give credit where credit is due—you taught me that."

She dumped juice into the cups a little too hard, splashing some on the counter. The tremble in her voice was masked by swagger.

"So, thanks to your ego over the years and a very hefty severance package, I'm good. Real good."

She celebrated inwardly at how shook he was. She saw it in the way his jaw moved, like he was chewing a truth he couldn't swallow.

"I never had an ego when it came to you," he said with conviction. "I was raised in a household where my mother stayed home and took care of me and my siblings, and my dad took care of the bills. That's still the case to this day. So naturally, I expected the same with my wife. When it became clear that's not what you wanted, I supported your career. Eventually. But that's not the point."

"No, that's exactly the point," she countered. "You didn't want to support me, you wanted to control me. And now that I don't need you? You're pressed."

His expression hardened.

"If I'm pressed, it's because you act like you've gotta be the mother and the father. That's not fair. I was always there for them. For you, too."

Autumn's eyes bucked. "You still using that tired-ass line, Chris?" Her head cocked to the side, eyes slicing through him. "At least you're consistent."

"I'm not saying everything between us was perfect. But I took care of this family. You never had to worry about anything—"

"Except losing my shit every time you were with another woman," she snapped, her voice sharp enough to draw blood.

They stood toe to toe, daring the other to look away.

Chris backed off slightly, his tone softening as tenderness flickered in his eyes.

"You really think this constant tension is good for Jordan and Layla? They don't need to see us like this. And they don't need to see you so angry with me all the time."

Her voice turned to ice. "I think watching me stand up for myself is better than watching me shrink for a man who lied and cheated the whole damn time we were together."

He exhaled, brows furrowing as his arms crossed over his chest. "There it is again. You refuse to let the past go."

"Because you act like it never mattered."

The tension was rising, the temperature in the kitchen elevating.

He stepped in closer, his voice dropping low and smooth.

"Maybe it still matters... because you still have feelings for me."

She sucked her teeth and pushed past him, returning the juice to the fridge with force. "First of all, don't flatter yourself. Second? I let the past go the minute I let you go."

"So that's it, huh? See, that smart ass attitude is why we didn't make it. And you don't see anything you did wrong, right?"

Her anger and his audacity collided as she stepped back and pointed toward the front door. "We're not doing this again. Get out."

He flinched, his eyes narrowing. "You serious?"

"Out. Now."

He stared at her for a moment, then turned and walked to the door, mumbling under his breath as he opened it to let himself out.

She followed, and before he could close it himself, she slammed it behind him with intention.

Autumn stood in the silence for a moment. Her hand still on the knob, her heartbeat a steady drum in her ears.

She didn't cry.

She didn't curse.

She breathed. Slow and deep, until the heat in her chest cooled into something more manageable.

Behind her, the faint clinking of silverware against ceramic pulled her back to the kitchen. The kids had come down and were seated at the table. Jordan sat with his elbows propped up, scooping oatmeal like it was his last meal. Layla pushed her spoon through hers, barely touching it.

Both were too quiet for a Saturday morning.

Autumn poured herself a small bowl and sat down across from them. The tension from moments ago was still thick, settled over the table like fog. She picked a raisin from her oatmeal and toyed with it absently.

She didn't notice how closely they were watching her until Jordan finally spoke.

"I'm sorry for telling Daddy your business. Is he mad at you?"

Autumn blinked out of her daze. She looked up, met his brown eyes, so much like Chris's, and softened.

"No, baby. And it's okay that you told him. He's just upset that he can't help. Grown-ups have big feelings sometimes, too."

Layla frowned. "Y'all sounded like you were arguing."

Autumn nodded slowly. "Yeah. We were."

"Why?" Layla's brows raised.

Autumn hesitated, her fingers brushing gently over Jordan's curls as she thought.

"Your dad and I have a difference of opinion on a lot of things."

"Is that why you got divorced?" Jordan asked.

"We divorced because we hurt each other and grew in different directions."

His voice was almost inaudible, his brows knitted together. "Was he mean to you?"

She nodded. "Sometimes. But we were mean to each other, and that's something your dad and I need to work through. He's always been a great father to you. And he loves you both so much. He's not a bad father, he's just not the right man for me." She smiled softly. "And I'm not the right woman for him."

The room stilled, heavy with the necessary truths she never shared with them before.

"So, we can still love him?" Jordan asked, his eyes searching his mother's.

Autumn reached for them both, pulling them into her arms when they came to her, holding them tight.

"You can always love your daddy," she said, kissing them both on the head. "That's never up for debate."

Layla lay her head against her mother's shoulder. "But he better not be mean to you again."

Autumn smiled faintly. "He won't."

After breakfast, she cleaned the dishes in slow motion, methodically, like muscle memory was all she had left. The kids had drifted to the living room, each sprawled on the floor with a tablet, wrapped in their personalized comfy blanket.

The argument with Chris still lingered in her head.

The way he said, "*You can't do it alone,*" like she hadn't been doing it for the last year and some change.

She stared out the kitchen window at the backyard fence. The same one he had promised to replace three summers ago. It leaned slightly, mirroring how she felt.

Tired. Yet, still holding it all together.

She had savings. She even had time, if she chose to take it.

What she didn't have was clarity.

And for that, she knew exactly who to call.

She bounded up the stairs and crawled into her unmade bed. She slid under the covers, phone in hand, and dialed.

It rang once.

His voice, calm as always, came through. "What's wrong, big head?"

She swallowed. "Am I that obvious?" she asked, letting out a light laugh.

"I can always tell. Besides, I know how antsy you can get."

Autumn sighed. "Yeah. And this morning didn't make it any better."

She told Amir everything: the knock at the door, the tension, Chris's offer wrapped in control, the weight of pretending she still had a plan.

When she finished, her voice softened. "I sit in this house every day, believing if I give it more time, things will fall into place."

"What exactly is it you're trying to accomplish?"

"I don't know," she sighed, looking at the black screen of the television across from her. "It's not like I need to go back to work right away. But every job application, every rejection, every condescending interview is a daily reminder that my old life is gone, and I'm not sure how to build a new one here."

"So why are you torturing yourself with all these applications and rejections?"

She took a moment to think about the question.

"Because I fear the longer I'm out, the harder it'll be to get back in."

She paused. "I think I need a change of scenery. A real one. A complete fresh start, miles away from all this."

"You mean... Ebondale?" Amir asked carefully.

She hesitated, her jaw tightening. "I don't know. Maybe. It's... there's so much history there. You know what that place took from us."

He didn't rush to respond.

When he spoke, his voice was lower. "Yeah. I know."

She picked at the hem of her T-shirt. "It's not only the memories. It's the fear. I don't want to bring the kids somewhere that might not be safe."

"It's not the same place, Autumn." His voice was firm, but not defensive. "I wouldn't still be here if it were. I wouldn't have started the youth center. I wouldn't be trying to raise up the next generation if I thought it was gonna be like it was back then."

She let that sit.

Amir wasn't the kind of man to give easy answers to make her feel better.

"You usually visit for a few days," he continued. "Holiday stuff, your sister's baby shower, but you've never stayed long enough to see how much has changed."

"I was afraid to look beyond a visit," she admitted.

"I know. But maybe it's time you came home and saw it through fresh eyes. Ebondale needs us. It needs you."

Autumn exhaled. "You really think we'd be okay there?"

"I don't think it," he said gently. "I know it."

As she leaned back on the bed, his words settled like a possibility. They landed, one by one, taking root.

She stared out the window for a moment, watching a lone bird take flight from a telephone wire.

"Alright." Her voice was quiet, but certain. "I tell you what. I'll keep my plans to stay with Mia for the summer. After that, I'll consider Ebondale. Otherwise, I may move to one of the suburbs."

She heard the smile in his voice. "Either sounds good to me. It'll be good to have my homie back, and my god-kids close."

"Yeah." She released a heavy sigh. "Now comes the hard part. Talking to Chris and the kids about this. He and I are not fans of each other right now, but he loves these kids to death. And they love him. I don't want to disrupt their lives to take care of mine."

Amir's voice softened. "Listen. Taking care of your life is taking care of theirs. You're giving yourself time, Autumn. That's the best thing you can do. And just know, we got you, whatever you decide."

By the time the call ended, her spirits were cautiously higher, prompting her to dial Mia.

"Girl, don't play with me," Mia exclaimed when Autumn told her about the potential change of plans. "Are you serious-serious?"

Autumn let out a small laugh. "I'm serious-serious. If that offer's still on the table..."

"You're moving in. Period." Mia clapped. "My spare rooms are already yours. I'll tell the boys."

"Hold on, now. I'm not saying I'm definitely moving to Ebondale, I still may choose to go to the suburbs—"

"I don't care. You're coming home, that's all that matters."

After Autumn hung up, she looked out the window at the Atlanta sky shimmering in the distance. A deep, resonant peace unfurled in her chest. The city looked beautiful from afar, like a memory—a past chapter—but it was no longer her future.

She was finally ready to say goodbye: not only to a place, but to the woman she'd had to become to survive it.

6

RUNNING VERSUS REBUILDING

The June sky was beginning to stir, unfurling the soft watercolor dawn that had once made her fall in love with Atlanta. That early light dusted everything in shades of lavender and rose, casting a serene glow over the street.

It wasn't even 6 a.m. yet, but the humidity had already claimed the morning, ushering a low, wet heat that clung to the skin and stifled the lungs.

A bead of sweat slid down the nape of Autumn's neck, soaking into the collar of her T-shirt.

In the driveway, movers bustled in tight, rotating loops from the house to the truck. They didn't waste a step as they loaded the last boxes marked "STORAGE" into the belly of the vehicle.

Bright neon straps snapped around dressers, beds, and bookshelves.

Chris was by the SUV, helping the kids cram the last of their duffel bags and backpacks into the trunk.

Layla was humming something off-key, Jordan rapped along, both too loud for the hour.

Standing on the porch, fingers curled lightly around the railing, Autumn didn't call out to shush them, even though she noticed the neighbor's blinds twitching across the street.

Let them make noise.

Let them be kids.

She would not hush them through this. They were leaving the only home they'd ever known. Today, the least she could give them was unfiltered joy.

But the noise made it real.

This was happening.

Not for a vacation. Not for one of her short, controlled visits to Chicago to see Mia and Amir. This was a severing.

And Chris, her first love, her ex-husband, her biggest heartbreak, was helping load her car.

That irony hit harder than she expected.

She'd been so focused on closing accounts, purging closets, sorting through furniture, deciding what to store and what to take that she hadn't given herself time to feel any of it. It wasn't until this moment, watching her kids with the man she once thought she'd grow old with, that the finality of it cracked the veil.

It had taken weeks of tense phone calls and one difficult face-to-face conversation to reach this point of peaceful cooperation. The first time she'd told him about her plan, his reaction had been exactly what she'd dreaded. He'd tried to charm her out of it, his voice smooth as honey.

"Come on, Autumn," he'd said. "Don't do this. A tiny part of me was always hopeful we'd find our way back to each other. Chicago is so far."

When she held firm, his charm evaporated, replaced by the bitter, familiar edge of jealousy. The final argument had been over the phone, his voice tight with an accusation she'd heard a thousand times.

"So that's it? You're just gonna run back to Chicago?" he'd sneered. "Or are you running to Amir?"

"Don't do this, Chris."

"Don't do what? State the obvious? You think I'm stupid, Autumn? Ain't no man trying to be just your friend. I told you that shit from the beginning. I never believed it."

But then, he had shown up at her door. His shoulders sloped, hands stuffed deep in his pockets. Not with cockiness, but with the meekness of a man unraveling old pride. They sat at the dining room table, the space between them filled with years of unspoken things.

"I was out of line," he'd started, not quite meeting her eyes. "It took my mom to help me see it." A small, sad smile touched his lips as he fumbled for his phone. His thumb hovered over the screen. "I, uh... I saved the voicemail. Figured it was better if you heard it from her."

He pressed play, and the tinny, warm sound of his mother's voice filled the quiet space. Autumn watched Chris as he listened along with her, his gaze fixed on the table, a muscle twitching in his jaw. He didn't look at her, couldn't look at her, as his own mother's voice laid his selfishness bare:

"Son, I thought more about what you said. I know it's hard, but you need to let that woman go. And not because you don't love her—hell, it's obvious you still do. You don't want her to stay because of the kids; you want her here for you. Autumn is a good mother, and she'll be a good mother whether she's in Atlanta or in Chicago. Your job now is to be a good father, no matter the zip code."

The voicemail ended, leaving a heavy silence in its wake. He finally looked up at Autumn, his eyes clear with a new understanding. "She was right," he'd admitted. "This move... It's you really moving on. Not only from us, but into your own thing. It was selfish of me to try and stop that."

That was when they'd made the deal about the kids: summers and holidays with him, unlimited FaceTime calls, and his promise to visit Chicago often. He had looked at her, and she sensed a shift. He wasn't seeing his ex-wife; he was seeing a woman he was finally beginning to understand.

Chris had insisted on being there on moving day and helping any way he could. "It's the least I can do," he'd told her.

He squatted in front of Jordan, tying his sneakers while nodding along to something Layla said. She envisioned him reassuring them he would visit, that they would video call all the time, that this wasn't forever.

That was the most maddening part. That he, somehow, could fail spectacularly as a husband and still show up like a damn hero for the kids.

That was his superpower.

Her chest tightened as she watched Jordan throw his arms around his father's neck, giggling at something Chris whispered into his ear.

Relief pressed against her ribs. No matter how they turned out, at least the kids still had him.

A trickle of regret slid in behind it. Not because she wanted him back, but because at one point she had wanted this to work.

The marriage. Her career. All of it.

So much of her identity had been wrapped in "making it." In the love story that was supposed to outlast the odds.

College sweethearts. Power couple. The girl who made it out of Ebondale and built something real. And for a while, she had.

Until life came for her in every direction.

A failed marriage. A job loss. And now, what felt like a retreat to the very place she'd once escaped.

Her throat tightened.

"Ms. Gardener?"

She blinked. One of the movers stood by the truck, clipboard in hand, sweat visible beneath his ball cap.

"We're locked and loaded. Ready to hit the road."

Autumn smiled. "Right. Thank you."

She stepped forward. "My friend Amir Jackson will meet you at the Chicago storage facility. He has the unit details and inventory list."

At the name, Chris looked up sharply. His jaw twitched.

She saw it but ignored it.

The kids were already in the SUV now, belted in and bouncing with excitement. She opened the driver's side door, but Chris stepped in front of it before she could climb in.

They stood, face to face, sunlight creeping into the space between them.

"I can work with the realtor," he offered. "You know, to help with the sale. Make sure it all goes smoothly."

"I've got it," she said, her voice soft but sure.

He nodded, like he expected that.

Autumn hesitated. "You sure you don't want any of the proceeds? You know you're entitled to half."

Chris shook his head. "Nah. That's for you and the kids."

She nodded.

"But if I need to borrow forty dollars…"

The corner of her mouth lifted despite herself, and they both laughed lightly, dispelling the heaviness of the moment.

His smile faded slowly, replaced with something more vulnerable as his eyes softened.

"I'm gonna miss you," he admitted.

Autumn didn't answer. She turned her head to avoid looking at him.

He stepped closer, gently lifting her chin until her eyes met his.

"I'm so sorry. For everything. I never stopped loving you."

Then came the unexpected kiss.

Soft and searching.

She didn't pull away. She let herself remember how it used to be, before love turned to ash.

Her lips moved with his, and in that moment, they weren't exes or failures or co-parents. They were two people grieving what could've been.

From inside the car, two delighted voices burst out in unison: "Oooooohhh!"

The moment was broken. They laughed awkwardly, stepping apart.

Autumn slid into the driver's seat and turned the key.

Chris patted the hood as she reversed, waving to the kids.

Before she turned out of the driveway, he said quietly, low enough for only her to hear, "I hope you find what you're searching for, Autumn."

She didn't look back. The words, genuine and gentle, settled on her like a blessing and a burden all at once.

* * *

THE GEORGIA SUNRISE had long surrendered to a blazing Tennessee noon, and now, as the SUV hummed north along I-65, the sky mellowed into a soft, powdery haze above sprawling Indiana fields. Flatlands stretched wide on either side, and endless rows of corn began to push through the early summer soil.

The air outside buzzed with that faint hum unique to rural roads. Distant tractors, birds in the brush, the occasional rustle of trees flanking the highway.

Autumn glanced back at the kids through the rearview. Jordan was knocked out, slumped sideways, with his headphones slipping from his ears.

Layla's head lay back against the headrest, mouth open as she slept quietly. Car rides were like melatonin for kids; a few miles after a rest stop, and they were out cold.

Mia's name lit up the screen of her dashboard, and she answered through the Bluetooth.

"Hey, sis."

"You alive?" Mia's voice was laced with playful concern. "You aren't pulled over in a Waffle House parking lot cryin', are you?"

Autumn laughed softly. "Not yet. But if this GPS reroutes me one more time, I will definitely start bawling."

"You halfway here yet, or halfway crazy from driving?"

"I think a little of both," Autumn giggled. "We just crossed into Indiana. Kids are sleeping like they worked a ten-hour shift."

"Cool. How's the drive been?"

"Quiet. Beautiful. Too much time to think."

Mia hummed knowingly. "Which means you're thinking about things you probably shouldn't."

Autumn let her silence confirm it.

Mia's voice softened. "Are you going to be okay with all of this?"

There was another pause, followed by a heavy sigh.

"I think so," Autumn said. "It's surreal. Like I blinked, and the whole life I planned and built in ATL is packed in a truck somewhere on I-65."

"You know you're allowed to grieve, right? You're mourning a version of your life that ended. Even if you were ready to walk away from it."

She rubbed her temple, one hand still on the wheel. "I keep thinking... What if this is me giving up? I don't feel like I'm coming home. I feel like I'm running."

"Girl, you're not running. You're rebuilding. Don't confuse the two."

Autumn didn't respond right away. Her voice was low when she finally did. "How'd you do it? After everything ended with Donovan?"

Mia took a breath. "I gave myself permission to start over. To stop surviving without his presence and start living."

Autumn nodded, the wind tousling her curls.

The road ahead curved slightly, fields opening wider as they climbed a gentle rise.

"And the kids?" she asked softly. "What if I'm uprooting them just to find myself?"

"They're watching you find yourself," Mia responded. "And that's the most powerful thing a mother can do."

She swallowed the lump forming in her throat. "You always say the right stuff."

"Hey, that's what a big sis does."

"Speaking of," Autumn switched gears. "I'm thinking of visiting my mother's and our dad's grave."

It was Mia's turn to go quiet.

"I know you hate him—" Autumn started.

"I don't hate him," Mia interjected. "I didn't like who he was."

"I get that. Neither did I. Which is why I want to go." She checked the rearview mirror to make sure the kids were still asleep. "I need to understand something. Because what are the odds that I would end up with a serial cheater in Chris, and you with a man who lied about having a whole other family?"

"So, you think we're cursed?" Mia asked.

"I'm just saying. Daddy lived two different lives; one with your mother, and one with mine."

"Yeah, but the difference is our mothers knew about each other."

"Eventually," Autumn countered. "But in the beginning, he lied to both of them. They made a decision to accept and live with it."

Mia let out a long, hard sigh. "Well, the good thing that came out of it was that I gained a sister. I hate we didn't get to know each other until we were grown."

"Same. Hey, have your sons met Donovan's kids?"

"Girl, we won't even go there," Mia laughed. "Anywho, let me let you get back to driving. Be safe, and I'll see y'all soon."

"Bye, sis," Autumn chuckled as she disconnected the call.

"Ma?"

Autumn checked the rearview and found Layla awake.

"Hey, baby. How was your nap?"

She blinked sleepily. "Good. You were talking to Auntie about your dad?"

"You heard that?"

"Some." She tilted her head. "You and Auntie have different moms, right?"

"Yeah, baby."

"Was he nice? Your dad?"

Autumn's grip tightened on the wheel. She blew out a slow breath before she answered, careful with every word. "To me, yeah. To Mia? He wasn't around her much."

"Why?"

"I don't really know. But some people... they don't know how to be what you need them to be. Doesn't mean you're not worthy."

Layla processed it quietly. "Okay."

Jordan stirred, yawning himself awake. "Are we there yet?"

"Almost," Autumn said softly, her gaze fixed on the horizon. "We're getting close, baby. Real close."

* * *

THE *WELCOME to Chicago* sign blurred past the windshield before the skyline came into view, sharp and sprawling against the sky. But it wasn't the skyline that tied her stomach in knots.

It was what waited on the lower south side of the city.

Ebondale.

As the SUV dipped off Lakeshore Drive and into the neighborhood, Autumn's breath caught in her chest. This was not the place she left.

The sidewalks were clean.

Too clean.

New trees, evenly spaced like ornaments, lined the block where wild roots used to crack the concrete. Murals now bloomed on walls that once bore gang signs and where candlelight vigils were held. On Oakenwood Boulevard, one of the old liquor stores had been replaced by a yoga studio, its windows crystal clear and sunlit.

A group of Black kids played on the corner, joyfully and with no fear, while a white couple strolled past them, the man holding a green juice and the woman pushing a baby stroller.

Autumn's heart tightened.

It was beautiful, yes. But it didn't feel like the home she once knew and sometimes feared.

Who got pushed out so a smoothie bar could replace Miss Charlene's beauty shop? What happened to the neighbors who couldn't afford this new version of safety?

Ebondale had changed. But at what cost?

She pushed the thoughts out as they pulled into Mia's driveway, just as the evening sun cast everything in amber light.

Mia came flying out the front door, and in that moment, Autumn took her in without the filter of FaceTime. She was a whirlwind of vibrant energy, all five-foot-three of her curvy frame radiating a confidence that three children hadn't diminished.

Her short, asymmetrical haircut, dyed a bold honey-blonde, highlighted her radiant mahogany skin. Dressed in stylishly distressed jean shorts and a thin, wide-sleeved hoodie that flapped like wings, she was every bit the successful, unapologetic woman Autumn admired.

Her arms were wide open, a joyful grin splitting her face.

"My babies!" she shouted as the kids tumbled out of the SUV and into her arms.

Autumn stepped out more slowly, stretching limbs stiff from the ride. Her eyes scanned the block, absorbing the newness and the nostalgia still lurking beneath it.

"Whew, girl," Mia said after hugging her, sizing her up as the kids ran to greet their cousins. "You look like you've been driving through hell."

"I feel like it," Autumn muttered, rubbing the back of her stiff neck.

"Uncle Amir!"

The ladies turned toward the dual squeals from Jordan and Layla and saw them being swooped up into Amir's arms.

The sun angled just right, catching on the silver chain around his neck as he lowered the kids and stood to his full height of six-feet-three. A gray tee clung to his torso like it was tailor-made, the sleeves hugging arms that had clearly never let the gym membership lapse.

Mia let out a low gasp at how his jeans hugged his thighs, and Autumn couldn't help but laugh at her reaction.

His skin gleamed like deep roasted coffee, smooth and rich. His beard was masterfully carved, lining a strong jaw with the precision of a man who took his grooming seriously. When a faint smile touched his lips, it revealed a single, deep dimple in his cheek.

The thick locs he once kept shoulder-length now spilled well past his waist, glossy and meticulously maintained, swaying gently as he moved. When he tilted his head and flashed that familiar grin, the one that had once made Asia doodle hearts in every notebook she owned, Mia grabbed Autumn's arm, her grip suddenly tight.

"Gawddamn," she said loud enough for only Autumn to hear. "That man is still foine!"

"Mia," Autumn warned through clenched teeth, playfully pinching her.

Mia wagged a finger at her. "No, ma'am. Don't try to gate-keep all that chocolate now. Especially when you keep friend-zoning it. Why didn't you snatch him up when you had the chance?"

Autumn looked at her sister like she'd lost her mind. "Girl, please. I've never had the chance, and for several reasons. Best friend. Godfather. That makes him off-limits."

Mia grunted. "Hmph, to you maybe..."

"Period." Autumn pinched her again. "Seriously. We've been friends since we were kids. And... he was in love with Asia."

"Psh," Mia rebutted, rolling her eyes. "That was forever ago. Asia would approve, and you know it."

Before Autumn could respond, Amir ran up to her, arms wide open.

"Ayyyeeee, look what the Chicago wind finally blew back in!" he exclaimed, smiling big.

"Hey, stranger," a tired Autumn replied.

He pulled her in, and for a second, she was enveloped in the solid warmth of him, a scent like clean laundry. She meant to hug him back, to sink into the comfort, but the exhaustion of the road had settled deep in her bones. Her arms stayed limp at her sides.

He seemed to sense the distance instantly and pulled back. The easy smile on his face tightened a fraction.

"Let's catch up later." The warmth in his eyes seemed guarded now as he turned to help the kids take in the boxes and bags.

It was Mia's turn to pinch Autumn.

"Ouch!" she exclaimed, grabbing the back of her arm to massage the sting. "What was that for?"

Mia shook her head and walked toward the house.

Inside Mia's home, the air smelled like warm cinnamon and lemon floor polish. The kids had already kicked off their shoes and disappeared up the stairs to their new room, Layla yelling dibs on the top bunk, Jordan trailing behind her.

Mia's four-year-old twin boys soon descended into a chaotic mix of toys and laughter, while Mia's fourteen-year-old offered a quick, cool nod before disappearing back into his room.

Amir finally hauled the last box into the guest room, as if it were filled with feathers.

"You sure you don't wanna stay and eat with us?" Mia called from the kitchen, where she was prepping dinner while Autumn assisted with cutting vegetables.

"Nah," he responded, tossing a playful wink toward her as he stepped into the space, filling it up. "I've seen Autumn burn noodles before. I value my taste buds."

"Boy, I can boil noodles. How do you burn *water*?" A wave of shared laughter with Mia swallowed Autumn's retort. She shook her head, a wide grin still on her face. "I swear, some things never change."

"Like your face," Amir teased, bumping her shoulder as he reached over to grab a baby carrot. "Still scrunches up when you laugh too hard."

"Don't start with me, Mr. Jackson," she warned, wagging a paring knife at him.

The kids, except for Mia's oldest son, brought the rancor downstairs, playing like they'd never had years or miles between them.

Amir joined in the fun as the kids shrieked and ran around.

Jordan ran to jump into his arms, and he caught him mid-air.

"You grow bigger every time I see you," he exclaimed, grunting playfully under Jordan's weight. "What you been feeding this boy?" he called to Autumn.

"Spaghetti," Layla replied. "And cereal. And the nuggets shaped like dinosaurs."

"Ah, you mean the delicacies," Amir winked at her.

A few minutes later, Layla was playing with the ends of Amir's locs, fascinated by their length. "Uncle Amir, why do you let your locs grow so long? Are you ever going to cut them?"

He laughed softly and planted a kiss on her cheek. "Well, you know how you get a little bit taller every year? My hair is kind of like that. Each bit that grows is a piece of a story from my life: a happy day, a sad day, a day I learned something new. They're like my memories. Cutting them would feel like forgetting all the things that made me who I am today."

Autumn watched from the background of Mia's open kitchen, arms crossed over her chest, smiling without realizing she was doing it.

He was so good with them. Patient. Attentive. Not performative... just present.

Mia looked over her shoulder, catching the exact angle of her gaze. She shot her a pointed look, her eyes narrowing as she let out a low "Mmhmm" that was pure indictment, meant for Autumn's ears only.

"What?" Autumn asked, startled.

Mia leaned on her hip, arms folded like a knowing big sister. "I'm just sayin'. That man is single, gainfully employed, emotionally intelligent, smells like a whole vibe, and fine as hell. Somebody better snatch him up before I do."

Amir grinned as he walked back into the kitchen after ushering the kids upstairs. "Y'all know I can hear you, right?"

"Good," Mia said, turning back toward the stove. "Just making sure you know you're on the radar."

Autumn shook her head, smiling to hide her fluster. "Y'all are ridiculous."

Amir didn't respond directly but glanced at her with a smirk.

Later that night, after the house had quieted and the kids were asleep in the guest room, Autumn sat on the side of the bed in Mia's decommissioned office, boxes unopened, bags still zipped.

She looked around the room, bathed in the soft orange glow of the street lamp outside.

Her phone buzzed.

AMIR

Are you okay?

AUTUMN

A little tired. But yeah.

And thanks for today. Really.

Three dots appeared and lingered for over thirty seconds. Then he responded,

AMIR

Anytime.

And always.

She set the phone on the nightstand and lay back on the bed.

Ebondale didn't feel like home yet.

But it was starting to feel less like running, and more like the very beginning of something she couldn't yet name.

7

THE GREEN BENCH

From the moment Autumn told her sister she was making her visit to Chicago permanent, Mia had transformed into a one-woman resource center.

She had the kids enrolled in every park district summer program she could find: field trips, reading clubs, and basketball camp at Amir's youth center for Jordan. Their days were full.

But for the first time since leaving college, Autumn's days were still, filled with a quiet she couldn't remember ever experiencing. Journaling more and learning to meditate should have felt like freedom.

By the second week, the stillness started to itch beneath her skin. Her thumbnails were raw from chewing her cuticles. Her journal pages were filled with half-started sentences crossed out before they could form into full thoughts. Without kid-and-work chaos to outrun her thoughts, she was stuck with an endless loop of doubt and second-guessing.

Why hadn't she moved on from Chris after more than a year?
What had truly pulled her back to Chicago?
Would she ever land a job on par with the one she lost?

Which is why, when Amir showed up on a Monday morning with a latte and that slow, sideways smirk she remembered all too well, she needed very little convincing to get outside.

"Let me take you around Ebondale," he said, holding the cup out like a bribe. "Get you reacquainted with the old hood. Plus, you owe me for clowning my fit in front of my godkids."

Autumn took a grateful sip, already smiling. "First of all, that fit clowned itself. I just gave it a mic."

"Oh, you got jokes!"

She turned to head upstairs, laughing. "Let me throw on a light jacket."

"A jacket?!" he cackled. "It's damn near seventy. You been down South too long."

"I can't hear youuuu," she sang over her shoulder as she bounded up the steps. "Give me ten seconds, judgmental."

The drive instantly snapped her out of the fog she'd been floating in all weekend. The moment they hit King Drive, the old rhythm between them took over. Jokes flew easily, laughter came without effort, and the vibe was light but charged... like no time had passed.

Amir's playlist, cheekily titled 'Triple A Vibes,' was already thumping: Brandy, Tupac, Mýa. Then DMX's gravelly bark exploded through the speakers like thunder.

Autumn's eyes lit up. "Ohhhhhh shiiiiit, that's my jam!"

She reached for the volume knob, cranked it with zero shame, and launched into the lyrics like muscle memory had been waiting to pounce. She rapped with ferocity, shoulders popping, head bobbing.

Amir beat the steering wheel in time, the car vibrating with every bark and versc.

By the time the track faded out, both were breathless, red-faced from laughter.

"Damn, I haven't zoned out like that in a minute," Autumn panted, peeling off the jacket.

"I told you," Amir chuckled.

He made a sudden U-turn, flipping his signal on too late, and the driver behind him blasted their horn.

"Ooh, you gotta see something." His voice buzzed with a mysterious energy.

She leaned forward as he cruised down Cottage Grove Avenue, her eyes wide as she took in what her old hood had become.

Blocks once littered with trash now gleamed with colorful flowers; the corner store that used to sell fruit-flavored blunts now served lavender lemonade.

There was a juice bar where Acme Hardware used to be. A gourmet sandwich spot with sidewalk seating outside replaced the old check-cashing place. Hanging planters bobbed above cafe tables where grandmas used to play the lottery and the old heads played Spades and chess.

"Remember when Mr. Bracey used to kick us from in front of that store at 6 on the dot?"

"Man! Every. Single. Day." Amir laughed, already slipping into character. "'Y'all ain't gon' sit up on my steps all day like y'all payin' rent.'"

His voice morphed into a raspy old-man's growl, and a laugh ripped out of Autumn so hard it ended in a snort.

"Stop!" she groaned, clutching her chest. "You play too much!"

"Asia used to clown you for that!" Amir wheezed, laughing harder. "You still got it, that legendary snort."

Their mirth was warm and familiar.

Amir's voice shifted, turning reflective, softer. "He always played mean, but Mr. Bracey let us hang out until the store closed. I didn't get it back then, but now? I know he was keeping us safe. No gangs, no drama. That stoop was neutral ground."

Autumn nodded slowly. "And we didn't even realize it."

They drove a few more blocks before Amir pulled to a slow stop in front of a freshly painted sixteen-story building. Autumn's brows knitted together as she took in the polished brick and gleaming glass.

"Wait... is this...?"

"Yup," Amir nodded. "One of the last standing project buildings."

"This used to be The Bricks..."

Amir turned off the engine. "Still is, technically. Just dressed up now."

Her eyes widened as she stepped out into the breeze. "I can't believe they didn't tear them all down."

Even the smell was different.

Gone was the thick scent of stale piss and trash that used to permeate the air like it was a part of the ecosystem.

Now it smelled like fresh-cut grass.

"This place was so bad," she recalled. "I remember asking my daddy if I could visit Mia here when I was ten. I wanted to see my sister, you know? He lost it. Said I wasn't allowed to come anywhere near this place."

The building, once a looming gray monolith of poverty and violence, had been reborn. Its new earth-tone exterior was warm and welcoming, softened by clean balconies adorned with potted plants and hanging succulents. A bold navy sign read "Ebondale Terrace Senior Residences" in gold script.

"I used to come here all the time," Amir said, nodding up toward one of the middle floors. "My aunt and cousins lived on the eighth. You had to walk through a gang of dudes before you even made it to the elevators. Most of them were strapped, and the rest were waiting for an excuse."

He scanned the peaceful courtyard, a flicker of old instinct in his eyes.

"My auntie never had to worry, though. And neither did my cousins when they were with me. They knew who I was. Who my brothers were." His voice dropped into a lower, quieter register. "They knew not to fuck with our family."

Autumn saw the echo of that boy on the block, the one who learned too young how to stand his ground.

His words, the tone, sent a shiver of memory through her.

His older brothers were legends in Ebondale, entrenched in a gang life Amir was fortunate to sidestep. She remembered the whispers, the way people would give them a wide berth on the sidewalk. It was a respect born from fear, a power Amir inherited by proximity.

But even then, she'd seen how he was different. The youngest of four boys, his brothers kept him shielded, making sure he walked a different path. Even early on, when he didn't want to.

He hadn't lost that edge; he'd mastered it. He'd taken that inherited power, that borrowed intimidation, and forged it into the quiet, unshakable foundation of the man who stood before her now.

And the respect she had for that, for the discipline it took to turn bravado into positive influence, sent an unwanted sensation through her, a feeling she purposefully left unexamined.

She sighed as she craned her neck to look up at the concrete behemoth that had devoured the corner. "Seeing this place now, it's hard to imagine things were ever like that."

Amir smiled faintly. "Mia's grandma still lives on the second floor, in that same apartment. She refused to leave when the revitalization started, told them this was her home before it became a war zone, and it'd be her home long after."

He slid closer to her. "I wanted you to see this especially. Because if this place can heal, Autumn, so can we."

They stood in silence, side by side, letting their memories collide with the moment.

"The sirens... the gang wars... the shootouts," she murmured, her voice taut with a familiar ache. "Even if I wasn't in these buildings, the rules still applied across Ebondale. You had to know which blocks were safe, who to avoid, even what time to be indoors."

Amir nodded. "Yeah. You practically had to memorize your own survival map."

They started walking. Around every corner, the past peeked out like a ghost dressed in new clothes. A mural spanned one red-brick wall; Black boys in capes leaping toward the sky, flanked by elders painted with halos. Another block down stood the old laundromat, where most of the machines never seemed to work. Now, it had transformed into Jasmine's Books, a cozy bookstore with chalkboard signs announcing poetry nights and Black Lit discussions.

Ebondale had shifted from a place people survived to a place they could stand tall in.

Autumn was embraced by longtime residents. Women hugged her, men offered nods of respect, and teen girls whispered behind her back in awe. She was one of theirs, one who'd made it out.

And yet the question rang out everywhere they went.

"Are you back for good?"

Dodging the answer with a smile each time, she wasn't sure of anything.

In every greeting, Asia's name was a gentle echo.

"She would be so happy to see you home, baby," said Ms. Davis at the bakery.

"I still think about that girl. Such a bright light," said their old fourth-grade teacher.

Each mention was a kindness. But each one was also a small, sharp stone added to the pile of grief she was already carrying. So, by the time they sat down at one of Amir's favorite lunch spots, Autumn's emotions hadn't just been poked at all day, they had been scraped raw.

An older woman approached their table, eyes wide with joy.

"Oh, my Lord, look who done come home!" she exclaimed.

Autumn and Amir stood to greet her, each kissing her on the cheek.

She felt like the prodigal child of the block.

"I remember the three amigos," the woman said, pressing her hand to her heart. "It was so sad when Asia passed."

The words sliced through Autumn.

Three more people repeated that exact sentiment before lunch was over. She smiled politely, but inside her molars ached from grinding.

Each time, it knocked loose a piece of something she'd been holding in place.

By the time they pulled up to their old high school, now rebranded with a fresh name and sleek logo, Autumn's steps were heavy, her mouth drawn tight.

Amir stopped walking and took her hand.

"Okay," he said gently. "Talk to me."

She opened her mouth, but what came out was a jagged sob, followed by hot, angry tears, a flood of sixteen years of polite nods and swallowed truths.

"Asia didn't pass away, dammit!" Her voice cracked, like the words physically raked her throat on the way out.

"She was taken from us. They killed her. People need to stop acting like it was natural."

Amir pulled her close, his arms steady around her back.

"I know," he whispered into her hair as her body shook. "I know."

* * *

THEY WALKED in silence for a while, the energy quieter now.

The sun sat high in the sky, but the weight between them made it feel like dusk had swooped in out of nowhere.

Amir led her through a few more blocks in the neighborhood, his steps slower, more deliberate. He didn't speak until they neared a small park.

"You sure you're up for this?" he asked gently, stopping at the edge of the entrance.

Autumn paused. Her fingers curled around the wrought-iron gate. The sign that once read *Whitmore Playground* now bore another name, fresh and bright: *The Asia Worthington Peace Park.*

Her stomach dropped, as if the ground had caved in under her. She took a shaky breath, her eyes tracing each letter of her best friend's name as if to be sure they were real.

She finally managed a nod, her voice a whisper. "I think I need to be."

They stepped through together.

The rusted slide and broken swing set were gone, replaced by a modern jungle gym with rounded edges and soft rubber flooring.

The basketball court had been repaved, the backboards gleamed, the chain nets clinked with each shot someone made in the distance.

A peace mural replaced the wall that once bore gang signs, with Asia's face front and center, her smile stretched wide beneath a painted crown.

Autumn saw the old bench, the infamous green one, now freshly painted, where the three of them used to sit like they ran the world.

Where they laughed loudly.

Where being seventeen had felt bulletproof.

Autumn's knees went soft, and she collapsed on it.

Amir sat beside her, close enough to offer comfort without a single touch.

A car horn blew in the distance. And suddenly, she was transported back to 2009.

* * *

It was late July.

Autumn was freshly seventeen, just a week into what should have been the best summer of her teenage life. She and Asia were coming down from the high of receiving their early acceptance letters to Spelman.

The Chicago heat was muggy and merciless, but not enough to keep the *Triple A* squad indoors. Autumn had her hair slicked into a side swoop, with deep waves cascading over one shoulder—a style she'd perfected with edge control and a satin scarf the night before.

Her giant hoop earrings caught the sun every time she turned her head. Her favorite lip gloss was poppin', as usual.

Amir and Asia sat beside her, the three of them claiming their usual spot on the bench by the court. It was the perfect angle for her to see Mario as he played pickup with the other neighborhood boys.

Today, she was looking extra cute, sporting a pair of tight denim shorts and a "Poetic Justice" crop tee.

As she sipped on a blueberry icee, Asia turned to her. "Girl. Are you ever gonna give in and step to Mario, or are you gonna keep being complicated? It's obvious you like him."

Autumn scoffed. "Girl, please. I am not complicated. I'm exclusive."

The trio laughed as Autumn adjusted herself to get a better view of the court.

Asia whispered something in Amir's ear, making him grin widely.

She was full of energy. Joyful and carefree.

Her long box braids were freshly done and gathered into a high ponytail; baby hairs sculpted into delicate swoops and held in place with Eco gel.

She rocked a pair of denim cutoff shorts, and she and Amir wore matching shirts she designed; hers pink, his black, both stamped with bold white block letters inside a heart that read "Asia and Amir."

"Y'all matching now?" Autumn teased, raising an eyebrow and sucking loudly on her straw. "Who said couples' tees were trending?"

Asia leaned into Amir, legs crossed. "First of all," she shot back, "we don't follow trends. We start them."

Amir smirked. "She made me wear it."

"And you didn't even fight it," Autumn said in mock disgust. "Whipped."

"Look, she bribed me with Flamin' Hots and her mama's peach cobbler. I folded."

They all burst out laughing.

Trash talk from the guys playing on the court grew louder as someone disputed a call.

Then came the screech of tires.

A black sedan tore around the corner, its darkened windows down. Hands already out.

Pop. Pop-pop.

"Get down!" Amir yelled, pulling both girls with him.

But it was too late.

Asia's body twisted unnaturally as the bullet hit. The pink shirt she'd been so proud of darkened in a spreading pool of red.

Autumn was frozen, tears streaming, mouth open in a silent scream as she watched her friend bleed out.

Amir crawled on his knees to her, clutching her body, trying to apply pressure as her eyes closed. "Asia? Asia, baby, stay with me!"

"Aye, somebody been hit!" someone yelled from the court. "Call an ambulance!"

The park was in chaos.

Sirens blaring.

Neighbors running.

Voices wailing.

Asia didn't move.

The last thing Autumn remembered, before the flashing lights and the coroner's van, was the pain in Amir's eyes and the way he screamed Asia's name, over and over, like it would bring her back.

* * *

AUTUMN JERKED when Amir touched her shoulder, the sob escaping like it was torn from her chest.

"She didn't just pass," she whispered. "She was killed."

Her voice cracked under the weight of the pain, each word feeling like lead.

"She didn't get sick. She didn't slip away in her sleep. Someone pointed a gun out a window... and fired into a crowd... and they killed her."

Amir's jaw worked silently, the muscle twitching.

"I know."

"She was so full of life," Autumn muttered after a few minutes, wiping hot tears from her face. "She had so many dreams... besides being your wife," she leaned her shoulder into Amir's, a wan smile forming. "She wanted to be a fashion designer. She loved making those cheesy ass matching shirts."

They both chuckled—a low, sad, hollow sound.

"I still have mine," Amir smiled. "It's in a box. I couldn't throw it away."

"Thank you," she said after a few seconds, her voice barely audible. "For bringing me here. I needed to remember."

He looked at her, eyes glossy but steady. "She'd want you to be here, Autumn. In Ebondale. I know you think staying away from this place was protecting you. But maybe coming back is how you heal."

Autumn exhaled.

"I'm not certain I know how to do that," she admitted.

"Listen, you don't have to have it all figured out right away."

Amir's hand hovered, then settled gently on hers... warm, steady.

A light breeze stirred the trees overhead, rustling like a sigh from the block itself.

"You just have to be willing to try."

8

CARAMEL SWIRL

The door to Mia's salon swung open with a soft chime, and the humid July heat seeped in, its oppressive warmth a tangible presence against the crisp, cool air blowing from the vents.

Inside, the cloud of freshly flat-ironed hair met the nose first, its buttery heat softened by the sugary scent of pink hair lotion and the warm notes of coconut oil.

To the left, women sat at stations with their hands cradled under small UV lights. Acrylic dust floated ghostlike in beams of sun slipping through the blinds, the scent of cherry cuticle oil cutting through the sharper bite of liquid monomer.

Laughter rolled in waves across the establishment, blending with the rhythmic snap of gum, the low murmur of gossip, and the pulse of a '90s R&B playlist whispering through a Bluetooth speaker hidden beneath a towel bin.

Autumn saw the magic of her sister's baby.

Fix Your Crown wasn't just a salon.

It was a sanctuary, a sisterhood under fluorescent lights.

Autumn sat near the back at Mia's private station, her legs crossed at the ankle, a soft pink sundress clinging to her curves like it was a second skin.

The delicate rosebud print and flirty, tiered skirt gave it a sweet, innocent vibe, but the way it snatched her waist and teased the top of her thighs was all woman. Thin straps framed her shoulders, and a small bow at the center of the bust hinted at softness.

A fresh mani-pedi, rose gold and glossy, popped against her rich, cocoa-brown complexion, her white sandals showing off the shimmer on her toes.

Her hands rested in her lap as Mia's assistant put the finishing touches on her hair: A sleek, tousled bob that fell just past her jawline, its deep waves curled softly, like they had an attitude all their own. The rich, glossy black strands framed her face perfectly, a subtle side part adding volume and drama.

Her lips were pressed into a tight line as she avoided the amused stares of Mia's best friends, affectionately known in the community as the Bag Ladies of Ebondale, a name born from the legendary group therapy sessions that started it all.

Mia was styling Brianna's hair, while other stylists were attending to Josie and Londyn.

"You know why we're all clocking you, right?" Brianna asked, and Autumn was reminded of the broad, teasing grin she'd received her first week back. At thirty-eight, she was the Bag Ladies' unofficial leader, the plus-size goddess with a head full of thick, natural curls who was fiercely protective of her tribe. As Mia sprayed them, Brianna sipped her green smoothie like it was the tea she wanted Autumn to spill.

Autumn met their collective gaze in the mirror, their eyes wide with a shameless, hungry anticipation.

She gave a slow, deliberate eyeroll that was pure performance, followed by a deep, put-upon sigh.

"I told y'all before," she feigned exasperation, her cheek twitching with suppressed amusement. "I don't have a man and have no intention of finding one any time soon."

Londyn, who at thirty-seven had the keen, hazel eyes of the Senior Property Manager she was, gave Autumn an observant, appraising smile. With flawless skin that spoke of her African American and Cherokee heritage, she leaned back in the seat like a sitcom auntie, arms folded, hair wrapped in colorful flexi-rods. "You're lookin' mighty cute today, you sure you ain't trying to catch nothing?"

Brianna sang out, "Amen! You been in Chicago for a few weeks, sis.

Don't you think it's time to loosen the notches on that refurbished chastity belt?"

Mia peeked over her stylish Michael Kors frames, shaking her head with a messy grin. "Lil sis over there tryna act brand new, but y'all, wait 'til I tell you what she did when she saw Amir that first day back."

Autumn groaned. "Mia. We are not doing this."

"Yes, the hell we are," she smirked, looking around at the ladies. "Chile, this woman saw that man and clutched her pearls so tight, I thought she was gonna pass out."

The ladies erupted in amusement as Autumn's eyes widened.

"She legit froze!" Mia continued.

"I did not freeze," Autumn defended, embarrassed by the exaggeration.

Brianna leaned forward, faux pity in her tone. "Ya froze up, sis?"

"She had to reboot!" Mia howled, causing the others to laugh just as hard. "And then had the nerve to act casual when he hugged her."

"I had just driven fourteen-plus hours with two kids," Autumn protested, trying to suppress a laugh. "He caught me off guard. I hadn't seen him in person in a while, and it threw me off how different he looked, that's all."

Josie looked up from her phone. Her chic bob framed a face with high cheekbones and buttered chocolate eyes that seemed to know a thing or two about life. At thirty-seven, she carried herself with the hard-won confidence of a woman who had seen some things but had come out on the other side, looking flawless as she fanned herself dramatically.

"Girl, Amir is always catching women off guard—old, young, and even those who wanna be women. That man walks around smelling like emotional stability and lookin' like a box of fine chocolate."

Mia co-signed on Josie's comment, her lips pursed like she'd just tasted something sweet. "Facts. But you know what's really attractive about him? The way he's out here for the kids. He started that youth center and even created a basketball camp for the boys in the neighborhood. He's like the community's bonus daddy."

Brianna hummed. "Lawd, if I had a man like that in my circle—"

"Um, Miss Thang," Mia interjected, tapping her on the shoulder. "You do have a man like that, all up and through your circle."

"Uh-huh," Londyn added. "You got a whole alderman, ma'am."

"Oh shit, I do, don't I?" Brianna laughed. "Carry on then."

"Y'all, please," Autumn sighed, waving them off. "Me and Amir have been best friends since we were eight years old. Besides, he and Asia were in love. My girl was determined to be the first and only Mrs. Jackson. You don't mess with your girl's man, even if she is gone."

That quieted the space for half a second.

Londyn nodded and voiced her agreement.

"Sis." Mia's look was gentle. "Y'all were teenagers when they started dating. You're grown now. Life has changed."

"It's still a line," Autumn murmured, her voice softer.

"But are you honoring the line?" Brianna asked. "Or are you hiding behind it?"

Autumn's mouth gaped open, her eyes wide with astonishment. "I don't believe we're having this conversation. Amir is my best friend. We could never be more than that. Case closed."

The salon's front door chimed.

Ms. Jenkins, Mia's 72-year-old client who loved her sponge roller curls and was always ear hustling on the latest shop gossip, shushed the chatter. "Bird in the bush," she whispered, eyes looking around as if they were all in on a conspiracy.

The women exchanged looks, half confused, half entertained. Brianna muttered, "What the hell is that old lady talking about now?"

Before an answer could be formed, Amir walked into the space, carrying a Styrofoam cupholder.

Well, more like floated.

He wore a fitted black crewneck tee that clung to the sculpted lines of his chest, framing his muscular arms with ease. His locs, which looked like they needed a re-twist, were pulled back today, gathered low at the nape of his neck, and brushed the small of his back.

He moved through the salon, easy and unbothered, in a pair of dark-wash jeans that knew their assignment. They weren't tight, but the thick denim clung to his athletic thighs with every stride, doing little to hide the powerful muscles beneath. They sat low on his hips, casual and confident.

He offered a small smile and a "Good morning, Queens," as he walked through the salon, like he'd just stepped into a room of royalty.

A collective hum rippled out, followed by a shudder of soft laughs.

"Oh lawd," Josie whispered as he neared. "He is fine-fine."

"Foine," Brianna corrected under her breath.

Even Autumn couldn't help but do a double-take as he approached, that familiar grin riding his lips. But the moment his eyes landed on her, something flickered in them.

He slowed his stride and lifted one brow with surprise.

His gaze swept from her laid edges to the soft curve of her sundress, and for a moment longer than was normal, it lingered on her exposed thighs.

The easy grin faltered, replaced by a look of unfiltered appreciation.

A definite spark ignited in his eyes, sending a current straight through Autumn's stomach.

"Damn," he breathed, the word escaping before he could stop it.

He immediately cleared his throat, seemingly wanting to swallow the sound back down. He held out one of the coffee cups, his movement a little too quick, a little less smooth than his usual rhythm.

"You look nice."

His fingers brushed against hers as she took the drink, and the brief contact seemed to startle them both.

He pulled his hand back, quickly breaking eye contact and focusing on the hair accessories case, the floor—anywhere but her.

"They, uh..." he coughed to clear his throat again, scratching the back of his neck. "They were out of oat milk, so I got you almond. Caramel swirl, right?"

She tried to fight the smirk, but it won, pulling at the corners of her mouth. This was the first time she'd ever seen Amir flustered. "I'm flexible," she said, taking a sip.

Londyn arched a mocking brow. "Are you now?"

The salon exploded in laughter.

Even Autumn let herself laugh as Amir handed the second drink to Mia, trying to regain his composure.

"Well," he stammered, glancing around, "just wanted to drop these off before my meeting. Y'all don't roast my girl too hard."

"Oh, we already lit that fire," Josie teased, winking at Autumn. "But thanks for fueling it."

Amir chuckled and waved goodbye, his exit not as smooth as his entrance had been.

The moment the door chimed shut behind him, an electric silence fell over the back room. Then, as if on cue, all eyes swiveled back to Autumn.

She immediately grabbed her phone, pretending to be engrossed in a social media feed. Her cheeks were still burning from the encounter, and she was trying to find her footing on ground that had suddenly, completely tilted.

Mia, however, was having none of her avoidance.

She picked up a pair of flatirons and resumed working on Brianna's hair, her movements deliberate while eyeing Autumn's reflection in the mirror. "So, sis." Her voice was deceptively casual. "How long has it been since you've had a man?"

Autumn didn't answer right away. She set her phone down and took a slow, deliberate sip from her cup, using the moment to gather herself. The heat from the coffee was just right, the warm combination of sweet and creamy perfect and soothing.

Everything the last five minutes had not been.

Setting the mug down on the station with theatrical slowness was a playful act of defiance against her sister's interrogation.

"I've had a serious relationship…" she replied, arching a brow, "… with my toy. We're emotionally compatible. It listens. Never talks back. And it's full of stamina, as long as I got the double AAs on standby."

The roaring oofs and laughter came swiftly.

"Not the battery-powered bae!" Josie guffawed with a dramatic sigh. "We've all been there."

Mia paused mid-press, glanced at Josie, and grinned mischievously. "You know I got a whole battery caddy, right? Bedroom closet. Top shelf."

"It's more like a damn altar," Autumn deadpanned. "I think she prays to it."

As the new wave of laughter finally died down, Brianna's expression sobered, her gaze cutting through the leftover humor. She studied Autumn for a few seconds, her tone leveling into something serious but kind.

"Autumn, what are you really afraid of? I mean, it's been what, over a year and a half since your divorce?"

Autumn nodded slowly.

"If hanging back is intentional, cool. No judgment. But if you're stuck in some kind of emotional time loop, you might need to unpack that. 'Cause one year turns into five real fast."

Autumn's gaze dropped to the coffee cup in her hands. The playful defiance drained out of her as she toyed with the lid.

"Actually," she said, her voice quieter now, "I lied about not wanting to get involved. I've been thinking about that very thing. Only, I want to date for a while. Nothing serious. But I don't know if it's too soon."

"Based on whose timeline?" Mia chirped. "Honey, the minute I left Donovan, I started going through my friend's list. Cos what I'm not gon' do is sit at home just because society has an opinion on how long I should be single."

A few older women nearby let out soft hums of agreement. Ms. Jenkins muttered, "Amen, baby," as she flipped through a magazine with well-worn pages.

Josie chimed in. "It's the double standard for me. Women are expected to sit back and clock in at some pre-designated timeline. Meanwhile, these men will have a woman on Monday, a situationship on Thursday, and can be engaged by Saturday after a breakup. And nobody gives a damn."

"Mmhmm," Mia added, her flatiron clicking closed with emphasis. "But let a single mama go on a second date before the ink's dry on her name change, and suddenly she's 'for the streets.'"

"Girl!" Brianna clapped her hand to her thigh. "Like she got dudes smokin' out the window or somethin'!"

That sent the room into another round of cackles.

Even the women under dryers perked up and leaned in, laughing and tossing in "that part!"

Londyn added, "It's like society wants women to disappear after divorce. But healing looks different on all of us. Some of us rest. Some of us travel. Some of us... worship our battery caddies." She tossed Mia a wink.

Ms. Jenkins adjusted the pink cap over her curls. The wrinkles of time were stamped into her forehead and puffed under her eyes, framing a wise, amused gaze. "Listen, baby. I was married twenty-eight years. When I left, folks told me I should find myself. I said, 'I have found myself. And she likes wine, fresh sheets, and dinner dates without having to clean up after two people.'"

The whole salon roared in solidarity.

A full-on debate broke out, funny, honest, and deeply layered.

The conversation stretched from expected modesty to "mom guilt," slut-shaming, and sacred self-care.

Everyone had something to add: those in their twenties with fresh heartbreaks, women in their thirties and forties juggling kids and careers, and the silver-haired aunties who'd been through all of it twice and had zero intention of sugarcoating the truth.

As the laughter from the dating debate wound down, Mia turned the focus back to Autumn.

"Sis, have you thought about going to therapy?"

Her friends nodded knowingly.

"I think Dr. Santos would be perfect for you."

"Is that the therapist who started the Bag Ladies thing?"

"Mm-hmm," she confirmed, adjusting her smock. "Brianna was the inspiration for it. Sis, she is the truth. She's soft when you need her to be, but she will drag your soul—in a loving, licensed way, of course."

Londyn chimed in from the dryer station. "She had me reevaluating every dusty dude I ever entertained. If it wasn't for her, Jeremy and I wouldn't have made it."

"I put in a 911 call after I almost texted my ex, Mike," Josie added, holding up a hand like she was giving a testimony. "Girl, it was December 23rd. It was cold. I was lonely. I was listening to sad holiday songs. I had those 'what if' vibes on me."

A wave of "Mmm hmm" and knowing chuckles swept through the salon.

"She stopped me mid-rant," Josie continued. "You're not missing him; you're missing the comfort he brought. Oof! I wanted to scream into the phone. But she wasn't wrong."

"You ain't gotta be in a full-on breakdown to need therapy," Mia said gently. "Sometimes you just need help unpacking stuff that's been sitting in your bag."

Autumn toyed with a stray thread on the hem of her dress. She'd thought about therapy more than once since her divorce, but saying it out loud made it real.

"I'll think about it," she said finally. "I've definitely been... carrying a few things."

Mia's look was pointed. "That's what I've been saying since you got here. Therapy ain't about saying you're broken, sis. It's about finally getting help to unpack all that damn baggage."

Just then, Ms. Jenkins stood from her chair, fluffing her curls and smoothing the back of her floral print dress. "You know," she said, clearing her throat, "I always thought therapy was for folks who didn't know how to pray. But the way y'all talkin'…"

She looked around the salon like she was giving an official announcement.

"Maybe I need to look into it. Lord knows I got a few past situations that still bother me."

The ladies clapped and encouraged her with warm applause and nods.

She reached into her purse, pulled out a few bills, and slid them into Mia's tip jar with a flourish. She turned around, pretending to whisper in Mia's direction.

"Also… can I borrow some of them batteries?"

The entire salon lost it.

Ms. Jenkins' grin was wide as she sashayed toward the door. "Well, y'all have a blessed day."

As the door closed behind her, laughter ricocheted through the shop again.

Autumn wiped tears from the corners of her eyes, her stomach sore from joy.

The therapy was a spot-on idea.

Opening herself up to date? That sounded good, too.

But this kind of camaraderie?

This was healing as well.

She no longer felt like she was unraveling. She felt like she was unfolding.

One layer at a time.

9

VELVET AND VOLTAGE

"Thank you, Dr. Santos—I mean, Jasmine," Autumn corrected herself. "I look forward to meeting you, too."

She ended the call, her thumb hovering over the screen for a second before she slipped the phone into her back pocket.

It was done.

She'd finally scheduled her first therapy session. The conversation at the salon a few days ago had been the push she needed. Her shoulders, which had been tense all morning, relaxed a fraction.

Mia, leaning against the kitchen island with her arms crossed, gave a satisfied nod. "I'm telling you, lil sis... once you sit on that couch, dots will start to connect. You'll be unpacking stuff you didn't even know was still buried."

"No spoilers," Autumn said with a small smile, though her fingers toyed nervously with the edge of the business card. "I just never pictured myself going to therapy. It always felt like something other people did."

"Yeah, same here," Mia admitted. "Until I hit a wall I couldn't climb over after learning the truth about my ex having another family. When I started digging into that baggage during my sessions, I found stuff that went back to childhood. And as you can imagine, Daddy was in that mess."

Autumn's brows lifted just a touch, a soft exhale coming through her nose. She definitely understood.

"Sis, we go to the doctor when our body's acting up. Our minds deserve the same energy. I didn't understand that until Jasmine held up a mirror and showed me what I had become, and I didn't like what I saw. Without her, I'd have continued to deal with that trauma on my own."

Autumn gave a slow nod, her thumb brushing across the raised ink on the card.

Her phone buzzed in her pocket.

AMIR

Hey, you free to stop by the center? Need your eyes on something. 👀

Oh—and be on your best behavior, nerd. I've got company. 😎

She smirked and rolled her eyes as she fired off a quick response.

AUTUMN

Asshole.

Then followed with,

AUTUMN

I'll be there shortly.

AMIR

"It's Amir," she announced to Mia, waving her phone like a receipt. "He needs me to stop by the center."

Mia grinned. "That man sure knows how to get you out the house."

"I swear he treats me like his personal assistant."

"Uh-huh. And you always go."

Autumn side-eyed her sister as she grabbed her purse off the island. "Back in a bit. Tell Ms. Layla not to blow up my phone if she gets in from dance camp before me."

"At least put some gloss on those crusty lips!" Mia yelled to her back when she started heading to the door.

Autumn threw up a middle finger over her shoulder as she walked out.

* * *

THE BUTTERY SCENT of fresh popcorn wrapped around Autumn the moment she stepped through the doors of "E Block", the youth center started and run by Amir. Born from his relentless determination to break the generational cycles of trauma that had claimed too many lives, including Asia's, E Block wasn't just a building. It was a refusal to let despair be the final word in their neighborhood.

In partnership with the alderman and local organizers, Amir had helped transform the once-abandoned community gym into a sanctuary for young people. Yes, there were basketball courts and beat labs, dance classes and arts clubs, but at its core, the center thrived on deeper values: safety, inclusion, cultural pride, and the pursuit of excellence.

In its fifth year, the center was legendary across the South Side, celebrated as a sacred space where Ebondale's youth weren't just kept off the streets, they were taught to dream beyond them.

The building buzzed with summer energy.

Fresh, loud, and chaotic in the best way.

A group of kids zipped past her in matching camp T-shirts, bagged snacks in hand, and screeching voices bouncing off the walls.

One of the staffers, Marcus, called after them with practiced patience, clipboard in hand and a box of juice boxes tucked under his arm.

"Y'all better stop running unless somebody's on fire!" he yelled.

"I'm on fire!" one of the boys yelled over his shoulder, erupting into giggles as he sprinted past the front desk.

"Hey, Ms. Autumn," Marcus greeted her with a smile and a "... you already know" shake of his head.

She returned his greeting, laughing out loud.

As she passed the gym room, she saw two teenage girls standing on either side of a long rope, turning it in perfect sync as another girl jumped in the middle, her knees high and braids flying. The rhythmic slap-slap of rope against the floor echoed through the room, and Autumn felt a rush of nostalgia rise in her chest.

She was instantly transported back to summer afternoons with Asia, the two of them battling for double-dutch glory on cracked sidewalks.

Asia always won. She was light on her feet, determination in her jumps and turns, and the whole block cheered her on.

Autumn continued down the corridor, nodding at a few volunteers and dodging a stray basketball that came bouncing out of nowhere.

"Sorry, Ma!" Jordan's voice called from down the hall.

"You're good, baby. I'm here to see Uncle Amir." She blew a kiss at her son, already halfway to Amir's office.

The closer she got to the administration wing, the quieter the atmosphere grew.

The buzz of the kids faded behind thickened walls and wooden doors, and she smoothed her shirt as she neared the meeting area.

Autumn rapped twice on the glass window and stepped inside a small conference room. Amir was at the front, wrapping up a pitch deck, his voice steady with confidence. The space smelled faintly of fresh-brewed coffee and the rich, clean scent of cologne that didn't belong to him.

She wore high-waisted skinny jeans that hugged her hips and a soft lemon-colored tank. A fitted white baseball cap sat low over her curls, with two small hoops peeking out beneath.

No makeup. No gloss. Just bare lips that she flicked her tongue over to moisturize.

She clocked the man standing at the whiteboard opposite Amir, one hand tucked in his pocket, the other casually spinning a branded water bottle. He looked over and paused mid-sentence, his words catching in his throat the moment he noticed her.

It was in that sudden, focused silence that she regretted not taking Mia's advice. With his attention so entirely on her, she was suddenly aware of just how crusty her lips were.

His hazel eyes, warm and amused, took a stroll from her head to her painted toes, then met her gaze with a smile that said he liked what he saw.

Autumn froze.

There was something cocky in the way he stood—intriguing but cool, and completely unfazed. He was tall—maybe six-one—and all presence. He wasn't bulky; his black tee and slim joggers hinted at a lean, confident build, like someone who knew his best angles. His low-cut fade was razor sharp, and his skin was a warm golden tone, like café au lait blessed by the sun.

"My bad, didn't mean to stare." His voice was smooth as he addressed Autumn. "But you walked in looking like the highlight reel of my week."

She wasn't easily rattled when it came to men flirting. But something about the way he'd looked at her, like he was slowly tracing every word on a page, memorizing her.

Amir's chuckle was a notch too loud, a sharp sound that cut through the room. He cleared his throat and glanced between them, bemused.

"Autumn, this is Ekon Carter. He's the social media influencer I told you about, the one volunteering to help promote the center. Ekon, this is Autumn Gardener. Recent volunteer and trusted advisor, pain in my ass, and the only person who knows all my dirty secrets. That's why I keep her around."

"Nice to meet you, Ms. Autumn," Ekon murmured, flashing a slow smile as he cupped her hand in his. "Looking forward to partnering with you."

Autumn smiled, brushing off the electric tug she felt. "Likewise."

She tried to pull her hand back, but he held it a half-second longer—subtle, just long enough for her to notice how smooth his palm was.

"You got a minute?" Amir asked her, his voice slightly edged, pointing to a stack of printed layouts on the table.

"Yeah, sure," she said, easing into the chair beside him as both men sat, grateful for the chance to focus on something that wasn't Ekon's perfectly lined-up eyebrows or how good he smelled.

Ekon settled across from her, that easy confidence still written all over his face. "So, what exactly does a 'trusted advisor' do?" he asked.

"She tells me when I'm full of shit," Amir answered dryly.

"You're welcome," Autumn replied tongue-in-cheek, glancing at him with a smirk.

Ekon laughed.

Deep.

Rich.

His eyes never left her face. "That's a hell of a job."

She shrugged, trying to play unbothered. "Somebody's gotta keep my guy from falling apart."

He leaned forward slightly, elbows on the table. "Well, judging by how he speaks about you, and how quickly you put him in his place, you should be the one running things around here."

"Flattery," she countered, arching a brow mockingly, "works better when it's not so obvious."

"Oh, it's obvious," he winked. "But that doesn't mean it's not real."

Amir cleared his throat, purposefully louder, dragging the stack of papers toward her. "Before he starts writing you a love song, can you look at the updated campaign rollout? I want your take before the graphics go live."

"Mmhm," she murmured, flipping through the pages, trying to refocus as her pulse betrayed her.

Ekon stayed leaned in, his eyes on her, his smile never fading.

She didn't look up, but she felt it. His attention was like static electricity in the room.

"So, Autumn…" he said after a brief pause. "You into digital marketing? Or just bossing Amir around?"

She snorted. "Both. I'm a marketing strategist. Was, I mean. Lost my job a couple of months ago. Took that as the universe saying, 'Time to try something new.'"

His smile softened. "Sorry to hear that." Then his smile returned. "Do you listen to the universe often?"

"Only when it says what I like to hear."

Their eyes met then, a spark of recognition between them.

But she was quick to blink it away.

"I like her," Ekon said, looking over at Amir. "You didn't tell me your friend was a marketing G."

"I didn't want her to upstage you," Amir replied with a tight chuckle and a shrug.

Ekon turned back to her. "Oh, I don't mind that at all. Listen, I know I just met you, but… would you be cool with me getting your number?"

Autumn hesitated. Not out of nerves. Not even out of disinterest.

It was the way he asked.

Smooth, yes. But respectful. Not assuming.

She hadn't been asked out since her divorce. It was almost as if there was a bright, flashing sign floating above her head with the words *"Damaged Goods"* in neon letters that only men could see.

Men flirted, but their advances never felt sincere.

Or maybe, if she was being honest, the icy exterior she projected was a wall too high for most even to try to climb.

Mia's words from earlier came back: "Sometimes you just need help to unpack the stuff that's been sitting in your bag."

And maybe, just maybe, she could try being open.

"Sure," she agreed, pulling out her phone.

Ekon passed her his and watched her fingers type. "I promise I won't blow you up," he said. "Just a 'hey' to see if I can make you smile again."

She glanced up. "So, you assume you made me smile the first time?"

"Didn't I?"

Damn. She hated how charming he was.

And how much she liked it.

Get it together, Autumn, she scolded herself, deliberately pulling one of the flyers toward her and avoiding his penetrating gaze. She skimmed the mockups Amir had printed for the center's fundraising campaign, occasionally tapping her finger on one of the flyers. Meanwhile, the two men shifted into quiet conversation in the next room.

She wasn't trying to eavesdrop exactly, but the walls were paper-thin, and the glass door was open. And their voices, though lowered, carried just enough to slip into her focus.

Moments later, from the adjoining room...

"So..." Ekon's voice was curious, amused. "You sure she's just a friend?"

There was a pause. A paper rustled.

"She said that?" Amir asked, his tone casual.

"You did." Ekon chuckled lightly. "But if I'm stepping on toes, say the word. You seemed a lil agitated in there."

Another pause.

"Nah. Nah, man." Amir's voice was calm, but something under it ran taut. "You're good. I just had something else on my mind. That's all."

Autumn glanced up instinctively, but neither man was looking her way.

Amir leaned against the wall, arms folded, his expression unreadable.

Ekon, meanwhile, flashed a grin as he tossed a glance in her direction, like he'd just gotten the green light.

"Cool. Because she's... nice." He exhaled a low whistle. "Yeah. I'm definitely feeling her."

Amir nodded once, slowly.

"Do your thing, bro." He reached out, and their handshake morphed into a brotherly clasp as he pulled him in and clapped him on the back.

Autumn's stomach fluttered as she quickly returned her eyes to the campaign materials, though she hadn't absorbed a single word on the pages.

* * *

MIA'S HOUSE was quiet by 10:30 p.m. The kids were all asleep, and the only sounds were the low hum of the dishwasher and the occasional click of the ceiling fan blades overhead.

Autumn was curled on the couch in the living room; one leg tucked beneath her and the other stretched toward the edge of the coffee table. She scrolled absently through her social feeds; her mind was still tangled somewhere between the graphics she'd reviewed earlier and the man who'd asked for her number with that velvet voice and those hazel eyes.

Mia plopped down beside her, draped in a silk robe, a bonnet perched on her head like a crown. She took one look at Autumn's expression and grinned.

"You're overthinking it," she observed.

"How do you know what I'm thinking about?"

"Because I know you." She reached for Autumn's phone. "Lemme show you what you really need to see."

"Mia—"

"Hush. You'll thank me in ten seconds."

A few taps later, Ekon Carter's TikTok profile filled the screen.

Autumn sighed as she looked over Mia's shoulder. "Seriously?"

"This is the latest one that went viral last week." She pressed play, ignoring her sister's plea.

The video opened in the low, moody lighting of a recording studio. The camera panned over a massive soundboard, glowing with dozens of lights. In the foreground, Ekon sat in a plush leather chair, headphones around his neck, nodding his head slowly with a look of deep, analytical appreciation on his face.

Across from him, a popular, Grammy-winning rapper named X, short for Xavier, lounged back, watching him intently. A snippet of a track played over the video.

The beat cut out, and the video ended with Ekon leaning forward to clasp hands with the rapper in a gesture of brotherly respect.

The on-screen caption read: "Got the exclusive first listen of the new X album. Y'all are not ready for this! 10/10."

The comment section was a firestorm of hype, with thousands of fans and other celebrities reacting to the sneak peek and Ekon's high praise.

Autumn watched, unimpressed but not blind. She could see the appeal.

"Okay, that was kind of nice," she admitted.

Mia clicked on another.

The video started with him on a basketball court at a youth center on the north side, dressed in a simple hoodie and joggers, laughing as he helped a young kid perfect his shot. The text on the screen read: *"Putting in the work that matters..."*

He then tossed the basketball toward the camera, and as it hit, the scene instantly cut. Now, he was in a sharp tuxedo, stepping out of a black SUV. The text changed to: *"... so you can show up for the moments that count."*

The final shot was of him on a stage at a glittering charity gala, handing over an oversized check to a foundation.

"He does a lot of stuff like that," Mia said. "And he's smart with his content. He knows how to stay relevant without being obnoxious. That's what makes him likable. He's one of my favorites."

Autumn pinched the screen to enlarge his image. "He looks good, and he seems to be extremely popular. And he knows it. That mix can be dangerous."

Mia chuckled. "And yet, you still saved his number."

Autumn gasped, dramatically splaying fingers across her chest as if mortally wounded. "Out of respect," she proclaimed, her voice dripping with fake sincerity. "The man gave a good pitch today. It's professional courtesy, and I may have questions about the campaign."

Mia sniffed with mockery. "Yeah, right."

Before Autumn could throw a pillow at her, her phone buzzed.

Ekon's name flashed on the screen.

She froze. "Oh no."

"Oh YES," Mia whispered, leaping off the couch like it was game day. "Answer it! Put it on speaker!"

Autumn swatted at her. "Go to bed."

"Don't mess this up," Mia warned, wagging a finger at her as she backed out of the room, then bounded up the stairs. She called down, "You deserve a little fun!"

Autumn took a steadying breath and hit accept.

"Hello?"

His voice was instant velvet. "Hope I'm not interrupting anything."

She smiled. "You are. I'm incredibly busy scrolling through social media."

He chuckled. "Fair enough. I just wanted to say thanks again for your input earlier. I really appreciated it."

"No problem. It's what I do."

"You sure that's all it was? Because... I felt a spark. Thought I should follow up and check the voltage."

Autumn rolled her eyes, but the smile lingered. "Smooth talker."

"I've been accused."

"And convicted?"

"Oh, definitely. Multiple counts. But I've been rehabilitated."

"Mmm hmm. That's what all repeat offenders say."

He laughed again, the sound low and easy. "You always play hard to impress?"

"Only when the other team's so used to winning."

"Indeed."

There was a pause. Not awkward. Just both of them, being in the moment.

"You've got a beautiful speaking voice," he said after a pause. "I bet you could narrate a documentary or something."

Autumn raised an eyebrow. "You flirting with my vocals now?"

"I'm just observant. And very, very interested in hearing more of it."

She didn't reply right away, letting the compliment simmer. She toyed with the frayed edges of the throw blanket, a smile plastered on her face.

"Well," she finally said. "That makes one of us."

"Ahh. So, you are a tough crowd."

"I'm not a crowd at all, Ekon."

She shifted on the couch, her voice dropping to a low, playful purr. "I'm a grown-ass woman with a pretty good bullshit detector."

His voice warmed. "And I respect that."

Autumn leaned her head back, eyes fixed on the ceiling.

This was nice.

And dangerous...

But not entirely unwelcome.

Somewhere between her laughter and his effortless charm, she'd moved to her bedroom without realizing it. The conversation shifted, sometimes playful, sometimes quietly profound. When she finally glanced at the time, it was 1:37 a.m.

"You're good at this," she said softly. "Talking."

"I've had practice," he admitted. "But you... you're the kind of woman who makes conversation worth having."

"Flattery again," she said, but she couldn't stop the wide, silly grin from spreading across her face. She bit her bottom lip, trying to hide the smile he couldn't even see.

"Observation," he corrected, his voice so smooth it made her toes curl.

She pressed her free hand to her warm cheek. "Noted," she finally managed to say.

"I'll let you go," he said. "I didn't want the night to end without saying, I look forward to seeing you again."

Autumn didn't respond right away.

But when she did, her voice was a little quieter. "Same."

When the call ended, she stared at her phone before tossing it onto the pillow beside her.

The flirting? *Slick.*

The charm? *Undeniable.*

But something inside her still pulsed with warning.

She wasn't sure if it was excitement or instinct.

Maybe both.

Either way, she was permitting herself to explore.

And that in itself was liberating.

10

THE HIGHLIGHT REEL

Two days later.

The golden hour hit Chicago just right. Sunlight bounced off the glass towers of downtown, casting amber reflections onto car hoods as pedestrians moved with summertime ease.

It was one of those evenings where the city buzzed with life: a warm breeze, the scent of grilled street food, and the low thrum of distant street music.

Autumn stepped out of the Uber in front of Zayah's, a well-known Black-owned restaurant tucked into a historic building near North Michigan Avenue. The awning, deep red with gold trim, fluttered in the lakefront breeze as suited hosts ushered guests in with leather-bound menus and friendly greetings.

She smoothed her dress, a curve-hugging satin wrap in bold teal that kissed every dip and rise of her silhouette, as if it had been stitched just for her. The thigh-high slit teased with every step. The plunging neckline was tasteful enough for dinner, but sinful enough for memory.

She adjusted the thin strap of her handbag and gave the bodice one last tug. Her curls were pinned half-up, a few strands tumbling down to frame her face. A soft nude gloss highlighted her lips.

This time, she had taken Mia's advice.

"Daaamn."

She turned to see Ekon standing beside a shiny black Escalade, his smile full. A crisp white button-down shirt stretched across his chest, wrists adorned with a leather-strap watch and a subtle silver bracelet. His low fade was flawless.

His eyes took her in with appreciation.

"You're really trying to have me out here acting unprofessional," he said, offering his hand.

Autumn chuckled, slipping her fingers into his. "So, you're being professional?"

"I'm trying to be. But you makin' it real hard."

He kissed the back of her hand slowly and opened the restaurant door.

Inside, Zayah's was a whole mood. The faint sound of jazz drifted from hidden speakers, mingling with the soft clink of crystal and polished silverware. The walls were adorned with striking art that evoked pride: Black expressionism and abstract portraits, each piece celebrating culture and history.

Leather booths in deep navy and burned copper curved beneath golden sconces, and the scent of rosemary, charred citrus, and smoked butter wafted through the air, promising savory delight.

They were ushered to a table already set with glimmering wine glasses and soft, flickering candlelight. Within moments, the owner appeared, and Ekon greeted him with a warm embrace before dapping up the head chef like they were old friends.

Autumn sipped her wine and arched a brow as a server passed, giving Ekon a familiar nod. Then another nod of acknowledgement from the bar. Even the hostess gave him a quick wink before returning to her post.

"Do you know everybody?" Amusement tugged at her lips.

He met her gaze, a slow, easy grin spreading across his face. He was handsome, obviously, but it was the relaxed confidence—the way he wore his own charisma so lightly—that was truly magnetic.

He leaned back, casually draping one arm over the top of the booth. "I show love. People remember that."

The food was nothing short of divine: shrimp and grits with a cayenne butter that danced on the tongue, blackened salmon on rich creamy spinach, and a peach cobbler with brown sugar crumble that made her close her eyes after the first bite.

But it wasn't just the food. Or the ambiance.

Ekon was attentive without being overbearing, charming without trying too hard. He cracked jokes, asked real questions, and, most surprisingly, he listened. His eyes stayed locked in, nodding slowly, confirming her words weren't just heard, they registered as he asked follow-up questions.

As their conversation deepened, he surprised her further when she asked what it felt like to be an influencer.

"I don't just want to be seen," he said quietly after dessert plates were cleared. "That's never been enough for me. Influence is cool, but impact? That's what I'm really chasing now."

Autumn tilted her head, swirling what remained of her wine.

"And what does impact look like for someone with your platform? Seventeen million followers, that's huge."

Ekon's expression shifted, the usual glint in his eyes dimming.

"My cousin lived in Ebondale years ago, before the changes. One of the old buildings in the Bricks. He got caught up in some mess, hanging with the wrong crowd... whatever." He exhaled. "That shit hit hard."

Autumn leaned in slightly, her voice softer now.

"What happened to him?"

"He was killed. Drive-by."

The words landed like lead. His jaw flexed for a second, then relaxed.

"Sometimes I wonder. If I could get millions of people to follow me using my voice and a camera, could I have used this so-called gift of gab back then to pull him out before it got too deep?"

His head dipped, just slightly, like the weight of that question still lived somewhere in his chest.

"I never lived in Ebondale," he went on, "but I've still got family there. Watching it transform and seeing what Amir continues to do, it hits me here." He pounded his chest, his voice cracking. "If I can use my name, my reach, to support what he's doing?"

He looked up, his eyes glistening. "That's what impact means to me."

Autumn swallowed hard. "I lost someone in Ebondale, too," she admitted. "My best friend. She was just seventeen."

Ekon's eyes narrowed gently. "Damn. Is that why you left?"

She nodded. "That's why coming back has been... complicated," she admitted, her voice trailing. "I've been here a couple of months and still don't know if I'm staying. I keep thinking I might move out to the suburbs. It's cleaner. Quieter. Safer."

"But is that you?" he asked, lifting his brow.

She smirked. "Still figuring that part out."

"Well, whatever you decide, don't let fear be the reason you leave. I've seen the change for myself. It still needs people like you, though."

Something about the way he said it—low, steady, with that magnetic gaze locked onto hers—made her forget, for a moment, why she'd even been so guarded to begin with.

"So, how long have you and Amir known each other?" She switched gears, attempting to bring the mood back up.

A waiter came and cleared their remaining plates, asking if they required anything else. Both declined.

"Oh, we go back to our college days. I met him at the Center for Inner City Studies. I've always been impressed by my brotha's commitment to making a difference. He didn't just talk the talk, you know what I mean?"

"I do," Autumn agreed. "He's been like that since we were kids. He hated seeing any kind of injustice. And when my best friend, who was also his girlfriend, was killed, it hit him differently."

Ekon's eyes lit up. "Oh, right, he mentioned that. Y'all grew up together."

She smiled. "Yeah. Her death made him stay in Ebondale, and from what I see, I'm glad he did. He's really making a difference, especially with all the gentrification going on."

"Quiet as kept," Ekon said, leaning in. "If it wasn't for people like Amir fighting for the community, they would have shipped everybody out of there. My aunt and many others got to stay because of his and other folks' advocacy, and they prevented them from being priced out. So, any time he needs me to do anything, I'm there."

The conversation stretched on, unbothered by the waitstaff even though they'd finished eating an hour ago. Their talk flowed easily from politics to some of the wild incidents he encountered as an influencer.

"How do you stand it?" Autumn laughed, shocked by some of the stories.

"Look," he said, putting his hands up in defense. "I just mind my business, let those folks do them, ya know what I mean?"

By the time they stepped outside into the warm hush of Chicago night, Autumn's stomach ached from laughing. The air buzzed with soft city life: the distant honk of a taxi, snippets of blues from an open restaurant patio.

When the valet returned his car, Ekon opened the passenger door with a gentleman's flair, but paused before she stepped in.

"I have a surprise," he said, his grin full of secrets.

They drove a few minutes to Navy Pier and entered a private section where a small riverboat bobbed on the water, decked out with string lights.

It wasn't fancy. But it was effortlessly romantic.

They stood at the railing as the boat pushed away from shore, the skyline behind them sparkling with starlight. The lake lapped beneath, rhythmic and calm.

"This was a nice surprise," she murmured, giving his forearm a gentle nudge with her head.

"I got a few more left," he said, his voice like warm silk. "But I figure I'll save something for next time."

Autumn glanced at him sideways, catching that look in his eyes again. Her pulse ticked up.

Lord, this man was dangerously sexy.

But she liked it.

The next few weeks of July flew by in a whirlwind of light, laughter, and velvet rope entrances.

One week, it was sunset cocktails at a rooftop bar, the skyline glowing with shades of lavender and gold. The next week, they wandered through a street festival, hand in hand, the air rich with the smells of jerk chicken and funnel cakes, kids chasing each other between street vendor carts.

Ekon thrived in every space.

He moved like he belonged everywhere; finger points, head nods, familiar handshakes that came from years of recognition.

"Ekon! You at this one, too?"

"Yo, lemme get a selfie real quick, bro!"

"You still comin' to that panel next week?"

He always smiled for the people; he always had time, always had the right energy. He was gracious, charming, and magnetic.

Club owners knew his name.

Artists waved him over at pop-ups.

Hostesses blushed when he glanced their way.

Autumn found herself riding the current. VIP wristbands appeared on her wrist. Velvet ropes lifted as they approached. Chefs sent out extra desserts "just because." It was a world adjacent to the one she knew in Atlanta, but louder, shinier, more effortless, and for a while, she let herself belong to it.

It was thrilling. Addictive, even.

And God, the man knew how to plan a night.

Without forgetting how to be a doting mother, she let herself have fun.

Let herself be seen.

After so long folding into emotional survival, it felt good to unfurl.

But somewhere in the slipstream of perfect dates, a tiny question began to thrum.

Is this who he is... or is this *his* highlight reel?

In the quiet moments, when the fanfare faded and the lights dimmed, there was a stillness in him. A flicker of something unreachable behind those eyes.

He asked about her childhood, but deflected when she asked about his. He told stories of success but never of fear. He showered her with attention and affection, but never real vulnerability, save for that one quiet moment about his cousin.

But she didn't press. She didn't know if it was too early to care... she wasn't even sure if she was only here for the ride.

Still, who she let into her space mattered.

Some nights, she'd lie in bed replaying the evening, trying to separate what was real from what was for show.

Was he always this polished? Or just this polished for her?

And then the texts would come in:

> You made tonight feel like magic.

> Just heard a song that reminded me of you.

> Send me a pic, I miss that smile.

And for a little while, that whisper of doubt would fade into the hum of excitement.

So, she smiled. She texted back.

She let herself live in the moment.

It didn't have to be heavy.

Maybe lightness had a place, too.

At least for now.

11

ALL EYES ON ME

August draped itself over Chicago in a thick, golden haze. It was the month of lazy afternoons and cicadas humming loudly in the trees.

Autumn walked into the youth center, carrying a tray with two coffees. The halls buzzed with life; basketballs thudded against polished floors, sneakers squeaked as teens dribbled, passed, and pivoted on the court.

She made her way through a cluster of middle schoolers, smiling when one of them shouted her name and waved. She returned the greeting, then entered the small conference room where Amir was setting up supplies.

"You're a brave woman." His smile held a tender admiration as she handed him his coffee. "Doing a marketing workshop with teenagers, and for free? You deserve an award."

She chuckled. "Gotta catch 'em early. Plant seeds while they're still young. I never even thought about marketing as a career when we were their age."

Amir nodded in agreement, then picked up a clipboard to organize sign-in sheets while she started setting up the room.

After a few minutes of easy silence, he casually asked, "So... how's everything going with Mr. Social Media?"

Autumn didn't hesitate, lighting up as her voice lifted with excitement.

"It's been amazing," she gushed, her words tumbling faster with each sentence. "We've gone to street festivals, rooftop bars, and art shows. He knows everybody! It's wild. I've never met anyone like him. He's deeper than I expected..." She trailed off for a moment, a soft smile playing at her lips. "He's really nice."

Amir cracked a half grin, slow and easy, nodding like he was genuinely happy for her. His hand shifted on the clipboard he held, the skin over his knuckles stretching taut before he relaxed his grip.

A muscle in his jaw twitched.

But Autumn, wrapped in the newness of her glee, missed the way his eyes dimmed for just a second, or how the warmth drained from his smile.

His voice was even when he finally spoke. "That's good." He coughed to clear his throat. "Good. You deserve to have some fun."

She bumped his shoulder lightly with hers. "Thanks for introducing me to all this again. It feels... good to get back to myself."

His chuckle was short and soft.

He slid a box of promotional stickers toward her. "Come on. Let's get these kids hyped up about marketing."

"Bossy!" she teased, grabbing the box.

The hallway noise swelled as kids started trickling into the room, half-finished jokes and laughter following them in.

Autumn hugged the box tighter for a second, nerves tightening under her ribs. It had been a long time since she stood in front of a room to present. And now she was praying she didn't bore these teenagers to death.

Without thinking, she looked over at Amir, seeking encouragement from her best friend.

He was already watching her.

There was something about the look in his eyes that caught her off guard. She cocked her head, mouthing, "You okay?"

He nodded, but his eyes didn't follow the curve of his lips.

Maybe it was just the light. Or maybe he was tired.

She made a mental note to take her buddy out soon. *He must be overworked,* she thought as she greeted the young people as they took seats.

That look in his eyes didn't sit right with her. It wasn't sadness—just a strange distance she couldn't place. She filed it away as the last person took their seat.

She turned her attention to the room, her professional voice bright and ready even as her heart hammered. The first few minutes were a blur of nervous energy, of trying to connect with a room full of skeptical teenagers.

But then she found her footing.

She started talking about branding not as a corporate concept, but as storytelling. She saw a flicker of interest in their eyes, and she leaned into it.

An hour later, she was a force of nature, laughing as a cluster of them argued passionately over whether their made-up brand should sell tees or slime kits.

Every so often, she'd glance toward the corner where Amir stood, catching the wistful smile that touched his lips whenever she animatedly high-fived one of the kids.

Autumn was in her element, glowing without even trying.

When the session was over and the kids were dismissed, she let out a long, happy exhale, wiping her palms on her jeans.

"You killed it," Amir said, a genuine smile finally reaching his eyes. "They were locked in."

"I think they were," she grinned back, the warmth feeling easy and familiar. "I forgot how much I love this."

Then she glanced at her watch, the easy moment vanishing. "Shoot, I'm gonna head out. Meeting Ekon for a late lunch."

And just like that, the smile in his eyes vanished. He gave a curt nod, his expression shuttered again behind an affable grin. "Be safe."

"Always."

She waved as she walked toward the exit, tossing a playful salute over her shoulder as she pushed through the front doors and out into the sun.

* * *

SHE CRUISED DOWN COTTAGE GROVE, her windows halfway down to catch the natural air. The radio station was playing her jam; she loved hearing SZA and Kendrick croon in harmony.

She felt good. Really good.

She drummed her fingers on the steering wheel, replaying pieces of her workshop with the kids and their enthusiasm, excitement bubbling at the thought of seeing Ekon again.

Then, flashing red and blue lights exploded in her rearview.

Her stomach clenched instinctively.

She slowed as she eased to the shoulder, her heart tapping a quick rhythm against her ribs.

A police cruiser pulled behind her, lights blazing.

She watched through the side mirror as the driver's door opened. A tall figure emerged: a staggering six-foot-three, she guessed, the same as Amir, his dark blue uniform a stark silhouette against the afternoon sun.

The sight of it, that uniform, sent an icy spike of adrenaline through her veins. Every muscle in her body tensed for a fight she didn't want. Her Ebondale instincts kicked in as he moved with that deliberate cop walk, a rhythm that lived in her bones as a prelude to something bad.

Then he stepped fully into the light.

His skin was the color of rich, brown cocoa.

The breath she hadn't realized she was holding escaped in a silent, shaky sigh. The tight knot of anxiety in her stomach slackened just a fraction.

He stopped at the driver's side, and as Autumn let the window slide down, her gaze took in the rest of him. It swept over the sharp crease in his trousers, traced the strong line of his clean-shaven jaw, and landed on the glint of the badge pinned to his chest. Above it all, his hair was a pattern of natural curls, tapered neatly around a perfectly shaped head.

He was handsome, an observation she filed away instantly.

"Afternoon, ma'am." His voice was deep and even, a calming baritone. "Pulled you over because you've got a taillight out. And..." his gaze flicked toward her bumper, "I see you got Georgia plates."

She let out a soft whoosh of air and dug through her purse. "I know, I'm so sorry. I just moved back from Atlanta. It's on my to-do list to change everything over."

A genuine smile broke through his professional mask. "Welcome home." He took her documents, and as he walked back to his cruiser, she noticed the confident, easy roll of his shoulders.

He returned a few minutes later, handing her license back through the window.

"Well, ATL. This is your lucky day." The warm tone matched his smile. "It just so happens to be Pretty Ladies Day. So instead of a ticket, I'm giving you a warning."

Autumn grinned. "Pretty Ladies Day? Is that in the official handbook?"

"It's an unofficial chapter," he shot back, dimples creasing his cheeks.

"Well, what if I was ugly?"

He stroked his chin in mock-seriousness. "Then you'd be getting two tickets."

Her laugh was genuine, and his followed, a rich sound that was as comforting as it was sexy.

"I'm DeMonte, by the way," he said, extending his hand into the car. "DeMonte Miller."

She took it. His palm was warm, strong.

"Autumn," she inclined her head. "Is giving out your first name official policy?"

"Nope." He chuckled, holding her hand longer than necessary. "And, this is the unofficial part, too. The part where I hope you'll let me call you sometime."

Oh, she thought, feeling a flush of warmth creep up her cheeks.

Wait... Ekon.

She blinked, the reminder slapping her back to reality.

But a sly voice whispered in her head: *Since when do you turn down options?*

She wasn't breaking any rules. By her own proclamation, she was in her dating phase. After years of being locked down to one person, maybe a little exploration was exactly what she needed.

Biting her lip to hide a smile, Autumn recited her number.

He tapped it into his phone, then showed it to her to confirm, his own smile never wavering.

"That's me," she confirmed.

He saved the contact, and she saw him add a winking emoji right next to her name before sliding the phone into his back pocket.

"What's the wink for?" She was genuinely curious.

He winked at her, his smile expanding. "I'll call you," he promised. "Drive safe, Autumn." He tossed a slow, confident nod before walking away.

She watched the cruiser in the rearview as she pulled back onto the road, her own grin reflected in the glass.

Well, damn, she mused. *This could get interesting.*

* * *

"Sis, we told you to be open to dating. Not start a damn harem!"

Mia and her salon patrons exploded in laughter as Brianna cut up in typical fashion after Autumn told them about the officer she met yesterday.

"But I'm happy for ya, girlfriend," she jumped up and high-fived her.

Saturdays were always busy in both Fix Your Crown and Fix Your Crown, Too—Mia's beauty salon and adjoining barbershop.

Today was no exception as she was running a special for fathers and their daughters. Brightly colored flyers proclaiming, "Bring Your Daughters to Fix Your Crown and Fix Your Crown, Too for Free!" were plastered all over the south side of Chicago, garnering attention on social media as well.

Autumn gave her the idea for the campaign, and it was such a hit that Mia decided to run it once a quarter going forward.

She was sweeping hair off the floor while Mia's friends roasted her, as usual.

"Open to dating means just that," she defended. "Dating without restrictions, if I so choose."

"Yessss, hon-tee!" Mia snapped her fingers in the air. "That's exactly the energy you should have. Because it's a whole new day out here and women are breaking all the so-called norms."

"As we should," Brianna chimed in, sass on full blast. "We're breaking all the other norms; we're running companies, building shit, and doing everything else men are doing. We have a right to date as much as we want, too, goddamit!"

The entire shop lit up with enthusiastic shouts of agreement.

As the chatter continued, the shop's chime announced the entrance of someone. Autumn's eyes bucked when she saw DeMonte talking to the receptionist at the front desk.

How did he find me? The thought was immediate, a jolt of paranoid surprise. She set the broom down, her heart thumping a little faster as she made her way over.

"Officer Miller?"

He turned, his brows knitting in confusion before recognition dawned and a large smile appeared on his face.

"ATL? Well, well, well. This must be fate."

"How so?" she asked, tilting her head and leaning a hip against the reception desk, playing along. She returned his smile, a genuine warmth spreading through her chest at the unexpected sight of him.

Without the formality of his police uniform, she could see the man beneath the badge. He wore loose-fitting cargo shorts that hit just below the knee, and a snug graphic tee stretched across his broad chest that read: "Super Dad. No Cape Required." His cocoa-brown skin was smooth, and his fade was freshly lined.

After paying the cashier, he stuffed his wallet in his back pocket and turned to Autumn.

"Well, I was thinking about you today and wondering if it was too soon to call. I come here to pick up my daughter, and I run into you."

"Your daughter?"

Autumn looked around the shop at the throng of women and young girls in seats.

"Yeah. There's my lil sunshine right there."

He pointed to a girl whose braids and curls shimmered under Mia's gentle spritz of oil sheen.

Autumn's eyes widened, her smile growing. "Oh! She's yours? She's such a beautiful princess. Do you bring her here often?"

"No. Actually, I saw this flyer and, since this is my weekend with her, thought I'd treat her to a pamper day while I got a shave and haircut next door. I've heard a lot about this place, so figured I'd try it out."

He noticed the smock she was wearing.

"You work here?"

"No." She was impressed at the thought of him treating his daughter out. "No, I'm helping my sister, who owns both shops."

DeMonte nodded, his smile deepening as his gaze locked with hers. She choked back a breath, a jolt of pure, unexpected chemistry pulling her forward without her permission.

The charged moment was interrupted when Mia walked up with his daughter.

"Hi, Mr. Miller," she smiled as she ushered the girl, a quiet eleven-year-old with a skeptical expression, by the shoulders. "Thank you for coming, and I hope you'll come back again. There's a coupon in your daughter's goodie bag."

"Thank you, we will definitely be back," he responded, winking at Autumn before taking his daughter's hand and exiting the door.

Mia smirked as she looked at Autumn, who watched them walk to his car. "Look at you, all googly-eyed."

Autumn couldn't suppress the grin that covered her face; she positively beamed. Turning away from the window, she met her sister's smirk head-on.

"That's the officer I was telling y'all about," she announced, her voice filled with a giddy pride.

"What?"

"Oh, hell yes!"

"You better go girl!"

The approving shouts rang out as Mia laughed out loud.

"Alright, now. Don't bite off more than you can chew. You are very new to this dating scene," she warned in jest as she walked over to start on another client.

Autumn smirked, not missing a beat. "Who said I was chewing? I'm just tasting."

"Oop!" Brianna praised. "And honey, please! Juggling two men is no harder than managing two jobs. You just gotta know when to clock in and which job you're doing."

The howling laughter continued as Autumn's phone rang.

"Shh, shh," she whispered as she placed a finger in her ear and answered the call in the other.

"Hey, ATL. It's DeMonte."

She could hear the smile in his deep baritone.

"Hi, DeMonte," she smiled in return as the ladies mocked her playfully in the background. "Did you forget something?"

"Actually, I did. I forgot to ask you out before I left."

The smoothness of his tone struck the right chord, and her temperature rose a few degrees. She fanned herself, smitten by his direct approach.

"Is that right?" She walked to the back of the salon to take advantage of the quiet.

"Yes, ma'am. So, I would love to take you out for dinner. Are you open to that?"

A giddy flutter danced under her ribs, a feeling she hadn't felt since passing a note back to her crush in seventh grade after checking "yes" in the box.

"Dinner sounds nice."

"Lovely. What day works best for you? I don't know your familial situation, so I don't want to assume anything."

The care he displayed for her time was even more of a mental turn-on.

"Well, my time is... somewhat flexible. So, we can make something work."

"I like the sound of that," he rumbled. "How about next Saturday? My daughter will be with her mom, so I can stay out past curfew."

Her laughter was light, enjoying the flow of the conversation.

"We can do a movie, then have dinner after. How does that sound?"

She leaned against the shampoo bowl, oblivious to the eyes watching her from the other side of the shop.

"That sounds amazing," she blushed, a warm calm spreading through her and manifesting on her face.

She finished up the call, floating into the main area where inquisitive eyes were locked on her.

"Why are y'all so nosy?" Despite her mock annoyance, the wide grin betrayed her.

Mia sucked her teeth. "Because we wanna know what happened, duh!"

Autumn grabbed the broom and continued sweeping. "We're going out next Saturday."

As the chatter ramped up again about Autumn's suddenly thriving love life, her phone lit up with another call. When she saw the name flash across the screen, she looked at the ladies, her face scrunching in a sheepish, uh-oh kind of grimace—the kind that said *y'all ain't gonna believe this.*

"Who is it?" Brianna asked, matching everyone's heightened intrigue.

"Ekon," she whispered like a plot twist.

The room exploded.

She held her hand up to silence the room while she answered the call.

"Put it on speaker," Brianna suggested mischievously.

"Hey, babe. What's up?" she answered coolly, ignoring the request.

"Hey, Beautiful," he beamed. "Checking in with ya, to see if you got some time for a brotha. I have a couple of events that I need to work this coming week, but I'm free after Thursday. How about we hang out next weekend? Can you get your sister to keep the kids?"

"Oh." Her eyes widened.

"I got a hookup on a nice villa in St. Lucia," he added, his voice a deliberate temptation.

Her heart quickened as she pondered spending a weekend with him on an island, or keeping a date with a man, although charming, she'd just met. Noting the eyes on her, she went to the back of the shop again as she debated with herself.

She enjoyed spending time with Ekon. The excitement he introduced into her life these last few weeks was magical.

Yet, a part of her liked the idea of slowing things down.

Going on a simple date without a crowd of people recognizing the famous person and infringing on their moments.

"That sounds amazing, Ekon." She steadied her voice. "But I actually promised to help Mia with the shops again on Saturday. It's the weekend before school starts and one of her busiest days."

She felt the weight of his disappointment, intermingled with a twinge of guilt for her lie.

"Ah, that's too bad, baby. But I definitely understand."

"You can still enjoy the island, so it doesn't go to waste," she threw in with a level of encouragement.

"Nah, it's not the same if my girl ain't there to enjoy it with me."

Remorse gnawed at her. "You know what," she said. "May... maybe I can talk to Mia—"

"No, no, don't skip out on your sis," he interjected. "I mean, she's always held it down for you with the kids at a moment's notice so you could hang with me."

Damn. Autumn closed her eyes against the sting of conscience.

"Hey, don't worry about it, baby," he coaxed, appearing to sense her internal battle. "We couldn't bask in this sunlight forever. I tell you what," he added, his voice lifting. "I actually turned down an event, and this will free me up to go to New York."

"Ooh, New York," she smiled, relief washing over her as he let her off the hook.

"Yeah, they asked me last minute, and I told them no. But that means I'll be leaving early Saturday morning. So, can I have you Friday night at least?"

Autumn stepped back into the main salon just as the words left her mouth:

"You can have me Friday."

Silence sucked the air out of the shop for a heartbeat, then laughter and shrieks exploded around her like confetti—bright, chaotic, and loud.

She hurriedly ended the call before he could hear the fireworks.

Brianna gripped and pointed her phone at Autumn. "Girl! You gotta warn us before you drop lines like that in public!"

"Oh, she *outside*-outside now," Josie cackled from under the dryer.

Mia looked up from her station, mouth ajar, brows raised in gleeful shock. "Ma'am. Friday with the influencer? Saturday with the officer?"

"Sounds like I got a full weekend," Autumn bragged coolly with a sly grin, sweeping up a section of hair clippings.

But as she turned and glanced up, her broom paused mid-sweep.

Across the shop, Amir stood just inside the door, a hand resting on Jordan's shoulder. They had just walked in.

"Hey, Ma!" Jordan ran toward her, wrapping his arms around her waist.

"Hey, my handsome man," she greeted, kissing his forehead.

"Hey Amir!" she beamed at her friend, who smiled like he always did—easy and warm.

But his eyes... they didn't look away when she expected them to. The moment stretched, silent and heavy between them.

And once again, she couldn't quite place the look on his face.

12

FLASH AND FLICKER

The salon still held the echo of laughter and gossip, even though the customers had long gone. The last of the loose hair was swept into neat piles, the dryers were silenced, and the music was now a mellow hum in the background.

Autumn sat cross-legged in one of the stylist's chairs, sipping from a bottle of lemon tea while she swiped through social media on her iPad.

Amir had graciously offered to take all the kids to the movies and dinner, leaving her and Mia free until after ten.

"Chile, thank God for Amir. I'm too tired to even think about cooking tonight," Mia called out as she wiped down her station.

Autumn nodded without looking up. "Yeah, same."

Then, casually, Mia asked, "So... you really don't see it?"

Autumn raised a brow, still absorbed in her device. "See what?"

Mia stopped wiping and turned to face her fully, one hip cocked. "Amir."

Autumn continued scrolling. "What about him?"

"You didn't catch that look he gave you today?"

With a light laugh, Autumn waved a dismissive hand. "Girl, Amir gives everybody looks. He's the king of facial expressions."

"Nah, sis," she countered. "This wasn't just a face. It was *that* look. That 'he's absolutely wrecked' look."

Autumn released a slow hiss of air as she sucked her teeth and rolled her eyes. "Sis, you're reaching."

"I ain't reachin', I'm observin'." Mia tapped her temple. "You were in here talkin' about having Friday with one man and Saturday with another, and that man looked like he was doing everything to hold it together."

Autumn shifted in the chair, the humor draining from her face. "Look, don't start that again. You know how I feel about that topic. Amir and I are friends. That's it."

"But what if he doesn't feel that way anymore? You ever think about that?"

Autumn leaned forward, elbows on her knees, her voice sharpening. "Even if that were true, it's not an option. Asia was—*is*—our link. I told you, that line doesn't just disappear because she's gone."

Mia softened, her voice edging carefully. "I get that. I do. But it's been sixteen years. Y'all were teenagers. That grief for your friend, for both of you, is real. But don't let it keep you from something good if it's standing right in front of you."

Autumn gave a defensive shake of her head. "It's not like that, sis. For either of us. Amir sees me as his homie, nothing more. And he only seems like the perfect guy for me because he's safe. Because he's always been around. That doesn't mean he's supposed to be more."

"Okay, let me ask you this, then. Can you tell me, straight up, you've never been attracted to him?"

"What?"

The high-pitched squeal was all the answer Mia needed as she laughed and threw a towel at her.

"That's what I thought."

"No, no, that's not fair," Autumn defended, tossing the towel back. "I mean, of course he's attractive—"

"That's not what I asked you," Mia shot back. "I asked if you've ever been attracted to him."

"What's the difference?"

"Why are you trying to play stupid all of a sudden? You know damn well what the difference is."

Autumn surrendered to her sister's point. "Fine. Yes, I know the difference." She paused. "And yes, I was attracted to him before."

Mia's face lit up. "That's what I'm talking about, girl! When?" She took a seat in one of the chairs, leaning forward with a huge grin of anticipation plastered on her face.

Autumn chuckled at the exuberance, shaking her head again. "You are so silly." She let out a long sigh before continuing. "Okay. I'm not proud to admit this, but there were actually a few times."

She took a steadying breath.

"The first time was when I was in college. He flew out for the weekend to attend my homecoming because I was always bragging about how bomb it was. Girrrllll..."

She leaned back in the chair, her eyes closing momentarily at the memory.

"He came at a time I was going through some mess with Chris. So, I was a lil vulnerable or something, because suddenly I felt this pull toward him."

Her eyes went distant for a second.

She could feel that moment: the heat of his hands on her waist, the shocking softness of his mouth on hers before he groaned her name.

The memory was so vivid it made her chest ache. She swallowed hard, pushing the most dangerous part of the memory down before she continued speaking.

"We both got a little tipsy, and things almost got complicated. *Real* complicated. I had to be the one to pull back before it went too far."

Mia nodded, listening intently.

"When he held me, he felt so good. He felt like..." she paused, eyes clouding over.

"Home?"

"Yeah," Autumn admitted. "He felt like home. I thought it was just comfort, familiarity, because we've known each other for so long. But, when I felt it again a few years ago, it scared me."

The soft, nostalgic haze on her face evaporated, replaced by a look of raw, wondering vulnerability. She met Mia's gaze.

"How could I feel anything for him besides friendship? It was wrong, and I got mad at myself for even going there. I vowed to never look at him that way again."

"But?"

She sighed. "But when we moved up here, it happened yet again. On that first day, that you tease me about."

Mia cast a knowing cock of the head.

"Yeah, yeah, I know. But I had to ask myself, why was I having these feelings? I realized, each time was after dealing with an issue with Chris. So, I think it's moments of emotional stress that trigger it."

Mia's eyes narrowed just a touch. "Is that an official diagnosis? Have you told Jasmine this during your sessions?"

Autumn grimaced. "Of course not."

"So then, you're just assuming that your attraction to him is a reaction, and not a reality?"

After a pause, Autumn asked, "Why are you so insistent on my getting with Amir?"

"Because it's obvious, you're running from and searching for something at the same time. And Amir is right there."

Autumn's brow furrowed as she returned to her iPad, letting out an exaggerated sigh. "I'm going back to social media. You're killing my vibe."

Mia hesitated, then wisely decided to retreat.

"Okay. Just... promise me you'll keep your eyes open. That's all I'm saying."

Autumn didn't respond. She sat back in the chair, chewing the inside of her lip, once again immersed in her device.

* * *

LATER THAT WEEK, after the sale of the townhouse in Atlanta finally went through, Autumn took stock of her savings.

Satisfied with the financial cushion she'd built, she made a decision: she wouldn't return to the workforce right away. Instead, she gave herself a year to breathe, to actually enjoy life.

She enrolled Layla and Jordan in the local magnet school and accepted Mia's offer to stay longer.

She was finding a flow that suited her.

And she was actively dating.

Not because she was searching.

Not because she was running.

Mia had that part wrong.

She was simply having fun. Not in the flailing, desperate way she remembered during that short breakup with Chris back in college.

This was different.

This was intentional.

One week, it was DeMonte, who opened car doors and walked her on the inside of the sidewalk like someone raised with old-school manners. His dates were simple: dinner at local joints, late-night strolls, and ice cream, even when it wasn't summer-hot.

She didn't have to perform.

Next, it was Ekon, who escorted her into VIP lounges like they were already a power couple. His energy was electric: roses for no reason, voice notes that made her blush, handwritten letters slipped into expensive gift bags.

Both men presented two very different energies.

Ekon dazzled, fast and magnetic, always pulling her into his orbit.

DeMonte was steady. Quietly commanding.

She floated through her weekdays, meeting DeMonte for lunch or coffee while the kids were at school. A few nights, she'd go to dinner with Ekon. On weekends, if the kids were hanging with Amir or visiting with Chris when he came up, she'd slip away with either man.

"You seem to be hella busy," Chris remarked as he handed her an envelope with the check from the sale of the house while they sat in Mia's kitchen. "Have you found another job yet? Where are you spending all this time?"

She sucked her teeth, her neck rolling slightly. "First of all, why are you checking my time? Second, no, I'm not working yet because I don't have to. And last, it's none of your business where I'm spending my time."

He chuckled dryly. "Yeah, okay. Well, it is my business how the mother of my children is spending her time. Especially if you're dating some dudes I know nothing about. I ain't paying child support for you to—"

Her palm shot up, a sudden, sharp wall between them that stopped his words cold.

"I told you this before, but let me refresh your memory," she snapped as her eyes narrowed. "When I left my job, I had enough money between savings, my retirement and investment funds, and my severance to last me a couple of years, longer if I'm conservative. The money you send for child support? It goes straight into a fund for the kids. It's never touched."

She pointed to herself.

"And as for how I spend my time? Being the mother of your children doesn't dictate that you know that. If you didn't let fatherhood stop you from doing whatever the hell you wanted, then don't try to regulate me now."

He dropped his head with a humorless sigh. "You always take it there."

"You're damn right I do," she hissed. "With your hypocritical ass. You have some nerve."

A slow grin spread across his lips. "Still get under that skin, don't I?"

She laughed, the sound sharp, humorless. "Yeah, you do," she admitted, sarcasm staining her tone. "But not for the reason you think. We've got history, Chris. And the fact that I let you control most of my adulthood, for better and worse, still pisses me off."

His grin faded when he saw the furious shimmer of tears that she refused to let fall.

The smugness drained from his face, replaced by something she hadn't seen before: a slow, dawning realization that shadowed his eyes, like he was actually hearing her words, not just weathering the storm of her anger.

"I poured everything into you," she continued. "Into the family we created. I became a wife and mother before I was twenty-five, built a career, and held it all down. Meanwhile, you played daddy when it suited you, cheated while pretending to be a husband, and wrecked my nerves in the process."

When he tried to lean in closer, she put a hand up between them.

"And that's another thing," she spat, steady and low as she regained her composure. "You still think you've got this hold on me. Love might not die, Chris, but it sure as hell evolves. And what I feel for you now, though it may be shaped by love, has shifted into something that teeters on the edge of..."

The sentence hung between them, unfinished, as the thunder of footsteps came crashing down the stairs. They both turned, their faces instantly rearranging into practiced plastic smiles. But the performance was thin. His eyes dimmed with regret; hers were still sharp with the lingering sting of his words.

As Chris shuffled the kids to the car for their weekend visit, he hung back while they buckled themselves in. His usual confidence gave way to something that looked like humility as they stood on the porch.

"I have a real talent for fucking these things up," he acknowledged, the words a low rumble of self-disgust. He finally met her eyes. "I'm sorry, Autumn. Again." He took a breath. "I'm trying to be better. And for what it's worth... I am proud of you."

She looked past him, focusing on the kids as they settled in the backseat of his car. But she heard it, the absence of his usual swagger, the raw edge of sincerity in his voice. And against her will, a small, tired smile lifted one side of her mouth.

When he finally left, she headed to her room and collapsed onto the bed, the mattress sighing under her weight.

Autumn was finally in her own rhythm. Not a frantic beat of survival, but something steadier.

One beat louder than grief, one beat softer than chaos.

It was the rhythm of a woman who had just fought for her own peace and won.

And damn, it felt good.

* * *

A FEW WEEKS LATER, on a lazy Saturday afternoon, the early fall sun filtered through the kitchen windows, casting a golden glow across the dining table where Autumn and her kids were eating lunch. It was a rare moment of calm for the trio. Mia's boys were with her twins' father for the weekend, and Mia was at the shop.

The scent of grilled cheese sandwiches and chicken noodle soup filled the air.

Jordan looked up from his plate, curiosity flickering in his eyes. "Mom, are we gonna live with Aunt Mia forever?"

Autumn paused, her spoon hovering mid-air. She glanced at Layla, who had stopped chewing, also waiting for her answer.

"Well..." she started slowly, "we've been staying here while I get things sorted out. But no, not forever. I'll be looking for us to have our own space again."

118

Layla frowned. "But we just started school here. I like it."

"I know, baby." She smiled softly. "Two weeks into fifth grade and you're already out here acting like you're on the school board." She looked at Jordan. "And don't think I don't see you trying to run the fourth grade now that you got voted class president."

Jordan beamed. "So, we're staying for a while?"

Autumn nodded. "Yep. Aunt Mia already threatened to lock us in if we tried to leave too soon. So, I think we're good here, at least until I figure out where we want to go next."

"Why can't we just live here? In Ebondale?" Layla asked through a bite of her sandwich. Then she puffed out her cheeks, fanning the gooey cheese burning her tongue.

Autumn's hand traced the edge of her napkin thoughtfully. It wasn't the neighborhood that gave her pause. Ebondale had grown.

Evolved.

She was proud of that. But what lingered were the memories. The grief stitched into its sidewalks. Some wounds were still healing.

"We'll see, baby," she said wistfully.

They were too young to carry those ghosts.

Switching gears, Jordan grinned mischievously. "So, Mama. Layla said you got two boyfriends."

The snort he let out was so extra, they all cracked up.

He laughed so hard he doubled over, then started coughing, sharp and whcczy.

Autumn's laughter faded just enough to side-eye him with concern. "Okay, okay, grab your inhaler. Top drawer."

Still giggling, he nodded and moved toward the kitchen.

"I have two friends," she corrected once the moment had settled. "And it's been nice meeting new people."

Jordan's eyebrows lifted. "Why can't Amir be your boyfriend?" he asked innocently, shaking his inhaler before giving it a quick pump.

Her smile faded, softening instead. "Amir is Mommy's best friend. He's been in my life since I was your age." She reached across the table and tapped his nose. "And sometimes, friendship is just that... friendship."

Jordan still didn't look convinced. "But he cares about us. And you. He treats us like a daddy."

Autumn's thumb traced a slow circle on the back of his hand. She looked past him for a moment, her gaze unfocused, as if searching for the right words.

"You're right, he does," she said finally, her tone a little heavier. "And what we have is so, so important. Sometimes… sometimes you get scared that if you try to change something that special, you might break it."

She met his eyes again, trying to give him a reassuring smile that didn't quite reach her own. "What matters most is that we have people who love and support us, and we have that with Uncle Amir, right?"

Layla nodded. "When I start dating, I want a boyfriend like Amir."

Autumn nearly choked. "While I support that in theory…" She shot her daughter a look. "That won't be happening until you're at least thirty."

The serious talk melted away as the house settled into the easy rhythm of a lazy afternoon. Soon, the clink of forks was replaced by the rustle of a popcorn bag and the opening credits of a movie marathon.

Autumn sank into the couch cushions, a familiar, comforting weight settling against her as Layla tucked herself into her side.

Jordan claimed the remote, crowning himself "King of the Movie Queue."

Outside, the sun drifted westward, shadows stretching across the yard.

Autumn let her gaze wander as the soft flicker of the TV danced across the room. The air was warm, tinged with butter and a peaceful joy.

Layla giggled softly beside her. Jordan's running commentary made her grin despite herself.

This. This was what she needed.

Not romance. Not answers dressed up in someone else's voice.

Just stillness. Peace. The chance to breathe without a deadline or expectations.

She wasn't searching for love, not the way people assumed.

She was searching for herself.

And this time, she wasn't afraid of what she might find.

13

THE FADED HUSTLE

Autumn closed her journal with a sigh.

The last words she wrote echoed in her mind like a gentle mantra. She sat still for a moment, letting the silence of the house settle around her. The late morning sunlight crept through the living room blinds in golden ribbons.

The kids were off to school, and Mia was attending a business conference for beauty and barber professionals.

Her chest ached with a heaviness that had no clear source, like a weighted blanket draped across her spirit. Was it idleness? Loneliness? Perhaps it was both.

She stood up from the couch and made her way to the kitchen, flipping on an eclectic playlist that always gave her the vibes of being in a cozy café, tucked in the corner of some far-off place. The coffee grinder, a recent gift from Amir, was already loaded with her new favorite blend: Asia's Ember, her own creation.

She'd been experimenting with coffee blends for weeks, chasing a flavor that was just right. And she'd finally found it: bold Sumatra for its earthy backbone, floral Ethiopian beans to lift the senses, and just enough Brazilian to smooth the edges like velvet.

It smelled like memories and blessings, like joy after pain.

As the blend brewed, the kitchen slowly transformed, steam curling into the air like incense, carrying notes of earth and brightness. The scent wrapped around her like a warm embrace, coaxing a soft smile from her lips. She'd always loved coffee, not just the taste, but the ritual of it.

Creating her own blend had been a dream tucked behind busier ambitions. Now, she was finally making space for it.

She reached for her favorite ceramic mug, the off-white one with the faint blue glaze and the tiny crack near the handle. It was flawed but still perfect in her eyes. She poured slowly, reverently, watching the dark liquid settle, as if this moment were a kind of ceremony.

It felt like a small act of rebellion to drink something this good, this intentional, without sharing it with anyone.

She sipped slowly, closing her eyes.

This was her new tempo. Not quite thriving professionally, as she was before the layoff. But not falling apart.

She was somewhere in between.

Her phone buzzed on the counter.

Amir's name floated across the screen.

She stared at it for a second before answering. "Hey."

"What's up, you?" His voice was acoustic warmth, a resonant sound she'd known her whole life. It was an easy, grounding tone that settled over her the way only something truly familiar can.

"Not much. Just trying not to let this stillness drive me crazy."

He paused. "Is everything okay?"

Autumn leaned over the counter, watching a bird peck at the grass outside the window. "I don't know. I mean, I should be good, right? I'm seeing my therapist. I've got free time I never had before. I'm dating. I've even started journaling again."

"But..."

She chewed on her bottom lip. "But it seems like I'm stuck in this weird limbo. Not working. Not grinding. Not striving toward anything. And as peaceful as the rest is, I'm starting to wonder if depression is circling the block."

He didn't jump to fix it, didn't offer the usual pep talk. He just listened.

"I'm not ready to go back," she added. "To the workforce, to deadlines, to pretending I care about things that drain me. But this... this stillness is playing with my head."

"I get that," he said after a moment. "It's hard to trust rest when all you've ever known is the hustle."

Her laugh came out soft. She tucked a stray curl behind her ear. "Exactly."

A lull fell between them.

Then Amir's voice shifted, lighter, but with a thread of nostalgia.

"Aye... you remember our old spot down by the lake?"

She blinked. "Asia's favorite spot?"

"Yeah."

"What made you think of that?"

"I don't know. Just in the mood to get out. Thought you could use the same?"

Autumn hesitated, staring down at her coffee.

"Yeah," she said finally. "Yeah, I could."

A little over an hour later, Amir pulled up outside Mia's house.

Autumn stepped onto the porch, holding two travel mugs filled with her specialty brew. The late September breeze tugged gently at her cardigan as she watched him get out and walk to the passenger side. He still had that smooth, unhurried energy that always made him seem to move to the beat of his own internal soundtrack.

The black hoodie was simple, the dark jeans unassuming, but the body beneath them was anything but. The sleeves, pushed to his elbows, revealed the hard, corded lines of his forearms. The fabric of the hoodie draped over a chest that she imagined was solid oak.

His locs, hanging loose around his face and down his back, weren't just a style; they were a statement, each one a thick, heavy rope that seemed to anchor his presence.

She'd looked at him a thousand times, but in that moment, she was seeing him. And the view was disarming.

"You ready?" he called out, holding the passenger door open, smiling at her with that calm gaze that melted hearts.

She hadn't realized she was staring. She shook her head, then moved toward the car.

"Sorry, I was lost in thought," she said, avoiding his eyes as she handed him a cup. "Thanks for picking me up."

"What's this?"

"That, my friend, is my own special blend of coffee. And you are the first to taste it."

He took a sip as she eased into the seat.

"Goddamn!" he exclaimed in delight, then took another sip. "This is good as hell, Aut."

He closed the door, then walked over and stepped into the driver's seat. He sipped again before placing the mug in the cupholder.

"So, you finally did it, huh?" he asked as he started the engine. "You've been talking about creating your own blends for a while."

"Yeah, well. I've got time on my hands."

"It's really smooth. Definitely different."

"Thanks." She tried to sound casual, but a wide, unstoppable grin broke across her face. It was a ridiculous feeling, this sudden, bubbling joy over a simple cup of coffee.

But it wasn't just about the coffee. It was that he'd listened all those times she'd rambled on about it. It was that he was here, the very first person to taste a dream she was just believing in herself.

She turned in her seat to face him fully, her eyes shining. "No, for real," she said, playfully punching his arm. "You really like it? Don't lie to me, Amir Raymond Jackson!"

He laughed and took another sip. "Not you using my whole government. But no, I'm being serious. This is amazing."

His eyes left the road for a second, locking onto hers. She saw the pride in them, and it sent a dizzying, happy flutter through her stomach.

"Thank you." Hearing him say it, and seeing his genuine approval, was like winning something she didn't even know she was vying for.

He took another slow sip, his eyes thoughtful. "So, what's the story behind it? I know you love naming-conventions. What slick name are you giving this?"

Her playful energy softened, her voice dropping a little. "I call it 'Asia's Ember.'"

The mood in the car shifted instantly. Amir's smile faded, settling into a look of quiet, profound understanding.

He didn't speak at first, then nodded slowly. "Asia's Ember," he repeated, the name a soft rumble from his chest. "Autumn... that's perfect."

The stillness that came next was full of shared memory. It lingered between them, a quiet tribute, until the trees lining the street finally gave way to the expanse of the lake, pulling them gently back to the present.

When they neared the spot that held so many moments of fun, laughter, and Asia's spirit, she couldn't hold back the tears.

This was exactly what she needed.

The gravel crunched under the tires as Amir pulled into the clearing, the lake revealing itself just beyond a row of thin pines.

Autumn stepped out slowly, inhaling the crisp air. The water sparkled under the sun, each ripple catching the reflection of nature's beauty.

The wind rolled in soft and cool, rustling the leaves just enough to make the trees murmur. A few golden ones broke free, floating down like memories.

"Looks the same," she observed.

Amir nodded beside her. "It does."

They went down to the rocks near the shoreline, where they'd spent so many long summer afternoons. Asia was always the loudest, daring someone to skip rocks farther than her.

Amir consistently let her win.

Autumn eased down first, sitting cross-legged on one of the large cragged boulders, letting her fingers skim the cool stone beneath her.

Amir followed, lying back with his hands placed at the back of his head, his locs fanning out behind him like roots.

For a while, they didn't speak.

"Do you remember when Asia freaked out because seaweed wrapped around her ankle when we dangled our feet in the water?" He chuckled as he sat up.

Autumn laughed, full and bright. "She screamed like she was being attacked by a monster. Then yelled at both of us for laughing so hard."

"Man, she hated any slimy thing touching her skin."

"Yeah, but you made it worse," she shot back, smirking. "You pulled some of it out and chased her around with it."

"Aye, I was in my immature phase," he defended, hands raised in mock defense. "I pulled all kinds of pranks back then."

They both snickered again, the sound fading into the soft hush of water lapping against the rocks.

"So..." Autumn said after a pause, her voice more thoughtful now. "The kids asked me about my two 'boyfriends'."

She encased boyfriends in air quotes.

"Ouch." Amir looked out at the water. A few seconds later, he asked, "How does it feel to be dating again?"

"It's... nice," she reflected. "I'm actually having fun."

He nodded, still looking away. "That's dope."

She glanced at him, tilting her head slightly. "Took me a long time to crawl out from under Chris's shadow."

He offered her a slow, approving smile. "I know. I'm glad you did."

A few more seconds of silence fell between them. Then,

"Amir, can I ask you something?"

"Of course."

She hesitated. "Mia's friend, Londyn, made a statement about me dating two men. Now, the kids are asking me about it." She looked out at the horizon beyond the lake. "Do you think I'm being a bad mother?"

"Hey," he called softly for her attention.

When she looked at him, his gaze was penetrating.

"Absolutely not. You are one of the best mothers I know. And you deserve to enjoy life. Besides..." he picked up a rock and tossed it in the water. "... it's not like you're bringing them around the kids."

"No, I'm not," she affirmed. "As far as they know, I'm just hanging out with two new friends."

A seagull flew overhead, its loud squawk punctuating the silence that followed.

"Can I ask you a question?" Amir inquired, squinting at the sun.

"Yeah."

He picked up another rock and tossed it in the water. "Are you getting serious with either of these dudes?"

Autumn shook her head. "Nah. I'm just having fun." After a few seconds, she added, "I mean, they're both really cool. But I'm not ready for anything serious."

Amir nodded, his expression blank.

"What about you?" she asked, nudging his knee with hers. "You're out here being Ebondale's number one Unc, but I never hear you talk about dating. The women love you, what's the deal?"

He gave a slight shrug, picking up another rock and studying it before tossing it. "Just been busy, I guess. Also, haven't found the right person."

She was curious. "What does that look like for you? The right person, I mean?"

He glanced at her, a glint of curiosity in his eyes. Then he looked straight ahead, into the vast waters.

"The right woman is a partner. She's not looking for me to complete her, 'cause she's already whole. She knows her worth, so she ain't tryna compete with my kids at the center. She's my peace, and I'm hers. She's the one I can build with, laugh with... the one who, when I see her, I just feel... home. That's the woman I'm waiting for."

He pushed a stray rock with his foot. "I can't settle for less than that."

It was Autumn's turn to nod as she let his raw admission settle. The weight of his words sat heavily in her chest, pressing down until she had to move around to shift it.

Then she perked up with a snicker, trying to change the temperature that had started to rise within her.

"Oh, guess what Jordan asked me? He wanted to know why *you* couldn't be *my* boyfriend."

She chortled like it was the joke of the century.

"Is that right?" His response was light, a quiet counterpoint to her booming laugh.

When her mirth softened, she looked at him. He was watching her, a strange, intense stillness in his eyes that made the air feel suddenly thick. All playful energy was gone, replaced by something weighted.

Then he cocked his head, his tone pensive. "What if..."

Autumn's eyebrows raised.

"What if you and me did get together?" he asked, his gaze locked on her. "Like, for real. What would that even look like?"

Her breath hitched. This wasn't just a question; it was a tightrope suddenly stretched over a canyon of guilt. She didn't dare look down, because her balance was already faltering. One wrong move, and she'd fall.

On one side was the safety of their friendship, a bond forged in their shared love for Asia. On the other side was this beautiful, terrifying unknown, a step that felt like it would betray that very bond. The thought of falling, of losing him as a friend, *and* breaking that sacred vow to the woman they both lost, was unthinkable.

So, she laughed. It came out too fast, too sharp, more armor than amusement. It was a reflex, a desperate grab for the one shield she knew could protect them both.

"Boy, you know that could never happen," she barked, still laughing to diffuse the sudden, thick tension. "Asia would haunt the hell outta both of us."

His mouth tugged into a half smile, but his eyes didn't keep pace as he turned to look out at the horizon. "You don't think she'd forgive us, huh?"

Autumn didn't even hesitate. "Nope."

She focused on the water, still laughing, scrambling to keep the moment light.

And because she was looking away, she didn't see the way his smile slipped, didn't catch the flicker of disappointment in his eyes, or the way he shifted just slightly on the rock like something in him had folded in on itself.

14

IN THE FRIEND ZONE

The next few weeks buzzed by like time was on a mission. October brought with it a smoldering late-season heatwave, blasting Chicago with a balmy seventy-seven degrees.

"Hey, Ma," Jordan called down to Autumn from upstairs.

"Yeah, baby?" she responded from the kitchen, where she and Mia were getting an early start on preparing Sunday dinner.

"Can I have a Black Panther costume for Halloween?"

"Of course, baby."

"Yay!"

Mia chuckled as she picked collards, the rhythmic snap of the stems filling the comfortable silence. "Every little Black boy on the block still wants to be Black Panther, and I love it."

"Yep," Autumn returned, distracted. She glanced at her phone, frowning when it showed no new notifications from Amir.

Things had been off with him since their trip to the lake a month ago.

At first, it was little things.

His responses to her messages started coming later and later, and they were brief, almost indifferent.

No more random memes or voice notes that used to make her laugh out loud in the middle of folding laundry or making the kids' plates.

No more "you up?" late-night texts just to talk about nothing and everything.

Now, he answered with one-liners.

AUTUMN

> Just passed the taco spot we used to hit. Remember that one lady who cussed you out over extra guac? 😏

AMIR

> Lol. Yeah.

That was it.

The rhythm between them, once so fluid, had become clunky. Their conversations stalled, without momentum, like strangers trying to find common ground.

She told herself it was just life. He was probably busy.

But she felt the shift.

In the way he called less.

In the way he didn't ask her to help at the center as often.

"Something's off with Amir," she finally said out loud.

Mia didn't look up from working on her greens. "What do you mean?"

"He's... distant."

"Distant like ghosting?" Mia asked. "Or distant like he got a new woman, and you don't like it?"

Autumn shot her a look. "What?"

Mia looked up, catching the surprise in Autumn's eyes. "You didn't know?"

Her eyes narrowed. "Didn't know what?"

Mia blinked, then set the greens down and wiped her hands on a dish towel. "He's seeing somebody. Thought you knew."

The words landed like a silent detonation in her chest.

It wasn't the thought of him with another woman that stung. Not exactly.

It was the secrecy.

The one-word texts, the late replies, the sudden space. It all clicked. His distance wasn't busyness; it was a deliberate wall he'd built between them. It almost felt like a betrayal.

Like, a quiet recalibration of their entire friendship that she hadn't gotten the memo for.

Autumn pivoted to the sink, grabbing the cool edge of the porcelain as she turned on the faucet. She needed an anchor, something solid, before the undertow of that thought pulled her under.

She tried to temper her voice as she glanced over her shoulder. "Who told you that?"

"Brianna saw them last week. They were at Bar Louie, looking real cute together." Her sister eyed her carefully. "You okay?"

"I mean... yeah. Why wouldn't I be?" She responded too quickly, her voice cracking on the last word.

Mia leaned a hip against the island. "I don't know, you tell me. Your whole vibe just changed."

Autumn scoffed. "I'm not jealous, Mia."

"I didn't say you were."

She could hear the infuriating smirk in Mia's voice without even having to turn around.

She switched off the faucet. "It just caught me off guard. He didn't mention anything. That's all."

Mia's voice softened. "So, what's really bothering you? That he's dating? Or that he didn't tell you?"

Autumn opened her mouth, then paused. "I don't know. Maybe it's both."

Her sister's grin widened knowingly. "And why is that, sis?"

Autumn turned, her eyes betraying her, and Mia burst out in laughter.

"Your ass really is jealous!" she cackled, ducking when Autumn threw a towel at her.

She watched the towel land on the floor, her cheeks burning as Mia walked out of the kitchen, still laughing.

Jealous? Ridiculous! she told herself as she retrieved the towel and tossed it into the sink with more force than necessary.

He's my friend. I'm allowed to feel weird about him dating someone I don't know. That's all it is.

The lie felt good enough to believe. So good, in fact, that the next afternoon, Autumn found herself turning into the parking lot of the center without fully thinking it through.

She hadn't texted first. Hadn't checked to see if he was busy. That was unlike her, and she knew it.

But curiosity drove her. Or was it something else?

Inside, the center was quiet as the staff prepared for the arrival of kids in a few hours.

Her gaze swept down the hall and landed on Amir without effort. He stood a full head taller than the volunteer he was talking to.

He did a double-take when he saw her approach.

"Autumn?"

She smiled brightly, lifting a friendly hand. "Hey. Just thought I'd stop by. See if you need help getting things ready for the Halloween party next week."

He glanced at his clipboard in his hand, then back at her, his brow wrinkling in confusion. "Oh. You usually call or text first."

"I was in the neighborhood," she said coolly, as if that explained everything.

He raised an eyebrow but nodded. "We can always use help."

Before either of them could say more, an unfamiliar female voice called Amir's name.

A woman was approaching, and the world seemed to shift into slow motion. She was tall and graceful, with an easy confidence in her stride that was more of a glide.

A soft, gray crop sweater hugged a frame that was all lean lines and gentle curves, paired with dark, relaxed-fit jeans that sat low on her hips. Her natural curls bounced with every step, perfectly defined and free.

But it was her face that truly held Autumn captive. High cheekbones framed a generous mouth that curved into a half-smile. She had the kind of radiant, bare-faced beauty that was completely effortless, her skin glowing with a warm honey-gold tone. She looked to be in her early thirties.

"Hey, babe," she chirped, walking up to Amir and placing a quick kiss on his cheek, then wiping the spot to remove the glossy smudge. "Sorry I'm late. Traffic on the Dan Ryan was insane."

Amir turned slightly, hand on her lower back as he returned her smooch. "It's cool, sweetheart. Moet, this is my homie, Autumn."

Moet smiled warmly. "Oh wow, so you're Autumn? I've heard so much about you."

Autumn nodded robotically, returning the smile. "Nice to meet you."

But something inside her pulled tight.

There was no reason for this to feel awkward.

No reason for her to feel... anything.

And yet...

The way Moet stood close. The way Amir leaned in. The easy, familiar way they navigated each other's space.

It shouldn't have stung.

But it did.

"You know what? I just remembered something—Mia asked me to grab some things for the shop. Nice to meet you, Moet. Amir, we'll catch up later."

She excused herself with a tight, polite smile, forcing her feet to move.

She turned and walked away, a desperate retreat before anyone could see the cracks forming. But the feeling followed her down the hall; a dull, heavy ache in her chest that she couldn't outrun and didn't understand.

* * *

LATER THAT EVENING, Amir brought Jordan home, a routine they'd done a thousand times. He gave his godson a high-five and told him to be good for his mom. But as he turned to leave, Autumn was standing in the doorway, blocking his path. Her arms hugged her chest, her expression unreadable.

"Amir, you got a minute?"

The easy smile on his face faltered when he saw the look in her eyes. "What's up?"

"We need to talk." Her voice was firm. She stepped out onto the porch, closing the door behind them for privacy.

He leaned against the porch railing, his expression turning wary. "About?"

"Moet." The name was sharp on her tongue. "You have a new girlfriend, and you didn't bother to tell me."

He didn't answer right away, his gaze dropping to a crack in the porch steps. When he finally looked up, his eyes were guarded. "It's not serious yet," he responded, but the calm in his voice was paper-thin. "I wanted to see if it was going somewhere before I made a big deal out of it."

It was a perfectly reasonable answer. One that she couldn't argue with. But after seeing them together, his hand on her back, the easy kiss, it looked like a big deal to her.

"Amir, we tell each other everything. At least... We used to."

There was raw hurt in her eyes, and something hard and defensive flickered in his own. "Look, Aut," he exhaled, exasperated, as he pushed off the railing, creating a deliberate space between them. "I don't tell you about every woman I go on a date with. You'll know if and when it's something *to* know."

She felt a steel door slam shut between them. Stung by the sound of annoyance in his voice, she fired back, her own voice dripping with sarcasm. "Wow. Okay. Good to know where I stand."

The explosion was immediate and unexpected.

"Why the hell does it even matter to you, Autumn?" he bit out, his control snapping. He bridged the gap between them in two short steps, his body heat a sudden, suffocating presence. He stared down at her, eyes blazing with a raw heat she'd never seen before. "We're just friends, right? That's what you said. That's what you want."

His voice dropped to a low, ragged whisper as he leaned in, his face inches from hers.

"Right?"

He was so close now she could see the frantic pulse beating in his neck, feel the warmth of his breath ghosting across her lips. Her own breath caught, trapped in her lungs. The world narrowed to the hard, working muscle in his jaw and the agonizing space between their mouths.

If she tilted her head a fraction of an inch...

"Uncle Amir, I thought you left!"

Jordan's excited voice sliced through the tension from behind the screen door.

Amir pulled back as if he'd been burned, his face a mask of stunned awareness. He scrubbed a shaky hand over his mouth, turning away from her, and when he looked at the door, his entire demeanor had shifted. The fire in his eyes had subsided, replaced by a soft, practiced warmth.

"Hey, little man," he called out, his voice impossibly gentle. "Just saying goodnight to your mom." He looked back at Autumn, but his gaze was distant, guarded. "See you around, Aut."

He didn't wait for a response. He turned and skipped down the steps, leaving her frozen on the porch, the ghost of his breath still tingling on her lips.

15

THE BRILLIANT STRATEGY

Jasmine's office always carried the scent of vanilla and lavender. Something about that aura made Autumn breathe in a little deeper, centering her.

She sat nestled in the corner of the sofa, legs folded beneath her, a soft throw over her lap. She gripped a mug of lemon ginger tea the therapist had offered the moment she arrived, her eyes focused on a speck of lint on her jeans.

"I'm not spiraling," she said, staring into her mug, responding to a point Jasmine had made.

"I didn't say you were," Jasmine replied gently, legs crossed as she sat in a chair on the opposite side, pen resting on her notepad like it wasn't even needed.

The therapist, a petite Filipino American in her mid-thirties, had a golden-brown complexion that seemed to glow in the room's natural light. She exuded an earthy, authentic vibe, from her minimalist makeup down to the calm, steady way she held Autumn's gaze. "But you seem like you're suspended."

Autumn looked up, her brow furrowed. "Suspended?"

"Like someone between trapezes. You've let go of one bar, but you haven't grabbed the next yet."

Autumn gave a soft laugh. "That sounds about right. And scary as hell."

"It usually is," Jasmine agreed. "But it's also where the transformation happens."

Autumn sipped slowly. "I'm just tired. Not sleepy-tired. Like, my soul is tired. And for once, I'm not trying to push through it. I only want to... *be.*"

Jasmine nodded. "So why does that scare you?"

"I don't think I've ever just *been*. I've always had something to chase. My ex..." she chuckled ruefully. "A deadline. A promotion. A fire to put out. Rest feels... dangerous. Like I'm losing ground."

"Or maybe..." Jasmine offered, "you're finally realizing that the ground beneath you is enough."

That landed harder than Autumn expected.

She swallowed, staring down at where sunlight painted soft patterns on the floor.

"A part of me feels guilty," she admitted.

"For what?"

"For starting to enjoy the stillness. For not hustling. For not being some type of warrior every damn day."

Jasmine leaned forward slightly. "Let me ask you something. What if this version of you—still, curious, choosing herself over the grind, what if she's the most powerful version yet?"

Autumn's eyes flickered, words catching in her throat.

She didn't know how to respond. So, she sipped her tea.

"Let's come back to that," Jasmine said. "You said you wanted to talk about something specific today."

After a few seconds, Autumn exhaled a breath that sounded like it had been waiting to escape for days.

"I saw Amir a few days ago."

Jasmine gave a light nod. "And?"

Autumn looked up, then away. The words sat heavy on her tongue. "He's dating someone."

There was a pause.

"Is that hard for you to say out loud?"

Autumn shrugged. "I don't know. I wasn't expecting it. And I didn't hear it from him, I found out by accident."

"Tell me how that made you feel."

She blinked at the steam rising from her mug. "Surprised. Irritated. Kinda stupid, if I'm honest. Like... why was I even caught off guard?"

"Why do you think you were?"

She exhaled slowly, her throat tight. "Because some part of me thought maybe..." She trailed off, shaking her head. "Never mind."

"No, finish that thought. 'Some part of me thought maybe'... what?"

Autumn looked up, her eyes flickering with embarrassment as she admitted the selfish, unspoken truth. "I guess I assumed he'd always be available."

"And are you mad that he isn't?" Jasmine asked softly.

"I'm mad that I'm mad," she confessed. "I shouldn't be feeling anything, yet I'm feeling everything."

"That's powerful," Jasmine said. "So, what is it, exactly, that you're feeling? Is it about him? About her? Or something deeper?"

"It... stung." The words were inadequate. "And I have no right to feel that way. None. So why do I?"

Jasmine leaned forward slightly in her armchair, her expression calm and open. She still didn't write anything down, continuing to hold the space for open, honest dialogue.

"Okay. So, a feeling came up that your logical mind says shouldn't be there. That can be incredibly disorienting."

Autumn nodded, relieved to be understood.

"Exactly. He's my friend. I want him to be happy. I rejected the very idea of us being together, for God's sake! I practically laughed in his face. And then I see him with this beautiful woman, Moet, and they look so... easy together. And it felt like a punch to the gut."

"Let's stay with those feelings for a moment," Jasmine said gently. "The punch. The sting. Where did you feel it most?"

Autumn blinked. "I... My chest got tight. And my stomach dropped."

"Okay. A tightening in the chest, a dropping in the stomach. Has this happened before?"

Autumn's mind immediately went to Chris, to the years of finding out about his infidelity and the subsequent feelings that she wasn't enough.

"Yeah," she whispered.

"So, what if the sting wasn't only about Amir dating someone?" Jasmine offered. "What if it was about the fear of being replaced in a core relationship, a dynamic that has been a constant, steady anchor in your life for years?"

That resonated.

It was more than jealousy.

It was the shifting of a foundation she thought was solid.

"He's been aloof," Autumn admitted, looking off into the distance. "Ever since that day at the lake. And I guess seeing him with her was the proof. That he was moving on... from me. I mean... from our friendship." She corrected herself, her cheeks flushing.

"You said, 'from me,' first," Jasmine affirmed gently. "And, his moving on feels like a loss."

"Well... Yes. But only of our friendship," Autumn insisted, her voice rising a little too high. "Because I don't want Amir in any other way. I... can't."

"Why can't you?" Jasmine challenged.

Autumn's eyes widened. "Asia..."

But she couldn't finish the sentence.

Jasmine nodded slowly. "Let's talk about that. It sounds like there's a rule you've created. The rule says, 'I am not allowed to have romantic feelings for Amir because that would be a betrayal of Asia's memory.'"

"It would be," Autumn insisted, her voice thick with emotion. "She was my best friend. He was the love of her life. That doesn't all disappear because she's dead."

"You say that a lot," Jasmine noted, her voice full of empathy. "That loyalty is a testament to the love you have for her. But let me ask you a question that might be uncomfortable. Do you think the Asia you knew, the vibrant, loving friend you've described, would want her memory to be a cage that keeps two people she loved from finding happiness? Even if it's with each other?"

Autumn flinched. The question was a direct hit.

"Of course not, but..."

"But the guilt is stronger than the logic," Jasmine finished after she hedged. "Grief and guilt get tangled up so easily. We start to believe that the depth of our pain is a measure of the depth of our love. That if we stop hurting, and we move on, we stop loving them."

Tears pricked Autumn's eyes. She'd never put it into words, but that was it exactly.

"Which brings me to DeMonte and Ekon," Jasmine pivoted, seamlessly shifting gears. "Let's talk about them for a second. What does it feel like to date these men?"

Autumn pressed the back of her hand against her cheek, her mood lifting slightly. "It's... fun. Liberating. Ekon is exciting. He makes me feel visible. DeMonte is steady; he makes me feel safe."

"Liberating. Visible and safe," Jasmine repeated. "Those are powerful feelings. Especially after a marriage where you often felt trapped, invisible, and unsafe emotionally. It makes sense that you would be drawn to those energies."

She paused, then asked, "Is it possible that you're dating two men, so you don't have to get too close to one?"

Autumn's mouth went dry. The question felt less like an observation and more like an indictment, like her therapist had held up an X-ray of her soul and pointed out all the hairline fractures.

Jasmine continued, her tone consistently gentle but persistent. "You keep things on the surface. One foot in the exciting world of Ekon, one foot in the safe world of DeMonte. It's a brilliant strategy, Autumn. It gives you the sense of moving forward, of having options and freedom.

But it also protects you. Because if you're not fully invested in either of them, no one can truly leave you. No one can truly replace you. You control the moment."

It was as if lights were being switched on in a dark room, revealing all the furniture she'd been tripping over.

"So..." Autumn started, absorbing the message. "The dating isn't just about freedom. It's about fear. Fear of repeating the pattern I had with Chris. Fear of being all-in and getting hurt again. Fear..." she choked back a sob. "Fear of losing someone again."

She dropped her head back against the couch.

The tea had gone warm in her hands, but she hadn't even noticed. For once, her armor was all the way down.

"That fear," Jasmine said softly, "that 'fear of losing someone again.' You're talking about Asia, aren't you?"

Autumn didn't look up, but she nodded, the admission a heavy weight in her throat.

"And *that's* the other thing we have to deal with," Jasmine went on. "The guilt. For not knowing how to draw the line between honoring her and moving on."

Autumn looked away. "If I'm being honest, that's probably why I'm out here dating like it's a sport; DeMonte one weekend, Ekon the next. I keep telling myself it's just fun. A little freedom. But you're right. It's also avoidance."

Jasmine leaned forward slightly. "Avoidance of what?"

"Of the truth. That, maybe, I do want a real relationship. But I don't want it with anyone who could hurt me."

"You said something interesting a few sessions ago," Jasmine recalled. "You said rest was like a threat because it meant giving up control. I think love is the same way to you... like the ultimate surrender of control. Something you crave, but don't fully trust yourself to handle."

Autumn let that settle, the word echoing in the quiet space.

Surrender.

Surrendering to Chris had meant losing pieces of herself. But surrendering to love... that meant confronting the guilt she carried for her friend. And *that* felt far deeper.

"I guess," she answered finally. "I... I don't know how to surrender without feeling like I'm losing."

Jasmine gave a soft, understanding nod. "And that's a completely valid fear based on your history. It explains why you're keeping Ekon and DeMonte at a safe, surface-level distance. It's another way to protect yourself from that feeling of losing." She paused, her gaze compassionate but direct. "But Amir... he's a different kind of fear, isn't he? It's not only about surrender with him. It's also about dealing with your grief over Asia."

Autumn looked away. The fear with Amir was older, more complicated. "Yeah," she admitted. "With him... that's where I don't know how to hold grief and desire in the same hand."

"You don't have to hold them equally," Jasmine replied. "But you do need to acknowledge both are there. And neither makes you disloyal to Asia."

Autumn's eyes welled again, but she didn't let the tears fall.

"I feel like we're heading somewhere, Doc," she chuckled softly. After a few seconds, she inhaled a breath, then blew it out slowly. "You're right. With Ekon and DeMonte, I'm controlling the space. I can keep them on the surface." She looked at Jasmine, the full weight of the realization dawning on her. "But I can't do that with Amir."

"Why not?"

"Because we're already deep. We have years of history; we've been friends since childhood. He's not a new door I can simply walk through."

"And that's terrifying," Jasmine concluded. "Because you can't control it. And because of the rule you made about Asia. It's the one connection that's both the safest and the most forbidden at the same time."

Autumn released a long, shuddering breath, grabbing and clutching a throw pillow tight. All the pieces were clicking into place, forming a picture she wasn't sure she was ready to see. The dating, the guilt, the jealousy, the fear. It was all connected.

"So, what do I do?" she asked, her voice small as fresh tears flowed.

"For now? Nothing," Jasmine said softly. "You don't have to do anything. The work right now is to simply notice. Notice the feelings when they come up—the grief, the guilt, the attraction—without judging yourself. Give yourself permission to acknowledge it all. The sting you felt when you saw him with Moet wasn't a sign that you're a bad friend. It was a sign that something in you is asking to be seen, by you."

Autumn wiped her face again and let herself sit in the quiet for a moment.

"Thank you," she whispered.

Jasmine smiled. "You're doing the work. Let that be enough for today."

16

GRACE FOR THE MESS

It was early Saturday evening, and fall had dipped the sky in soft amber and subdued lavender across Ebondale.

The scent of taco spices floated from the kitchen downstairs, blending with the muffled sound of kid squeals, giggles, and racing footsteps in the hallway just outside the bedroom door.

Autumn modeled in the mirror, tugging the sleeve of her silver lightweight knit sweater far enough off one shoulder to showcase moisturized caramel skin that was smooth like silk, glowing like royalty. The sweater snatched her waist with the subtle grip that said sexy without shouting.

Her hair was fresh; a voluminous twist-out laced with warm brown highlights that caught the light when she moved. Slate hoops bobbed with each tilt of her head. High-waisted dark denim jeans cinched her hips, and her ankle boots clicked with the authority of a woman who knew she turned heads.

Was she trying to go full tilt on the sexy High Striker?

Hell. Yes.

And tonight, DeMonte was gonna hear that bell ring.

She'd added the final touch, a soft neutral-colored lip oil, when someone tapped lightly at the door.

Layla peeked in, one puff ponytail sitting lopsided on her head.

"Hey, mommy," she beamed.

"Hey, baby." Autumn reached for her favorite perfume. "Come on in."

Layla stepped inside, eyes wide. "You look really pretty."

"Thank you, pumpkin."

"Are you going on a date?"

Autumn paused, spraying a soft mist of vanilla musk at her collarbone. "I'm going to hang out with my friend."

Layla wrinkled her nose. "Is it the friend from last week? Or the other friend?"

Autumn nearly choked on a laugh. "Excuse me?"

Layla giggled. "Well, you have two boyfriends. So, which one are you going with tonight?"

Autumn shot a mental dagger in Mia's direction. "Stop listening to your auntie," she chided with a soft pinch of her daughter's nose, then turned to check her reflection, fluffing her curls one last time.

Layla shrugged, totally unbothered. "Is it bad to have two boyfriends?"

She watched her daughter through the mirror, then turned and crouched before her, brushing a stray piece of lint from her cheek. "Here's the thing, baby. Mommy's not doing anything bad. I'm getting to know two people at the same time. And they are my friends. Before I make any big choices about a boyfriend, I need to be sure about what I want... and what's right for you and your brother."

"Okay." Layla nodded like she was mentally scribbling it all into an invisible diary. "Are they friends with each other?"

Autumn laughed, a real one this time. "Not exactly."

"Then you better be careful," the now ten-year-old rang out, with a smirk way too grown for her age. She turned on her heel and headed for the door.

Autumn blinked. "Okay... wait, Little Miss Ma'am, where did that come from?"

Layla tossed a shrug over her shoulder. "TikTok."

And she skipped off, leaving Autumn staring at her reflection as she shook her head.

She'd always monitored not only what her kids consumed, but what seeped into their minds and spirits.

That conversation with her daughter would be revisited. Soon.

What side of the app was she even on? Autumn wondered, a familiar knot of parental anxiety tightening in her chest.

She was careful. She gave them space, freedom within reason.

Yes, Layla could scroll, but only through a restricted, child-safe account. She had enabled every parental control the platform offered. Still, she knew the internet had a way of slipping past firewalls, and Layla, wise beyond her years, always picked up more than she let on.

But it was her daughter's final question that echoed back.

Is it bad to have two boyfriends?

They're friends, she repeated to herself, adjusting her sweater.

Totally normal. Totally under control.

* * *

"Autumn!" Mia's voice floated up the stairs. "You tryna be fashionably late for your own date or what?"

"I'm coming!" She called back down, getting out of her head and grabbing her bag.

Laughter bubbled from the kitchen where Mia and her friends were preparing a taco feast.

Josie was chopping tomatoes, Mia and Londyn were layering warm tortillas onto a serving tray, and Brianna was busy perfecting the homemade guacamole, smacking hands away from the bowl every few minutes.

The scent of cumin, lime, and slow-simmered beef filled the air, mingling with the fresh bite of cilantro and the tang of salsa verde.

The room paused for half a second as Autumn sashayed into the kitchen, just long enough for Josie to raise both eyebrows and Londyn to give a low, appreciative whistle.

"Well damn," Brianna praised, licking lime off her finger. "You said it was a casual dinner, but you lookin' like you tryin' to slay a brotha tonight."

Autumn grinned and did a slow spin.

Josie smirked. "You dressing like you 'bout to change a man's life."

"Or get yours changed," Londyn added, eyebrow arched playfully.

"Okay, see now y'all doin' too much," Autumn laughed as she sampled the guac.

"You know who else got a man taking her places tonight?" Brianna's grin was sly.

Everyone paused.

Autumn turned, a finger filled with a second scoop of guac at her lips. "Who?"

Brianna dragged out the name like a slow pour. "Mo-et."

The playful light in Autumn's eyes vanished. The scoop of guacamole paused halfway to her mouth. "Moet," she quipped, her voice dripping with sarcasm. "Who names their child after a damn bottle of champagne?"

The room went silent, broken only by Doechii on the speaker.

Then the kitchen exploded with laughter.

"See!" Mia shouted, pointing a spatula at her. "I knew she felt some type of way!"

Autumn fought a smile and lost, the corners of her lips twitching upwards as she finally brought the guacamole to her lips.

"Oh no, not the shade before the girl even gets in good," Brianna cackled.

"You sound like a haterrrr," Londyn sang, leaning against the fridge.

"I don't know what y'all are talking about," Autumn protested, though her lingering smirk said otherwise.

"She *mad*-mad," Mia added, popping a lime tortilla chip in her mouth. "Gotta be, if she's dragging somebody over a name."

Autumn lifted a tortilla and dipped it into the homemade salsa. "Fine. Maybe I feel some type of way, but it's not like y'all think."

Josie clapped. "Progress! The Bag Lady sessions are working!"

Autumn laughed again, holding up both hands after gorging on the chip. "Y'all are wild. I'm not feeling anything for myself. I guess I see Amir as a brother, and I'm protective of him like he'd be over me."

Brianna shot a look at the other women, a quick, silent poll that said 'Can you believe this?', before turning her gaze back to Autumn. "Uh huh. So, you're trying to tell us that the only thing you see when you look at all of that is a brother?"

Mia fanned herself. "Chile, that brother is sex on a six-foot-three stick."

Autumn didn't flinch. "That's all I see. He's just Amir to me, the same goofball from back in the day."

She tamped down the small voice in her head that whispered, "Liar."

Brianna shook her head, tossing down the rag she was using to wipe the counter. "See, you keep looking at him like the teenager who was in heavy like with your friend when y'all was kids. That's a grown ass man right there."

The ladies co-signed loudly.

"I'm so glad you joined our group sessions and you're having your own, because you got some more unpacking to do, sis." Mia tapped her on the shoulder as she walked past. "I keep telling you, letting go of the past is going to free you in so many ways."

Josie slid Autumn her purse after her phone vibrated with an incoming text. "Well, right now, sissy's got two boyfriends to keep her distracted."

Autumn snorted, her thumbs already moving as she texted DeMonte back. "Correction: two friends," she stressed without looking up. "We're just hanging out. That's it."

Right on cue, a little voice floated down the stairs. "Is it the tall friend or the one with the nice car?"

The women froze, eyes widened, mouths framed in laughter.

Autumn turned around slowly.

"Layla Marie Gardener!" she yelled, a frown covering her face.

"Sorry!" the little voice yelled back.

"And stay off TikTok!"

"Awww!"

Josie nearly dropped her taco from laughing so hard.

Shaking her head at the chaos, Autumn grabbed her leather jacket from the hook by the door. She blew a kiss to the room, ignoring the chorus of "get some!" and "be safe!" that followed her out.

The sun's descent was almost complete, casting the neighborhood in a soft, golden glow that kissed every porch and windshield with warmth. Autumn took a deep breath as she stepped onto the front porch, letting the cool air clear her head.

She zipped up her jacket, arms wrapped lightly around herself, her twist-out bouncing gently in the breeze. The subtle smell of tacos and lime still lingered on her skin, but now she carried the scent of vanilla as she refreshed the perfume on her neck and wrists.

DeMonte pulled up in his midnight blue Charger, tires crunching softly over the gravel. He stepped out, and the word that came to Autumn's mind was *solid.*

He wore a button-up in deep olive, the dark fabric a perfect complement to his rich skin tone. Paired with dark jeans, he looked put-together without being formal. His smile was genuine behind a neatly lined beard, and he carried himself with a quiet strength that was becoming dangerously more attractive.

He paused with his hand on the car door, his gaze taking her in fully. A low whistle escaped his lips before he caught himself. "Okay, Autumn," he grinned. "You sure this is just dinner? Because you're looking like you're ready for a red carpet."

Autumn blushed as she slid in. "I clean up well. I'm a mother, I'm allowed."

He shut the door behind her and jogged around to the driver's side. As he got in, he glanced her way again.

"Seriously, though. You look good."

Her own gaze swept over him then, a slow, deliberate inventory. The way the olive shirt set off his skin. The clean, confident line of his jaw.

"So do you," she said, her voice a little warmer than before.

A soft blend of amber, vanilla, and delicate musk lingered in the car. She immediately recognized the scent—Maison Berger, her favorite, the sleek diffuser nestled in the vent.

His music hummed low through the speakers, classic D'Angelo's "Lady" sliding through like an admission.

"Appreciate you hanging out with me tonight," he said as they pulled off. "I know this was a last-minute thing, but I really wanted to see you."

"And I appreciated the bouquet and chocolates you sent today. Ain't nothing wrong with a little old-school courtesy."

"Oh, my mama raised me right. Gotta keep it classy for a lady."

She smiled, settling into the seat as they merged onto the road. The cityscape shifted from residential calm to the soft glow of street lamps and storefronts. The ride was filled with low music, easy conversation, and a few moments of comfortable silence. He touched her thigh lightly when she made a funny comment, and she didn't move his hand.

The restaurant setting was a vibe: dim lighting, leather-bound menus, and low chatter. The host greeted them with warmth and led them to a corner booth. Autumn slid into the seat with practiced ease, DeMonte sitting across from her with a relaxed confidence.

"Okay," she started, picking up her menu. "Should we order drinks first?"

DeMonte grinned devilishly, his eyes crinkling at the corners. "You're grown. Do whatever you want. I'm just here to enjoy the show."

She smirked, feeling a genuine glow spread through her. They ordered drinks, red wine for her, bourbon neat for him, and shared appetizer bites while DeMonte made her laugh with stories about his coworkers.

Then, just as Autumn reached for her glass, a subtle shift in the restaurant's atmosphere pricked at her senses. A new energy surged as the low buzz of chatter near the entrance quieted, then started again with a more electric hum. Her eyes were pulled there instinctively.

And then she saw him.

He walked in like he had his own theme music, wearing sleek black slacks and a pristine white dress shirt opened just enough to reveal a flash of chest. No coat. Like his charisma was enough to keep him warm.

Autumn's lips parted, her breath catching in her throat. Her heart plummeted as she mumbled a silent, frantic prayer in her head: *Please don't see me, please don't see me, please don't see me.*

Across the table, DeMonte noticed the sudden change in her expression, the way the joy drained from her face. "Everything okay?" he asked, his voice a low murmur.

She could only manage a tight, jerky nod. "Yeah. Just... didn't expect to see someone I know."

As if summoned, Ekon's gaze swept across the room and landed directly on her.

His smile was slow. Deliberate. He didn't even blink as he started moving toward their table with a slow, controlled walk.

"Autumn," he greeted when he reached their booth. His voice was smooth as the jazz playing in the background as he leaned down to press a kiss to her cheek. It was intimate, lasting with intent, his familiar, expensive cologne a heady cloud she couldn't escape.

A polite smile spread across her face, a fragile mask for the way her heart was suddenly hammering. One clear thought cut through the noise: He's making a statement.

Her spine went rigid. The warmth that had been in her chest from DeMonte's easy company curled into an icy knot of tension. "Ekon." The name came out as a tight, breathless whisper. "What are you doing here?"

"Client dinner," he said, his eyes finally flicking to DeMonte with a cool, dismissive assessment, as if he'd already run a background check. He extended a hand across the table. "Ekon, my man."

DeMonte met his grip like a silent negotiation, a brief, firm contest of wills that ended in a stalemate. "DeMonte."

"Nice to meet you," Ekon replied, though his attention snapped right back to Autumn, his smile a little too wide, his head cocking to the side. "Looks like y'all are in for a good night. The lamb is excellent."

Autumn was hyper-aware of DeMonte across from her. He was still and observant, calmly taking a slow sip of his bourbon, his eyes trained on her.

"Well, don't let me interrupt." Ekon gave her a final, conspiratorial wink, as if to say, *You and I have secrets*. "Enjoy yourselves."

He walked off with the same casual swagger he'd walked in with, leaving a trail of nervous chaos in his wake like he hadn't just stirred a pot and left it to boil over.

The moment he was out of earshot, the breath Autumn had been holding escaped in a shaky rush. She reached for her wine, her hand trembling slightly as she lifted the glass and guzzled it like it was water and she'd just crossed a desert.

DeMonte leaned forward, his forearms resting on the table, his voice calm but weighted. "Friend of yours?"

Autumn nodded, the movement small. "Yeah."

A few seconds ticked by, thick with tension.

"Is there anything more?" he asked with a quiet steadiness that made her stomach twist.

"We've gone out a few times."

She tucked a strand of hair behind her ear, suddenly unsure where to rest her hands.

He didn't respond right away. He just nodded slowly, his gaze unreadable as his eyes never left hers. She'd braced for an argument, for ego, for the accusation she deserved. Instead, he gave her space. And that quiet, unexpected grace was more disarming than any argument could have been. It was an invitation to be honest, and she found herself wanting to accept it.

"Actually, it's more than that," she admitted, meeting his gaze. "Ekon and I are... dating."

There was a flash of disappointment in his eyes, but a calm acceptance just as quickly replaced it.

"Look, we never said we were exclusive, right?" he said evenly as he sat back in his seat. "You're figuring things out. You made that clear in the beginning. I knew what that meant. And I respect it."

This was so not the toxic script she had learned after her entire dating life and marriage with Chris. She had not been prepared for this easy, grown-up grace.

"I appreciate you," she breathed, sincerity in her eyes. "But still, I should've said something before. That wasn't fair to you."

DeMonte leaned in and reached across the table, placing a warm hand over hers.

"Autumn." His voice was low and certain. "It's okay."

She nodded, but emotion cracked through anyway.

"I've spent so many years making every move about someone else," she admitted, a frown creasing her brow. "Being someone's girlfriend, someone's wife, someone's foundation builder and safety net. I just... I need room to find out what I like. What I want. And I need to do that without it meaning I'm being reckless."

"You're not," he affirmed, thumb brushing softly over the back of her hand. "You're being honest, right now. With me. With yourself. That takes guts."

He leaned back again, watching her, the corners of his mouth lifting into a small smile. Then, the smile faded as his expression sharpened with intention.

"But... let me be clear. I like where this is going. I like *you*. So, while you're out here exploring and healing and figuring it all out, I'm not bowing out. I'm in this. For real. I just want to stay in the running. That's all I ask."

Her chest fluttered at the words, something soft and powerful spreading where panic had once lived.

She looked at him, meeting his gaze head-on. "I can give you that," she voiced, barely above a whisper.

* * *

LATER THAT NIGHT, Autumn sat in bed, legs tucked under her, a silk bonnet fitting loosely over her hair. The house was settled, a quiet that echoed after a day full of laughter and layered drama. Her phone lay face down on the nightstand. Two unread messages waited: one from Ekon, the other from DeMonte.

She didn't read either. Not yet.

Instead, she opened her journal.

The pages smelled faintly of ink and lavender.

Note to self: my ten-year-old is coming for my entire life with her observations. And those therapy sessions are no joke. Turns out my baggage isn't just a carry-on; it needs its own damn cargo plane.

Tonight was proof. A whole soap opera played out in a booth at a steakhouse. I swear, I wanted the floor to swallow me whole when Ekon did his peacock strut over to our table. This is what Jasmine was talking about. I thought I was being slick, keeping things light and easy with two guys, so I wouldn't have to get real with one. But the universe really said, "Oh, you think you're in control? Okay. Let's put them in the same room and see what happens."

I keep telling myself this is my 'freedom tour,' but tonight, freedom just felt like anxiety in a cute sweater.

The old me would have panicked. Definitely would have over-apologized. But... I told the truth. It was shaky, but it was honest. And DeMonte didn't flinch. He just listened, looked me in my eyes, and said he wanted to be in the running. Lord, be a fence.

It's making me question everything. Who am I still trying to please with all this caution? Asia's ghost? Those critical of my choices? The remnants of the wife I used to be?

I know I owe these men honesty. That's true. But I'm

learning that I owe myself grace first. The space to be messy while I'm growing.

Maybe this is what evolving is supposed to feel like: a bit like falling and flying at the same time.

She capped her pen, closed the journal, and let out a breath.

Outside her window, the wind rustled the leaves just enough to remind her that the seasons were shifting.

So was she.

17

CLARITY OVER COMMITMENT

Autumn couldn't sleep. The run-in at the restaurant had left a raw, anxious energy buzzing under her skin. She went down to the kitchen in search of a snack, using movement to pacify the angst in her heart.

It wasn't regret that had her unsettled; it was the shock. The unexpected, jarring collision of the two separate lives she'd been so carefully curating. Dating freely in her own private bubbles was one thing. Having those bubbles merge and pop in the middle of a crowded restaurant? That wasn't on her bingo card.

When Ekon's name lit up her phone for the third time, she finally answered.

"Hey." Her voice was a soft exhale, the fight gone out of it.

"Well damn," he teased. "I was starting to think you were ghosting me."

"I almost did," she admitted. "But that would've been unfair."

There was a pause as she quietly rummaged through the snack cabinet.

When he spoke, his tone was grounded. "So, talk to me."

The kitchen was still, illuminated only by the stark, digital glow of the microwave clock. Losing her desire to snack, she closed the cabinet and walked over to stand in front of the patio door, watching the porch lights spill gold over the deck.

"I owe you an apology," she started. "I should've said something to you. About DeMonte."

Ekon was quiet, prompting her to continue. "I wasn't trying to hide him. I just didn't think we would cross paths like that. And when it happened... I saw your face..."

"Yeah," he replied, measured. "I wasn't ready for that. I mean, I knew. Or I suspected. We both said we weren't exclusive. But seeing it? I gotta admit, that hit different. And that whole scene I made... that wasn't me, for real. That was my ego talking. My whole brand is being the guy who's never pressed, and for a second there, I was pressed."

His chuckle was wry, but the honesty was a gut punch of a different kind. This wasn't the familiar sting of toxic ego she knew how to navigate. This was accountability. A quiet, mature ownership of his feelings.

Chris could never.

The sudden ache in her chest wasn't from a past wound; it was the strange, sharp pang of recognition. This was what growth felt like. She was attracting a different kind of man because she was becoming a different kind of woman.

She sank into a kitchen chair, the weight of that realization settling deep in her bones.

"And that's why I'm so sorry," she said, the words a direct consequence of her new clarity. "Because I know what it's like to experience that kind of carelessness. I never should have done that to you."

"No need to apologize. You're just living your life."

She let the words sit between them for a moment before replying. "Still, I could've been more upfront. With both of you."

"You don't owe me anything," he said, softer now. "But I do appreciate this. Us talking about it."

Autumn's exhale was filled with relief. "I just want to make sure we're okay. I mean, I get it if you'd like to stop—"

"I'm good, Autumn." His voice was reassuring. "You're still good with me."

She smiled, the tension easing from her shoulders. "You free this weekend?"

"Yeah." The familiar warmth slid back into his voice. "Come through. We'll crack a bottle of Moet—"

"Let's have something else," she cut in, her nose wrinkling before she could stop herself.

* * *

A FEW DAYS LATER, the city was quiet as fall chased the summer crowds indoors early. The air was cool, but the winds were gentle, and the fire-pit on Ekon's rooftop burned low in front of them, soft orange light flickering across their faces.

Autumn curled her fingers around her wineglass, legs tucked beneath her in a wide-knit sweater and leggings that looked effortless, but the effect was intentional.

Ekon sat beside her in joggers and a long-sleeve tee. His body was relaxed, but his attention on her was sharp, making her feel like she was the only one in his orbit.

"I've been thinking a lot about that night," she said, her eyes on the skyline.

"You're not still feeling some type of way, are you?" He took her hand in his, moving closer.

"Not exactly," she replied. "But I do want to own my part. I should've told you I went out with DeMonte the first time it happened. I didn't because I honestly didn't think it mattered."

"Didn't it?" he asked, gently.

Her head tilted slightly when she saw the sincere glint in his eyes. "I guess maybe it did."

She sipped her wine as she stared into the flames. "With you being who you are, I figured you wouldn't care. And for me? Like I said, I'm not looking to lock you or anyone down. I'm trying to give myself space. I've spent so much of my life belonging to someone else. And now I just want to belong to myself."

Ekon nodded slowly. "That's fair. I'm in that space too, so I get it more than you know."

"Really?"

"Yeah," he admitted, his eyes steady. "I'm still dating. Still moving around. Still keeping things low-key. I don't do public entanglements. I'm

156

careful about who I connect with, especially in this industry. Image is everything."

Autumn nodded, a new level of understanding clicking into place. He wasn't a carefree influencer; he was a man protecting a brand. In a way, they were both doing the same thing, carefully managing their public lives while trying to figure out their private ones. "That makes sense," she said quietly.

"I value what we have, though," he added. "You've been fun to be around. Chill. No drama. I like that. I'm not trying to change it. I only want to be clear about what we're doing."

Autumn nodded. "Clarity matters more to me than commitment right now."

A moment passed.

"I wish I could get everyone else to understand," she continued, "that I'm not looking for love. Not yet. I'm looking for air. For autonomy. For space to make mistakes and not apologize for wanting more than one flavor."

Ekon's eyebrow raised. "Well damn. I don't know why that's a turn-on, but that's sexy as hell."

They both laughed, a moment of levity to break the night's heaviness.

"I guess..." he said as he took the wineglass from her hand and set it on a nearby table. He rose and pulled her into an embrace. "It's because a grown ass woman standing on business and owning it is a flex all its own. And there ain't nothing sexier than that."

He planted a soft kiss on her lips, then pulled her in closer. "Here's to having your Red Velvet and your chocolate cake. And, to not settling for anything until you get what you want."

It wasn't perfect. But at least now, it was honest. And when his mouth settled over hers again, the kiss wasn't a frantic dance; it was a conversation. A slow, deliberate exploration. His tongue traced the seam of her lips before sweeping inside, a warm, searching question that tasted of wine and unspoken truths.

A quiet thought settled in her mind: *sometimes, this kind of raw honesty was the most powerful intimacy of all.*

18

AN EMPTY SEAT AT THE TABLE

"What's going on with you and Amir?"

Mia's voice was softer than usual, curiosity replacing her normal teasing tone.

They sat at the kitchen island on a crisp Sunday morning, surrounded by recipes and scribbled Thanksgiving prep notes. The scent of maple syrup and bacon still clung to the air, but even that sweetness couldn't cover the unease in Autumn's gut whenever the thought of Amir surfaced.

She didn't answer right away.

"I mean..." she finally said, her eyes on the grocery list, "We're okay."

Mia let out a soft murmur of doubt. She picked up her coffee mug and squeezed Autumn's shoulder as she passed by. "Okay. Well, I'm gonna go fold that mountain of laundry that's been sitting for the last two weeks. Holler if you need me."

Autumn watched her go, and the silence she left behind was louder than their conversation had been. The words *we're okay* echoed in the quiet kitchen, feeling wrong, hollow.

Because truthfully? She didn't know how else to answer. What do you call it when a friendship begins to unravel without a fight? When no harsh words are spoken? Just a slow, silent shift, like fall leaves drifting from a tree that no longer tries to hold them.

They were still speaking, yes. Still texting here and there. But the rhythm —their language—the shared shorthand of inside jokes and unspoken understanding, had thinned out.

She could pinpoint the beginning of the shift. It wasn't just the lake trip anymore.

It was Moet.

Since she came into the picture, everything between Autumn and Amir had been rewired; still familiar, but nothing sparked anymore.

Autumn had thrown herself into the noise of life. Into the kids' schedules. Into helping Mia at the shop. Into the messy, thrilling chaos of dating.

That last part, she knew, was a deliberate distraction. What started as a way to explore freedom and choices was now being used as a balm for a wound she refused to fully acknowledge.

The sound of tires crunching over gravel pulled her from her thoughts. She glanced up and saw Amir's black Jeep pull into the driveway.

And this was the hardest part. He was still here, a constant presence woven into the fabric of her family. Days like today, when he came by just to be "Uncle Amir" and she had to pretend she didn't feel the chasm between them, were the moments when the ache was most acute.

Jordan bolted out the door before Autumn could make it to the living room. "Put on a coat! And grab your inhaler," she yelled as he ran to the car.

"Somebody's hype," Amir called, stepping out with his usual grin. "Aye, boy, go on back in there and put on a coat like your mama said." He winked at Autumn as she stood in the doorway, arms wrapped around herself to ward off the cold. "Told you Top Golf would be a hit."

He leaned against the passenger side of the car while Jordan ran back in and grabbed his coat.

"Thanks for taking him," Autumn said, coming down the porch steps.

"Always," he replied, pulling her in for their classic one-arm hug. It was familiar, but brief. A little too much space left between their bodies, a new caution she wasn't used to.

He may as well have given her a distant dap.

The sharp pang of loss hit hard. Amir was supposed to be the one thing that never changed, the one person whose hugs were always an anchor in a storm.

And now, even that felt different.

"You know I got him."

It had always been like that with the kids. He was never just their godfather; he was the constant. The uncle, the protector, the stand-in while Dad was in Atlanta. He didn't just show up; he stayed.

But lately, he wasn't staying as long. At least, not for her.

Later that afternoon, when he dropped Jordan off, and as Autumn waved goodbye, she noticed a figure in the passenger seat of Amir's car.

Moet.

Her curls were pulled back in a sleek bun, nails resting on the lowered window as she gave Autumn a wave with her other hand, her smile bright and genuine.

Autumn's smile was polite, cordial even. Why couldn't she reciprocate the same level of excitement for a woman who appeared to be making her best friend happy?

Then, the void started expanding.

There was the day Layla came downstairs with a glittery picture she'd made for his office, a masterpiece she insisted on framing. He picked it up himself later that week, but he didn't come inside. Just a honk, a smile, and a wave from the car as he took the art through the window, their eyes meeting for a brief, warm, but painfully distant moment.

And the Saturday before Thanksgiving, when Jordan came home still giddy from their barbershop visit, laughing about a joke Amir had told.

He didn't come in.

"Uncle Amir said if I keep missing open layups, he's cutting my hair like this." Jordan showed a picture on his phone.

Autumn arched a brow. "The high-top fade?"

"No," he laughed, thoroughly amused. "The real short one, with the bald spot down the middle."

Autumn chuckled, ruffling his hair. "Mmm. Motivation through threat of looking like an old man. I love that for you."

She watched Amir's Jeep pull away, the laughter still on her lips, but a new thought surfaced as she closed the door.

The holiday was just around the corner.

A small, quiet panic tightened in her chest. Before she could overthink it, she pulled out her phone, her thumb moving quickly, reaching for a piece of their old, easy rhythm.

AUTUMN

Hey, big head. You coming for Thanksgiving?

The bubbles popped for seconds, then stopped. Then started again. Finally, he responded.

AMIR

Nah, Moet actually invited me to go with her to her family's home in Indiana.

The sting was so deep, her nerves tingled.

The thought of Amir not being at the table on their first Thanksgiving together in years—carving the turkey, arguing with Mia over the last piece of pecan pie, being a loud, laughing fixture in their family chaos—felt fundamentally wrong.

They weren't in conflict. They were in quiet decay.

And Autumn, wrapped in her own growth, had no desire to pull him back. He seemed to be enjoying his new girlfriend, and rightfully so. But she also couldn't lie to herself about what she felt, a dull ache that she still couldn't quite place.

Weeks passed in a soft blur, like the stretch of sky between dusk and dawn.

She moved through time, cocooned in her new flow; writing in her journal, parenting with purpose, and dating on her terms. She forced Amir to the back of that list, where it became just a little easier to deal with that persistent ache.

While continuing to attend the monthly Bag Lady sessions with Mia and the ladies wasn't something she ever imagined doing regularly, it was becoming more of a blessing in her healing journey.

Both of her situationships carried on; different flavors, same loose ends.

With Ekon, there were more rooftop nights filled with wine and music, short weekend getaways to Miami and Nashville, long, grown-folk sexy talks that dipped just below the surface, but never quite deep enough to plant anything lasting.

With DeMonte, the energy was steadier. There were late-night phone calls, Netflix marathons, grilled steak and sweet wine, his hand finding hers when they walked together.

They'd grown closer. He was still respectful of her space and pace, but he was also letting her in. He'd told her he was 'all in,' and his actions were the quiet proof: he asked about her therapy sessions with genuine curiosity, shared stories about the frustrations of co-parenting, and remembered the small, silly details she'd told him weeks before.

She was a woman living two different lives. One was a glittering escape. The other felt dangerously close to building something real.

And some days, she wasn't sure which one scared her more.

January rolled around like a tide change, subtle at first but shifting everything. While she didn't need to rush to figure out a living situation for her and the kids, she was getting restless again.

Maybe it was the whole *new-year-new-me* vibe that was going around.

On her resolution list were three things:

– Figure out where she wanted to move.

– Figure out when she was ready to return to work.

– Figure out the emotional mess her life had quietly morphed into.

As much as she hated to tackle that third one, she knew things were not as she expected them to be.

This was supposed to be a time of fulfillment in her journey: dating, exploring life, and having fun. But everything was off.

Was it her? Did she want more?

One Thursday afternoon, just as she'd settled into a post-holiday lull, her phone lit up:

EKON

You free next weekend? I wanna fly you out to LA. Big label event. Real Hollywood type shit. I want you there with me.

Autumn stared at the message, then typed:

AUTUMN

What kind of event?

EKON

> Black carpet, awards-week adjacent. Fancy.
> Exclusive. I got the plus one. You in?

The idea stirred something in her. A thrill, yes, but also curiosity.

A new city.

A high-profile scene.

And maybe, if she were honest, a way to pull herself out of the emotional fog that had settled in during the holidays.

She sent back a simple:

> I'm in.

Mia, of course, lost her mind.

"L.A.?! With Ekon?!" she shrieked, throwing a dish towel over her shoulder. "Girl, you better bring me back a picture with Kendrick or Kehlani or somebody!"

Autumn laughed as she helped with the dishes. "It's just a quick trip. Three nights, max. I'm not even sure what I'm wearing."

"You better borrow or buy something stunning," Mia demanded, hands on her hips. "You are not going out there in anything that says Chi-Town Target run."

"I'll leave the tags on and return it like a responsible adult," Autumn joked.

"Pictures. Autographs. And I want the uncensored tea when you get back. I mean all of it." She gave one of her twin sons a cookie when he smiled his way into the kitchen.

"You got it. Thank you again for keeping the kids."

Mia waved her off. "I love hanging with my niece and nephew. And I'll take any excuse to live through your single season, because my theme park is closed until further notice."

As she lay in bed that night, scrolling through pictures of L.A. hotspots, she knew exactly what this was.

A part of her knew this trip was a distraction, a way to outrun the emotional mess she'd listed on her New Year's resolutions.

But another part of her felt a jolt of the old Autumn, the ambitious, adventurous woman who wasn't afraid of a little chaos.

Maybe she wasn't just running away from her problems.

Maybe she was running toward a different kind of answer.

And for now, that felt like more than enough.

19

ALL THAT GLITTERS

By the time the plane touched down in Los Angeles, the sun was kissing the edge of the Pacific, smearing streaks of molten orange and blush across the sky, a beautiful, almost surreal vision.

Autumn stepped off the jet bridge into a world that felt manicured within an inch of its life: sleek architecture, marble floors that gleamed like wet glass, and the scent of designer perfume clinging to the air.

Ekon waited near the terminal in a cream knit sweater and tailored slacks that probably cost more than her sister's monthly mortgage. His smile was polished, his arms open. He leaned in and kissed her deeply, pulling her closer as the kiss lingered.

"Happy to see me much?" she grinned when he finally released her.

"Girl, you have no idea. It's been a long week, so I'm ready to get loose. This party is going to be amazing," he murmured, lacing his fingers through hers like it was second nature. "Welcome to the wild."

The mansion in the Hollywood Hills looked like it belonged on a magazine cover: gated, glowing, perched high above the city, as if watching from a throne.

Autumn took it all in: valet attendants in slick black suits moving with choreographed precision, women in bodycon dresses painted onto bodies that seemed to defy gravity, teeth bleached and bared in permanent media-ready grins. A DJ tucked under string lights spun house remixes with bass that thumped in her ribs.

For a while, she floated through it, mesmerized by it all.

She let Ekon guide her like a seasoned tour host, introducing her to other influencers with platforms on par with his, A- and B-list celebrities, and men and women who looked like they were made of money. She sipped champagne from fluted glasses, posed for selfies next to infinity pools, and laughed politely at jokes she didn't get.

It was all shine and glitter. The kind of surface-level thrill one got while ascending to the top of a rollercoaster ride, but it didn't last past the descent.

The shift happened slowly.

It started with the girls.

They were beautiful... and young. Too young for this kind of scene, the youngest bragging when Autumn asked that she'd just turned eighteen. Fresh-faced, with baby hairs laid and eyes that darted around the room like they were trying to remember their roles.

Some tugged at thigh-high dresses every few minutes. Others laughed too hard at unfunny comments. Autumn caught one girl in the bathroom mirror practicing a pout, then smoothing out invisible fly-aways before whispering, "You belong here. You belong here," to her reflection.

A familiar anxiety pooled in her stomach.

Because she remembered that voice.

Because she'd said it to herself before, in a different place, for different reasons.

A few minutes later, she caught a girl, who couldn't have been older than nineteen, whispering something to a man in a red velvet blazer. He laughed, tugged her by the waist like she was made of Velcro, and whispered something back. The girl smiled and giggled. He looked old enough to be her father.

And that was being generous.

And then she saw the pills, and the small baggies of powdery substance.

Autumn's throat went dry.

She saw hands slipping into pockets. Fingertips brushing palms in a quiet exchange.

Quick looks.

Quick nods.

A guy in a slick blue suit offered her a tiny pink tablet and called it "*California Confidence.*"

She blinked, then waved him off with a cordial smile.

Ekon just shrugged when she mentioned what she'd been seeing, a flicker of boredom in his eyes, as if she'd asked about the weather. "That's L.A., baby. This city runs on ego and enhancers."

As if that explained it. As if that made it normal.

She tried to laugh with him, to act unbothered. This wasn't her scene, fine. But she could adapt.

Except, she couldn't convince her gut.

The music got louder. The lights seemed harsher.

She needed to find a space that was less... everything.

She was heading upstairs to find a quiet balcony when another girl caught her eye.

Mascara smudged like war paint. Eyes wide. Lips trembling.

Like she'd seen something or been through something.

She brushed past Autumn on the stairs, practically sprinting, being followed by a friend who kept repeating: "It's okay. You're okay. Just breathe. You're okay."

Autumn stayed frozen on the staircase for a long moment, watching as the barefoot girl disappeared around the corner, still trembling, still being coaxed by her friend.

What if this were Layla? she thought as anger scorched her veins.

She moved before she could form an answer, gripping the handrail as she descended the steps and scanned the crowd, following the last thread of the girl's path.

She finally found them near the back patio, huddled in a corner just past the sliding glass doors. The girl was sitting on a lounger, arms crossed protectively around her waist, her head hanging down. Her friend sat next to her, shoulders tight, whispering something low while patting her on the back.

Autumn stepped into the glow of a hanging lantern, standing cautiously in front of them. "Hey," she said gently, holding her hands out like she was approaching a wounded animal. "Are you okay?"

The friend looked up first, her eyes wary. "She's fine. We're fine."

Autumn knelt beside the chair, ignoring the pain in her ankles.

"Sweetheart, did something happen? I saw you on the stairs, and you looked terrified."

The girl didn't answer.

Her eyes darted toward the glass doors. She rocked her head back and forth, refusing to look Autumn in the eye.

"She just needs a minute," her friend said, more forcefully now.

"A minute from what, though?" Autumn's voice stayed low, steady. "I've got a daughter. I'd want someone to step in if something wasn't right."

"She just had too much to drink," the friend snapped. "It's not a big deal. It happens."

"But why does she look scared?" Autumn pressed, her tone sharpening. "Did someone hurt her? Was she given something?"

Before the girl could even try to speak, a man stepped out from the shadows of the patio doorway.

Tall. Black shirt unbuttoned at the collar. Smiling, but the smile didn't reach his eyes.

"There you are," he purred casually, walking toward the girl like she was a misplaced accessory. "I was looking all over, babe."

The girl flinched, a slight, almost imperceptible movement, and shrank back into the corner of the lounger.

Autumn's focus locked on the girl as she pivoted to squat directly in front of her, hands intentionally on either side of the chair's arms. She kept her voice low, remembering the workshop she took years ago on recognizing victims of trafficking. Her goal: to be a steady anchor in the obvious tension. "Sweetheart, are you okay? Do you need help?"

For a second, the girl's terrified eyes met hers. She glanced at her friend, then back at Autumn, and gave a tiny, almost invisible shake of her head. But Autumn saw the petrified look in her eyes.

Please say the words, baby, Autumn prayed internally as her eyes pleaded with the girl's.

The man laughed lightly, a sound devoid of any real humor. "Excuse me, Ms. This is my friend, and she's fine."

Autumn ignored the man, keeping her eyes on the young lady in front of her, searching for any signs that said help me.

"She's fine. Aren't you, babe?" the man repeated, this time the impatience evident in his tone.

The girl kept her eyes trained on the floor. Autumn stood up slowly, deliberately placing herself between the man and the girl. "Can I have a few minutes with her?" she tried to force a smile. "It'll just be a few minutes," she continued, plastering a friendly tone she didn't feel.

"Let's go, babe." His icy blue eyes swept past Autumn, his voice edgier now as he reached around her for the girl's hand. "We've got to get going, yeah?"

"I don't think so." Autumn's voice dropped, losing all its forced pleasantry and hardening into something cold and immovable.

She felt his gaze sharpen on her, cold and heavy.

"Back off, lady. You obviously don't know who I am."

"No, but I know what it looks like when a girl's scared out of her damn mind and no one around her is doing a thing about it."

At that, two security guards appeared from the perimeter, gliding in with earpieces and matching expressions. One gently but firmly put a hand on Autumn's arm.

"Ma'am, we're going to have to ask you to step away."

"Are you serious right now?" she snapped, turning toward them. "She needs help, look at her!"

The man was already leading the girl away, arm around her shoulder like he hadn't just been called out. The friend followed, silently.

"That baby looks terrified!" Autumn shouted after them. "Did you even ask her if she was okay?"

One guard moved slightly closer, his look almost sympathetic as he gently gripped her arm and whispered in her ear. "Ma'am. She's not a baby—no one in here is. And that's one of the most powerful men in this city. Please don't cause a scene, or I'll have to ask you to leave."

Autumn yanked her arm free, chest heaving. Her hands turned to fists. Her mouth was tight with fury, frustration, and helplessness. It didn't matter who that man was. In a mansion full of glitter and shine, her gut instinct screamed she was witnessing something ancient and ugly: a predator cornering his prey.

And no one was doing a damn thing.

She watched the girl vanish into the crowd again, swallowed by the music and movement as if she had never been there. The glitz of the party suddenly appeared like broken glass, and every polished smile seemed threatening.

It took her a full minute to unclench her jaw. When she finally moved, it was a cold, determined march. Heat flushed up her neck like a physical manifestation of the righteous anger building in her veins. She was looking for an ally, an anchor in this glamorous, ugly world. She was looking for Ekon.

She found him leaning against the bar, sipping something golden and grinning with two men in designer hoodies.

He turned as she approached, his eyebrows raising in a lazy, amused way. His eyes slowly skimmed over her, taking in her rigid posture and the storm brewing on her face.

"Hey, baby. I've been looking for you," he said. "You good?"

"No. I'm not good," she snapped, her voice a low, tight tremor. "There was a girl on the patio who was either drugged or traumatized, and nobody seemed to care. I tried to step in, and some man had security pull me away like I was the problem."

He blinked slowly, as if processing. His smile tightened. He shot a quick, almost imperceptible glance back at his friends, a silent signal that read, 'Give me a second to handle this.'

He lowered his voice and placed his hands firmly on her shoulders, forcing her to meet his unsteady gaze.

"Autumn, was this a little girl? Or was she a young adult?"

The question threw her. "I... I don't know. She was young, she looked... maybe eighteen? But Ekon, she was..."

He cut off her rambling with a small, patronizing sigh. His tone was practical, firm, as if he were closing a business deal.

"Baby, you can't save everyone. This ain't Ebondale. This is how it is out here. You learn to look away, or you go crazy. It's not our business."

Autumn's mouth fell open as he turned to the bar to finish his drink. He wasn't hearing her words; he was managing her tone. The horror of what she saw was, to him, just a vibe to be curated.

"I saw her, Ekon," she retorted, her voice sharp with disbelief. "That girl was terrified. And that man... he was—"

Ekon exhaled, a long, weary sound, and turned his body fully toward her, creating a private bubble as he gently cupped her chin, his thumb rubbing her skin. "Hey. Look. I get it. It's a wild set, not everybody's used to this. We can dip if it's too much for you."

She stared at him, her head swaying in bewilderment. He was offering her an exit, not an alliance. The thumping bass from the other room seemed to fade to nothing. All she could hear was the booming echo of his indifference.

"I want you to myself anyway," he added, his voice dropping into a low, seductive gear. "Let's go back to the suite."

Before she could form a protest, he dipped his head to kiss her, his lips mashing against hers with an unfamiliar, urgent pressure. One hand slid down, clamping onto her backside with a blunt, possessive force that was unlike him.

Her face turned to stone as she pushed back, fast and firm, her palm flat against his chest. It was then that she saw the glassy look in his eyes and the sideways smile.

"Whoa! Are you drunk?"

All the months they dated, she'd never seen him past tipsy.

"We're done here," she snapped, the previous tremor gone and replaced by a definitive clarity. "Let's go. Now."

Without waiting for a response, she turned, her heels punishing the marble floor in a sharp, staccato rhythm all the way to the exit.

He followed behind her quickly after dapping up the two men he was talking to before.

"Aye... Autumn..." he called, skipping to catch up.

But she kept moving until she made it to the elegant double doors, pushing them open with force, ignoring his pleas.

The wait for a ride was a brief standoff on the curb, a foot of charged silence between them as they both stared at their phones, avoiding each other's eyes.

As they rode back to the hotel, Ekon sat in the back of the Uber beside her, his hand resting on her thigh. With his other hand, he covered his eyes as he propped his head against the headrest.

Autumn angled her body toward the window, arms crossed tightly, staring out at the city rushing past in a blur of neon gloss.

"I'm sorry about that back there," he muttered. "Got a little carried away. The vibe was wild, and I got swept up in it."

She noted the steadiness in his voice, as if the cool air from the open window was dulling the edge of his intoxication.

"No worries," she replied, her voice even. But it was a lie. She was still trying to process what she actually felt.

Her mind was back at the party.

On that young woman's mascara-streaked face.

On the man who smiled with entitlement and left with her.

On Ekon's easy dismissal of her concerns, as if she was overreacting.

She couldn't shake any of it.

She liked Ekon. More than she planned to. She'd let herself enjoy the champagne charm, the electric energy, the whole vibe. But tonight, something cracked open.

It wasn't just the scene; it was the way he reacted.

The ease with which he shrugged off what felt deeply wrong. And the way his apology now hung in the air like a throw pillow on a house fire.

She wasn't sure if it was a deal-breaker yet.

But she was sure it was a red flag.

A woman learns to pay attention to those. Especially when she's spent years ignoring them.

So, she didn't push his hand away. But she didn't hold it either.

She kept her gaze fixed on the blur of L.A. lights outside the window, her reflection barely visible in the glass.

This trip had shifted something in her.

And come morning, she planned to find out just how deep the cracks ran.

20

CHAMPAGNE AND UNO CARDS

The opulence of the penthouse suite felt out of place. The chilled champagne in its gleaming silver bucket stood untouched, its promise of celebration now seeming absurd. The rose petals looked like scattered, wilting wounds on the pristine white duvet.

Ekon stumbled past her, his hand clamped over his mouth, and disappeared into the marble bathroom. The click of the door was followed by a series of harsh, guttural retches that echoed in the room's silence.

Autumn didn't go in to help. She collapsed on the sofa, the plush fabric cool beneath her tense fingers as she clutched a decorative pillow to her chest. An ache throbbed at the base of her skull, a dull, persistent drumbeat of stress. Through the floor-to-ceiling windows, the city lights of Los Angeles glittered with a cold, indifferent beauty.

The toilet flushed, followed by running water. A few seconds later, a pale Ekon emerged, his face beaded with sweat, the collar of his expensive shirt damp. He fell into the bed, face-first.

"This is why I don't get drunk," he moaned into the mattress, his voice muffled.

Autumn's gaze pinned him to the bed, a mixture of weighted sadness and resignation. Her voice was stripped of its usual affection. Now, it was sharp like the chipped ice in the silver bucket.

"I've never seen you like this before."

He turned over on his back, looking at her with sorrow in his eyes. "Hey," he said softly. "I'm sorry. About all of that. That whole scene."

Her eyes narrowed. "Sorry about what, Ekon? About the girl? About not giving a damn? About shrugging off my concerns?"

Shame crossed his face as he ran a hand over his head. "Everything, babe. You're right. I was drunk, I was acting like an idiot, and what I said to you... There's no excuse."

His eyes pleaded for understanding.

"Autumn, I've been in this world for some years now. You see enough ugly things, and you learn to tune them out. You build a wall so you can function. I didn't even know I was doing it until I saw it through your eyes tonight."

She listened, her anger slowly giving way to a sad, hollow ache. It wasn't an excuse, but she recognized the truth in it.

She knew Ekon. She'd seen him in action at home.

He wasn't a monster.

He was just desensitized. Numb to a world she could never, ever get used to.

"I believe that you're sorry," she acknowledged with a firm edge to her voice. "I do. But I don't think I can unsee what I saw tonight. It's not just about that one girl. It's about that whole culture."

He eased off the bed and slowly moved to the couch next to her, clutching his stomach. "But it's not my world all the time. We can—"

"Can we, though?" she interrupted with a small smile that didn't reach her eyes. "My first thought tonight was about my daughter. About protecting her from a world exactly like that. Your first thought was to dismiss it. We see things different, Ekon. Our instincts are different."

She wasn't trying to prove she was right. She looked at him, her gaze clear and steady.

"I need you to understand this from my perspective. Silence in the face of harm... is harm, too."

The stillness in the room was palpable. The glamor had evaporated; the thrill was dissipating. She'd thought he was more grounded beneath all the glitter. That they had shared values, especially since he was so involved in giving back to the community.

Ekon dragged a hand down his face, his jaw tightening with a frustration that made him look cornered. He wouldn't meet her eyes.

"I'm gonna go wash this night off," he sighed, his voice drained as he stood.

He disappeared into the bathroom, and a moment later, the shower hissed to life, a steady, white noise that interrupted the tense silence of the suite.

Autumn didn't move from the couch. She listened to the water run, replaying the night in her head. His apology had been genuine; she believed him. But did it matter? Could an understandable justification erase the casual indifference he'd shown?

With a sigh that felt like it came from the soles of her feet, she pushed herself up and walked over to the bed, sitting on the edge of it. Right now, it was the path of least resistance, a temporary truce in a war she didn't have the mental strength to keep fighting.

She was staring at the rug's intricate pattern when the shower cut off. A few minutes later, Ekon emerged, a towel slung low on his hips, water droplets glistening on his skin.

He dropped beside her, his body still warm from the steam. "You okay?"

"I just can't get that party out of my head," she admitted after a few seconds.

"I guess I can understand that."

"Some of those girls… they looked so young. Like they didn't even know why they were there."

"Most of them don't," he said as he scooted to the back of the bed and lay against the headboard. "This environment is built on dreams, and it preys on dysfunction. But everybody's grown. Nobody's forced into anything."

She glanced down. "But that doesn't make it right. And eighteen, although it may be the age of consent, is not grown."

"C'mere," he whispered, the word a soft invitation for her to join him fully in the bed. She moved into his arms, laying her head on his chest. She could feel the thump-thump of his heart.

God, why did he have to feel so good?

"Are you really good with all that stuff?" she asked after a while, her fingers tracing the muscle lines of his chest.

"Honestly? I never saw it as my business before," he acknowledged. "I didn't get involved. I always just kept my head low."

She let that sit for a minute. She didn't expect him to save anyone, but she couldn't ignore how easily he'd allowed himself to go blind to it.

"You talked about giving back and making an impact," she reminded him. "So, it's kind of hard to reconcile this side of you in my head."

"I give back... to my people," he defended. "That's what I meant. The folks back home need us. These people here, they've had the world handed to 'em on a gold-plated platter."

"I hear you, but I'm a mother, Ekon," she countered. "And I'd be ready to burn a place like that down if my daughter—"

"Babe." He sat up, pulling her up with him, his eyes boring into hers. "Those girls are not the little precious princess you have at home. They were all adults. Young adults, maybe. But adults. Some of them have trust funds bigger than our wildest dreams."

A buzz from the nightstand pulled her attention. She rolled over and grabbed her phone, instinctively panicking when Mia's number and image flashed on the screen.

"Sis, what's wrong?"

Mia's voice came fast and low. "Don't panic... but we're at the hospital. Jordan had an asthma attack. He's stable now."

Autumn's heart thudded frantically, blood draining from her face. "Oh my God! Is he okay?"

"He's better now. He's getting a breathing treatment. They want to keep him overnight for observation."

"Wait... why didn't you call me when it first happened? I could've—"

"I tried, but it went straight to voicemail."

Autumn cursed the bad reception she'd been complaining about since she first arrived.

"I'm getting a flight home," she said with finality.

"Autumn, he's okay—"

"I'm getting a flight," she repeated, her voice cracking with intensity. "Tell him I'm on my way."

She ended the call, her heart banging against her chest as she jumped out of bed. Her hands moved on instinct, suddenly clumsy with panic as she threw open her luggage.

"What's going on, babe?" Ekon watched her with worry creasing his brow.

"I need to get to the airport." Her voice trembled as she moved through the room with an anxious stride, tossing things in the bag without care for order. "Jordan's in the hospital. He had an asthma attack."

"Damn," he muttered, pulling the blanket up to his chest as the room's automatic air conditioner kicked on. "Is he going to be okay?"

"He's stable. But he needs me. I have to get back."

Ekon nodded slowly. He sat up a little straighter.

"Do you need help packing?" he asked, his voice quieter now as he watched her.

When Autumn didn't answer, he continued, "I mean... Mia's with him, right? You don't have to bounce tonight, do you? Flights ain't even gonna be easy right now, it's almost two in the morning."

She stopped mid-toss, a shirt dangling between her fingers. He was still snuggled under the blanket, and although his eyes held concern, his movements suggested comfort.

The gap between them opened like a curtain at showtime. It was wide as a canyon and carved with different instincts.

"I'm going home, Ekon," she quipped, her voice even as she threw things in her bag with more force. "Now."

The flames of tension quickly tempered the coolness in the room as he raised his hands in defense. "Alright. No need to trip. I was just saying."

"You were just saying that my kid can wait."

He blinked. "That's not what I said."

"It's what I heard," she snapped as she zipped her bag.

He tossed the blanket aside and leaped from the bed. "Whoa, whoa. Hold on, baby." His tone shifted as he grabbed her waist, stopping her frantic movements.

"Ekon, I'm going home. I can't stay here—"

"I get it," he interjected softly, peering into her eyes. "Let me make some calls, I'll get you on a flight somehow."

Autumn paced the floor while Ekon took his phone into the next room. Her fingers trembled as they moved through her curls.

Her mouth went dry. Her imagination started flashing images of Jordan in a hospital bed, small and struggling; the beep of a machine she couldn't see, giving him life-saving oxygen.

She stopped in the middle of the room and closed her eyes, forcing herself to calm down.

"Mia said he's stable," she whispered. "He's not alone, she's with him. He's fine."

"Aye, thanks, I appreciate this, Stephanie," Ekon was saying as he entered the bedroom, his charm on display.

Autumn's eyes opened, a hopeful glint focusing on Ekon as he hung up his call.

"Hey," he said softly, gently taking her by the shoulders and bending slightly to meet her eyes. "Breathe. It's going to be okay. My contact got you on a 4:30 a.m. flight."

Autumn's relief was palpable as she threw her arms around his neck and buried her face against the solid wall of his chest. "Thank you so much."

He pulled back and kissed her full on the lips.

"Again, I am so sorry for this entire night." He pressed his forehead against hers. "And I wasn't trying to be insensitive about your son. You deserve better. I'll make all of this up to you."

She nodded, but something in her had already shifted.

Sudden gratitude didn't equal trust, and intermittent tenderness didn't undo a lack of instinct.

* * *

THE RED-EYE FLIGHT from L.A. to Chicago was a world unto itself, a quiet, humming tube suspended in an ocean of darkness. Outside her window, the vast blackness was occasionally pricked by tiny, glittering constellations of stars.

Autumn was cocooned in first class, a privilege Ekon had insisted upon, but the soft blanket and plush leather seat offered little comfort. It was a luxury she couldn't afford, with her son sitting in a hospital bed, and she wasn't there with her eyes on him.

With her journal open on the tray top, she let the pen move, trying to keep her mind busy.

This was supposed to be an escape. A fun weekend to get me out of my rut. But the thing about escaping is, you can't outrun yourself. You just end up face-to-face with reality again, this time in a nice hotel room.

I spoke to my baby. He's upbeat and chipper. He kept giggling, like his normal self, and that gave me a sense of relief until I can get to him.

I keep replaying that party in my mind. The gloss and the glamor were nothing but a costume, and underneath it was something dirty. Is it always like that? Ekon didn't lie to me about who he was, not really. But I wasn't getting the full picture, either.

I was getting—what's my favorite phrase for him? The highlight reel. I didn't like that all of that was happening around him, around so many people who I am certain saw what I saw, and it was dismissed as 'the price of admission.'

This life, this flashy, distant, glass-house persona? I can admire the view. But I could never live there. It's not built for people like me.

I belong to a mother's world. A world where my heart lives outside my body. A world where I would see any kind of disrespect to a young woman as an affront to my own daughter. A world where I would drop everything, burn everything, the moment one of my kids needed me.

That's not Ekon's world. And for him, that's okay. But it's not okay for me.

A lump rose in her throat. She swallowed it down, but the sadness lingered.

She closed the journal and leaned against the cool window, the engine's vibration a steady thrum in her bones.

The plane began its descent, the city lights of Chicago growing from a distant nebula into a familiar, sprawling grid. The moment the wheels touched down with a soft jolt, a sense of relief washed over her.

She was home.

The cabin's chime signaled it was safe to use electronic devices. Autumn powered on her phone and texted Mia.

AUTUMN

Just landed. I'm coming straight there.

MIA

Okay, sis. See you soon.

The freeze of the Chicago Hawk, that bone-chilling cold, was a stark contrast to the warm illusion of L.A. as she made her way out of the airport and walked to the Rideshare platform.

By the time her Uber pulled up to the hospital entrance, the morning sun was high over the city. Her carry-on bumped behind her as she rushed through the sliding glass doors and toward the pediatric wing.

Mia was standing in front of a vending machine, bolting to hug Autumn when she saw her walking with urgency.

"Hey, sis. Calm down, I see it all in your eyes," she said knowingly. "Jordan is fine. Like I told you over the phone, the inhaler wasn't working right when he started having breathing issues, so I brought him here just to be on the safe side."

Autumn squeezed her hands. "Thanks, sis. I appreciate you. Go on home, I know you've been here a while. I got it."

Mia nodded. "Okay. I just got off the phone with Malcolm, and he says Layla is still sleeping."

"Ok, and thank him for me. Tell him his Tee Tee owes him big time."

"Go on with Jordan, he's in room 229. I'll see you later."

Autumn made her way through the corridor, navigating the quiet halls with nervous tension. She offered a quick smile to the lone nurse at the station as she scanned the walls for Jordan's room number. When she found it, she pushed the door open softly, not wanting to wake him.

Her breath caught in her throat at the sight before her.

Jordan was wide awake, sitting up in bed, a small oxygen tube looped gently beneath his nose. His small hands were fumbling to grip the ridiculously oversized fan of giant Uno cards he was holding.

Amir, wearing joggers, a hoodie, and a lopsided smirk, sat across from him on the side of the bed.

"Draw four, my guy," he taunted casually, like they were back at his apartment.

Jordan groaned, the giant cards slipping in his fingers. "Uncle Amir, you cheated!"

Her knees nearly buckled. In that moment, everything—the party, the flight, the anxiety—collapsed into a single breath of gratitude.

Tears sprang forward freely, unleashed by the swell of relief that overcame her. She quickly wiped them away, plastered a smile on her face, and walked in fully.

Amir looked up, and something tender gleamed in his eyes when they landed on her, before he covered it with a grin. "Hey, you. Welcome back."

"Mommy!" Jordan exclaimed, his face lighting up.

She dropped her bag, ran to the bed, and wrapped him in her arms.

"How ya doin', buddy?" she asked, straightening the tube behind his ear.

"I'm fine," he said. "Uncle Amir's cheating, though."

"Oh, he always cheats," she pretended to whisper, smiling at Amir.

She gathered her son's face in her hands and filled it with kisses, her eyes unable to hold back the second wave of tears. She checked him thoroughly, firing off questions in rapid succession. "Does your chest hurt? Can you breathe okay?"

Satisfied Jordan was good, Autumn promised she wasn't going anywhere, and then pulled Amir into the hallway, finding a quiet spot away from the throng of rooms.

She leaned against the wall, her arms crossed, trying not to let the emotions swallow her whole.

"Thank you so much for being here," she said softly. "You have no idea how much I appreciate you."

He leaned beside her. "I know."

Of course, he knew. He always knew. The simplicity of his answer, the complete absence of ego in it, made her heart do a slow, painful somersault.

She smiled, nudging him gently with her elbow.

Then he said, "There was no other place I was going to be."

Autumn's heart jolted like it had been hit with a thousand watts of electricity. She turned to him as his head lay against the wall, his eyes fixated on the ceiling. She noticed the way the harsh hallway light carved a shadow under his beard, the sheer length of his eyelashes as he stared upward, the quiet strength in the set of his shoulders.

She wasn't just seeing her sometimes goofy, dependable best friend. She was seeing a man. Someone whose loyalty never wavered, no matter what.

"I just needed to say thank you," she repeated.

His hands rested in his pockets. "You don't have to. That's my guy in there. He called for you, but if he couldn't have you, he was gonna have me."

Her throat tightened. He didn't say it for points. He said it as if it were a given. Like he'd never needed a reason to be exactly where he belonged.

His eyes met hers. Autumn nodded, looking away quickly lest he see the new tears forming. She cleared her throat and tilted her head.

"How's... uh... Cristal?"

Amir's brows furrowed. "Who?"

She blinked. "I mean... Moet."

He snorted. "Cristal? Really?"

"I'm jet lagged," she muttered, followed by a fake shrug.

"She's good," he chuckled with a shake of his head. "We're chillin'."

Autumn nodded again. "That's good."

There was silence. Not awkward. But heavy.

"How was your trip?" he ventured, looking down at the glossy floors.

"It was... interesting," was all she would admit.

Another moment of silence.

"Thank you again," she said, breaking it. "For being you."

Amir bumped her shoulder gently. "That's my job."

Jordan's discharge came an hour later.

Amir carried both their bags out of the hospital and loaded them into his jeep. He blasted old-school Kanye the entire way to Mia's, bopping while Jordan rapped offbeat.

Autumn observed from the passenger seat without directly looking at them, her heart full and her spirit recalibrated.

The noise and glitter of the last few months seemed to fade, replaced by the simple, grounding rhythm of this feeling of home.

When they pulled up to the house, Amir turned toward the backseat. "Alright, my guy. No more asthma attacks, *capisce*? Scared the hell outta me, dude."

Jordan laughed, ending in a slight, wheezy cough. "*Capisce.*"

They exited the vehicle after he took a pump from his inhaler. Then, he walked happily between Amir and Autumn as they entered the house.

Inside, they moved in a familiar, friendly cadence. Autumn tucked Jordan into the bottom bunk while Amir checked on a still-sleeping Layla on the top, planting a soft kiss on her forehead. He caught Autumn's eye and gave a small, tired nod, a silent promise that everything was going to be okay.

And she allowed herself to feel it.

"Can I get you anything?" she asked as they descended the stairs together.

"Nah, I'm good. Gonna go home and catch a few hours of sleep, then head over to the center."

She walked him out to his car. "It's Sunday, and you're working?"

Amir tilted his head up, squinting at the sun. "Yeah. It's quiet. I get more done when it's like that."

She nodded, trying to find something to do with her hands. She stuffed them in her pockets.

"Well—"

"Don't you say thank you not nan other time," he joked as he slid into his jeep.

She smiled, pulling her coat tighter around her.

He let the passenger window down. "Now get on in the house before you freeze, Hotlanta."

He gave her a long look, then pulled off with a peace sign in the air.

She watched his car until it disappeared around the corner, processing a myriad of emotions that she couldn't untangle.

Autumn finally got a moment to herself later that afternoon. With Jordan napping and Layla busy showing her auntie her latest hair twist style on a mannequin's head, she sat on the bed in the bedroom, phone in hand.

She opened the contacts to Ekon. She didn't have the energy for talking. So, she clicked "new message."

Her thumbs hovered for a moment. Then moved.

AUTUMN

> Hey. Jordan's home and in bed. Thanks again for the invite to L.A.

A moment later, she typed again.

AUTUMN

> I wanted to say this clearly. Last night showed me something important. And I've realized I need to step back from what we've been doing. I have loved hanging out with you, it's been exciting and fun. But it's a little too much for me. Not judging you—it just hits different being a mother. No hard feelings at all. I just need to move differently.

The dots blinked almost immediately.

EKON

> Damn. Figured that might be coming. Still think you're special as hell. If this were a different time, I'd be trying to wife you for real. But I get it. Respect. No love lost. Keep me in the contacts?

He ended the message with three red heart emojis.

Autumn smiled softly at the screen, but it didn't reach her eyes.

"Some people you let go gently," she said out loud as she typed "of course" and closed the messaging app, "not because they aren't good, but because they aren't good for who you are."

She stood and walked toward the window, watching the afternoon sun pour over the backyard.

Jordan was safe. Her daughter was happy. The noise had settled. The fog had cleared.

And now, playtime was over.

Not because the idea of fun was gone—but because focus had returned.

She thought about that party again, those girls, that glitter, those shadows.

And then she thought about Layla.

What my children see becomes their roadmap.
So, I need to be sure I'm showing them what they should be following.

2 1

SAVORING THE SIMMER

February came in soft, like a peace offering. The frantic energy of the holidays had faded, replaced by the deep, insulated hush of a Chicago winter.

There was no drama. Just the muffled sound of life outside, the city's sharp edges softened by fresh snowfall.

It was this muted atmosphere that made Autumn realize just how loud things had gotten.

It had been a month since she broke it off with Ekon.

It was an amicable ending, but it brought more stillness.

Truthfully, she missed him.

His smile. His style. His charisma. Sometimes, she'd let herself venture to his TikTok page and smile at his content, even leaving a like on something that caught her interest.

Was it just her ego noticing? Or was there a little sadness behind his eyes when he smiled into the camera?

Then she'd remember that last night.

The party. The girls.

The way his silence felt like complicity.

She often wondered what had happened to some of those young ladies and berated herself for not doing more.

But Autumn knew she had to move past it. Journaling became routine. Reading became an escape.

She dove deep into books on the history of coffee cultivation until the pages were dog-eared, sticky-noted, and inked with highlighter. The kitchen was always filled with the scent of toasted beans and chicory as she tested blends, labeling them by hand and gifting them to a select few.

And slowly, without fanfare or fireworks, DeMonte drifted closer.

He wasn't trying to replace anything.

He existed beside her, warm and steady, demanding nothing she wasn't ready to offer.

There were long phone calls that stretched into the middle of the night, debates about the best hip-hop albums of the '90s, stories about parenting wins and fails, and deep dives into nothing and everything.

On his free weekends, he invited her into his world, his kitchen alive with the scent of garlic and oregano while she helped him perfect his spaghetti and meatballs.

On other nights, they'd order in and binge documentaries on Black inventors, their legs touching beneath a throw blanket. Their bodies curled together under the soft glow of the TV, not urgent, not performative... just present.

The intimacy was comfortable. Unforced.

There had even been a couple of sleepovers when she stayed too late. Their lovemaking was slow, deliberate, more like exhaling than igniting.

And to her own surprise, Autumn didn't miss the spark. She savored the simmer.

Like landing after a lifetime of turbulent flights.

Alone in the house on a Friday morning, she stood in Mia's kitchen, a mug of her Asia's Ember roast blend warm in her hand, watching the snowflakes fall outside the window.

Her jam hummed low through the Bluetooth, Lauryn Hill's *Nothing Even Matters*, a perfect backdrop to her thoughts.

A text notification chimed.

DEMONTE

Morning, gorgeous. Thinking about dinner
tonight. Chicken Alfredo or baked salmon?

> Or I could surprise you…

A soft smile touched Autumn's lips.

She could picture him on the other end of that text: probably leaned forward in his police cruiser or at his desk, thumbs moving with purpose. She imagined the tip of his tongue peeking out from the corner of his mouth, that little tell of intense concentration, as if he were carefully crafting the perfect, playful line just for her.

AUTUMN

> You know how I do. Surprise me. Just no mushrooms on the salmon. 🐟

DEMONTE

> LOL, noted. No mushrooms. I don't want no smoke. Just good food and good…😏

She chuckled, set the phone down, and took another sip.

She felt anchored.

No high-wire tension.

No anxious second-guessing.

Just a steady, predictable ease, something she might've once labeled boring.

But now, after navigating so many storms?

This felt like stability.

It wasn't perfect, nor was it permanent. But it was peaceful.

And for now, that was more than enough.

Still, every so often, she wondered,

What if peace means I'm playing it safe?

But after the chaos she'd survived—losing her best friend, the emotional shitstorm with Chris, losing the career she thought she was tailor-made for, Ekon—maybe "enough" didn't need to be more.

* * *

A WEEK LATER, when Amir invited her to dinner with him and Moet, Autumn wasn't sure what she expected.

They'd finally had the official conversation about his girlfriend.

"I mean, I still don't know where it's going," he'd told her as they sat in Mia's living room after he dropped by for a visit. "But, since you dragged me for not saying anything in the beginning, I wanted to make sure I properly introduced you two."

When the moment had arrived, a tight knot of anxiety rose in her gut as she wondered how the night would play out.

Maybe awkward small talk. Perhaps a few tight smiles.

Maybe the mild ache that sometimes sprang out of nowhere when the person she used to lean on... leaned elsewhere.

Amir was already at the restaurant when she arrived, standing near the hostess podium in a fitted black sweater and dark gray slacks. She was so used to seeing him in his signature joggers that the man standing before her barely registered as the same person. He was sharp, tailored, and radiated a quiet, potent confidence. It was a jarring, breathtaking upgrade.

His locs were freshly braided, cornrowed tight along the scalp in neat rows that fed into two long, thick ropes down his back. Mia had warned her earlier about his beard.

"Girl. When I tell you that man walked out the shop lookin' like he got hand-carved by angels. My new barber hooked him up, and let me just say, not a hair outta place. And..."

She had paused for dramatic effect, fanning herself. "Don't get me started on the way it framed his mouth, like the Lord personally commissioned those lips to test a woman's strength."

Autumn had shaken her head, knowing what her sister was trying to do.

"Do you have to be so damn theatrical?"

But now she understood.

The soft lighting caught the warm undertones of his deep brown skin, and his eyes, those sharp, steady eyes, found hers instantly, like they'd been waiting.

Moet stood beside him. Her long curls were down, her high cheekbones glinting under the warm lights, wrapped in a lavender sweater dress that hugged her curves.

"Aut!" Amir beamed with a smile, stepping forward and hugging her tight. "Glad you made it."

"Hey," she smiled in return, shifting her purse on her shoulder and returning his embrace. "Nice to see you again, Moet."

Moet surprised her by pulling her into a hug —not a polite air-kiss kind of hug, but a genuine, tight squeeze like they were old friends.

Autumn stiffened for half a second, an involuntary defense mechanism kicking in. But the warmth was undeniable, and so was the simple kindness of the gesture. So, she let herself soften, melting into it.

They dined at a trendy Black-owned soul-food eatery tucked in the west end of Ebondale. The air inside was thick with the rich scent of braised short ribs and brown-sugar candied yams. A low hum of conversation mingled with the smooth sounds of a Maxwell track playing in the background, and candles on each table flickered like the ancestors were celebrating.

Moet complimented Autumn's earrings, a vintage pair from a small boutique in Hyde Park. Before the appetizers even arrived, the two of them had fallen into an easy, rapid-fire conversation about thrifting, nineties R&B, and the shared, sacred struggle of finding the perfect edge control for natural curly hair.

Moet was hilarious, animated, and unexpectedly down-to-earth. She was a makeup artist who had just launched her own brand that catered to Black skin; she loved cheese fries and called Amir out without hesitation, especially when he tried to pretend he didn't cry during their re-watch of The Lion King.

"Yep, Mufasa's death always makes baby cry," Autumn pouted, teasing as both ladies ribbed him.

Amir shook his head, grinning. "Why are both of y'all like this?"

The ladies leaned back in their seats, laughing.

As the night went on, there was a moment when Autumn caught him watching them as she and Moet giggled over something silly. There was a softness in his expression she hadn't seen in months, an unreadable affection in his eyes that wasn't directed at one of them but seemed to encompass them both. Then he blinked, smirked, and looked away.

When the check came and Amir reached for it, Moet waved him off.

"I got this," she retorted playfully. "I'm not gonna let you flex all night."

"You see what I deal with?" he directed the question to Autumn, feigning exasperation.

"It's called balance," Autumn replied.

After settling the bill, they bundled up against the cool night air and stood outside a few minutes later, beneath the warm wash of street lamp light.

Moet pulled Autumn in again. "Seriously, girl. This was nice. We should hang out sometime, just us."

Autumn's smile was genuine. "Yeah. I'd like that."

As they all walked toward the parking lot, Amir leaned over to Autumn.

"You good?" he asked, his voice low enough for only her to hear.

"I am," she affirmed.

And this time... she meant it.

* * *

LATER THAT WEEK, Thursday night wrapped itself in serenity. The kids were fed and tucked in, a curated playlist of 90s and early 2000s love songs hummed through the speaker, and Autumn was nestled on the couch in an oversized tee and fluffy socks. A half glass of Sweet Red rested on the end table beside her, while she was engrossed in an e-book on her Kindle.

Her phone lit up, showing DeMonte's picture.

She smiled before answering. "Hey, you."

His voice was smooth, low, delivering that late-night softness that came after long days. "Hey, gorgeous. How was your day?"

She could hear him settling in for the night, likely sitting up in bed, back resting against his headboard.

They traded updates: DeMonte's latest excitement on the force, a funny thing Jordan said during dinner, until the conversation settled into a gentle lull.

Then he cleared his throat. "So, I've been thinking."

Autumn leaned her head back on the couch. "About?"

"Us. Where we're headed."

Her breath caught just slightly. Not out of panic or fear, just a pause, a flutter in her chest that came at the idea of moving in another direction.

Was she ready for that?

A small part of her wanted to double-check the exits. Just in case.

"We've been spending a lot of time together," he continued. "Getting closer. And I'm really feeling this, Autumn. You... Us. It just feels right." He paused. "I know how we started. Casual, just having fun. I'd like to think we've progressed beyond that. Or am I imagining things?"

A fleeting image of Amir and Moet holding hands flashed through her mind, and she forced herself to dismiss it.

"No," she said quickly, catching herself. "You're not imagining things."

"And I also know I'm not dating just to date. I want to build something solid with someone who's on the same page."

He paused again before continuing, encouraged by her silence. "I think it's time we met each other's kids."

Autumn sat up straighter, her hand tightening on the phone.

This was the line. The one she hadn't crossed, not even for a second, with him or Ekon.

She'd built a firewall around her children's lives, a strict policy against turning their home into a revolving door of 'mommy's friends.' It was her most non-negotiable rule.

"You do?" Her voice was tight.

"I do. And they can all meet each other as well. No pressure, nothing too heavy. Just a little family-style fun. Bowling, maybe. I remember you saying Jordan and Layla liked to bowl."

She hesitated, the weight of his proposal settling in her chest. Her hesitancy wasn't about his daughter; she remembered the girl's shy, sweet smile from the salon.

It was about Jordan and Layla. About letting another man into their small, safe world, a world she had fiercely protected since the divorce.

But the more she thought about it, the more she realized DeMonte was different. He wasn't just some guy asking to enter her sacred space; he was a father, offering to open his own. He understood the weight of what he was asking in a way Ekon never could have.

She inhaled, then let it out slowly, a decision solidifying in the quiet of the room.

"Okay," she said, the word coming out softer than she expected. Then, with more certainty, "Yeah. That sounds... actually kind of perfect."

The relief in his voice could be heard through the phone. "Good," he replied. "I want them to see us together. And I want Ashley to see what a real, positive woman looks like. She hasn't had many to look up to. I think she'll love your energy."

His voice softened, losing its playful edge and gaining a new, vulnerable weight.

"I'm really looking forward to this, Autumn."

"Me, too, DeMonte," she admitted, and the truth of it surprised even her.

"Sleep well, beautiful," he said as their call wound down. "Tell Layla I heard about her love for chocolate chip cookies, so I'll make sure to bring a fresh, unburnt batch."

Autumn laughed, a real, bubbling sound. It wasn't just the joke; it was the easy, thoughtful way he was already trying to impress her kids with the skills he was still cultivating. They ended the call, and she was left with a feeling that was both foreign and deeply welcome.

But also just a little nerve-wracking. Because there was one person she needed to at least consult before introducing them to a new man.

She dialed Chris's number.

"Hey." He picked up on the first ring, his voice holding a slight edge of panic. "Everything okay?"

She should have known he would still be in alert mode after Jordan's last asthma attack.

"Yeah, yeah. Jordan's fine. They both are."

"Okay." She could hear him relax. "What's up?"

She explained the situation to him: how she'd broken things off with Ekon, and how she and DeMonte were growing closer, which had led to his proposal for a family date.

"Are you getting serious with him?" Chris asked.

"That's the thing," Autumn replied. "I still don't know if I'm ready to be serious with anyone. But I don't see the harm in a family date. We've been going out for months now, and I've technically already met his daughter."

"So what's the problem?"

She hesitated. "Well," she paused, "I guess before I introduce a man to the kids, even if in friendship, I'd want you to know first."

She could hear the smile in his voice. "I appreciate that, Autumn. That means a lot."

"It's only right. But, to also give you the choice of meeting him before he meets the kids."

"But you said you're not ready for anything serious, right?"

"Right…"

"Then this is just a friendly family date, the way I see it. If and when you start to discuss something more formal, then I for sure would like to meet this man."

Autumn nodded. "That's fair."

"Listen, I trust you one thousand percent. The fact that you even called me before you introduced them tells me everything I need to know about who you are as a mother. So I know whoever is invited into that circle, dude's gotta be worthy."

Autumn ended the call, a quiet certainty settling in her chest. There was no rulebook for this, no official protocol for co-parenting after betrayal and heartbreak. But in that moment, she knew she'd made the right decision.

She and Chris might never be husband and wife again, but they would always be a team when it came to their kids. And finally, that felt less like a burden and more like a blessing.

The next morning arrived with high energy. The kitchen was already buzzing by the time Autumn poured pancake batter into the sizzling skillet. As Layla attempted the latest viral TikTok dance behind her, a video game explosion echoed from upstairs. With school closed for the day, the house was at full capacity and volume.

She smiled, flipping the flapjack. She loved this for her kids, who did not get this level of family engagement in Atlanta. They hung out with Chris's nieces and nephews, but only on special occasions, such as birthdays or holiday dinners.

This level of regular connection was golden.

"Guess what?" Autumn said with excitement, handing her daughter the batter bowl to stir. "We're going bowling this weekend with my friend."

Layla perked up, peeking over the edge of the bowl, eyes wide. "Yay! Which one?"

"Mr. DeMonte. And his daughter, Ashley."

Layla's smile grew. "That's so cool!" Then her face shifted. "Wait. Is his daughter mean?"

"I don't think so."

"She better not be. I don't fight, but I do know how to defend myself. Uncle Amir taught me."

"Girl…" Autumn shook her head, chuckling. "Give me the bowl and go get your brother and cousins for breakfast."

Jordan's only response when told about the outing was a nonchalant shrug and a "Bet." He was just happy bowling was involved.

By Saturday morning, Autumn found herself double-checking the kids' socks to make sure they were matching, slicking down Layla's baby hairs with a toothbrush, and making sure Jordan had on clean underwear.

She tried to ignore the flutters in her stomach. Tried to remind herself this wasn't a performance, it was just life moving forward.

But deep down, she knew this was more than just bowling. It wasn't just about strikes and spares; it was about seeing if their two separate worlds could fit in the same lane.

DeMonte was making his intentions clear.

It was a window.

And windows always showed the light.

And the cracks.

2 2

IT'S COMPLICATED

The Family Fun Center was packed, bustling with the sounds of crashing pins, kids squealing, and the low murmur of grown folks trying to have a moment between frames and french fries. Neon lights, blinking arcade games, and the smell of nacho cheese made the setting a neutral, harmless space, just as DeMonte promised.

Autumn arrived with Jordan and Layla in tow, both bouncing with energy, their colorful duffel bags of bowling gear in hand.

Jordan had already claimed victory.

Layla wore her pink bedazzled ball glove and cherry lip gloss.

"It's giving… confidence," she had announced with all the sass of a ten-year-old diva as she flicked her ponytail.

From the entry, Autumn clocked that DeMonte was already there with his daughter, who wore a Canada Goose jacket, a tight-lipped smile, and AirPods plugged in while scrolling through her phone. When she briefly glanced up, she looked like she was at an unnecessary board meeting.

Autumn crouched beside her kids for a pre-game huddle before they joined them.

"Be kind," she warned gently while tying Jordan's shoe. "Be cool. And please don't clown too hard if you win."

The nine-year-old's grin was devilish. "Okay. I'll just clown a little."

Layla crossed her arms, smacking her lips. "Depends on her attitude."

"Layla..." Autumn's voice was a soft but firm admonition.

She gave a dramatic sigh, then smoothed down her shirt.

"Fine. I'll be nice."

A smile played on Autumn's lips despite her nerves vibrating on a ten. Taking a deep breath, she led them toward the lane where DeMonte was waiting.

As he watched them approach, he broke into a wide, relieved grin. He met the trio halfway, placing a warm hand on the small of Autumn's back as he leaned in to speak just to her.

"Hey, you," he greeted, his voice a comforting hum beneath the alley's chaos. "Glad you made it."

"Wouldn't have missed it," she replied, grateful for his steadying touch.

Autumn felt a familiar, nervous flutter as his focus shifted to Jordan and Layla. He knelt, bringing himself to their level, his smile sincere and genuine.

"You must be Jordan." He extended a friendly fist. "Your mom tells me you're the king of the court. I'm gonna need to see that crossover sometime."

Jordan, looking visibly impressed, met his fist with a solid bump. "Yeah, maybe," he said with a sideways grin, trying to play it cool.

DeMonte then turned to Layla. "And you must be the famous Layla. I've heard a lot about you."

She preened, tossing one of her braids over her shoulder. "All good things, right?"

DeMonte chuckled, a deep, warm sound. "The best things. Your mom told me you were the real boss, and I can see she wasn't lying. I also heard you have amazing style, and the reports were definitely accurate with that bowling glove."

Watching him, Autumn felt the knot of tension begin to loosen. He wasn't just talking at them; he was seeing them, connecting with each of them.

"I'm really happy to finally meet you both." He rose, then winked at Autumn.

He then pivoted and led them toward his daughter. Ashley remained seated as they neared the reserved lane.

"Ash, put the phone down for a minute," DeMonte prompted gently. "This is Ms. Autumn. And these are her kids, Jordan and Layla."

She pulled one white pod from her ear, but left the other one in, her expression neutral. She offered a polite nod, barely looking up. "Hi."

"What's up?" Jordan spoke with a cool dip of his head, his attention already captured by the glowing rack of bowling balls nearby.

Layla, however, stepped forward, unbothered by the lukewarm reception. "Hi, Ashley. I like your jacket."

"Thanks," she mumbled. She glanced at her dad, then quickly looked back down at her phone.

Autumn and DeMonte exchanged a quick, knowing look over the kids' heads. He offered a slight, almost apologetic shrug.

"So how old are you, Ashley?" Jordan asked, cocking his head as if he was sizing her up.

"I'm eleven, why? How old are you?" The response came with a challenge that Jordan quickly took on.

"I'm nine, and I just need to know how big this victory's gonna be when I beat two old ladies." His laughter was smug as he stuck his tongue out at his sister.

Layla rolled her eyes, directing her comment to Ashley. "He always thinks he's the champion of everything."

"That's 'cause I am," he returned with mock swagger, grabbing a neon green bowling ball that looked way too big for his hands.

Layla and Ashley exchanged a look of pure, unadulterated secondhand embarrassment, dissolving into a fit of giggles as his fingers fumbled to keep a grip on the heavy ball.

Autumn exhaled quietly as she nudged DeMonte and whispered. "We might survive this."

His chortle was warm, comforting. "It's gonna be fun. And don't worry, if things get too tense, I got food on standby. Ain't nobody mad when they're eating chili cheese fries."

The first half hour was smooth enough.

DeMonte ordered snacks in abundance, handed out game cards, and raved about the kids' bowling styles like he was the supportive sports dad of the year. Jordan ate it up.

Ashley still didn't talk much, but Layla kept trying as they sat on the bench waiting for their turns to bowl.

"You like Beyoncé?"

Ashley shrugged. "She's alright. My dad says she's kinda overrated."

Layla blinked. Hard. Like someone had just insulted her mama. Her lips parted, disbelief radiating off her like heat. "Well, your dad is kinda wrong."

Autumn, sipping her Coke beside them, nearly choked. She masked a laugh behind her palm, careful not to fuel her daughter's fire but also not mad at the loyalty. Layla's love for Beyoncé bordered on obsession. Any criticism of her idol was always met with a strong adolescent attitude.

Ashley sucked her teeth. "I don't think so. And why is she always parading her kids on stage like that? My dad says—"

"Layla, you're up, baby," Autumn interjected quickly, ushering Layla toward the pins with intention.

A half hour later, Jordan let out a loud cheer after his third strike in a row, beating his chest and doing a V-Step victory dance.

"Yeah, boy! That's what I'm talkin' about!"

Autumn laughed, clapping from her seat. As she turned to look at DeMonte, about to raise her hand in the air for a high-five, she noted the tightness of his smile. Then, he caught Jordan's eye and gave him a look—a quick, almost imperceptible head shake.

"Alright, champ, bring it down a notch," he admonished, his voice gentle but firm enough to carry. "Celebrate the win, but always act like a gentleman in public. Humility is a good look."

Jordan's dance stuttered to a halt. His shoulders dropped, but he nodded, the grin slipping from his face as he went to sit down.

Autumn's own smile faltered. She knew it was good advice. The kind of advice Black boys were given their whole lives to keep them safe. But seeing the unadulterated joy snuffed out of him, even for a second, sent a sharp, protective pang through her chest. Something about the reminder tugged at her, how early the world demanded her son shrink.

She wondered, fleetingly, how Amir might've handled the same moment. Probably would've cracked a joke about Jordan needing to teach him that dance, then slipped the lesson in sideways without fading his shine.

The thought passed quickly.

A few rounds later, as the throwback playlist shifted into Destiny's

Child, Layla couldn't help herself; she started dancing between frames, throwing in a few hair flips and hip pops for good measure.

Autumn watched, amused.

DeMonte leaned in. "She can really dance, huh?"

"The only thing she loves more than fashion," Autumn replied, chuckling.

"She reminds me of my niece," he added. "Full of confidence. But I always tell my sister, let our girls keep that spirit... but also learn when to tone it down. There are too many dudes out here watching, ready to pounce on our little princesses."

Just then, Layla finished with a final, dramatic spin and skipped back toward them, her face flushed with joy. "Did you see that last move, Mama?"

DeMonte smiled at her, but it didn't quite reach his voice. "That was great, Layla. You've got a lot of energy." His tone shifted from amused to something more instructive. "But a lady also knows how to compose herself in public. You might want to turn it down, just a little."

The light in Layla's eyes dimmed a fraction. She gave a small, respectful nod and sat quietly beside Ashley.

Autumn's posture stiffened. She thought about how Amir always called Layla his little superstar, hyping her spins and silly dances like she was already headlining a stage.

He never clipped her wings. He let her fly.

The difference pressed on her chest now, heavy and undeniable.

"Oh, she's fine," she said, trying to keep her voice light. "She's just feeling the music."

DeMonte gave a short, curt nod. "Sure."

And she felt it then. That subtle tug of reality pulling her coattail.

DeMonte wasn't being harsh. He was measured. Thoughtful. Protective even.

The kind of man any mother would be lucky to co-parent with—if she were on the same frequency.

But Autumn *wanted* her children to be bold. Loud when it mattered. Unafraid to dance and celebrate, even when the world stared. Especially then.

Her taut smile held, her eyes stayed on Layla. "She'll learn balance. But I want her to hold onto that innocent light for as long as she can."

"I hear that," he agreed, nodding. "She's a star, for real. They both are. We just have to watch them closely and prepare them for when we can't always be there to see."

They exchanged a look, exposing a bridge between conflicting approaches.

He wasn't wrong. Her mind drifted back to the party in LA. She knew predators were real. But she wasn't wrong, either. In safe spaces, surrounded by people they loved, kids shouldn't have to shrink themselves.

Perhaps they were aligned in values but misaligned in temperature.

The games continued, but for Autumn, some of the joy had drained from the day. She found herself getting antsy when Jordan hit another strike or when Layla started dancing to a favorite song.

When the outing reached its end, and as they made it to her car in the parking lot, her hug with DeMonte was stiff. "Thanks for today," she said, her voice tight.

The kids, having finally found a rhythm together, laughed and joked about the rounds.

DeMonte looked into her eyes, concern etching his own. "Are you okay?"

"Yeah," she said, forcing a tight smile. "Just got some things on my mind."

She called the kids. "Come on, guys, we need to get home. It was nice meeting you, Ashley."

This time, the little girl was brimming with life.

"You too, Ms. Autumn. Bye, Layla and Jordan!"

As she turned onto the expressway, Autumn looked at her kids in the rearview mirror, each looking out the window with a happy, joy-filled expression. They didn't appear to harbor any of her apprehensions, and for that she was grateful.

Later that night, the house was still after the kids went to bed. They had fallen fast asleep, worn out from a day that, for them, had been pure fun.

Autumn sat on her bed with her phone in hand, staring at DeMonte's contact photo.

Her mind kept replaying the day with a quiet, aching clarity. Jasmine's voice echoed in her head: "When someone shows you who they are, commit it to memory."

And DeMonte had shown her exactly who he was: a thoughtful, protective, and loving father who saw the world through a lens of caution.

But was it too cautious?

Her phone buzzed with a text from him, as if summoned by her thoughts.

DEMONTE

Hey you. Just wanted to say again what a great time I had today. Ashley is already asking when she can see Layla again.

Autumn smiled. Then she hit dial. He answered before the second ring.

"Hey, beautiful." His voice was warm.

"Hey. I had a really nice time today, too." She took a breath. "But DeMonte... can I be really honest about something that's been on my mind since the bowling alley?"

There was a slight pause. "Of course." His tone shifted from casual to attentive.

"I loved watching you with your daughter today. And the way you look out for her, and even for my kids... It's admirable. It really is." She hesitated. "But I think we see the world, and how we need to prepare our kids for it, a little differently."

She paused, fiddling with the edge of her pillowcase.

"I want my kids to be loud and take up space, to be unapologetically themselves. And I worry that my 'let them be free' style doesn't quite mesh with your more careful, protective one."

He was quiet for a moment. "Do you think that's a problem?" he asked gently. "A difference in parenting styles? Because, baby, that's stuff people figure out."

He paused again, and she gave him space.

"I really want this to work," he continued, his voice low and earnest. "Autumn... Look, I'm just gonna say it. I could see myself falling for you. Hell, I think I already am. And I want to take this to the next level."

Falling. Next level.

The words floated in the air, full of a sentiment and promise she wasn't ready for. How could she even think about the *"next level"* with him when her heart still did a complete somersault every time Amir walked into a room? The unfairness of it all made her chest ache.

"DeMonte," she started carefully, her voice thick with regret. "You're ready for the next level. And you're falling for me in a way that I'm not sure I can be there to catch you. At least, not right now…"

"What are you saying?" The confusion was evident in his voice.

She took a deep breath.

"I'm saying this isn't about parenting styles, or anything you did wrong. You're a great man." A tear she didn't expect slipped down her cheek. "This is about me. My heart… It's just not fully available. And I can't, in good conscience, keep taking up your time when I know I can't give you what you deserve."

The silence on the other end was heavy, and she could feel the energy shift.

"Wow," he said finally, his voice low. "Okay. I… I don't understand, but I hear you."

"I'm so sorry," she whispered.

After a few moments, he murmured, "I'm not asking you to catch up to me, Autumn. You're worth waiting for."

And that single, selfless sentence was what finally broke her. A ragged sob escaped her, sharp and involuntary.

"DeMonte." She took a breath to quell the tremor. "I can't do that to you."

His own breath was torn, weighted. "Then, is this over?"

She closed her eyes, her face awash with tears.

"Yes." Her voice was barely a whisper as it cracked with regret. "I… am so… sorry," she choked out.

There was a long moment when neither of them spoke, as the quiet settled into a new, heartbreaking rhythm.

"Yeah," he answered finally, his own voice burdened with emotion and full of a quiet resignation. "Me, too."

The call ended gently, with a finality that left her feeling hollowed out. After several moments of a soul-purging cry, she pushed herself to the back of the bed and opened her journal, writing with frustration.

What the hell is wrong with me?

I just let a good man go.

A man who is protective, and steady, and available.

Yes, the parenting differences matter. But was that really a deal breaker? DeMonte's instinct is always caution. He wants to protect, even if he has to dim.

Amir is different. He corrects without clipping wings. He lets the joy stay big, lets the shine stay loud. With him, my kids don't feel the need to shrink.

Wow, I've done it again. I keep comparing him to Amir. If I'm honest, I did the same with Ekon.

I wish I could feel more for DeMonte. I know, without a doubt, he would have been an emotional safe harbor, no drama.

But my heart doesn't want safe. My first thought is that it just wants what it can't have, like a complicated, foolish attraction to the forbidden.

But that's not it. Not really.

It doesn't want just any complication. It wants <u>our</u> complication. It wants the storm. It wants the history.

It wants Amir.

She capped the pen, the weight of her honesty wrapping around her like a thick fog: difficult to see through, but something she could no longer ignore.

23

THE BEAUTIFUL ESCAPE HATCH

The scent of coconut oil, hot flatirons, and edge control wrapped Autumn in a familiar warmth as she stepped through the door of Mia's salon. The hum of chatter, laughter, and Toni Braxton crooning from the speaker lifted her spirits, providing a much-needed emotional reprieve.

It had been a week since the family date, and the heartbreak that followed.

DeMonte had called a few times since. Sent texts she couldn't bring herself to open. But last night, he showed up at the house.

* * *

"I NEEDED TO SEE YOU," he said, standing on the porch with hands in his pockets, his expression open but weary. "Not to beg. Just to understand."

She stepped outside, closing the door softly behind her.

"It's my fault." His voice was rough with emotion. "I shouldn't have told you I was falling for you so soon. If I had just played it cool, maybe we'd be having dinner tonight instead of this."

"Would it have changed how you feel?" she asked gently.

He hesitated for a brief moment. "No. But maybe it would've kept you from pulling away."

She took his hands in hers, her gaze soft but unwavering.

"What we had was fun... amazing. And what we could have had might have been just as amazing. But I'm not there, DeMonte. And I won't let you wait for something that may never be."

He looked away, the muscles in his jaw tightening as he blinked up at the sky, as if searching for strength in the stars.

When he looked back at her, his gaze was filled with sorrow, but also clarity. "You don't have to worry about me waiting," he said quietly. "I won't put myself in limbo. I deserve to be somebody's first choice."

A tear slipped from Autumn's eye. "You do," she nodded. "You absolutely do."

He shook his head, slow and solemn, and gently pulled his hands from hers.

"Well, damn," he whispered, a wistful smile touching his lips. "A man can't argue with a woman's honesty." He let out a sigh. "You take care of yourself, Autumn."

"You too, DeMonte." Her voice was thick with tears.

He leaned in and pressed a soft, lingering kiss to her forehead. And with a final look of bittersweet regret, he turned and walked away.

* * *

THE MEMORY DISSOLVED, but its weight lingered. Autumn blinked at her own reflection in the salon mirror, the echo of DeMonte's goodbye still clinging to her as she sank into the stylist's chair.

Her phone had felt heavy all night.

She'd almost called Amir—thumb hovering, screen glowing—but something in her gut pulled back. That comfort wasn't hers to seek anymore.

He had Moet.

And calling on him now felt less like friendship and more like betrayal to his new woman.

"Bout time you showed your face," Mia called from her station, hands deep in a client's twist-out. "We've been waiting for you, Sunshine."

"Girl..." Autumn shook her head. "Please don't tell me you put all my business in these salon streets."

Brianna, perched under the dryer with a drink in her hand, grinned like a cat with good tea.

"Damn heifer," she said, loud enough for the whole shop to hear. "You out here dropping dudes like calls in a dead zone; if that connection's weak, buh-bye."

The whole salon erupted.

"Two-piece combo!" Londyn fake-coughed.

Josie, sitting on the couch scrolling her phone, looked up just to add, "Honey, I'm with you. Swipe left and keep it movin'."

Mia's eyes landed on Autumn with concern. "Y'all let my sister breathe. Autumn out here doing the Lord's work, what a lot of women should be doing: clearing space for what don't serve her before it breaks her soul later."

"I'm not out here just cutting men off," she clarified, her voice low. "Me and Ekon, that was a values clash. We don't see the world the same. But DeMonte—" She paused, her breath hitching as a fresh wave of sadness washed over her. She closed her eyes. "That one... that one just hurts."

"Hey, sis." Brianna's eyes were earnest now. "We get it, baby. You did what you had to do."

The vibe in the room shifted, still light but layered, as Londyn leaned in. "Real talk, Autumn. I know it's hard. Letting go of someone, even when they're not good for you, means admitting that your hope was misplaced."

Josie nodded. "And sometimes, we'd rather stay in something halfway decent than risk having nothing at all. I've been there."

Autumn looked at herself in the mirror, the cape now fastened around her neck as one of the stylists sectioned her hair.

"I used to shrink and fold to keep peace with Chris for that very reason," she said slowly, the words tasting like old bruises. "But now? I want peace that doesn't cost me my dignity or make me feel like I'm settling for good enough."

She paused, her voice thick. "And, as much as it pained me to see DeMonte hurt, I can't stay in something that's not real just because it fills a void."

Mia smiled at Autumn through the mirror. "And that, baby girl, is growth."

The conversation became a tapestry of shared healing, each woman adding in her own thread: stories of starting over, loving smarter, and learning the brutal, beautiful art of letting go. The younger clients leaned in, eyes wide, soaking it all up like gospel.

Combs clacked against counters. The playlist swirled between Mary J. and Anita. And amid the sound and spirit of sisterhood, Autumn felt something inside her settle, like the click of a lock finally turning the right way.

Later that day, the sun was melting into the horizon when Autumn stepped out of the salon, its golden rays catching the soft sheen of her freshly styled curls.

Her scalp tingled from Mia's signature conditioner, a lavender-mint blend that lingered in the air around her like a fragrant crown. Her hair bounced with every step, light and full, brushing her shoulders with a freedom that felt earned.

She closed her eyes for a brief moment, letting the evening air cool her cheeks before unlocking her car door.

Ebondale hummed with its usual evening playlist; a distant siren, cars bumping music. The noise was the perfect background to the quiet, settled space she now occupied in her own head.

A small, satisfied smile played at her lips.

As she slid into the driver's seat, her phone buzzed against the console.

Kendra's number popped up.

Autumn's brows lifted. That name hadn't crossed her screen in almost a year. Not since the layoffs gutted her department and carved open wounds that no HR exit memo could soothe.

But she was curious...

"Kendra?" she answered, putting the call on speaker.

"Well, look at that," came the familiar voice, warm and amused. "Still answers on the first ring."

Autumn smiled. "It's been a minute."

"It has. I saw your post on Facebook. Bag Lady of the Month, huh?"

She groaned, laughing. "Yeah. I don't know why I posted that."

"I'm glad you did. You look... different. At peace. Like somebody who finally knows who the hell she is."

Autumn's smile faded into something more thoughtful. "I'm getting there."

Kendra paused.

"I'm actually calling because I have an opening," she said. "Director of Brand Strategy. The position that should've been yours before everything fell apart."

Autumn sat up straight, a tiny alert flickering to life as her fingers curled around the steering wheel.

"Titan and Lewis has been restructured," she continued. "New leadership, new team. The office culture's different now. Better. You'd have autonomy, a team of your own, and more flexibility. We're even offering hybrid schedules. Full relocation benefits. The pay is... significant."

"How significant?" Autumn ventured, her tone even, but her pulse quickening.

"More than what you left with. And more than what they were offering you for the promotion back then. I made sure of that."

A contemplative silence stretched as she chewed the inside of her lip. Then, her grip on the steering wheel eased as she leaned back, her eyes shifting to the streaks of gold and purple painting the sky.

"I'm not offering this because I feel guilty," Kendra added. "I'm offering it because you're still one of the best I've ever worked with. And I know you'd build the hell out of this next phase."

"I appreciate that," Autumn said. "Really."

"So... think about it. I'll fly you down. You can walk the floor, see how things are. No pressure, just to get some perspective."

"I can do that," Autumn agreed. "Let me sit with it for a few days."

"Good," Kendra replied. "You always move best when you listen to your gut. I miss that about you."

After their goodbyes, Autumn sat in the stillness, her phone resting in her lap like it held the weight of her past and the outline of her future.

She pulled down the visor, staring at her reflection.

It wasn't just a job offer.

It was a door.

She wasn't running toward it or away from it.

She was deciding.

She had promised herself a year.

A full year to breathe, to rebuild, to remember who she was without the roles that had once defined her: wife, employee, fixer, shadow.

Living with Mia had been an unexpected gift. The laughter, the late-night talks, the kids forming their own little tribe; it was the family she'd never known she needed.

Layla and Jordan were thriving.

And her sister? Mia had become her anchor.

In that time, Autumn had also found her rhythm. She'd forged new friendships. Real ones, the kind with shared wine, secrets, and unfiltered truth.

And she had dated on her terms.

Not as Chris's other half.

Not as someone's placeholder.

But as Autumn. Unapologetic. Untethered. Figuring it out in real time.

She'd opened her heart to new experiences, to new men, to herself.

And yes, the past few months were a whirlwind of dizzying highs and gut-punching lows.

But now...

Now came the inevitable fork in the road. The one she always knew she'd arrive at on her journey. The time to settle back into the reality of a career.

The Atlanta offer presented a known variable. A title, a salary, a version of herself she knew how to perform flawlessly. The thought was seductive. To just... go back. To be a successful career woman again. It would be so much easier than dealing with the suffocating stillness here in Chicago and navigating the messy, uncharted territory of her own heart.

And a small, cowardly part of her whispered maybe that was the point. To avoid the messiness of feelings that were too tangled to touch just yet.

On one hand, there were the feelings for Amir, which felt like a trespass on sacred ground. On the other hand was the ghost of DeMonte's affection, the memory of his forehead kiss, a tender bruise left by a man she'd had to hurt.

Maybe Atlanta wasn't a step forward; maybe it could be a beautiful, high-paying, corner-office-shaped escape hatch.

* * *

THE AIR inside the house felt like a cozy hug; the scents of roasted hazelnut and warm vanilla drifted from the French press and simmering candle.

Autumn moved through Mia's kitchen with ease, scooping her special blend into the coffee maker, humming faintly to herself. The kids were upstairs, the boys in the middle of yet another video game war, while the late Sunday afternoon sunlight poured through the windows like God's favor.

"Still making that bougie-ass coffee?"

Autumn looked up to see Amir leaning against the doorway, watching her with a familiar fondness. He'd come by early to help Jordan with a school project before their Bulls game, but had been pulled into the video game chaos between Jordan and his older cousin.

He nodded up toward the source of an occasional triumphant shout. "They're wrapping up. Figured I'd come see you before we head out."

Whether he knew it, his presence—so easy, so at home in this space— was shaking her to the core. It was one thing to decide she wanted him in the quiet of her own mind; it was another thing entirely to have him standing right there, a walking, talking temptation in her sister's kitchen.

Autumn smirked at his comment about the coffee. "Bougie? Yet, folks still drink it like it's crack in a cup."

He chuckled and walked over, grabbing two mugs from the cabinet like he lived there.

"' Filler Up' or the battle-scarred '#1 Coffee Fan' mug? Pick your weapon." He paused, grin pasted on, like there was a memory tucked in that old chip.

"I'll take the chipped one. I like things that speak to my character."

She filled both mugs without asking how he took it, adding three sugars and two creamers to his cup, as if it were muscle memory. He accepted his with a slow, knowing smile pulling at the corner of his mouth.

"What?" she asked, smiling in return, assuming he was about to tease her about the chipped mug.

"Nothing," he said, but his gaze lingered, sending a quiet, unnerving message straight to her gut: *Of course you remember.*

He sipped and closed his eyes like he'd just had a spiritual experience. He raked his tongue over his lips, exhaling slowly. "Whew. That's disrespectfully good."

She laughed, her chest loosening in a way it hadn't in months. For a heartbeat, the world bent backwards to when it was just them and their old rhythm.

He gazed over the rim of his mug, eyebrows lifted with concern. "So. Another one bites the dust, huh?"

Autumn paused mid-sip.

"I'm guessing DeMonte's out?" he continued.

She set her mug down slowly, fingertips tracing the crack in the ceramic. "Ya know, you know a lil too much of my business." She tried to sound lighthearted.

He grinned, waiting for an answer.

"But, yeah," she sighed. "Unfortunately, I had to let him go." The steam from her cup curled upward.

"Messy?"

She gestured with her head. "Not really. Just... misaligned. In more ways than one." She averted her eyes, suddenly fascinated by the pattern on the floor tiles.

He observed her, as if he could read the fissures in her composure. "Are you okay?"

She tipped the mug to her lips, letting the warmth soothe her. "Yeah. I will be."

Silence settled around them, tender and familiar, but carrying an undeniable, magnetic undercurrent.

Amir's smirk shifted, half-tease, half-concern. "Should I even ask what you're looking for at this point? I say this with love, but... for months, you hopped between these two dudes like it was a game of musical chairs. Is there someone out there who can make you stop dancing?"

Autumn cocked an eyebrow, though her heart rate spiked at his question. "Seriously?"

"I'm just saying," he shrugged, still grinning mischievously. "You're starting to move through this dating phase like it's seasonal."

She crossed her arms, a playful glare surfacing. "What are you implying, Mr. Jackson? You calling me a—"

"Nope!" he laughed, setting his mug down, dashing around the island as she gave chase with a damp dish towel, their giggles echoing in the kitchen.

When the easy play between them settled, he reclaimed his mug, his voice softening. "All jokes aside. What I'm calling you is a woman who knows how to exit with grace... but won't admit she's still guarding the door."

Her smile faded, just a little.

"That's because I'm not looking for anything right now." She leaned on the island, cradling her cup. "Not love, not a relationship, not even a deep text thread. Ekon and DeMonte were both no more than fun distractions."

Amir raised an eyebrow. "Is that right? So, you're telling me that neither of them came close to being a 'what are we' moment?"

"Well..." she hesitated. "DeMonte came the closest." She stared just past his shoulder, thoughtful. "But, aside from some differences we have in how we view things, he was ready for something I wasn't able to give. I had to be honest with him. And with myself. I'm not chasing a relationship status. I'm only chasing clarity."

Amir nodded slowly, his eyes fixed on his cup as he processed her words.

When he looked up, the teasing glint was gone from his eyes. "Then let me ask this instead," he ventured. "What would make you stop and look twice at a man? Not fall in love right away. Just... be with someone."

The question sat between them, and suddenly the mug felt heavy in her hands. She met his gaze, trying to read the intention behind the query; was this a friend's curiosity, a protector's interrogation, or something else entirely?

"I guess..." she started, her voice a little rougher than she intended. "A man who doesn't flinch at who I am. Who doesn't need me to dim my light for him to feel like he's shining. Someone," she paused, the final words feeling more like a confession, "who knows me better than I know myself."

He held her gaze, and she saw it in his eyes: a look of such profound, startling recognition it seemed to short-circuit every thought in her head, leaving her speechless.

Autumn's first instinct was to look away, to break the spark that had just flared to life between them. It scared the hell out of her because it was less like a new discovery and more like an old, undeniable truth.

"That's fair," he said softly, clearing his throat.

He leaned closer over the counter, the inches between them shrinking until she could feel the warmth radiating from his body. His voice dropped to a low, serious rumble that vibrated straight through her.

"For what it's worth... you've always been too bright to shrink. Any man who tries to box that in? He's not your man. He's just another delay from what you truly deserve."

It was too much. He was getting too close to a truth she wasn't ready to claim. She needed an out, fast.

She released a forced, breathy chuckle. "Okay, dude. Not you trying to goose me up so I can talk Mia into catering your awards ceremony."

He winked after a few seconds, taking the hint and shifting gears. The easy-going mask snapped smoothly into place. "You picked up on that, huh?" But he didn't pull back right away. The air was thick, and suddenly very, very dangerously charged.

A sharp ring from his phone cut through the tension.

He pulled it from his pocket, glancing at the screen.

"It's Moet," he said, and his shoulders dropped just a fraction, the easy grin replaced by a flicker of apology as he met Autumn's eyes for a half-second before answering.

"Hey, babe." His tone shifted. "Please tell me you were able to score an extra ticket for the Bulls game. Jordan's cousin really wants to come. He beat me in Mortal Kombat for that seat."

His words, so normal and domestic, gave Autumn the reprieve she desperately needed. She walked to the sink, her back to him as she gripped the edge. It was her chance to reboot her system after the overload, to find her footing in a world that had once again tilted her emotions.

He ended the call as Autumn was finally turning around, her own mask of casualness firmly back in place. "Sounds like you guys are gonna have fun."

"Yeah, man," he sighed, running fingers through his beard and massaging his chin. "Looks like I'm taking the whole crew now." He looked at her, the intensity from before still simmering, but carefully banked.

An awkward stillness rushed in, taking its place between them.

"Guess what?" she perked, needing desperately to switch gears again. "I got a job offer."

Amir's brows lifted. "Yeah?"

"From Kendra. In Atlanta."

"Oh!" He stood up straighter. "That's big."

"She said the position is mine if I want it. It's the promotion I was slated for before the layoff. Huge salary increase, flexible schedule. They'll even pay for relocation. The works."

Amir didn't speak. He took a slow sip from his mug, his eyes focused on something beyond her shoulder. The soft, dangerous heat from moments before was gone. In its place, his expression was hardening, settling back into the familiar, focused lines of the man who had seen her through every crisis of her life.

"I'm almost a year into this rest season," she continued. "Part of me is like, girl, take the money. Get the title. Lock it in."

"And the other part?" Now he was looking directly at her, his eyes penetrating.

She hesitated. "The other part is scared that going back means going backward. That I'll lose this peace I worked so hard to build. I mean, I loved what I did. The career climb was exhilarating. But now that I've experienced life without the hassle, I kinda like it."

She glanced at him after he was still silent. "What do you think?" she asked as she refreshed their cups.

He didn't answer. Instead, he placed his mug on the counter with a quiet, definitive clink. He pushed back from the island and crossed his arms over his chest.

"What is it that you want, Autumn?"

The question hit different; it felt more like an excavation.

"That's the real thing, right?" he added, his voice now carrying the blunt, familiar cadence of a man who'd never lied to her, not once. "You've probably asked Mia. Your therapist. Even your journal. But you haven't asked yourself, not really. So, I'm asking for you."

Autumn opened her mouth, a knee-jerk defense already on her tongue. She closed it quickly, the truth of his words landing like a lead weight in her gut.

"I don't know," she admitted finally, the words a quiet surrender.

He gave a single, sharp nod, his gaze unwavering. "I think you do," he countered softly. "You just haven't said it out loud yet."

Autumn stared into her coffee like the steam might produce the answers.

"I want freedom," she said quietly. "But I also want stability. I want to build something, to let my creativity flourish, but I'm scared of losing myself in the corporate mire again."

Amir nodded slowly as he moved forward, putting his elbows on the island counter and leaning toward her. His voice held earnestness.

"Don't retreat, Autumn. You're stronger than you think. And whatever decision you make, it should be because you chose it. Not because you're scared of not being chosen."

She looked up at him, and the return of the intensity in his eyes sent a shiver straight through her. This wasn't simply support; it was a profound belief in her that left her breathless.

Then—BOOM! The boys thundered down the stairs, their noise and energy so explosive it felt like the quiet, fragile bubble they'd been in had physically burst.

"Uncle Amir, we thought you were coming back," Jordan yelled. "Malcolm beat your high score!"

Amir straightened, knocking back the rest of his coffee. "Say less, lil homie. Can't let that stand!"

He headed out of the kitchen with Jordan and the twins in tow, but not before stopping at Autumn's side and whispering,

"You already know the answer. Be fearless in your choices. I believe in you."

He was gone before she could respond, the warmth of his words lingering in the air long after the sound of feet bounding up the stairs.

You already know the answer.

And in the sudden quiet of the kitchen, she had a terrifying, thrilling feeling that he was right.

2 4

CORNER OFFICE VIBES

The plane dipped below the clouds, and as the skyline came into view, Autumn felt it before she saw it, a slow beat pulsing under her ribs.

Atlanta.

The city that once held her ambition in its palm, squeezed it, and then released it like forgotten dust.

Now, as the wheels kissed the runway with a jolt, the city just seemed familiar. It was no longer home. It had been reduced to a place she used to orbit.

An early Tuesday flight brought her back, her only luggage an overnight bag, a laptop, and a sharpened sense of self she hadn't owned the last time she was here. After bypassing baggage claim, the cool February air greeted her, the light breeze playing hide-and-seek with the sun and tugging at the edges of her tightly wrapped trench coat.

The Uber ride to Titan and Lewis was a trip down memory lane and ego alley. Autumn passed the billboards she once pitched campaigns for. Eateries and bars that were her spots to sit and cry in silence after twelve-hour workdays and being overlooked for promotions she practically bled for.

She stepped out of the ride and into the sleek lobby of the office building, where she was once wrapped in a different kind of determination.

This wasn't nostalgia; this was reconnaissance.

Today, she wasn't desperate for recognition.

She was evaluating alignment.

The new waiting area was all glass and statement furniture. Cush seating, curated plants, abstract art with just enough edge to look posh. It was beautiful. Intentionally so. Like it was designed to allure before there was a chance to question whether you were all in.

Autumn recognized the tactic. She'd helped create it once.

She opened her coat and adjusted her blouse, quietly steeling the jitters in her stomach while moving to the receptionist's desk.

"You're here to observe," she whispered to herself. "You're not proving anything today."

Before she could announce herself to the redhead sitting behind the large oak desk, Kendra burst through a set of glass double doors.

"Autumn Gardener, back in the flesh," she grinned, arms open wide.

Autumn's smile was genuine as she returned the hug. "This place looks incredible."

"It should," Kendra smirked, leading her down the hall. "We gutted the entire space. New money, new vision, new energy."

They walked past bustling departments, whiteboards filled with creative briefs, and young interns typing as if deadlines were a sport. The air smelled of industrial-strength coffee and new paint, underscored by the low, constant hum of over-the-phone pitches and team huddles.

They moved into a private meeting room. A charcuterie spread sat on a corner table, and Kendra waved toward it like it was part of the presentation.

"I wanted this to be personal," she said, handing Autumn a sleek folder. "You're not here to interview. You already know the position is yours if you want it."

Autumn sat before slowly opening the folder. Her eyes were immediately drawn to the highlighted sections, standing out in bold, confident font.

Director of Brand Strategy.

$220,000 salary.

$25K signing bonus.

Remote options. Full benefits.

Team of five. Creative lead authority.

Kendra continued. "It's not only the promotion you were supposed to get; it's what you deserve. I said that before, and I'm saying it again now, with real numbers attached. Leadership fought me on the salary, but I kept your name and past accomplishments in every room."

Autumn read the offer twice. It was solid, more than expected, and the one thing she used to fantasize about.

Her fingers paused, hovering over the paper.

The old Autumn would have burst into tears of pure, vindicated joy.

This Autumn had a strange, unnerving stillness in her chest.

There were no fireworks. No shortness of breath. It was a disconnect, as if she were watching someone else's dream unfold.

She looked up, forcing a smile.

"This is... incredible, Kendra. Really."

"It's yours," she replied. "If you want it. I don't need an answer today, but I do need to know you're considering it seriously."

"I am," Autumn affirmed, placing the letter back into the folder. "I would like to think it over, though."

Kendra nodded, her expression softening. "That's fair. And wise."

They wrapped up after an extensive tour of the updated space. Autumn met a few new team members and ran into a few old colleagues, some of whom had returned. She sensed both hospitality and pressure in equal parts.

By the time she stepped into her hotel room that evening, she dropped the folder onto the pristine white duvet. The heavy thud was the only sound in the quiet room, like a giant question mark lying on the bed.

So why didn't it feel like a yes?

* * *

Tuesday Evening—Atlanta.

The restaurant was one of her and Chris's favorite spots when they first married, tucked into the edge of Midtown. Dim lighting, comfortable booths, and an eclectic playlist that catered to every musical taste were the first sense of happy nostalgia she'd experienced since landing.

Autumn arrived first. She sipped on water with lemon, taking advantage of a quiet moment to sit with herself. She'd been moving all day, catching up, shaking new and old hands, pretending she was more interested than she was.

Now, she was about to have dinner with the man she once built a life with.

Chris walked in a few minutes later. He spotted her immediately, smiled, and raised a hand in casual greeting as he made his way to the table.

An acoustic guitar played low in the background as he slid into the booth across from her. Autumn glanced at him, struck by how little had changed. He wore a crisp white button-down, the top buttons undone at the neck to reveal a hint of his smooth, caramel skin. Much like the atmosphere, he hadn't changed much. Still handsome. Still polished. And still devilishly beguiling.

His eyes did a slow, appreciative sweep of their own. She wore a tailored, wide-leg jumpsuit in a deep forest green, cinched at the waist with a thin leather belt. It was a power outfit: sleek, modern, and unapologetic.

"Well, well, well," he grinned, his eyes twinkling. "Look who's still gorgeous."

Autumn met his gaze, letting a small, unimpressed smile touch her lips. "Don't start."

A low chuckle rumbled in his chest as he flagged the waitress. "A glass of red," he said, his gaze quickly returning to her.

They caught up lightly at first; kids, Chris' traveling more for work, how he was managing work-life balance and fatherhood from a distance. Their conversation was familiar, but neutral.

"So..." He cut into his salmon. "How'd the interview go?"

Autumn shrugged as she chewed on her tender steak. "It really wasn't an interview. The offer was made. It's actually the promotion I was supposed to get before the layoff. On steroids."

Chris raised a brow. "That's huge."

"It is. But I don't know. I thought I'd be more excited. Instead, I just feel... flat."

He chewed slowly, nodding. "That makes sense."

Her brows shot up. "It does?"

"Autumn, you're not that woman anymore. You're not hustling for the top spot or seeking approval the way you used to. Back in the day, we both were chasing stuff that we assumed would make us whole. You were chasing validation. I was chasing... everything else."

He cast a wry grin as he sipped his wine.

The faint clink of silverware paused as her eyes widened slightly at his admission.

"I keep asking myself," she said after a pause, "if I'm making it harder than it needs to be. Like, what if I'm the problem?"

Chris studied her for a moment, setting down his fork. "Are you looking for a job, Autumn? Or are you looking for something to mold and control because you're scared if you don't, you'll lose it?"

She swallowed. He sounded like Jasmine.

He leaned forward slightly, his voice softer. "It's the same pattern with love, isn't it? I hear about you dating, and I have to wonder if you're looking for someone real, or someone so perfect they could never hurt you."

The truthfulness of his words was a direct hit but not original, as she'd heard these same things in therapy. Still, it left a sting, especially coming from him.

"Well, your grapevine is old. I'm not even dating right now," she finally managed, the words a weak defense.

"I hear you," he said gently. "And look, I'm not judging. In fact, I have to take some accountability for a big part of that fear. I need to own up to my part."

His eyes held the regret that echoed in his tone. He took a slow sip of his wine, the admission settling between them.

Autumn sat back in her seat, her eyes wide as the plates on the table.

"But you can't let my mistakes be the fortress you build around your heart," he continued. "Love ain't a checklist, you're the one who taught me that. You're holding out for perfection because you're tired of rebuilding, and I get it. I respect it. I hope you don't wait so long for 'perfect' though, that you miss out on what's good. What's right... for you."

This was Chris, the man who had once left so many bruises on her confidence that it was unrecognizable. But tonight, his words didn't torment, they sobered. Uplifted.

"Who the hell is this man, and where is the father of my children?" she chuckled, her head shaking in amazement. "Where's all this coming from?"

He looked out the window before returning his gaze back to her, remorse clouding his expression. "After our divorce, I still had access to you, so I never fully appreciated how much you meant. When you left Atlanta, it hit me harder than I thought it could."

He stared past her shoulder. "I spiraled for a while, Autumn."

Her eyes softened, but she stayed quiet.

"You were gone. My kids were gone. One of my frats is a psychologist. When I confided in him, he recommended I get counseling."

Autumn's eyes grew wider.

Therapy. Chris?

The two concepts belonged to different universes, and she struggled for a moment to make them connect.

"I've been in therapy for a few months now." He said it quietly, his gaze dropping to his plate for a moment before he met her eyes again, a flicker of vulnerability showing.

Her smile beamed, a pride she hadn't felt for him since he became VP at his job. "Chris! Why didn't you tell me? That is so amazing! Not many men, especially Black men are willing to do that."

He shrugged, a rare humility in the gesture, before diving back into his food. "Yeah, I know. I'm trying to change that, too. Me and the brothers started a chat room for men to pop in whenever they need to connect, vent, whatever it is. It's small, but it's a start."

Autumn stared at him with widened eyes, trying to reconcile this version of Chris, this man building a safe space for other men to be vulnerable, with the man she used to know. The cognitive dissonance was dizzying.

"Here's something else that's gonna throw you," he said after they both passed on dessert. He shook his head with a small, wry grin. "I never gave you shit for it back then, but I always hated that you insisted on making Amir the kids' godfather."

Autumn rolled her eyes. "He's my best friend, Chris."

"I know," he held up a hand. "I always thought he had a thing for you. But I get it now. The man is legit, especially how he shows up for Layla and Jordan. That man sat in the hospital with our son when you or I couldn't be there. I can't even hate on that. In fact, I owe the man a beer."

For the first time since their divorce, Autumn laughed with Chris, a genuine, heartfelt chortle. This was unexpected and so refreshing.

"Thank you, Chris," she said after they fell into a comfortable silence. "For sharing with me tonight. For being vulnerable."

"I only wish it hadn't taken me so long to figure shit out."

When the dinner finally ended, it wasn't with the familiar tension of their past, but with a warm, respectful hug at the valet line and his soft, "Take care of yourself, Autumn."

As she rode back to her hotel, the Atlanta lights blurred outside the Uber window like scattered jewels. The weight of Chris' words, of his stunning growth, settled over her.

She thought of his final, tender, "Take care of yourself, Autumn," and it was less like a goodbye and more like a genuine blessing. A gift of finality to do just that.

She leaned her head against the cool glass and whispered to her own reflection, "I'm trying."

And with that admission, a quiet shift happened. The thought of what came next was no longer a void to be filled, but an open, tranquil space waiting to be explored.

2 5

SOMETHING'S BREWING

Wednesday afternoon—headed home.

The plane's cabin buzzed with low conversation and rustling snack wrappers, but Autumn was somewhere else entirely, floating in the strange headspace where clarity was whispering.

She took the window seat, tray table down, her journal open and waiting. Atlanta's horizon had faded behind thick clouds, and all she could see now was sky. Gray, layered, and serene.

The folder from Kendra was tucked inside her carry-on, unopened since last night.

She hadn't needed to reread it.

The numbers were clear. But her spirit wasn't. Not yet.

She picked up her pen.

> *Atlanta is the same. But I'm not.*
>
> *It's strange to return to a place and realize your soul didn't follow.*
>
> *The offer is everything I used to hustle and pray for: Power. Respect. A seat at the table.*
>
> *But now I'm asking, do I even want that anymore?*

She paused as the plane tilted slightly, shifting through turbulence like her thoughts.

Chris asked if I'm looking for perfection. I'm just afraid of settling again.

Afraid of pouring into something that looks good but empties me slowly.

But maybe perfection was never the point.

It truly is all about alignment.

She paused again.

And... I've outgrown chasing titles.

She looked down at her own hands, at the pen they held, at her ability to create something from nothing. She turned to a new, blank page.

I think it's time to build something of my own.

She closed the journal gently, letting her hand rest on the cover.

Autumn rode the rest of the flight with her eyes shut, needing no music or phone distractions.

After the captain announced the final descent, she looked out the window, the clouds parting to reveal faint patches of land below, familiar roads leading home.

Finally, she wasn't running away from a life that had ended. She was flying toward one that was being renewed.

* * *

FRIDAY AFTERNOON—THE youth center.

Basketballs echoed like thunder inside the small gym as sneakers squeaked against polished hardwood.

Autumn stood on the side of the bleachers, watching Jordan throw up a wild shot that somehow swished clean through the net.

Amir stood behind him, coaching with ease, calling out plays and throwing high-fives like he was handing out candy.

Jordan listened intently, nodding in acceptance and celebrating joyfully when he followed through.

Autumn smiled softly as she watched them, warmed by the sight. Neither of them saw her yet.

Her friend was in his element; baggy heather-gray joggers, locs freshly re-twisted, whistle around his neck as he ran up and down the court with the boys.

He was a coach, a godfather, and in all things, the steady hand the community had grown to count on for helping to mold its young people.

She thought back to the incident a few months ago when there was a fight between rival gangs—relics of the past that still held on to a false sense of power—just a block away from the youth center. One of the young men was a hothead, known for carrying a gun, and Amir knew it was only a matter of time before a simple fistfight escalated with deadly consequences.

He'd run up the block with the speed of a track star, immediately throwing himself in the middle of the fray. He pulled the boys away from the crowd with no fear and talked them down. Afterward, he found the leaders of both gangs and brokered a truce, preventing any form of retaliation.

He was respected, and his influence carried weight even among the hardest of the community's young men, who were still figuring life out. Both boys later joined the center with scholarships from the community fund Amir established, and one was working toward a basketball scholarship to attend one of the Big Ten universities next year.

His eyes landed on her, a wide smile spreading on his face as he walked over. "Hey, look who finally decided to grace the gym."

Autumn met him halfway, both embracing in a friendly hug. "I came to pick up my future NBA star."

Jordan shouted from the free-throw line. "Hey, Ma, take a video! I'm posting all these buckets!"

"See what you've created?" she teased Amir.

He shrugged, feigning innocence. "Ayyeee, genius recognizes genius."

They stepped back while Jordan continued practicing with the other kids, the gym noise fading into background chatter.

"You good?" he asked, leaning against the wall, the same question he'd asked a thousand times. But this time, she answered differently.

"I think I'm actually getting to 'better'."

He waited, sensing more, but didn't push.

She sighed. "Atlanta was... familiar. The job offer was... is... solid. Kendra even called me the version of myself she always envisioned."

"But?" he nudged.

She looked out at the court as Jordan scrambled to catch his own rebound.

"The old version of me was always fighting to be chosen."

She smiled at her son after he made a shot from the three-point line and held his hands in a "swish" pose.

"Good job, baby!" she praised. She turned back to Amir. "This version of me is working on choosing myself."

Amir nodded slowly.

She cocked her head to the side. "You once asked what I wanted. I answered then, but still didn't fully know at the time. But I do now."

He raised a brow. "Hit me."

"I want something that gives me peace. I want full autonomy. I want to explore my creativity. Something that's mine. Something that won't be stifled when someone else makes a decision about my worth."

He folded his arms, curious. "And what is that?"

She paused.

She had thought about the idea a few weeks ago after receiving constant praise for her coffee blends. Nothing serious, it was more a fleeting, "what if?" After spending the last 48 hours mulling over Kendra's offer letter, the idea grew bigger.

She took a deep breath, her hands twisting together in front of her. "I'm thinking about opening a coffee shop," she blurted, the words rushing out before doubt could steal them. Her eyes sparkled, her smile wide and electric. "I saw a cute, empty storefront right here in Ebondale. It would feature my blends, and I can sell local pastries, cos you know the women in this hood can throw down in the kitchen."

A slow, undeniable warmth spread across Amir's face, his eyes softening with a look of pure pride.

"I see it so clearly," Autumn continued, her excitement building. "Black art on the walls, some of it on consignment with local artists. Maybe a small event space in the back for poetry nights."

Amir blinked, then gave the slowest, widest smile she'd seen in weeks. "Now that's the Autumn I know. Grounded. Ready. With her vision clear."

She laughed, eyes misting. "You think it's crazy?"

"Not at all. I think it's overdue."

They stood there a minute in silence, the weight of her idea settling gently between them like the first snowfall.

Amir slid closer and bumped her shoulder with his. "Just so you know? I'd be in your shop every damn day, drinking the hell out of that coffee."

She looked up at him, something tender passing between them as her eyes met his.

"Hey, Coach!"

One of the young boys waved for Amir's attention.

"Go ahead, we'll talk later," Autumn encouraged as he looked at her apologetically.

As he hustled over to the court, Autumn leaned her head against the wall, attempting to still the sudden quickening of her pulse.

Something was simmering again between her and Amir. And it was more than ideas about coffee.

* * *

THE NEXT FEW weeks unfolded like puzzle pieces clicking into place. February rolled out in a blur of planning, learning, and rediscovery.

She had officially turned down the job offer. Kendra understood, and before their call had ended, she told her how proud she was.

Each morning after that, Autumn woke up with fresh energy, her coffee pot brewing blends she was now measuring and testing with precision. The journals she once used to vent and heal had a new purpose: they had become the blueprint for her dream.

On the cover of a fresh notebook, she wrote in bold black marker:

Asia's Ember Coffeehouse—Vision Book.

She pressed her palm gently over the words, as if to bless them. Her throat tightened.

Asia. Her first, and outside of Amir, only true friend.

Ember. The flame that refused to die.

It was more than a title. It was a resurrection.

She let out a soft exhale, tears stinging her eyes as she stared at the words. The ink stood bold against the clean cover. She ran a fingertip over the name that was a tribute heavy with grief, but light with possibility.

A smile touched her lips, soft and sure. It felt like planting a flag in the ground of her own future. And this time, she wasn't scared of the territory. She was ready to claim it.

That night, and many nights after, she sat hunched over her laptop at Mia's kitchen table, researching startup grants, city codes, and business plan templates. Though she still had significant savings, she was clear: she'd only touch those if grants didn't come through.

Loans were out of the question. She was not building her dream on a mountain of debt.

She attended small business workshops, her hand constantly in the air with questions. She was no longer simply dreaming; she was designing.

One Tuesday afternoon, Autumn stopped by a vendor fair, sipping and sniffing different coffee beans from growers. She caught the subtle notes in each batch: the earthiness, spice, cocoa, hints of citrus, and took her time chatting with every merchant, asking questions about sourcing, roasting, and shelf life. By the time she left, she had several sample bags and a head full of ideas.

Back at home, Mia's kitchen turned into a test lab.

Cinnamon sticks boiled in almond milk.

Lavender syrup cooled on the counter.

When Mia sampled one of her creations and clutched her chest like she'd tasted heaven, Autumn knew she had something special.

She met with a local print shop to brainstorm logo designs, and when they landed on one with deep purple script curling around the silhouette of a steaming cup and tangled roots, the artist looked up and said, "This has your essence all over it."

Even Amir was looped in. He dropped by the house one evening to bring Jordan a new pair of sneakers and left with a to-go cup of Autumn's newest blend.

"This the one?" she asked, arms crossed with expectation.

He took a sip, raised his eyebrows, and gave a small, approving nod. "Okay... this the one."

"I call it Triple A," she beamed.

His eyes widened, then softened as he walked over to her. In an unexpected move, he bent down and kissed her gently on the forehead. His lips, still warm from the coffee, lingered for a few seconds.

"You are so awesome," he praised as he took another sip, his eyes rolling in pleasure.

The next day, she sat on her bed, laptop open to the application she'd been perfecting for days. It was a woman-centered grant for small business startups, designed for those starting over with big dreams and a clear vision.

Autumn reread every answer on the application twice, her heart thumping a steady, hopeful beat in her chest. She took one final, deep breath, and with a prayer on her lips and a tremor in her finger, she hit submit.

Later that night, her journal was open again, but this time, her tone was different. She scribbled freely, her handwriting loose and certain:

> This is no longer about proving I can do it. This is about creating something that feeds people in more ways than one. And the best part? I'm not building for survival. *I'm building a legacy.*

She underlined the last line twice as she placed her pen down and curled up under her blanket, a smile on her lips.

There was no messiness. No swirling questions about what she was or wasn't doing right in a relationship.

There was only this. A dream with roots. A legacy brewing. And the steady, unstoppable thrill of a woman who was finally choosing herself.

2 6

A BEAR IN THE HANDS

The grant application had been submitted weeks ago.

Asia's Ember Coffeehouse, her vision in black and white and poured into every text box and formatted line, was now in someone else's hands.

A review board. A faceless panel of decision-makers. People she'd probably never meet, but who held a piece of her dream between their thumbs.

This was the worst part: the waiting.

But before she applied, she'd picked up the phone and made a call she'd been sitting with for days.

The one person whose blessing mattered most.

Asia's mother.

She had stood in the kitchen one afternoon, staring at the number Amir had given her. Her thumb hovered over the call button, a tremor of fear and guilt running through her.

Their years of silence weren't awkward: that silence was sacred. Stained with grief and guilt, and the question that always lingered in the back of Autumn's mind:

Why her and not me?

Another scary thought: what if Ms. Worthington's voice were cold?

What if she thought Autumn was selfish for asking to use her daughter's name after so many years?

Taking a deep, fortifying breath, she pressed the button. The line rang; once, twice, three times, until finally:

"Hello?"

The voice was older, etched with the gentle rasp of time, but unmistakably hers. The sound of it unlocked a part of Autumn's heart she had kept sealed for years.

"Ms. Worthington?" Autumn's own voice was a nervous whisper. "It's... It's Autumn. Autumn Gardener."

There was a sharp intake of breath on the other end, followed by a moment of stunned silence. Warmth flooded the line, thick and immediate. "Autumn? Oh, my baby girl. Is that really you?"

Tears instantly pricked Autumn's eyes. "Yes, ma'am. It's me." She sank into a chair, her composure crumbling.

They spoke for almost two hours, the years folding in on themselves as they caught up, softly and carefully.

"The last time I saw you and Amir was at his mama's funeral," she reminisced. "I tell you, both of you have always been in my heart. Y'all lost both ya parents, and I lost my only dawtah. That's a helluva lot of loss, ain't it?"

Autumn sighed. "Yes, ma'am, it is. But what can you do?"

"I know that's right. All we can do... is keep breathin'. Amir calls me every once and again, but he sends me a birthday card every year. That boy is the sweetest thing."

Autumn smiled. "Yes, he is."

"You know, I still got the lil box Asia kept, with all the trinkets he used to give her. And I went through it the other day. I do that sometimes when I'm thinking about her. My Asia loved her some Amir, and he loved her, too."

Autumn's heart tightened as she closed her eyes, grateful the woman couldn't see the pain behind the smile.

"I found that cute lil plastic forever ring he gave her a few days before..."

Her voice choked, and Autumn gripped the phone.

"Well... you know. Anyway..."

Ms. Worthington let out a ragged sigh, her voice gaining strength. "I still call him son-in-law, he tell you that?" she asked with a raspy laugh.

"No, ma'am," Autumn chuckled softly.

"Chile, all him and Asia talked about was how they were gonna get married after college and move away from Ebondale. But I guess the good Lord had other plans."

A peaceful silence stretched between them.

"So, how's those babies of yours?" Her voice perked up as she switched gears. "I gotta see 'em, I bet they've gotten so big."

Autumn was grateful for the conversation shift as she caught Ms. Worthington up on her life; the return to Ebondale, her divorce, and the kids.

She told her about the coffeehouse. The vision, the name.

"I named it for Asia," Autumn finished, her voice thick. "But I won't move forward, Mama, until I know it's okay with you. I would never want to disrespect her memory. I can send you whatever percentage of the profits—"

"Baby girl," Ms. Worthington interrupted, her own voice choked with emotion. A soft, wet sniffle came through the phone. "Listen, you are still a dawtah to me. You and Asia were thick as thieves. I know you loved her like a sister." Another pause, heavier this time. "She *was* your sister."

Autumn pressed a hand to her mouth, trying to hold in a sob mixed with grief and relief, as something old and buried was finally unleashed.

"You don't owe me nothing, you hear me?" the elder woman continued, her voice a balm of understanding and love. "I am honored, so deeply honored, that you would do this. That you would keep her fire burning like this."

When that call ended with promises of keeping in touch, Autumn couldn't move for a while. She sat there, phone clutched in her hand, letting the tears fall freely.

It wasn't only permission she had received.

It was a blessing.

The final piece of alignment she needed to truly, fearlessly chase this dream.

* * *

Autumn sat on a cushioned bench on Mia's porch, her journal balanced on one knee, her other leg tucked under her.

The early spring breeze tickled the edge of her fluffy robe, and the smell of Mia's rose bushes drifted up as faint reminders that change was coming. Whether it came with good news or another lesson, she couldn't tell yet.

Everything seemed suspended, as if life were waiting for the next step.

She'd nearly rushed the process with the coffeehouse. Almost cracked open her savings to kick-start the dream herself; lease the space, call a contractor. Skip the waiting altogether.

But she kept hearing the voice of her assigned mentor from the women's business accelerator program:

"I have money," she'd told the older Black woman, who had been an entrepreneur for twenty-plus years.

"Use grant money to build the dream," came the sharp advice. "That's what it's there for. Use yours to secure your future. Be smart and intentional about every move you make."

So, she waited. And journaled. And prayed that all her intentions would bear fruit in divine timing.

She flipped the page in her journal, writing slowly.

> *This isn't only a business venture. It's so much more. It's healing. It's creativity. It's culture. It's a place for people to be inspired. I don't want it fast. I want it right. I'm not building to prove anything. I'm building for legacy. Mine, and my children's.*
> *And I'm building for Asia.*

The screen door swung shut with a soft bang. Small footsteps approached.

"Mommy?"

Layla sat next to her, carrying a sparkly notebook and a pink pen with a boa feather. "Can we do the menu stuff now?"

Jordan followed close behind, holding a basketball under one arm and a banana in the other hand. "Let's goooo! Because I already named your best drink."

Autumn smiled and closed her journal. "Okay. What's the name?"

"Jordacious... Mocha... Vibes." He punctuated the name by tossing the basketball high in the air and catching it with a smug grin.

Layla rolled her eyes and sucked her teeth. "Basic."

Jordan lifted a nostril and sniffed. "Your face is basic."

"Okay, timeout," Autumn laughed, holding up her hands in a T-formation. "No insults during brainstorming."

Layla flipped open her notebook with a dramatic flair. "I want a drink called Princess Sparkle Latte. With edible glitter. And whipped cream that's shaped into a crown."

Jordan gagged. "Ugh. Nobody wants to drink glitter."

"I think it's creative," Autumn praised. "And if your sister wants it on the menu, we'll find a way."

"Fine," Jordan muttered. "But can I still design the basketball special? Like, me and Amir came up with a smoothie with protein powder. We call it a Clutch Shot."

Autumn laughed heartily, overjoyed by her children's excitement. She wrote their suggestions down on a fresh sheet of paper.

It was adorable. And it was real.

The way their ideas flowed. The way they saw themselves in the dream.

Amir's car pulled up, evoking an eager "Yooooooo!" from Jordan.

He walked like time was on his side, white joggers slung low on his hips, black hoodie unzipped just enough to flash a glimpse of the fitted tee underneath. His locs were pulled back, catching light at the tips, and he had that easy, unbothered stride that made it hard not to look.

Autumn hadn't realized she was staring until his eyes met hers when he made it to the bottom step and looked up. He grinned, slow and smooth, one dimple deepening.

"What's up, superstar baristas?" he teased, gaze dancing between Layla's glitter pen and Autumn's open notebook. "Y'all still coming up with ideas?"

"Yep!" Layla beamed, looking up from writing. "You like my pen, Uncle Amir?" She waved the feathered ballpoint in the air.

"It's awesome, just like you, Beautiful."

He looked back at Autumn, and the easy amusement in his eyes softened into something quieter, more focused.

As his gaze lingered, the bustling porch, the kids, and the entire neighborhood faded into a soft, distant hum.

"Hey," she managed to speak, sounding a little breathy. She was suddenly, acutely aware of the worn terrycloth robe cinched at her waist and the silk bonnet she hadn't bothered to remove. *Damn it,* she thought. *Of all the times for him to look at me like that.*

"What's up, you?" His grin returned. "Man, summer's trying to come in early, ain't it?" he said, noting the unusually warm weather. "I think you brought this heat back."

A warmth that had nothing to do with the weather spiked in her veins, and she had to look away, scoffing playfully to hide the smile spreading across her face.

"Oh please," she fiddled with a loose string on the bench cushion. "Chicago weather is nothing but a tease. This is only a preview of what we can expect, tomorrow it'll be in the forties again."

They laughed together, and as his head tilted down, she noticed the small diamond earring in his right ear.

"Oh, that's different," she commented, pointing at the glittery accessory.

He hesitated, then nodded. "Yeah... Moet gave it to me as a birthday present."

Before Autumn could process his admission, Jordan jumped down the steps.

"Yo, Coach! I told mama about the Clutch Shot. We gonna be famous!"

Amir ruffled his hair. "She better put it on the menu or we're gonna have a whole boycott."

"I already wrote it down," Autumn said, lifting her notepad with a playful glare. "Y'all are relentless."

Amir chuckled, but the playfulness in his eyes was gone, replaced by a raw sincerity that hit her square in the chest. "That's because we believe in you."

And just like that, her heart did that slow, subtle lurch it had no business doing.

Why won't you stop it? Stupid heart! she thought, her mind scrambling for a place to put the emotions. *It's only relief. Gratitude because he's being a good friend.*

But the excuse felt thin, even to her.

"I'll have him back before dinner," he said, guiding Jordan toward the car. "We're working on that layup today."

"Don't fill him up with junk food," she called after them.

He turned back and smiled. "Okay, I will," he teased.

She stood there as they pulled away, the porch too quiet once the taillights disappeared down the block. She didn't realize Layla had gone inside, didn't even know how long she'd been standing, when Mia poked her head out the screen door.

"You good, Sis?"

"Yeah," Autumn murmured, pulling her journal against her chest. "A little tired. Might crash for a bit."

Mia nodded. "Your favorite spot on the couch is free. I just washed the throw blanket. Got it smelling all Downy fresh."

Autumn stepped inside and curled up on the oversized sectional. She flipped through channels on the television, settling on a National Geographic documentary about grizzlies. Within a few minutes, her eyes fell shut.

* * *

THE WORLD around her blurred and softened. She was sitting on their favorite park bench—hers, Asia's, and Amir's—but the park looked more like a distorted memory. The sky was a swirl of bruised purple and impossible orange, like twilight and sunrise had collided. The air was thick with the scent of honeysuckle and coming rain.

She looked at the empty basketball court. The rim on the pole was cartoonishly large, and the net was made of what looked like gleaming silver chains. A vintage ice cream truck sat in the middle of the court, its paint slightly faded. A haunting, tinkling music box version of an old Aaliyah song drifted from its hidden speakers.

Autumn turned her head, and there she was, sitting on the other side of the bench.

Asia, with long, thick synthetic braids in a high ponytail, wearing her "Asia & Amir" tee with a pair of cutoff shorts and her signature glossy lips, waved at her.

She was still vibrant, smiling as if she knew the world's secrets.

"It took you long enough," she called out, motioning for Autumn to come closer.

"Long enough for what?" Autumn asked as she slid next to her friend.

They sat for what felt like an eternity, their conversation fun and playful, a murmur of inside jokes and shared history that Autumn couldn't quite hold on to.

Her chest ached with a joy so pure it was almost painful; the forgotten, everyday bliss of being with her best friend.

Suddenly, the scenery shifted. They were standing side by side in front of the ice cream truck.

Asia leaned closer, nudging Autumn's shoulder, her eyes bright with mischief. "I know what you want."

Autumn squinted at the menu board, but the letters swam before her eyes, jumbling into a beautiful, illegible script.

"What's that?" she asked.

Asia held out the faded, well-loved teddy bear, its button eye missing, and the body softened by time. "Here."

Autumn's chest tightened. "But that's your bear, Asia. It's your favorite," tears welled in her eyes. "I can't take this."

Asia's smile softened, a knowing glint in her eyes. She pressed the bear into Autumn's hands. "Girl, I can't keep it."

She glanced over Autumn's shoulder at something far away, a serene expression crossing her face. "I want you to have it. And I know you'll take care of him."

As Autumn's fingers closed around the bear, Asia's image shimmered, a translucent edge forming around her silhouette.

Autumn heard her name called, almost like a whisper in the wind. She turned toward the sound. In the distance, she saw a figure emerge. It was Amir, emitting a silent, joyous laugh that shook his whole body. Moet appeared beside him, her hand tucked into his, their faces lit with an easy, unbreakable connection.

Autumn's breath caught. The bear in her hands was suddenly a dull, heavy weight. She took a step forward.

"Hey Amir."

He didn't appear to have heard her as his focus stayed on Moet.

She called his name again, louder this time, but the thick, heavy air swallowed the sound.

It was like shouting underwater.

He didn't look her way. He wrapped his arm around Moet's waist, and together they turned and dissolved into the hazy, orange light, leaving her alone on the court with the silent ice cream truck and the weight of the bear in her hands.

* * *

Autumn gasped as her eyes flew open, her heart racing, breathing shallow. She was still on the couch; the blanket was tangled around her legs.

Her phone chimed loudly, SZA's *Good Days* vibrating against the floor, startling her. She sent the unknown caller to voicemail.

She sat up slowly, her eyes stinging.

Her hand pressed instinctively to her chest, feeling for the teddy bear that wasn't there. But the phantom weight lingered.

The room smelled faintly of onion and garlic, signaling that Mia was starting dinner.

She inhaled again, slower this time, like her body was trying to piece together where the dream ended and the ache began.

I want you to have it. And I know you'll take care of him.

Asia's words echoed, and the image of Amir, happy with Moet, flashed behind her eyes.

Something settled deep in her gut. It felt like the universe had whispered a message she wasn't quite able to translate.

RUNNING FROM THE RUB

The scent of citrus cleaner and hair products clung to the air like humidity, thick and bold. It was Easter weekend, and Mia's shop was jumping. Every dryer buzzed, every chair spun, and every client walked in with Pinterest visions and zero patience.

Autumn was busy with curl mousse and edge brushes, moving with the confident rhythm of a woman who'd assisted a million times.

Mia's top stylist had to leave unexpectedly, her baby had come down with a fever, and Autumn, already at the shop to help for the holiday rush, had simply nodded and stepped in.

Now, as things wound down and the last client fluttered out with a fresh silk press, Mia exhaled and leaned against the doorway, towel slung over her shoulder like a battle-weary soldier.

"Autumn, you're a real one," she said. "I owe you dinner and a foot massage."

"I'll take a mani-pedi and I like my steak medium-well," she replied, wiping her hands on a towel.

Mia chuckled. "One last favor, and then I swear I'm locking the door. I need you to head over to the barbershop side. One of my guys had to leave, some baby mama drama, and there's only one client left. Should be easy.

He's been shaved, he only needs the hot towel and moisturizer treatment. That's it."

Autumn nodded, already walking toward the connecting door. "I got it."

"Thank youuu!" Mia called after her. "Tell him to tip heavy!"

The barbershop side, Fix Your Crown, Too, was like stepping into a cool, private lounge for men. It was dimmer, the air a masculine blend of cologne and warm clipper oil. A massive flat screen, muted and tuned to ESPN, was mounted on a brick accent wall.

The real magic, though, was in the back. What was once a storage room had been transformed into a neighborhood sanctuary with a vintage Pac-Man machine, a well-worn chess table, and a dedicated corner for the weekly Spades tournament. It wasn't simply a place for a haircut; it was a space for Black men to have community.

Autumn entered through the connecting door, calling out to the customer. "Hey, I'll be with you in a second," she said as she grabbed the hot towel canister and the warmed moisturizer from the prep station.

She rounded the corner... and stopped cold.

Her breath snagged.

Amir was relaxing in a barber chair, looking like temptation incarnate.

Black leather cape across his chest. White tee peeking from underneath. Locs loose and splaying across the back of the chair.

She'd kept her distance since that dream about Asia two weeks ago, tossing a casual "*hey*" when he came to pick up Jordan and a cursory, "*take care*" when he dropped him off.

The unsettling symbolism: Asia giving her the bear and telling her to take care of it, and seeing him with Moet.

It was all too heavy.

Each night since, the dreams had shifted, morphing into emotional labyrinths she couldn't seem to escape. Sometimes she chased him through thick fog, screaming his name with no reply. Other nights, he was just out of reach, fading before she could speak.

But the most recent one... that one left her shook.

In it, Amir heard her. Saw her. Closed the distance between them and kissed her like something buried had finally clawed its way to the surface.

Now, he was sitting in the chair.

His eyes were closed, head tilted back as if waiting for something...

Oh, hell, she murmured to herself.

As if he heard her thoughts, he opened one eye, then both widened in surprise when he saw her.

"Look at this," he grinned, his voice low and playful. "Am I in for the VIP treatment today?"

Autumn blinked. "I—Mia didn't say it was you."

He smiled, wicked and devastating. "You disappointed?"

She walked toward him before her nerves could argue, trying to force a confident smile. "Depends. You tipping?"

"Depends..." he quipped in return, "on how good you are."

His tone suggested he was teasing. But his eyes...

She stood in front of him, the hot towel canister suddenly feeling like it weighed a ton. Her training from the salon side evaporated. She didn't know the proper process here, so she moved on instinct, stepping into the space between his legs.

His knees brushed against her outer thighs, and a sharp, involuntary jolt shot straight through her.

She opened the canister, the hiss of steam a loud sigh in the quiet room. As she removed the towel and inched toward his face, her fingers lightly grazed the top half of his jaw. His skin was warm, and she felt the faint, sandpaper texture of a fresh shave on her fingertips.

Steam rose between them like a visible confession.

He didn't move. Didn't blink. He watched her, his lips curving into a slow, knowing smile.

"You sure you're not trying to seduce me for that tip?" he murmured, his voice a smooth, low vibration that seemed to travel straight through the floor and up her spine.

His grin suggested he was trying to be funny. But again, his eyes...

Her heart thudded in her chest, and her mouth went dry.

"I mean...." he added, his gaze dropping to her lips, "If this is the new service menu, Mia's about to be booked out for the year."

He plays too much, she thought as she laid the towel across his face, her movements a little too fast, a little too jerky.

"Shut up." She tried to give off annoyance, but the words came out breathy and soft, betraying her.

God, did I just sound giddy?

She cleared her throat, fumbling with the towel's edges. "I meant—hush."

He chuckled beneath the cloth, the sound a husky rumble that pulsed right through her stomach. She could smell his cologne now, an unfamiliar scent, but she liked it.

She took a shaky step back.

Why does this keep happening?

A different kind of steam started rising between them. It was suddenly hard to breathe. That look in his eyes? The way her stomach did a slow, dangerous flip?

Girl! Get it together. You can't go there! You shouldn't even be thinking it...

When she peeled the thick cloth away, his skin glowed, looking impossibly soft. She swallowed hard.

"Moisturizer," she announced, her voice a near whisper.

"Take your time," he murmured, eyes still closed. "I ain't got nowhere to be."

She scooped a dollop of the warm moisturizer. Her hands were clumsy, the movements uncertain.

Just act like you know what you're doing, she told herself.

Her thumbs started at his temples, pressing in small, firm circles, tracing a path she didn't know she knew. He made a low sound in his throat, a rumble that seemed to vibrate straight from his chest, through her palms, and up her arms.

Her touch softened, her fingers now exploring, discovering a terrain she had only ever known from a distance.

The strong arch of his brow. The sharp angle of his cheekbone.

Her thumb traced that line with a slow massaging motion, stopping just shy of the corner of his mouth.

So close.

Dangerously close.

There was a whole universe of unspoken history in that single inch of space.

A shaky breath escaped her, and she felt his own exhale ghost across her knuckles in reply.

"Is this good?" she asked, her voice barely there.

His eyes fluttered open, heavy-lidded, his gaze a sensual fire that threatened to burn through her.

"Exquisite." His voice was an unfamiliar rasp, the playful edges completely sanded away. "You tryna kill me with this TLC?"

Her hands didn't move. His gaze didn't break.

"You look... different," he said finally, his head tilting slightly, like he was studying her face.

"Different how?"

"I don't know." His eyes moved to her mouth. "Just... different."

She didn't have time to respond.

Mia's voice cut through the heat like a cold breeze. "Y'all done over here? I'm locking up!"

Autumn jolted back, her foot catching on the mat, her body pitching sideways.

Amir caught her.

Smooth. Swift. One arm at her waist, the other bracing her elbow. His grip was solid. Steady.

"All good!" she called out, voice cracking like a tween as she gained her footing.

Amir smirked. "You sure?"

"Don't start," she shot, embarrassment creeping in.

"Too late," he responded, eyes still smoldering.

She wished he would raise that damn voice level an octave or two. It was doing crazy things to her nerves.

Things it shouldn't be doing.

He stood and pulled the cape off, taking his time as his gaze lingered, penetrating, like he was reading a page she didn't mean to leave open.

"Thanks for the steam," he said, his voice thick. "It was... eye-opening."

Autumn didn't answer. She turned, grabbed the cloths, and headed for the back, blazing with a heat that had nothing to do with hot towels.

* * *

AUTUMN SAT in Mia's passenger seat, body facing forward. Her thoughts were a tangled mess, replaying the last ten minutes in a frantic, endless loop of heat and confusion.

The steam.

The way Amir's skin felt beneath her hands.

The way he'd looked at her, like he was seeing her in a new light.

She gripped her thighs, fingers curling into fists as Mia climbed in.

"You good over there, sis?" Mia asked, her voice cutting through the haze. She put the car into gear.

Autumn hesitated. "Yeah. I got a few things on my mind."

Mia glanced over with a smirk. "You sure it's only on your mind?"

Autumn exhaled through a tight grin. "Mia..."

"Okay, okay," she chuckled, holding up one hand, feigning surrender. "I'm just saying. You got that look like somebody messed around and flipped on a switch."

Back at the house, she tried to force a sense of normalcy. She helped Layla with her homework, her own voice sounding distant and foreign as she explained a math problem.

She went to the kitchen to wash the few dishes left in the sink, needing a mindless task. But as she plunged her hands into the hot, soapy water, she was instantly transported back to the barbershop.

Her hands on his face. The steam rising between them like a declaration. His hand on her waist...

She snatched her hands from the water as if she'd been burned, hastily drying them on a towel.

After the kids were finally tucked into bed, she ran to her room. She needed a refuge. She needed to wash him off her.

She stumbled into the bathroom, turning the shower knob to full blast.

Cold. She needed cold.

Freezing water pelted her skin like pinpricks, but it wasn't enough to erase the memory of his voice. The rasp in it. The rumble when he moaned from the moisturizer rub.

It wasn't enough to cool her off when she replayed that brief, loaded comment.

"Thanks for the steam."

Good Lord.

Wrapped in a towel, she collapsed backward onto the bed, her body still damp and humming with a fire the cold water couldn't touch. She stared at the ceiling fan as it circled with lazy indifference.

Her hand reached for the phone like it had a mind of its own. Then, she typed two words:

Hey you.

The reply came faster than she expected.

Hey Beautiful. You good?

Her fingers hovered over the keys for a second before she typed:

Can I come through?

A pause.

For sure. I'll leave the door unlocked.

The drive was a blur.

Her jeans were snug, her black top dipped low in the front, and the gloss on her lips shimmered.

When she pulled up, the building's light glowed a soft yellow. Once inside, she dashed to the elevator before it closed, pressing the button rapidly.

Ekon opened the door before she could touch the knob, wearing gray sweatpants, his bare chest smooth and cut, glistening like he had been working out.

"Hey," he greeted, leaning against the frame, already knowing.

She didn't answer.

She stepped inside like her feet didn't belong to her. Like her body had already made the decision.

The kiss was instant. Eager. Like a hunger that needed to be fed.

His hands cuffed and squeezed her curves. Clothes hit the floor.

His hands gripped her waist.

Their tongues silenced her guilt.

They tumbled clumsily to the living room.

They did it on the couch. The floor. The edge of the bed.

And when the fire burned through, when the stillness came, so did the truth.

Autumn lay on her back next to him, staring at the ceiling. The air, which had been hot and frantic moments before, was now cool against her damp skin. The only sounds were the hum of the fan and the distant, lonely wail of a siren somewhere in the city below.

Ekon's voice, still rough with exertion, cracked through her thoughts.

"So. You wanna talk about what you're running from?"

She didn't respond.

He didn't press. He lay there, one arm tucked behind his head like a man who knew what this was—and what it wasn't.

When she finally stood to gather her things, he watched her from the bed, eyes soft but grounded.

"Even if it's yourself, Beautiful," he said, "you still need to face it."

She met his gaze for a moment.

"I know," she whispered.

Outside, the night air had cooled. She hugged her jacket close as she walked to the car, body still warm from Ekon's last embrace.

But as the door shut, and the engine started, one thought echoed like a soft confession:

You didn't choose him tonight.
You're just avoiding someone else.

2 8

GRIND WITH ME

*I*t had been two weeks since the barbershop heat and the aftermath that followed.

Two weeks since she slipped into Ekon's arms, trying to quench a fire she had no business igniting.

And there was still no word on the grant.

The application had been submitted months ago; each passing week was a reminder that sometimes, divine timing moved slower than human patience.

Autumn sat in the kitchen, absentmindedly making lazy circles in her coffee. Her robe hung off one shoulder. The mellow, mournful horns of Solange's *Cranes in the Sky* hummed low through the Bluetooth, a sound that was smooth and calming, but with lyrics that spoke directly to the chaotic rhythm of her own thoughts.

She'd been trying to stay productive, anything to keep her hands and her mind occupied.

Ekon hadn't pressed her. If anything, he'd been cool. He gave her space; no shade, no demands, just a steady, grounded vibe that only made her feel worse for using him as a landing strip for her emotional fly-by.

He'd sent a text the next morning after that heated night in his apartment:

"Hope you're good today. No pressure. Last night was good, but I know you. Don't get down on yourself. Just be easy."

The kindness of it made the guilt coil even tighter in her gut.

As for Amir?

Since their steamy encounter, sleep had been a stranger. She'd toss and turn, the memory of the hot towel and his gaze slamming into her mind at random moments. In the shower, while stirring her coffee, while watching an intimate scene on television.

Every time she closed her eyes, she was back in that barbershop, feeling the heat from his skin, the low timbre of his voice.

"Where is this coming from?" she asked herself over and over.

But the question was a lie. She knew exactly where it came from. She hadn't let herself fully remember.

Until now.

Her mind spiraled back to 2011, in a cramped campus apartment her sophomore year of college, a space that always smelled faintly of stale pizza and her Cherry Blossom Jubilee body spray.

* * *

IT WAS HOMECOMING WEEKEND, but Autumn's roommate, Chris's sister, had gone home. Amir was visiting, wanting to experience all the Spelman extravagance Autumn bragged about.

But instead of partying, Autumn needed to blow off steam. Chris had cheated. Again. Amir vowed to take her mind off all of it.

"I'm so sorry, Amir," she had said, pulling a throw pillow onto her lap and hugging it like a shield. Her eyes were heavy with guilt. "I know you wanted to go out tonight. But I don't have it in me. You can still go, though. I'll call one of my classmates—"

"Nope," he protested. "I'm here for you. We can have our own party."

A genuine smile—the first to touch her lips that entire day—broke through the numb haze of heartbreak, her gratitude so strong it almost hurt.

He wouldn't let her fall apart.

Amir pulled out all the stops. They played Band Hero, the plastic clicks of the guitar buttons a frantic rhythm against their shouted, off-key lyrics

249

until their hands cramped. They played Twister until they collapsed in a heap of tangled limbs and helpless laughter on the worn-out rug.

They invented a game involving movie quotes and dares, fueled by the syrupy sweetness of the Bartles & Jaymes wine coolers he'd triumphantly produced from a plastic grocery bag when he first arrived.

Tipsy and giggling, Autumn swayed to Beauty by Dru Hill, moving her hips, singing the song with off-key passion.

"Why you stay with him?" Amir asked, half-drunk, lying back on the couch.

When she opened her eyes, he was watching her.

"I don't know," she said, spinning in a lazy circle. "Because I'm stupid, I guess."

He didn't return her laugh.

"You're not stupid. You're just used to the wrong things."

Autumn stopped spinning and looked at her friend.

"Chris is the one that's stupid," he continued, picking at a loose string on his shirt. "You're damn near perfect, and he out here acting like you're a side dish and not the main course."

He was being supportive. Her loyal hype-man, saying the things a best friend is supposed to say. But hearing those words, "damn near perfect," "main course," from him, from the one person whose opinion had always been a steady anchor in her life, hit differently.

Dru Hill's chorus swelled from the speakers, and the lyrics, which had been a fun sing-along moments before, now landed like a punch to her gut. Drunken tears she couldn't stop welled in her eyes, blurring Amir's image on the couch.

"This," she whispered, her voice thick and trembling as she gestured vaguely to the music. "This is how love is supposed to sound. Why isn't it ever like this for me?"

The question wasn't really for him. It was for the universe. But he was the only one there to hear it.

She flopped down next to him on the couch.

"That's how I want someone to see me. And I always thought Chris did."

"Aht aht, none of that." Amir jumped up and changed the song, selecting the punchy "Grind With Me" by Pretty Ricky.

He gyrated in front of her, a goofy swaying of his hips that made her giggle. He pulled her up to dance with him.

The distraction was immediate and total. The fun, pulsing beat was a world away from her heartache, and she let herself get lost in it. A real laugh escaped her at their movements, silly and uncoordinated, a return to the spontaneous joy that had always been their native language.

"Ooh, wait," she said, her words slurring playfully. "Lemme show you the routine the dance team does to this. Watch."

She did a slow twirl in front of him, turning her back and pressing her body against him before sliding down, then back up. She turned around and, goofy and emboldened by the alcohol, pushed him back onto the couch.

Amir laughed harder, happy to see his friend back to enjoying herself. He cracked up as she straddled him, finding the performance cute.

Getting lost in the music, Autumn started a slow grind on his lap. His amusement slowly faded as the song's suggestive lyrics guided her movements.

She could see the thought process in his eyes, the playful energy dissolving, the friendly walls crumbling.

The air thickened, hot and heavy, charged with a question neither of them dared to ask. He put one hand around her waist, the touch grounding and electric all at once, lifting himself as she leaned in.

The kiss started soft, like a curiosity. A gentle press of his lips against hers, tasting of sweet wine coolers.

For a split second, the world stopped.

There was no Chris, no heartbreak, no campus apartment. There was only the surprising softness of his tongue and the low, steady hum of want.

He groaned, a low, guttural sound in the back of his throat.

And that was the spark that lit the fuse.

His hand tightened on her waist, pulling her flush against him as the kiss deepened, turning from a curiosity into a desperate, fevered exploration.

Her hands tangled in the front of his shirt, bunching the fabric in her fists.

His other hand came up to cradle the back of her neck, his thumb stroking the sensitive skin below her ear, sending shivers down her spine.

The scrape of his five o'clock shadow was an electric friction against her soft skin.

It was both messy and perfect.

As her fingers hooked under the hem of her Spelman sweatshirt to pull it over her head, the sharp, ugly blare of her phone on the coffee table sliced through the haze.

Her heart seized. It was Chris's ringtone. And, as soon as her eyes swung to the table, they landed on the picture frame that held the funny, crazy pose of her, Amir, and Asia, taken the week before she was killed.

The phone... the picture... it was like a bucket of ice water had been thrown in the room. Autumn flinched back as if she'd been struck, her body going rigid.

The spell was shattered. The heat vanished, replaced by a sobering, reflexive panic.

She scrambled off Amir's lap and lunged for the device, answering it before the second ring could finish, her back turned to him.

"Hey," she said into the phone, her voice already shifting, softening for the very man who had broken her heart just hours before.

Without a backward glance, she waved a phantom apology in the air as her entire world narrowed to the voice on the other end of the line.

And because her back was turned, because she was already choosing the familiar pain over the terrifying possibility, she didn't see it.

She didn't see the way the passion drained from Amir's face, leaving a hollow, stunned confusion. She didn't see his hand, which had been so warm on her neck, fall to his side like a dead weight. She didn't see the light in his eyes flicker and die out, replaced by a deep, shuttered devastation that he immediately tried to hide.

* * *

Autumn had lied to Mia, giving her the Cliff's notes version of that night. The truth was, she had been lying to herself because she didn't want to remember. The guilt was overwhelming.

How could she go there with Asia's man? With her best friend?

But that moment ignited a spark she'd never been able to extinguish.

So, she buried it.

In Chris. In her life in Atlanta. In Ekon. In DeMonte.

Because Amir was the one thing she was never supposed to want.

And now, it all came crashing back. Only this time, she wasn't sure she could contain the blaze.

Especially now.

He'd been his usual charming, involved self whenever he picked up or dropped off Jordan. But there was a different charge in the air now.

He hadn't said anything about the barbershop moment. Neither had she.

But the tension?

Oh, it was real.

They just smiled their way through interactions, making small talk about the weather while their eyes engaged in silent communication. They intentionally kept a distance when in person.

Autumn blinked and realized she'd been stirring her coffee for a solid minute without sipping. She snapped out of the daze and grabbed her phone from the counter.

Hey, is that spot still available?

She hit send before she could second-guess it. She'd been checking on the storefront she'd eyed for Asia's Ember regularly.

Her realtor, a no-nonsense older woman named Brenda, replied almost instantly.

BRENDA

It's still available, honey. That spot is waiting for you. Want me to set up another walk-through?

Her thumb hovered over the screen.

AUTUMN

Not yet. Hold it for me a little longer if you can.
Still waiting to hear about the grant.

She locked the phone and took a sip, the warm coffee hitting her chest like a reminder to breathe.

She pushed away from the counter, pacing the short length of the kitchen. The truth was that everything felt like it was in limbo.

The grant. The business. Her damn emotions.

She needed movement. Something, anything, to break the stillness before it swallowed her whole.

A text from Jordan came through right on time, stating he'd left his sneakers at home. And he had basketball practice today.

She grabbed her keys, slid on her Crocs, and headed to the youth center.

The building was muted, sunlight cutting in through the wide front windows as staff moved about with purpose, sweeping, stocking equipment, and checking clipboards.

Autumn was greeted by the familiar blend of lemony floor cleaner and the faint hum of fluorescent lights. She clutched Jordan's gym shoes in one hand, her keys jingling softly in the other.

A few strides down the hall, she spotted Amir through the glass window of his office, bent over a crate of fresh basketballs.

She knocked lightly before letting herself in.

"Jordan forgot his gym shoes," she said by way of greeting, holding them up like a hall pass. "Texted me from school like it was a national emergency."

Amir straightened up with a grin; the movement pulling his t-shirt taut across his chest. He chuckled and wiped his palms on a towel slung over his shoulder. The subtle movement made the muscles underneath the shirt flex, ever so lightly. Autumn forced her gaze away, focusing instead on a scuff mark on the floor.

"That boy. He's always forgetting something. Thanks for bringing 'em. I do keep an extra pair here for him, just in case."

Of course he did.

The thought hit Autumn with a quiet force. Amir was always the one with the backup plan, the one who anticipated the need before it became one.

"He claimed these are his lucky shoes," she said, matter-of-factly, as she set them down on a nearby chair. She glanced around, searching for a safe topic. A neutral one. "Quiet in here today."

"I gave half the staff the day off. The others are just getting everything ready for afternoon programming." He motioned toward the hallway where two team members were organizing snack boxes. "It's the calm before the chaos, because spring break is going to be crazy."

"I can imagine," she sighed, the single breath carrying the weight of her own suspended dreams and the simmering chaos of her heart.

Silence sat between them for a few seconds.

Amir leaned against the edge of his desk, arms folded, watching her like he could see a thought passing behind her eyes.

"You been okay?"

Autumn offered a half-smile. "I'm trying. Staying busy. Distracting myself from checking my email every ten seconds."

"Still waiting on an update about the grant?"

She nodded. "It's been months now. I even called last week to make sure I didn't miss something."

He tilted his head, voice warm. "I get it. I remember when I started this place. It took forever to get my approvals. Heck, I'm still waiting on funds from several places."

Her phone buzzed.

"Hold on," she said as she grabbed it from her pocket, intending to put it in silent mode. She paused, her stomach doing a sudden, hopeful lurch when she realized it was an email from the women's grant program.

The subject line from the floating notification glowed:

APPLICATION DECISION: Asia's Ember Coffeehouse Grant Request

She inhaled sharply. Her blood went cold, then hot, all at once. A bubble of tension rose in her chest, so tight it felt like it might choke her.

"No way... we were just talking about this."

Amir straightened. "What is it?"

Her eyes went wide with a mixture of worry and excitement. "It's an email about the grant," she whispered, holding the phone up.

He stepped closer, his own eyes widening. "Open it. Read it out loud."

She hesitated as her nerves stood on end, her stomach doing somersaults.

He reached out, gently gripping her shoulders, his gaze holding hers.

"You got this, Autumn. No matter what." The simple, solid pressure of his hands was an anchor, silencing the panic.

With trembling fingers, she tapped on the email. Her voice quivered as she read out loud:

"Dear Ms. Gardener, we are pleased to inform you that your application for the Women in Business Small Business Grant has been fully approved..."

She covered her mouth, unable to continue as emotion tumbled out in a choked laugh, her eyes blurring with tears.

Amir whooped, loud and genuine. "Yoooo! That's what I'm talking about!"

"I can't believe it," she whispered, her voice full of awe.

"You better believe it!" He grinned like he'd won something himself. "You earned every bit of that. I told you it was gonna come through."

She beamed, bouncing where she stood. "Asia's Ember Coffeehouse," she said aloud, every syllable feeling like a living, breathing testament to her purpose.

Amir opened his arms, and she didn't hesitate. She moved into his embrace like she belonged there, arms wrapping around his neck, his around her waist, lifting her slightly as she laughed in his ear.

It was warm. Familiar, yet different.

When he finally set her down, the movement was slow, a deliberate unfurling that seemed to stretch time.

His hands didn't immediately drop from her waist; hers still rested on his shoulders. The air between them crackled, suddenly thick. This wasn't just a celebratory hug anymore.

Their eyes locked, and there was a dangerous acknowledgment of tension, of timing, and a terrifying feeling of fate.

She drew in a breath, slow and ragged.

His gaze lingered on her lips.

"Amir—" she started, her voice hushed.

"Hey, Amir!" one of the staffers called, just outside the office, loud enough to snap the moment in two. "Oh, hey Moet!" the same voice greeted, the casualness shifting to a tone of warm respect.

The sequence of words hit like a cold slap. Autumn froze; her eyes locked with Amir's. She watched the warmth in his gaze vanish, replaced by a flicker of something she could only describe as panic.

His hands fell to his side like lead. Her eyes darted to the door, noting the movement outside. She heard the faint jingle of keys, followed by a laugh. The unmistakable click of heels.

Autumn stepped back, smoothing her shirt, trying to regain some semblance of control over the nerves that were still buzzing,

"I should get out of here," she blurted, her tone a notch higher than before.

"You sure?" Amir asked, but his voice was guarded now. Like he was back in coach mode.

She nodded. "Yeah. I got a lot to do." She flashed the cell phone with a swift movement.

Before he could say more, she was out the door, her gym shoes delivery mission accomplished, her joy suddenly tangled with emotions she was still afraid to name.

* * *

As Autumn hit the sidewalk, the cool afternoon air wrapped around her, a distinct contrast to the heat that simmered in her chest. She stopped, leaning against the brick wall to catch her breath.

She looked at her phone, the congratulatory email still glowing.

She had won.

So why did it feel like she had just lost something, too?

Pull it together, sis.

She had jumped into Amir's arms like a giddy high-schooler. Felt his arms wrap tight around her. Watched his smile break wide, soft and proud.

And then, just like that, the moment had faded. Not from her, but from him, at the sound of Moet's name.

Her feet kept moving down the block, but something inside her stalled.

This ain't it, Autumn, she chided herself. *Right now, Moet is the obstacle. But the real wall is Asia.*

You. Can't. Cross. That. Line.

She understood this clearly now. Moet was the practical barrier, the memory of Asia was the sacred barrier, and her own denial of what she was truly feeling for Amir was the final line of defense against the one thing she wanted and feared the most.

By the next morning, she was intentionally in motion, driven by the grant approval letter. It was go time, and she couldn't afford any distractions.

She created task lists. Held phone calls with vendors.

The steady rhythm of entrepreneurship was exactly what she needed. It gave her something to reach for that didn't feel complicated.

She spent half a day at the storefront with the realtor, mapping out where tables would go, where sunlight would hit just right. She could already smell the roasted beans and hear the laughter echoing from soft-seated corners. They put in an offer to lease with an option to purchase that day.

Over the next few weeks, she poured her energy into the bones of the café, using floor plans and paint swatches as a shield against her own complicated heart.

Hours flew past in a blur of branding ideas and color palettes.

But even with the noise and movement, her mind kept circling back. Not to the moment in Amir's arms, but to the dream. The one where Asia had handed her that old teddy bear and told her, "I know you'll take care of him."

Autumn had clung to it like a sign. A green light. Permission.

But maybe that wasn't what Asia meant.

Maybe she wasn't passing Amir off like some cosmic hand-me-down. Maybe she was telling her to watch over him... like he had watched over her all these years.

Maybe it was never about romance.

Maybe it was about friendship.

That thought hit her like cool water on a smoldering fire. And with the release of steam came something close to peace.

Acceptance.

She journaled a few days later, following her attendance at the Bag Ladies session, writing with deliberate reflection:

I've loved before. Deeply. So, I know what it is, and what it isn't. Love isn't always meant to bloom the way we imagine. Sometimes it's soft. Protective. Sacred. Maybe that's what Asia was saying. I think she was reminding me that some connections aren't meant to turn into something new, but to be honored for what they are.

Every time we've come close to having a moment, there's always been some kind of interruption. It's almost as if fate itself is rebuking the thought of us together.

Amir has Moet. They seem good together.

Maybe I'm meant to walk differently this time. Not with him, but beside him.

As his friend.

Just like I thought in the first place.

That last line was more of an admonishment, a chastisement for allowing herself to step beyond a barrier she had held dear.

She sat with the weight of those words, letting them settle instead of fighting them.

A month after the grant was approved and the lease was signed, Autumn let herself into the empty storefront alone. This time, with her earbuds in, blasting a playlist that blended old school with new soul, she moved through the space like an owner, feeling the future stretch wide before her.

Asia's Ember Coffeehouse.

It wasn't just a name.

It was a promise fulfilled to her friend, one they made in high school about rising from the trenches of Ebondale together.

A legacy for her children.

A love letter to resilience: her own.

As for anything else? She was bowing out of the fight before it could even get started, choosing not to deal with the parts of her heart that she couldn't control.

Because the love she was building now... her business, her creation... it was all hers.

And it was finally something she *could* control.

29

THE WEIGHT OF EXPECTATIONS

June's warmth clung to the pavement in shimmering waves as the kids dragged their roller bags toward Chris's SUV. Layla wore her Minnie Mouse ears, bouncing with each step, and Jordan's grin was wide enough to split his face. Autumn watched from the porch, arms wrapped around herself, heart tight.

Her babies were leaving to spend the summer with their dad, and it would be the first time without them longer than a few days.

The kids had just found out about the Disney trip this morning, which had been an add-on at the last minute. Autumn had kept it to herself because Chris wanted it to be a surprise. And judging by the way they'd screamed and bolted to pack, she'd nailed it.

"You knew the whole time?" Layla had gasped between suitcases.

Autumn smirked. "Yep."

"*Mommm!*" she squealed, hugging her tight. "You're the best."

Chris stepped around the car, helping Jordan load his bag into the trunk. Autumn watched the woman standing at the passenger door, helping Layla adjust the strap on her bag. She had smooth cinnamon skin, and sunglasses were perched on her head.

Her name was Shari.

Chris surprised her when he told her his new friend was going to Disney with them. Autumn knew he was dating again; they'd had that conversation when she saw him in Atlanta, and he'd introduced them on a video call a few weeks ago. But seeing her here, now, interacting with her daughter with such gentle care? This felt official.

"Hey," he said, coming to stand next to her on the porch. "Thanks again for keeping the trip a secret. You know how I like to be the hero." He managed a self-deprecating grin.

Autumn laughed softly. "You better enjoy it now, because they'll be teenagers soon. And from what I see with Mia's teen son, parents become 'bruhs' who 'suck'." She punctuated the phrase with air quotes and a satirical eyeroll.

They stood for a second, letting the moment breathe as they laughed at the wild days to come.

"Shari seems really nice," Autumn noted casually, nodding toward the smiling woman, who was talking animatedly with the kids.

Chris rubbed his neck. "Yeah. Figured it's a good time to introduce her to them in person, and for them to be around each other more. She's been solid."

Autumn raised her brows. "So. This means you're serious about her?"

He looked at the ground, then back up. "I think so."

Autumn playfully tapped him on the arm with her fist. "Look at you! I knew something was up when you introduced her to the kids on FaceTime last week."

"Well, like I told you in Atlanta, I've done a lot of growing up," he admitted, meeting her gaze. "Been taking a lot of pages from your book."

She nodded slowly, the words landing with a surprising softness in her chest. For years, she had been the one learning from his mistakes. The idea that he was now learning from her growth settled a genuine, profound respect between them.

"I can tell," she said softly. "And I know the kids are going to love her."

Chris slid his hands into his pockets after a brief pause. "What about you?"

"What about me?"

"Are you seeing anyone? I mean, seriously."

Autumn looked out at the street, where the kids were now building out a road trip playlist with Shari. She shrugged. "I've been more focused on getting the coffeehouse off the ground."

Chris tilted his head, an old knowing smirk tugging at his lips. "You were always good at handling business." He paused. "But just know our daughter hears and talks. A lot."

Autumn rolled her eyes, her head swaying as she chuckled.

"Of course she does."

Then his voice softened. "Listen. Don't let my past mistakes dictate your future with love. Strive to build your business, yes. But don't discount falling in love again. You've always loved love, Autumn. Don't let that change."

Her eyes stung, just a little, from both sadness and recognition.

She swallowed. "Thanks, Chris."

"I mean it."

He headed to the car, then turned around. "Just a reminder. While they're staying the summer with me, I'll have Shari around a lot, if that's cool?"

"Of course," she said. "This is all actually perfect. Gives me time to focus on getting everything ready for the launch."

The kids ran to the porch for last-minute hugs and kisses, then sprinted back to the car. Shari walked back as well, giving her a hug and a reassuring eye about the kids.

"I'll make sure Chris doesn't overload them with junk food," she promised with a smile.

As the car pulled away, her hand waved long after they disappeared down the block. The street fell quiet again, the scent of summer heat and cut grass permeating the air.

Autumn felt like the pieces of her life were falling into place.

Not perfectly, not all at once.

But gracefully.

Maybe this was what life was all about: creating alignment.

She had been treating her dream like a fortress, a safe place to hide from the messiness of her heart.

But watching Chris drive away with the kids and his new lady, seeing him find his own hard-earned peace, she realized something with a clarity that hit her right in the heart.

The coffeehouse wasn't a fortress. It was a foundation.

And a foundation is meant to be built upon. You don't build a beautiful house to leave the living room empty.

The kids were happy. The business was coming to life.

And that one missing piece, the one thing she kept trying to box up: she didn't have to chase it.

She just had to stop running from it.

* * *

It was pre-opening day.

The soft ding of the coffeehouse doorbell hadn't stopped since morning, with all the shipments and supplies coming in.

Autumn stood behind the counter, her laptop open and a checklist in front of her. Flyers had been sent, vendors were confirmed, pastries ordered, and signage delivered.

Ekon even volunteered to do a live shout-out on his channel. He said he'd be front and center with a full camera crew on opening day. "Your soft launch is about to look like Essence Fest," he'd texted, followed by three fire emojis and one heart.

She smiled now, thinking about it as she walked toward the window. The vibe was going to be insane.

The coffee bar gleamed, the tables were dressed in soft linens with subtle metallic accents, and the scent of vanilla, fresh paint, and the sharp, promising aroma of the first test-ground beans floated through the air.

Her coffeehouse. Her dream.

Asia's Ember.

Autumn stared at the engraved name on the front window for a long moment, then pressed her fingers to the glass. "We made it, Sis," she whispered.

Her phone buzzed.

AMIR

> Had to make a quick trip to New York, Moet's launching her makeup line and needed some help. I'll be back in time tomorrow. Wouldn't miss your big day for the world. Proud of you, Aut.

She exhaled slowly, the words a balm on her ragged nerves.

He's proud.

She reread the text, trying to force the simple comfort of them to be enough. She shook her head slightly, attempting to dismiss the anxiety.

He's supporting his girlfriend. This is good, that's who he is. Be happy for him.

But the logic couldn't touch the ache. It was a physical weight in her chest, stubborn and real.

Another text came in.

EKON

> Don't forget, camera crew's pulling up at 10am sharp tomorrow. I want these folks to know this ain't no regular launch. You're a vibe, Autumn.

She chuckled, genuinely grateful for his over-the-top energy. It was exactly what she expected from him. She texted back a simple red heart emoji.

Later that night, the café lights were dimmed, casting warm shadows across the polished countertops and freshly waxed floors. Autumn walked through slowly, her heels clicking softly against the tile, a checklist in hand.

Every detail was in place: the chalkboard specials written in curly, deliberate loops, napkin holders stocked, playlist queued to start with Erykah Badu and loop into Jill Scott. A small vase of sunflowers, Asia's favorite, sat on each table, their yellow heads tilted like they were already soaked in joyfulness.

Autumn lowered her checklist and took a slow step back. She let her eyes defocus from the details, allowing herself to feel the space she'd built.

The intentional vibe she had carefully, painstakingly curated.

The air was the first thing to be noticed; a thick, perfect, intoxicating blend of roasted coffee and a sweet hint of local pastries stacked high under sparkling bakery glass. It was the smell of comfort, of a place that made each person feel at home.

The walls were painted a rich, warm terracotta, giving the space a mood of baked earth and sunshine. It made the room glow when the sun beamed through the windows, as if it were perpetually caught in the golden hour before sunset.

The walls were also a living, breathing gallery of Ebondale's spirit and creativity. Just as she had envisioned, they were covered in the vibrant, unapologetic canvases of Ebondale's own artists.

There were bold, abstract color bursts, stunning black-and-white portraits of neighborhood elders, past and present, and scenes of everyday life. Each piece was labeled with a small tag: *'On Consignment. Support the Culture of Ebondale.'*

The glossy tile floors gleamed under recessed lighting, making the reclaimed wood four-top tables in the middle of the room feel even richer and more grounded.

Booths lined the entire left side, upholstered in a regal plum vinyl that invited patrons to slide in, get comfortable, sip, and talk for hours.

And in the back, past the main counter, was a wide, inviting archway with a handcrafted wooden sign that led to *'The Poet's Lounge (A Space for the Unheard).'*

This wasn't just a coffeehouse. It was Black Joy personified.

She checked off the last task on the list with a satisfied sigh.

Tomorrow, it would all be real.

Her phone buzzed just as she started turning off the lights.

AMIR

Everything's gonna be perfect. I wish I could see
your face right now. This moment's yours,
Autumn. You earned every bit of it.

She stared at the text longer than she needed to, her thumbs hovering before typing back:

AUTUMN

I'm trying to stay calm, but these butterflies
keep doing line dances in my stomach.

Autumn breathed in, then exhaled slowly.

He was right. His words cut straight through the frantic buzzing in her stomach, grounding her instantly.

She smiled, a real, bone-deep beam this time, and tucked the phone in her pocket. She locked the door after she exited, the sound sharp and definitive in the quiet night.

* * *

Opening day arrived.

The sun rose like it had an appointment with destiny, casting a golden, hopeful glow over Ebondale.

By 10 a.m., the sidewalk outside Asia's Ember was a beautiful sea of Black joy. The air was electric, thrumming with the bass from a curated playlist. The rich, intoxicating scent of roasted coffee and Mia's fresh-baked lemon loaf slipped into the streets like a warm, loud invitation.

Local news vans were double-parked, their antennas reaching for the sky. Neighbors, old and new, lined up on the pavement, their laughter and excited chatter a symphony of community support.

Autumn stood near the entrance, dressed in an all-white summer dress with a delicate gold waist belt. She exuded radiance, grace, and confidence, a universe away from the woman who had arrived in Chicago a year ago, feeling like a failure.

She greeted every guest, her eyes sparkling, her energy magnetic. A warm hug from Ms. Davis from down the block, a firm handshake with Alderman Nkosi, a shared, tearful glance with Asia's mother, who had arrived with a bouquet of sunflowers. In the older woman's eyes, Autumn saw a reflection of her own grief and a deep, wordless pride.

They both knew who this day was truly for.

Kendra had sent her a large gift basket and a note of praise. "If I didn't have to be in Japan this weekend, I'd be there with you, celebrating your accomplishments. Keep doing big things. I always knew you could."

An hour later, the coffeehouse was officially open, humming with a life of its own. Baristas moved with the fluid choreography of a seasoned team, the hiss of the steam wand and the clatter of ceramic mugs creating a steady rhythm.

The playlist flowed from Erykah Badu to Jill Scott to Ledisi. Kids from the youth center, who were volunteering, ran in and out, offering cookie samples on trays to patrons outside. The air inside was a heady blend of dark roast, sharp citrus, and melting brown sugar.

Ekon stood near the entrance with his hype crew, his phone capturing it all.

"Ebondale!" he shouted, his voice booming with genuine excitement. "Y'all are witnessing history today! Black-owned, Black-woman-led, community-rooted! Now make some noise for the visionary behind it all. The incredible Miss Autumn Gardener!"

A roar of applause and cheers went up from the crowd as Autumn stepped beside him, her cheeks flushing. She leaned into the mic, voice calm but electric.

"So, tell everybody what inspired this," Ekon instructed.

"This coffeehouse isn't just about coffee," she said. "It's about culture. About healing. About creating a place that feels like home when the world shuts us out. I wanted to build something that honors where we've been and helps us imagine where we can go. Ebondale deserves that."

The celebration moved indoors, and Mia wiped a tear from the corner of her eye as a local poet took the mic to deliver verses about culture, resistance, and rebirth.

The entire day was magical.

And yet... it felt like something was missing.

Autumn kept glancing at her phone, hoping to see his name.

Finally, she felt the familiar buzz against her hip. She discreetly pulled it from her pocket, turning away from a conversation with a local blogger to steal a private moment. Her heart leaped when she saw the notification next to Amir's name, a wild, ridiculous hope surging through her.

Maybe he made it. Maybe he's outside.

AMIR

Flight's still delayed. I'm trying to get on standby. I'm sorry, Aut. I swear I'm coming.

She closed her eyes for a moment, forced a smile, and typed back:

AUTUMN

Be safe. I appreciate you trying.

But her heart dropped anyway.

Because no matter how full the moment was, his absence was loud.

Later that night, the guests were gone. The blinds were closed. The lights were dimmed again, but this time it wasn't for setup; it was for soul-soothing. Autumn stood at the counter, wiping it down even though it was already spotless.

Her feet ached. Her cheeks were sore from smiling. And her heart was bleeding.

Outside, the moon spilled its glow across Ebondale's quiet streets, and inside, the faint smell of coffee and fresh paint still lingered in the air. The grand opening had been everything she'd hoped for, and then some.

The coffeehouse had buzzed with life. Faces she hadn't seen in years showed up with smiles and warm hugs.

The poet had stirred the crowd with verses that landed like truth-tipped arrows.

Ekon's livestream had pulled in hundreds of thousands of views and likes within minutes. Her face was now floating across timelines she hadn't even imagined.

But somehow, it felt incomplete.

Amir had missed the whole thing.

She'd checked her phone too many times. Each ping sent a little thrill of hope through her until the last one:

Standby is a no go. I'm so sorry.

That one had sent something else through her: A dull ache that settled behind her ribs and stayed there all night.

She thought about the moment she'd walked onto the small makeshift stage to thank everyone. She'd worn her smile like armor, but inside, she'd scanned the room, praying to see his smiling face.

When she didn't see him, that hope had crumbled. And her heart broke.

She folded into herself, arms crossed tight like a barrier, trying to quiet the thoughts ricocheting off the inside of her skull.

Why did it matter so much?

Why him? And why now?

It wasn't his absence that hurt the most. It was the fact that deep down, she'd expected him to make a miracle happen and just show up. Like always.

Whether that part was about the friend she knew, or the feeling she hadn't yet found the courage to name... she did not know.

Autumn let her head fall back against the wall, her eyes fluttering closed as she whispered aloud, "I just wanted you to be here."

Suddenly, the bell jingled, a sharp sound in the exhausted quiet. She straightened, a jolt of alarmed adrenaline shooting up her spine.

She forgot to lock up. Her lips parted before her brain caught up, about to announce the shop was closed.

But it was him.

Amir stood in the doorway like a delayed promise, his small suitcase dragging behind him, and his eyes locked on her.

"I know it's too late," he said, his voice scraped raw, like he'd spent hours arguing with airline agents. His eyes showed a weariness she hadn't seen since the days after Asia's death. "But I had to come anyway."

30

ON THE SAME SIDE OF THE LINE

The sight of Amir standing there, tired, slightly disheveled, and suitcase in tow, sent a contradictory jolt straight through her—half raw relief, half blinding rage.

Autumn blinked slowly, her mind needing a minute to catch up with her emotions. Every instinct screamed at her to run to him, to melt into the embrace she'd been craving all day.

But she fought it, shoving the feeling down with a familiar, bitter force. It was a defense mechanism she'd perfected with Chris, turning hurt into a weapon before it could turn on her.

"How did you know I was still here?" she demanded, her eyes narrowed into angry slits.

He gave a small, weary smile. "Because I know you."

"Why did you even bother showing up, Amir?" Her voice rose, the tone biting. "The event was over hours ago."

She turned her back to him, picking up two empty coffee cups that didn't need picking up, sitting them on the opposite end of the counter, like they'd betrayed her.

He turned and locked the door behind him with a soft click. The silence suddenly pressed in like humidity after a storm.

"I got here as soon as I could. The flight was—"

"Don't." She cut in, spinning around. "Don't make this about logistics."

He took a step forward, his eyes pleading. "I'm not—"

"You were supposed to be here, Amir!" Her voice cracked under the strain of a day spent holding herself together. "Not with Moet. With me."

She hadn't meant to say that last part. Not out loud.

But it hung there now, naked, aching, and true.

Amir ran a hand over his face, dragging his palm down his cheek. "Autumn, I told you... she had this event, her support bailed. She asked me to—"

"And you said yes," she snapped, her voice echoing in the quiet space. "Even though you knew my opening was this weekend."

The air, which had smelled like vanilla and possibility just hours before, now felt thick and suffocating as the resentment she'd been swallowing all day came pouring out.

"You weren't here when it mattered. I needed my people. And I guess I thought..." Her voice faltered, the anger cracking to reveal the hurt underneath. "I thought you were one of them."

His face shifted. The exhaustion vanished, and for a split second, his eyes went wide with a raw, unguarded devastation. Then he blinked, and it was gone. His entire posture went rigid.

"You think I didn't want to be here? I was stuck 800 miles away—"

"And that's the problem!" she fired back, taking a step toward him, the words pouring out before she could restrain them. "You've been so wrapped up in *her*, I barely even matter to you anymore."

Amir's jaw clenched, a muscle feathering along his cheek. "Wow. That's rich, coming from you." He took a half-step forward, his normal calm demeanor replaced by a rigid intensity. "You mean like how you were so wrapped up in Ekon and Officer Friendly that I just became background noise?"

Autumn flinched as if he'd struck her. A stunned silence fell, broken only by the low hum of the drink cooler.

"That's not fair," she spat. "And you know it."

"Isn't it? My birthday came and went while you were juggling your boy toys, and all I got was a text and a crusty-ass card from Walgreens." There was a bitter, unfamiliar edge to his chuckle. "Even the kids were more thoughtful than that."

A raw heat flooded Autumn's face as shame coiled in her stomach, sharp and nauseating. He was right. God, he was right. She had treated his birthday like an afterthought, a task delegated to the kids while she drowned in her own drama. The memory was an ugly jab of guilt.

But the shame was quickly consumed by a wave of defensive fury. "So now we're just gonna hit below the belt?" she snapped, forcing herself to meet his hardened gaze. "I had a lot going on, yeah, but I was always there when you actually needed me. Always."

"And you really think I didn't want to be here today?" His voice cracked, the sound raw and desperate, bouncing off the high ceilings. "You think I enjoyed being stuck hundreds of miles away while you were launching your dream? I fought like hell to get back, Autumn. I thought I could be there for both of you."

She let out a short, disbelieving laugh. "Right. 'Both of us.' Guess we know who won *that* coin toss."

His eyes flared, the last remnants of his exhaustion incinerated by pure rage.

"You've got a lot of goddamn nerve," he hissed.

"Excuse me?" she shot back, hands flying to her hips, her own anger surging to meet his.

He closed the space between them in two long, angry strides, invading her personal space until she had to tilt her head back to look up at him. His body radiated heat, his fists clenched at his sides.

"Let's talk about your priorities, Autumn. You had Ekon and his whole damn hype squad ready to turn this place into Coachella. Before that, you were playing house with Officer Friendly. But *I'm* the one who hasn't been prioritizing *you*?"

Her mouth fell open, a strangled gasp lodging in her throat. The proximity, the accusation, the sheer force of his anger... it was overwhelming.

"What does any of that have to do with today?" Her voice trembled, thick with unshed tears, but she held his fiery gaze, refusing to back down. "I needed you here. Today."

"Why?" he pressed, leaning in closer, his voice dropping to a low, dangerous growl, laced with a pain that seemed to vibrate through the floor.

His eyes were wounded, furious. "You had Mia. You had Brianna. You had your whole damn fan club lining up outside. What the hell did you need me for? To move some goddamn chairs? To pour coffee? Or just to be another face in your crowd?"

The sarcasm was a blade, and she felt every cut.

"What are you even saying? I needed my friend."

"No." He leaned even closer, his voice a raw, devastating whisper. "You needed your backup."

Backup.

The word hit her with the force of a physical impact, silencing the angry retort already forming on her tongue. Her entire body went still, processing the cold, ugly truth of it.

Not a friend, not a partner, not the man she secretly wanted. Just a contingency plan.

The accusation was so brutal, so unlike Amir, it stole the very air from her lungs.

"And I've needed *you* to see *me*." His voice cracked as he continued. "Not as your safety net. Not as the nice guy you keep on the bench while you test out every other player. But when I got close, you laughed it off. You acted like nothing was there. And now you get mad when I don't break down every damn wall to get to you in time?"

They stood just inches apart now, but it might as well have been a canyon.

"I didn't know you felt like that." Her voice was soft, yet her defiance remained intact.

"No," he retorted. "You didn't want to know."

Then, his eyes softened, the fury draining away, leaving only an exhausted vulnerability. His shoulders slumped.

And just like that, the brittle wall of Autumn's own anger dissolved, replaced by a sudden, aching empathy.

She put her hand on his chest without thinking, tears pooling but not falling. He looked like how she felt: raw, undone, stripped down to something primal and real.

"Amir..." she began, but the rest got stuck.

The need to put some space between them suddenly felt overwhelming —a firewall against the feeling threatening to burn her to the ground.

Their friendship was on the line.

Her loyalty to Asia was on the line.

His own relationship with Moet was on the line.

"I think we're both emotional right now," her voice trembled as she took a step back and wiped a hand across her brow. "Maybe we should talk tomorrow. When we've both calmed down."

She swung around to walk toward the sink, desperate for the safety of dishes and denial.

But Amir caught her wrist. His grip was warm, solid, impossible to pull away from.

"Autumn."

The way he called her name... Jesus.

It wasn't the sound of the easy tone she'd known all her life. It was gravel and smoke, rough with hunger, curling low in her belly. She turned and nearly crumbled at the sight of him. His eyes burned, fierce and unguarded, a fireball of desire she'd never seen aimed at her.

He stepped in close, slow and deliberate, giving her every chance to run.

Move, Autumn. Step back.

The thought was a warning. But she didn't... she couldn't convince her feet to move.

"Yes," she answered back, shocking herself. The word spilled out, traitorous, her body taking over.

As if her response was an invitation, his mouth crashed onto hers.

The kiss was a wildfire. Not careful, not safe. His tongue swept hers with a hunger that set her ablaze, and she met him stroke for stroke. Her fingers tangled in his locs, tugging him closer as if on instinct.

And when he groaned—God, that sound. It vibrated straight down to her center.

Is this Amir?

Her knees almost buckled at the thought.

"This what you've been running from?" he rasped against her lips, voice shredded with need. "Me wanting you like this?"

Thought evaporated. There was only the heat, the pressure, the reality of his mouth on hers.

Yes. No. Maybe. The words were meaningless static.

But her moan told the truth. And he heard the admission.

His mouth blazed a path down her neck, tongue hot, teeth sharp enough to make her gasp. She clutched the counter behind her; dizzy with a desire she'd never known was possible.

"Tell me to stop," he growled in her ear, then softly nicked her lobe with his teeth. "Say the word, and I'll walk away."

His hand was already sliding under her dress, palm burning against her thigh.

Stop? The word was foreign.

Instead, she pulled down the straps of her dress and unclasped her silk bra, allowing both to fall to the floor.

"Goddamn," he groaned, his gaze dropping to the soft, heavy swell of her breasts. His voice cracked, wrecked. "You're so fucking beautiful."

An inferno spread through her under his gaze.

Amir: her best friend, the boy who teased her in gym class, who once lit a firecracker under her chair just to make her scream, was looking at her like she was a feast. Like she was his to devour.

She didn't recognize this man, but God help her, she wanted him more than she'd ever wanted anything.

He palmed her breasts, his thumbs brushing her taut nipples, and a low, involuntary cry ripped from her throat.

"Yeah," he muttered as he leaned in, rough against her ear. "I wanna hear the noise. Give me every sound. Don't hold back from me now."

She needed to touch him.

All of him.

Her hands found the hem of his shirt, tugging it up with a desperate groan. He got the message, lifting his arms to let her pull the fabric over his head and toss it aside without breaking their gaze.

Her palms skimmed his chest, greedy, desperate, cataloguing every ridge of muscle she'd never let herself touch before. Then, her hands moved lower, dipping into his unzipped jeans, past his briefs, and sliding down the length of his dick. She gripped the thick, rigid flesh as her hand glided up, her thumb caressing the wet, sticky tip.

His answering groan was feral, vibrating through her until she thought she'd break.

Their mouths collided again, hungrier, sloppier, both devouring the other. His hand slipped into her panties, fingers parting her folds like he'd been waiting years to make her this wet.

"I feel you," he muttered, his voice shaking with restraint. "Is all this for me, Autumn?"

"Yes," she gasped, the word tumbling out before she could stop it. "Hell yes."

Oh, fuck. Her mind was a tempest.

This man, this version of Amir, was going to break her.

She'd never heard him like this. Never heard any man like this. Talking her through it, dragging the pleasure out of her like it belonged to him. It terrified her. It thrilled her. She was on fire as the rare possession in his voice sent a fresh wave of heat through her.

In one swift move, he scooped her up, her legs locking around his waist. She felt the thick, solid hardness of his dick rubbing against her core through their clothes, and a sharp gasp escaped her, her vision momentarily whiting out at the delicious friction of it.

"You feel that? That's every thought I've had about you since that night in your dorm room, even when I knew better. And now, I don't give a fuck about better."

This is Amir! Her mind screamed, the room tilting, the scent of him overwhelming her senses.

This wasn't the goofy teenager she once knew. This wasn't the silly college sophomore she almost got busy with.

This was a man. And he was taking her to a level of desire she hadn't even known was possible.

He effortlessly carried her to the couch and laid her down, eyes wild, body trembling with the effort of control. "Is this what you want? Say it, Autumn."

Her voice cracked, but her truth was steady as she met his gaze. "Oh, I've wanted this for a long ass time."

"Goddamn, girl," he growled, his voice deep with need as he pressed his forehead to hers. "You don't know what that does to me."

He pulled back slowly, his eyes dropping to her chest. A low rumble rose from deep in his throat. "So... fucking... beautiful," he breathed, before his mouth descended, rotating between her breasts, sucking hard until she cried out in sweet agony.

"That's it," he muttered, voice dripping heat. "Sweetest fucking sound I've ever heard. Give me more."

One hand trailed between her thighs, slipping into the last scrap of silk fabric between them. His fingers found her clit, thumb circling until she was arching up, clutching his shoulders.

"You like that?" His breath was like hot gravel against her skin. "Say it. Don't hide from me."

"Yes, baby!" she gasped, shameless now as her hips moved with ecstasy. "I fucking love it."

Who was she right now? Letting him pull sounds from her just by command. And the sick truth? She wanted more.

"Good girl. I want you to say my name every time I get you there."

When his fingers slid inside her, curling deep, she nearly shattered. He worked her slowly, steadily, until she was shaking uncontrollably, then pulled them out, stripping her bare.

"Not yet—not like that," he panted, lowering himself. "I need to taste you."

He pulled her legs over his shoulders, lifting her hips to his face.

The first flick of his tongue across her pearl dragged a whimper from her, her hips jerking. Then he gorged.

"Shit," he groaned against her, his voice vibrating through her clit. "Sweetest pussy I've ever tasted. Cum for me, Autumn. Don't hold back, baby."

Her whole body clenched at the command as he licked, then sucked, then licked again, a relentless, greedy rhythm that overloaded her senses, short-circuiting thought itself.

No man had ever told her what to do with her pleasure.

And she was loving it.

The ecstasy was insane. Her fingers gripped his locs, her cries of unabashed euphoria echoing through the room.

"You're gonna make me cum," she breathed, her body climbing to crescendos unknown before as her legs tightened around his neck.

He pulled back, face slick, eyes dark with need.

"Nah, not yet," he rasped. "I need to be inside you when you let go."

He moved up her body, lying on top of her with a controlled gentleness.

Then he was off her, a blur of rough, urgent motion as he tugged his jeans off. They hit the floor a second later.

When he slid inside her, a single, shared gasp tore from both their throats. For a moment, neither of them moved, rocked by the sudden, absolute pleasure of their joining.

"Fuck," he growled into her neck, his voice wrecked. "So tight... so damn perfect. You're gonna kill me, baby."

Her walls instinctively clenched around him, pulling him in further.

He started to move, in and out, slow at first; then harder, each thrust going deeper, until she was clawing at his back.

"Say my name." His voice was a husky command in her ear.

"Amir," she cried out, choking on the sound.

"Louder." His hips slammed forward as he drove even deeper and precisely, hitting that upper wall.

This man was breaking her open, talking her through every point like he knew her better than she knew herself. And she wanted every filthy second of it.

"Ohhhhh fuck... Amir!" she shouted as she crested, so loud she was afraid the whole block might hear.

"Shit... that's it," he groaned as his hips moved rhythmically, and he strained to hold back from releasing. "Now let go for me. Cum on this dick, baby. Give it all to me."

That was it—she was done for. Her body shuddered, the orgasm ripping through her so violently she screamed his name over and over, her walls milking him until he broke too, his body seizing, a single, guttural roar of her name tearing from his throat.

When he collapsed on top of her, shaking, she realized her world had just split wide open.

"Damn, baby," he whispered, his voice wracked, trembling as he pushed in one last time. "Feels like I've finally come home."

As the heat simmered, they lay with limbs intertwined, chests heaving, their mingled scents clinging to the air.

Regret had no room to breathe in this moment. There was no shame.

Only the profound, grounding weight of what they had just become to each other.

And the echoing, earth-shattering possibility of everything it might mean.

* * *

THE SHOP WAS QUIET, cloaked in the hush of dawn. A low hum came from the fridge behind the counter, and somewhere near the entrance, the wall clock ticked in steady defiance of suspended time.

They lay tangled on the couch, bodies still warm, skin cooling slowly in the open air. Autumn rested her cheek against Amir's chest, rising and falling with the rhythm of his breathing. She could feel his heartbeat beneath her fingertips.

His arm was draped around her back, palm pressed gently between her shoulder blades, like he didn't want to let go just yet.

For a long moment, neither of them spoke.

Then Autumn broke the silence.

"A crusty-ass card?" she grinned, lifting her head slightly.

They burst into laughter.

When it softened into quiet smiles, Amir murmured, "I've been crazy about you since that first time I came to see you in Atlanta."

Autumn didn't respond; she just let the words settle.

"I didn't want to be," he added quietly. "Wasn't even looking at you like that back then. Shit, we were friends. And I'd finally gotten over Asia. But something changed. I saw you standing in your apartment, hair wrapped up, wearing that old college hoodie, and I don't know..."

He trailed off, staring at the ceiling like it might offer the rest of his thoughts. "You were different. Maybe I was, too. But I felt something. And it scared the shit out of me."

Autumn swallowed. Her heart beat a little faster, but she stayed still, letting him continue.

"And when we kissed later that night..." He paused, and she felt the rumble in his chest as he took a deep, shaky breath. "Man. It was all over for me."

He gently brushed his fingers across her brow, like tracing the memory.

"When I realized it wasn't just a moment, that I couldn't shake it, I tried to smother it. I'd tell myself it was just grief messing with my head because of our connection to Asia. Then I'd see you again. And those feelings would come right back."

He sighed and kissed the top of her head.

"When you married Chris, I really was happy for you. You deserved happiness. But it hurt... more than I expected. I figured whatever it was I was feeling would fade. Life would move on. And for a while, it did."

She shifted slightly, curling closer into his arms. He exhaled, a deep, comfortable sound.

"But when you got divorced, it was like my heart picked up where it left off. No questions asked. Just opened the door and let all those old feelings back in."

A soft chuckle escaped his lips.

"When you said you were moving back here, I told myself I'd finally be real with you. Say how I felt. Let the cards fall where they may. And then..."

He shook his head, smiling ruefully at the memory.

"You stepped out that car and I almost folded right then and there. Hair all over the place, looking tired as ever. I could've wrapped you up and never let go. But your hug? It was kinda loose. Not even polite. And I thought... damn. Maybe she's not as happy to see me as I am to see her. So, I chickened out. Again."

Autumn stayed silent, letting him unload the weight he'd clearly been carrying.

"Then the lake happened." His voice dipped into something more fragile. "I asked if you ever thought about us getting together, and you said Asia would haunt us..."

He paused, then swallowed hard.

"That messed me up, Aut," he admitted, his voice rough. "It wasn't just the rejection. It was that you made my feelings for you feel... dirty. Like I was dishonoring her memory just by having them."

Autumn lifted her head slightly, eyes searching his face. "I didn't mean it like that," she said, her voice an earnest admission. "I was scared. I felt guilty. And confused as hell."

He gave her a small nod. "I get it. But that moment shut me down. I started thinking, maybe I was just imagining everything. That it was always just me."

She exhaled hard through her nose. "Trust and believe. It wasn't just you."

His brows lifted slightly.

"I was scared for it to be real because it made everything more complicated," she admitted, the words feeling foreign and freeing all at once. "I kept thinking about our history, about Asia. The friendship we've built since we were little kids. You're the godfather to my children. I was afraid of breaking this beautiful thing we have."

She sighed.

"But eventually the feelings caught up to me, and I could no longer outrun them."

Their eyes met, and in that shared gaze, every defense dissolved. There was no more pretense, no more hiding. Just the undeniable truth between them.

They had finally crossed the line.

And this time, they were both standing on the same side of it.

31

AIN'T NO HALF-STEPPING

They didn't say much as they left the coffeehouse. Autumn locked the door, her movements slow, her body still trying to catch up with the emotional whiplash of the last few hours. Beside her, Amir adjusted the strap of his bag, his silence as heavy as her own.

"You good?" he asked for the umpteenth time, like he needed to keep checking the temperature.

She nodded, though it was more reflex than truth. A placeholder until she could figure out what 'good' even meant. "Yeah. I just need to grab a shower and change clothes. I'll come by your place after."

Amir hesitated, then gave a small nod of his own. "I'll be there."

They lingered on the sidewalk for a second, the air between them thick, charged with the invisible residue of everything that had happened, and everything that still needed to be said. There was no kiss. No dramatic goodbye.

He saw her to her car. Made sure she buckled up, then smiled and walked away. Autumn watched him head off down the block toward his jeep, his frame slowly shrinking in the distance. She exhaled hard, the coolness of morning doing nothing to settle the warmth still tingling beneath her skin.

The short drive home stretched into an eternity. Her mind was a war zone, thoughts coming in sharp, painful volleys.

His hands.

The raw heat in his eyes.

The way he said her name. The way he said... everything.

The guilt.

The want.

The goddamn guilt!

She cranked the radio until the speakers crackled, as if the furious lyrics of Kendrick Lamar's *TV Off* could drown out the noise in her own head.

Her fingers tapped the steering wheel in time with the beat; one strike for guilt, one for desire, one for the panic setting in.

They should be awakening to a lazy morning in his apartment, the smell of fried bacon and coffee filling the air. They should be laughing about all the clues they'd missed for more than a decade before tumbling back into bed, getting reacquainted, and learning the new landscape of their old friendship.

But that was the fantasy.

This was the messy reality. Her, alone in her car, with nothing but a Kendrick Lamar beat and the sharp sting of the emotional conflict that always arrives with the morning sun.

When she pulled in front of Mia's house, the tires gave a screech that matched her nerves. She stepped inside quietly, letting the door click shut behind her. Morning light filtered through sheer curtains, casting long strips of gold across the hardwood floor.

The silence wrapped around her like a soft shroud, a moment of deceptive peace. And then her thoughts returned, rushing back in to fill the quiet with a familiar, anxious noise.

On autopilot, she climbed the stairs, grabbed a towel, and headed into the bathroom. The shower knobs squeaked, and as the water warmed, she went and planted her palms on the sink, staring at her own reflection in the mirror.

Her eyes were wide, as if startled. Lips slightly parted. She looked altered. Not just post-glow but cracked wide open. Something had shifted, and not just in her body.

Amir's confession replayed in her mind.

"I've been crazy about you since that first time I came to see you in Atlanta."

He said it scared him. And the truth was, it scared her, too. Because that attraction had never been one-way.

But was it really that simple? Was it ever only "attraction"? The thought slammed into her, so sharp and undeniable it felt like a physical assault. She scrambled into the shower, needing the roar of water to drown out the sudden, deafening truth in her own head.

She closed her eyes and let her mind drift back to something her therapist had said months ago.

"I'm going to hit you with something else that you may not receive," she'd told her after blindsiding her with the observation about her true feelings. *"I think you've been crazy about him for a long time, Autumn. That first moment of genuine attraction, in your college apartment? It sealed something in your heart. But you couldn't admit it, so you kept finding ways to avoid it. Asia became your shield. Chris became your sabotage."*

Back then, the words had felt like a wild, outlandish guess. Now, standing under the scalding water, they landed with the chilling, undeniable weight of prophecy.

She pressed her palms against the cool tile, letting the hot water pound across her back as if it could singe the truth away. But it couldn't. The realization stayed, sharp and stunning in all its painful glory, leaving her reeling.

I've been afraid of my true feelings all this time.

Not because I didn't want them.

But because I was scared they would cost me something sacred.

My loyalty to her.

My friendship with him.

When she stepped out, her body was cleansed, but her emotions were still a chaotic mess.

One thing, though, was clear.

She couldn't run anymore.

Not from Amir.

And definitely not from herself.

When she wrapped herself in a towel, she heard the ping of a FaceTime call. Jordan's face lit up on her screen.

"Hey, Mama! We saw the TikTok video for the launch party. You got over a million views. You famous now!" his voice rang out, full of excitement. Behind him, Layla chimed in with her own hype.

Autumn's laugh was soft, easing the tension in her chest as she sank onto the bed, the warmth of her children's excitement centering her. "I'm not famous, baby. Just grateful."

They talked for a few more minutes—jokes, hugs, "we miss you," and "Disney is amazing!"—before they signed off with kisses blown through the screen.

As she set the phone down, a knock came at the bedroom door.

"Come on in, sis," she said, applying shea butter lotion to her arms.

"You stayed out celebrating all night, huh?" Mia teased, leaning against the doorframe with a sly grin. "Hooked up with Ekon again?"

Autumn paused, then let out a shaky exhale.

"No," she breathed, the word barely audible. "That was one time, and it was a mistake." After a brief pause, "I was with Amir." She glanced upward cautiously. Saying it aloud felt like pulling the pin from a grenade she'd been holding for years.

Mia's smirk vanished. She blinked hard. Then her eyes widened into saucers. "Wait—*Amir*-Amir?! Ohhhhh shiiiiiit!" She threw a hand up in the air. "It's about damn time!"

Autumn sighed heavily, rubbing lotion on her feet.

"Girl, you know I gotta ask," Mia said, moving into the room with excitement and sitting on the bed, her voice lowering to a conspiratorial whisper. "Was it good?"

Autumn smiled despite herself, a slow, soft expression that was full of memory. "It was more than good," she admitted, then gave her sister a knowing look. "He's a talker."

Mia's eyes bulged and her mouth gaped, like she'd been given the juiciest piece of gossip. "*Amir? A talker?*" Her expression quickly changed to one of mischievous envy. "Umph, that's hot as hell."

"Girl, it was a three-alarm fire." Autumn's hands stilled, the lotion forgotten, her gaze drifting unfocused past her sister's shoulder. A slow, almost involuntary smile spread across her face as the memory replayed: the heat, his voice, the sheer force of him. "I mean, I've never experienced anything like him."

Mia's eyebrows raised. "Um, sis. You still here?" She laughed as she waved a hand in Autumn's face. "And, you know, you said *him*, and not *it*. Right?"

Autumn's brow raised, a question in her eyes.

Mia shook her head. "*It...* is just sex. But *him*, that's the man."

Autumn looked at her dubiously, trying to dismiss the words. She picked up the lotion bottle again, but her movements felt suddenly stiff, less certain.

"No, I'm serious," Mia insisted. "Ms. Jenkins told us at the shop one day that no matter how many times she had sex, she's only made love once. And that was with the man who literally poured everything into her. His body, his heart, and his soul. She said it was a different kind of feeling and no one else had even come close."

She stared just beyond Autumn, shaking her head in wonderment. "I always wanted to know what that felt like."

"Well, don't get too excited," Autumn warned. "We still need to figure this out."

But even as she said it, she wasn't sure if her heart was bracing for complication or already surrendering to the inevitable.

* * *

AUTUMN STOOD outside Amir's apartment building, the simple act of pressing the buzzer feeling monumental. Her stomach was in knots, her breathing shallow. The door clicked without preamble, and she stepped inside, clutching her bag like it might anchor her. Before she reached his unit, she steeled her nerves.

This is Amir, dammit! And you are not in high school. Suck it up, Buttercup!

He swung the door open, a crooked smile softening his features. Barefoot in casual shorts and a snug t-shirt, spatula dangling loosely in his hand, he exuded a quiet ease that tugged at Autumn's thudding heart.

Focus, she told herself. *You can't get lost.*

"Hope you're hungry," he said, stepping aside to let her in.

The apartment smelled like fresh coffee and bacon. The vibe was warm and familiar. It was so him.

She smiled faintly, glancing around the space. It was always clean, minimal, and lived-in. Cozy in a way that made her want to let her guard down. She had to fight the dangerous urge to just sink onto his couch and forget the complicated reality waiting on the other side of his door.

Is this how Moet feels when she's here?

The thought slipped in before she could block it. She shook her head gently, as if trying to toss it loose.

"I need coffee more than food," she admitted, setting her bag down by the door. "But it smells amazing in here."

Each tranquil movement—him pouring coffee, her buttering toast—was laden with the tension of conversations not yet had, and the fragile anticipation of more honesty waiting to break through.

Finally, after they had been seated a while, their plates only half-touched, Autumn spoke.

"I've been thinking," she said softly. "About what you said. About Asia. About us."

Amir finished chewing, then deliberately set his napkin down on the edge of his plate. His gaze locked onto hers, the easy morning vibe replaced by a quiet, focused intensity. "Okay."

Autumn took a breath. "I've carried her memory in my heart and ruled much of my life by the dreams we set," she admitted. "I didn't even realize that until recently. I have been very careful, overly so, I think, when it came to you. I put you in this box and locked it with a moral code. Like, if I crossed certain lines, I'd lose her all over again." Her eyes shimmered. "But I've also used her memory and our friendship as a barrier. Against feelings. Against possibilities."

"Against me?" he asked gently.

She didn't answer right away. "Maybe," she conceded, toying with a piece of toast.

He leaned forward, forearms resting on the table, his eyes searching hers. "Or maybe you've just been afraid. Not necessarily of dishonoring her memory, but of what happens when you let your heart want something again."

She closed her eyes, a sharp intake of breath betraying how precisely his words had just landed.

"I get it, Autumn," he said, his voice softening. "Chris did a number on you back then. That kind of betrayal, hell, it builds walls you don't even realize are there until someone's on the other side, knocking."

Her eyes fluttered open, meeting his steady gaze.

He paused, his own gaze thoughtful. "So let me ask you this. Are you truly honoring Asia's memory by keeping yourself locked away? Or is hiding behind that loyalty just easier than facing the truth about what you feel for me?"

The question was a silent detonation in the middle of Amir's kitchen, but it wasn't the first time she'd heard it. In fact, it had been on repeat ever since she set foot in Chicago.

"So... you think I've been hiding, too, huh?" She shook her head. "Using Asia and Chris as a shield?"

"I think," he said gently, "you've been more loyal to pain, so you don't have to risk falling in love again."

She exhaled, sharp but soft. "Damn. I think I'm getting tired of hearing the same thing."

"But is it untrue?"

Her eyes met his, but she didn't answer his question.

He propped his elbows on the table, chin resting on his folded hands. "So now what?"

"Now," she sighed, "I'm still scared. But I'm not walking around blind anymore."

For a few minutes, they sat, neither speaking, both settling into that strange space where familiarity and uncertainty coexist.

"What about Moet?" she asked finally. "What does this mean for you and her?"

Amir rubbed the back of his neck. "That's on me. I like her. A lot. She's smart, funny, sharp as hell. But I wasn't honest with myself. Or her."

Autumn tilted her head. "How so?"

"I never stopped wanting you," he admitted.

The words hit, straightforward, and for a second, her own heartbeat felt impossibly loud in the stillness of the kitchen.

"Even when I tried. After the lake, I thought there was no hope for us. Moet's been asking me out for a while, so I went for it. But we're not aligned. Not just because of my feelings for you. She doesn't want kids. We... just don't want the same things."

"You think she knows?"

"She knows how I feel about everything... except you. However, I think she suspects," he admitted. "But I'm gonna talk to her tonight. I owe her that much."

Autumn swallowed the lump in her throat. Then, she cautioned, "I'm not saying I know what this is between us. Or where it's going."

"I'm not asking you to," he said. "I'm just asking you not to run from it."

Their eyes met. No matter what, it felt good to have no more pretenses. To no longer hide behind what-ifs and memories.

An hour later, the dishes were cleared. The coffee had gone lukewarm. And yet, neither of them made a move to break the spell, to let the real world and all its complications rush back in.

Autumn sat with one leg tucked under her, nursing the last sip in her mug like it held answers.

Amir leaned back against the sink, arms crossed, watching her in that quiet way he did when his thoughts were brewing under the surface.

She stood and walked toward the sink to put her mug in. When she reached him, he didn't hesitate. That strong arm slid around her waist like it belonged there, anchoring her in the curve of his body.

He dipped his head and kissed her, soft, assured, unhurried. Unlike the raw urgency from the night before, this kiss held patience, an unspoken promise.

She leaned into it, swept away by the feeling of him. Her fingers pressed lightly into his chest, the warmth of him sinking into her. When she pulled back, it was reluctant, like easing a pacifier from a baby who'd finally stopped crying.

But she had to.

She needed her thoughts clear, her heart steady. No blurring lines, not when clarity was finally in reach. She still needed to figure out what last night meant.

And Amir had a woman.

That alone was another layer of complication she wasn't prepared to deal with.

"I should probably go," she murmured.

He nodded, though his hand lingered at her waist.

"Okay."

The raw intensity still burning in his eyes sent an immediate echo of last night's fire licking up her spine, and it took everything she had not to melt right there against his chest.

"I'm not running."

"I know," he said, tucking a curl behind her ear.

She looked at him squarely, her voice steady but soft. "I need to be sure. That what we're stepping into is real. Not just a release of years of what-ifs, timing that never lined up, and all that jazz. We can't build on nostalgia, or even longing. I want us to build on truth."

His jaw flexed once, but then he nodded.

"I get that."

They stood there, only a breath between them. No longer just friends. Not officially lovers. Something in between. Something... becoming.

"I can't do halfway," she added. "Not with you."

Amir leaned in closer, brushing a thumb gently across her cheek. "Then we won't."

His voice was quiet, but firm. "Whatever this is, we'll figure it out. No more hiding. No half-stepping."

She smiled; the kind that pushed tears into the corners of her eyes.

When he walked her to the door, she stopped with her hand on the knob. "This isn't a pause," she promised.

Amir nodded. "No, it's not. It's just the part where we stop pretending."

He walked with her to her car, reaching his head into the window when she rolled it down. "I'll call you tonight," he said, then kissed her, a soft touch of his tongue to hers that sent a warm hum spreading low in her belly.

When she opened her eyes, lips still puckered, he'd already pulled back and was watching her, a beautiful smile plastered on his face.

"Go home before I snatch you out this car, woman," he teased, the restraint in his voice betraying him.

She smiled, started the engine, then drove away as he jogged back to the building.

The ride home was quiet.

But for once, the silence wasn't a void being filled with anxiety.

It was a quiet space where she finally felt comfort.

32

BAGGAGE CLAIM

ia's living room was alive with laughter and layered voices when Autumn walked in. The scent of lavender incense lingered in the air, soft music humming low in the background. It was a playlist curated for soul-work, all honeyed vocals and gentle bass lines.

Fourteen women were already gathered in a tight circle. Pillows, blankets, and half-empty tea mugs were scattered across the floor like a patchwork of comfort and courage. The Bag Lady sessions had grown. What started with four had blossomed into a therapeutic movement of fifteen.

Autumn took her seat slowly, folding her legs beneath her and wrapping her arms around her knees. Her smile was faint. She felt like she was in a bubble, the camaraderie of the other women sounding distant, their mirth a frequency she couldn't match. Her own secret was a heavy, buzzing thing in her heart and mind.

Jasmine caught the heaviness in her eyes. "Are you okay?"

She started to nod yes, but the movement felt like a lie. She took a breath, knowing this was not the environment for holding back. "I need to share something with the ladies."

The room shifted as the energy settled, ushering in a hush of readiness.

She exhaled, then stood and walked over to the long table where fifteen drawstring bags were sitting. Hers was the color of fall, a burned-orange silk sack that held four ten-pound sandbags, each labeled with a single word: "Loss," "Grief," "Heartache," and "Confusion."

She reached in, as was customary for the ladies when sharing their progress in the sessions, and pulled out the bag marked "Confusion," holding it up for the circle to see.

"It happened. Me and Amir."

There were gasps, a couple of wide eyes, and one exaggerated "Girl, when?" from the back of the circle.

Brianna and Josie clapped.

Autumn's gaze stayed fixed on the bag. "Two nights ago, after my opening ceremony ended. We didn't plan it. I didn't even know I felt all of that... not fully. But it was like everything that's ever been buried between us just came up all at once."

She lifted her head then, voice trembling but steady, and confessed, "I've avoided dealing with my grief for Asia. About what happened to her. Questioning why not me. And now," she said, her voice dropping, "I'm about to add guilt to this baggage. For even thinking I could ever look at Amir in that way, let alone sleep with him."

She walked to the end of the table and grabbed a blank sandbag and a marker. The ladies watched, a profound sadness in their collective gaze, as she wrote "Guilt" on it in large, black letters.

She moved back to her drawstring bag, holding the two sandbags together for a moment: confusion and guilt, a matched set of her own making. She placed them both inside with the others, pulled the drawstring tight, took a breath, and tried to lift it.

Her bicep strained, her arm shaking from the new, impossible weight, and she had to set it back down with a heavy thud that echoed in the quiet room.

Brianna leaned forward. "Oh, sis," she said softly, empathy creasing her brows. "That's an awful lot of baggage you're putting on yourself. Asia's been gone for what... sixteen years?"

Autumn nodded. "Yeah. But I told you before, grief has no clock. And guilt?" She let out a short, hollow chuckle. "That thing latches on like a leech, sucking away at your conscience."

Mia reached for her hand and squeezed it. "Sis, you're not wrong for feeling that way. That man has been in your life since y'all were nine years old. But it ain't betrayal if what y'all feel is born from truth. I mean, neither of you intentionally sought out the other. Circumstances happened, and it lit a spark that refuses to die. That much is obvious."

Autumn's shoulders relaxed a fraction at her sister's words. She desperately wanted to believe it was that simple.

Then the sharp click of a mug hitting a coaster cut through the supportive murmurs. "Mia, I hear you. But we can't act like lines don't matter," Londyn quipped. "Some things are sacred. Some people are off-limits. It ain't about what Asia would want now that she's gone. It's about the lines you respected when she was here. That loyalty doesn't just disappear."

Her words hit like a cold stone of reality, because it was the exact argument Autumn had been having with herself in those dark hours. A buzz of agreement went through the room, and her fleeting relief vanished.

She nodded, accepting the contradiction. "I know. That's why this is so hard. I'm not even sure what kind of woman this makes me. What kind of friend..."

There was a long pause.

"It makes you a woman who's still healing," Josie broke through the silence. "You're still human, sis. Still trying to figure out where love fits into all that pain. And that's okay."

Autumn wiped the tears from the corner of her eye. "I just... I don't want to build anything with Amir on guilt. Or confusion. I need to know it's real. That it's right."

Mia squeezed her hand again. "That's why you're here. To sort through it. And trust me, you are still a friend. A damn good one. Because you care. You're not ignoring it. You're facing it."

A chorus of "That's right" and "Mmm hmm" went around the circle, the women nodding, their voices a wave of affirmation that washed over her.

"I don't think you're dishonoring Asia at all," someone in the back called out. "You're still respecting your friendship, while trying to accept your own truth."

And for the first time since that night in the coffeehouse, Autumn let herself believe it might be possible to do both.

* * *

Later that day.

Autumn had just finished washing her face when her phone buzzed. The screen lit up with a name that made her lips twitch into something resembling a smile.

Ekon's gorgeous face flashed on the screen.

"Hey, buddy."

His voice was upbeat, smooth. "Hey, Beautiful. Was wondering if the boss lady's schedule could spare a little time for a humble fan."

She chuckled, easing onto her bed. "Oh, you are not just a fan, sir. You helped blow this whole thing up. Folks have been tagging me every day, saying they came in because they saw your livestream."

"That's what happens when you build something real. People wanna be part of it." He paused. "That's why I'm calling."

She leaned back against the headboard. "What's up?"

"I was thinking... do you ever celebrate your wins? Like really let yourself enjoy the moment?"

"I'm learning to," she said airily.

"Well, how about I help with that? Brunch. My treat. We'll toast to your coffeehouse and your future book signing tour. Because girl, you got a story to tell."

A quiet comfort settled over her. The offer was a lifeline, a return to something easy, fun, and uncomplicated. It was so tempting that she almost said yes reflexively.

But she couldn't. Not without being upfront. Although they were friends now, she wanted there to be no room for misunderstandings.

"There's something I should probably tell you first." She took a steadying breath. "Something happened between me and Amir." She paused, then said, "We slept together, the night of the opening."

The silence on the other end was a dead-air vacuum that felt more damning than a scream.

The tension caught Autumn off guard, and she squeezed her eyes shut, her knuckles straining as she gripped the phone.

When Ekon finally spoke, all the warmth had been leached from his voice, leaving it cold and flat. "With Amir."

He wasn't asking a question. He was casting a verdict.

She swallowed. That voice, so smooth before, now felt like gravel dragging across her skin.

"Yeah..." Her affirmation was laced with confusion over his dramatic reaction.

Another moment of silence, then a short, brittle laugh crackled through the phone. "Wow. Okay. Say less."

"Ekon—" she started, but he cut her off.

"No, it's cool. I see it now. I guess I always knew what my role was here." The words were clipped, sharp.

"Wait... It wasn't like that," she tried, sitting up straight. "You and I were friends after the breakup; I never hinted at anything different. And this thing with me and Amir... It's always been complicated."

"Was it? Or was it simple? Let me get this straight." His voice took on a raw, biting edge. "I flew you out to LA. You saw some things you didn't like, and I respected that. We pulled back. But we started talking again. I'm thinking something is building here.

I'm stepping up to help you launch your dream, and now I'm calling to take you out to celebrate *your* win. And this whole time... I was just the opening act? The understudy until the headliner decided to show up?"

Autumn's heart lurched with a fresh wave of remorse. "No! You were never that."

"Then what was I, Autumn?" he demanded, his voice dropping, the sarcastic tone replaced by something callous and genuinely wounded. "The fun guy? The one you just slept with when the mood hit? Because it damn sure feels like I was just the convenient one, the one you called when the man you really wanted was busy with his girlfriend."

The accusation was a gut punch. Autumn flinched, physically recoiling from the phone as if it had burned her. "That's not fair, and you know it. You and I were friends—"

"You know what's not fair? You told me you weren't looking for anything serious. Was that ever true? Or was it code for 'not with you' because you were waiting for him?"

Her own anger flared. "I was being honest!" she shot back, her voice rising. "I *wasn't* looking for anything serious—"

"But you obviously found it anyway!" he yelled, the sound distorted through the small speaker. "Just not with the man who was actually showing up, putting in the time. You found it with the ghost from your past. The fucking 'what if'. How the hell is that supposed to make me feel?"

There was a brief, tense-filled silence as she tried to reconcile where things got lost. "I'm so sorry, Ekon," she whispered, the fight draining out of her. "I didn't know you were catching feelings for me like that. I never meant to hurt you."

He released a long, heavy sigh, the sound of a man trying to wrestle his anger back into its cage. "Yeah, well. You did. I knew shit felt off that day at the youth center when I first met you. Talkin' bout y'all was just friends." A rueful grunt came through the line. "See, that's what happens when a brotha puts himself out there."

She didn't respond. The silence between them had the gravity of a black hole, pulling everything into it.

Then, he muttered, "Look, I wish you the best. For real. Him too. He's a good dude."

The shift to resignation was almost as bad as the anger. She let his words breathe, then asked timidly, "So... we're good?"

There was a humorless scoff. "Hell no, Autumn. We're not 'good.' I'm not gonna be your friend. I'm not gonna be your backup plan for when things get complicated. I don't play those games."

"Ekon, wait..." The words were a desperate plea.

"Nah. I gotta go." His voice was cool, final. "You go be with your man. Just do me a favor. Don't call me again unless it's for a business plug. We're done here."

The line went dead, the silence that followed leaving an icy void in its place.

* * *

THE SHOP HAD BEEN BUZZING for days, and she'd been working non-stop; blending and brewing, greeting customers, mentoring her teenage barista, smiling for photos, checking the numbers. It felt good to be walking in her purpose, to have built something from scratch and see people show up for it.

She should've been basking in the glow of her success, letting it wash over her like an earned reward.

But she missed him.

Not just romantically.

In a bone-deep, soul-stirring way.

When things got quiet, when the espresso machines weren't hissing and no one was asking for another chai latte with oat milk, Amir's face would appear in her mind's eye, uninvited.

The easy way he grinned. The sound of his laugh.

The intrusion wasn't loud, just a constant, quiet hum that would intermingle with the noise of her new life.

Autumn exhaled, her body sinking deeper into the mattress. Her fingers hovered over her phone.

She opened her photos and scrolled.

There he was.

It was a snapshot from the youth center picnic during spring break. He was crouched between Jordan and Layla, arms flung wide, flashing a big, goofy grin. Layla was mid-eye roll, Jordan cheesing like he just won a trophy. Amir looked carefree. Joyful.

He wore a ribbed tank top and jeans. The sunlight had hit his skin just right that day, casting a warm bronze glow over the curve of his shoulders. His locs were pulled back, but a few tendrils had escaped, framing his face like the perfect portrait. She loved his new beard growth—full, precise, and somehow both rugged and neatly groomed.

But it wasn't just the outer package.

She pinched the screen, zooming in on his face. There was a tenderness in his eyes, even in play. The kind of quiet strength that held space for everyone around him. He wasn't just handsome. He was safe, solid like oak.

Autumn let the image linger, staring at it until her vision blurred. Her heart gave a subtle knock against her ribs.

Yeah... she was in trouble.

She hadn't seen him. Not since that talk in his kitchen a few days ago. And he hadn't pressed her, for which she was grateful. Besides, he still had his own thing to figure out with Moet.

But the ache in her chest wasn't letting up. She had told herself she needed time. That space was wisdom.

But space wasn't quiet. It was loud with memories.

And she was tired of pretending the silence didn't hurt.

She switched to the Messages app. Her fingers moved before her overthinking could catch up.

AUTUMN

Can we talk?

She stared at the words for a long moment before hitting send.

The bubble disappeared. Message delivered.

The thought didn't dawn until after it was too late: *what if he's with Moet right now?*

She dropped the phone on the nightstand, trying to still the nerves that had suddenly begun teeming.

It wasn't like this was new. They had crossed every line. Shared breath. Shared truths.

Shared skin.

But clarity sometimes came slower than passion.

Her phone buzzed.

She snatched it up, breath lodged halfway.

AMIR

Yeah. Come by.

A wave of relief, so potent it left her lightheaded, made her sink back against the pillows, her whole body suddenly feeling weightless.

Three little words.

And yet they carried so much weight.

She sat up and smoothed her hair back.

It was time.

Not for answers, maybe. But for movement.

At the very least, the first step toward whatever came next.

A few minutes later, Autumn was in front of the mirror, the bathroom still faintly fogged from her shower. A bead of water traced the curve of her shoulder as she wrapped herself in her plush robe, the cotton soft and worn from years of comfort.

She stared at her reflection in the mirror, a practice that had become common since her divorce. Except now, her features reflected the entire journey that had led her to this point.

Eyes that held questions. Lips that remembered kisses she hadn't planned.

What are you walking into?

She didn't know.

Her fingers moved on autopilot, twisting her hair up into a soft bun, pinning back the strands that framed her face. She kept her makeup light, just a thin layer of mascara, eyeliner, and lip gloss.

She padded into the closet and paused, her hand hovering over the hangers.

What do you even wear to a conversation that could change everything? And what, exactly, do you wear to meet the man who was once a childhood friend, but is now... so much more?

She didn't want anything too loud. At the same time, nothing too quiet.

She reached for a soft cream top that hugged her curves without calling attention to itself. Paired it with stretch jeans and her favorite open-toe sandals. It was comfortable and grounded.

As she dressed, her mind strayed, inevitably, back to that night. Amir's words echoed in her head. The feel of his body was still a warm, phantom weight against her own.

But it wasn't just about the heat they shared.

It was about the new space they were stepping into.

When she was done, she grabbed her bag and keys off the dresser and gave herself one last glance in the mirror.

"You're good," she whispered to her reflection. "Whatever this is... You can handle it."

Outside, the evening air was warm on her skin, fragrant with the scent of blooming jasmine from a neighbor's yard. She took one deep, steadying breath and jumped into her car.

The engine purred to life.

And with it, so did her resolve.

FALLING INTO FINALLY

When Autumn had arrived at his apartment, the tension was a thick, unspoken thing between them. He met her at the door before she could knock, his eyes searching hers, and simply said, "Let's go somewhere we can really talk." He'd grabbed his keys and driven them to the one place that held all their history.

The lakefront was quiet, just a few joggers in the distance, and a couple walking their dog. The golden wash of sunset stretched across the water like a sigh: soft, warm, unhurried. Amir had picked the perfect spot, low-key and familiar.

Autumn sat beside him on a big rock, hands folded loosely across her lap. She said little since they arrived, but he didn't push. He just waited, like he always did when the moment needed space.

She finally spoke, her voice subdued, but certain. "This place... this community. It broke me, and it built me."

Amir tilted his head toward her, an encouragement to continue.

"When I first came back to Ebondale, I felt like a failure. I'd lost my job, my confidence, my marriage. Hell, even my reflection didn't look like me anymore." She looked out at the lake. "But it gave me my voice back. It gave me space to fight for myself."

He nodded slowly. "I get that."

She was quiet again.

"Can I share something with you?" he asked, looking out into the horizon. When she nodded, he continued. "I became who I am because of the women in my life," he said. "My mother, before she died of cancer, told me to be the one to make a difference. Not allow my environment to make the difference in me.

Even Asia. She was my first mirror, showing me what it meant to love someone. But I was still a boy, just learning how to handle life."

He turned to look at Autumn fully now, his eyes reflecting the last light of day. "But you... You're the one who saw me grow up. Who saw me become a man. Falling in love with you didn't hit me all at once, Aut. It crept in, quietly, year by year, until it exploded. And when it did... It damn near crushed me."

Autumn's breath stopped.

Hearing him name it—*falling in love*—was too big, too direct. Her mind went blank, unable to process the sheer, stunning reality of the words.

He'd said it. He'd finally said it.

Her foundation was rocked. It was devastating, dizzying, and overwhelming, all at once.

"I'm scared," she admitted, her voice trembling.

Amir took her hand and pulled her to sit in front of him. He cradled her in his arms, and she let her body relax against his, the solid warmth of his chest a sudden, grounding reality. The fear didn't vanish, but it receded, muffled by his steady presence.

"I know. I'd be lying if I said I wasn't."

"I've never had to tread a relationship this carefully," she said. "Because this? It's not just about being a couple. This is history. And it's too important to get wrong."

"Agreed. Because if we mess this up, there's no easy return."

They sat in the pause, letting the weight of that truth settle around them like dusk. A soft wave of water crested on the rocks below, the sound of a thousand tiny bubbles popping as the foam dissolved.

"I ended things with Moet," he said, breaking the silence. "I told her the truth. That my heart's somewhere else."

Autumn looked out at the vastness of the lake, unable to tell where the horizon ended and the sky began.

"How did that go?" she asked ruefully, thinking back on Ekon's reaction.

"About as good as you'd expect," he rested his chin on her shoulder. "She uh... she told me that she loved me..."

Autumn could hear him struggle to get the words out. She squeezed his hands gently.

He cleared his throat, then continued. "She told me she loved me and thought we were heading somewhere. Said she'd even started liking the idea of wanting children."

Autumn glanced back at him, her brows lifting, a sharp pang of secondhand guilt twisting in her gut. She knew exactly what that kind of rejection felt like.

"So yes, she was hurt," he chuckled without humor, an edge to his voice that said he was angry at himself. "But she wasn't surprised," he paused. "She said something that stuck with me, though. She said, 'You've kept your heart locked away, waiting for the one person who held the key. You don't run from love like that. You run to it.'"

Autumn's stomach clenched.

The key.

Had she been holding it all this time without even knowing? Or worse, knowing and pretending it was for a different lock entirely?

"I feel so bad for her," she finally said. "Because I could tell she was really into you."

"Yeah," he acknowledged with a sigh. "But I don't regret my choices, or my decision." He kissed Autumn's neck. "I do regret hurting her, though."

She pulled back from his embrace just enough to turn her body and face him, needing to see his eyes.

"So. It's you and me then?" she asked.

"You and me," he affirmed, his gaze locking with hers.

She reached for his hand, her fingers lacing through his. The touch wasn't a thrill or a spark. It was solid like a current.

Because... *damn.*

After a lifetime of maybes, this felt like a finally.

And that hit different.

They settled into a peaceful intimacy for a few moments, the only sounds the gentle lapping of Lake Michigan against the shore and the distant hum of traffic on Lake Shore Drive. The sky above was a deep indigo, and the moon cast a shimmering silver path across the dark water.

Then Autumn broke the stillness, the corners of her mouth already lifting as she moved to sit next to him, hip to hip.

"Soooo..." she bumped his shoulder with a smirk. "Does this mean we're actually dating?"

"Sounds like it," Amir agreed, his silhouette framed by the glittering city skyline behind him. "Feels like it too."

A soft laugh escaped her, a sound of pure, unburdened relief. "This feels different."

"Because it is," he said. "It's us."

Autumn leaned her head on his shoulder. "So, what now?"

He reached down, his calloused fingers lacing through hers, his warmth a stark contrast to the cool night air. "Now, we try. But we do it right."

She nodded slowly. "We protect the friendship. If this starts pulling us apart instead of bringing us closer—"

"We pause," he interjected, finishing her thought. "We check in. And if we gotta step back, then that's what we do."

Her eyes flicked up to meet his. "No anger. No shutting down. Just honesty."

"Always."

A shared exhale stuttered between them, the sound lost to the gentle lapping of the waves. The tension of the last few days finally drained away, leaving a quiet, almost fragile peace in its place.

Amir's smirk returned, the familiar, easy one that crinkled the corners of his eyes. "So... I guess I'm your mans now."

Autumn felt a small, genuine laugh bubble up in her chest. She gave him a playful, teasing shove. "Guess so. Should we get matching varsity jackets or something?"

"I'm down. Yours can say 'I Bagged Him,' and mine'll say 'I Folded.'"

She laughed, the sound easy and light, as she leaned into his side. "You're such a fool."

"But I'm *your* fool now," he teased, breath warm against her ear as he wrapped an arm around her, pulling her close. He gently mussed her bun, adding a dramatic, pseudo karate-style "Bwaah!"

She rolled her eyes. "You really can't help yourself."

"But apparently you like it, though."

"Apparently I do," she laughed again, smiling harder against his shoulder. They fell into an easy silence, just listening to the lake, his chin resting gently on her head.

Then, a new thought surfaced. "We should probably tell the kids."

Amir sighed with a dramatic groan. "You know Jordan's about to make it a whole thing. I'm gonna owe that boy money. He bet me twenty dollars that we'd be 'going together'."

"Layla too!" Autumn laughed. "You ready for this?"

"Let's do it."

Autumn pulled out her phone, the bright screen a small, intimate bubble of light in the darkness. The kids' faces popped up quickly, split between Layla sprawled on the couch in her bonnet, and Jordan mid-snack, the crinkling of his Takis bag audible through the speaker.

"Hey, y'all," Autumn chimed.

"Where you at?" Layla asked, squinting. "It's dark. Are you outside?"

Jordan leaned closer to the screen. "Is that Amir next to you?"

Autumn cleared her throat, a sudden, nervous flutter starting in her stomach. "Yes, and yes. Okay, so we wanted to tell you something."

Layla immediately sat up, her eyes going wide. "Are y'all going together? Because I totally knew it."

Jordan blinked. "Wait, for real? You and Amir?"

Autumn's jaw went slack. She and Amir exchanged a quick, stunned, almost-laughing look over the phone, a silent "Are they for real?" passing between them.

Amir jumped in, a wide grin on his face as he looked into the camera at Layla. "You've been spying on us, haven't you, baby girl?" Then he looked at Jordan. "Yep, lil homie. It's official. I'm ya mama's boyfriend."

Layla gasped and squealed. "I knew it! I told you, Jordan!"

Jordan grinned widely. "This is so cool!"

Layla clapped like it was Christmas. "Does this mean we can all do family vacations now? I want matching shirts!"

Autumn pressed a hand to her chest. The sheer joy of her kids—the one thing she'd been afraid of complicating—was so pure, it almost made her dizzy with relief.

"Y'all love matching stuff, don't ya?"Amir chuckled, his voice thick with his own emotion.

"I love this so much! OMG, Auntie Mia's gonna pass out. I have to call her!"

"No, ma'am," Autumn warned, finally finding her voice. "Let us breathe for two seconds before we hit the group chat."

"But this is big!" Layla beamed. "Y'all are like... Beyonce and Jay Z!"

Amir laughed, throwing his head back. "Wow, thanks, baby girl. You hear that, Autumn? We're like royalty."

Jordan nodded. "Just don't get weird about it. Like kissing all the time or slow dancing to old people music."

Autumn cackled, a real belly-laugh this time. Her chest felt achingly full, a kind of joy so potent it was almost scary. "Noted."

"Oh, and you owe me twenty dollars, Uncle Amir!"

"I thought you woulda forgotten that, my guy..."

"Nope! Gimme my muh-nay," Jordan sang, doing a crazy dance in the camera.

They said their I love you's and ended the call, the screen going black on Layla and Jordan's still-giddy, laughing faces.

In the sudden quiet that followed, Autumn turned to Amir. He was already watching her, a soft, unreadable expression on his face, illuminated by the glow of her phone screen. In his eyes, she saw the reflection of her own smile.

A sudden exuberance filled her chest. Gratitude, yes, but also just the simple, staggering weight of what was finally real.

He smiled. "So we passed the first test."

She leaned her head back against his shoulder, letting his solid presence hold her. The rough-but-soft texture of his hoodie was a familiar comfort against her cheek. "Now all we gotta do is figure out the rest," she murmured.

He kissed her forehead, his lips warm and firm. His voice was a low, steady vibration against her ear.

"We've already started."

34

SOAKING IN THE SOFTNESS

Summer stretched its arms wide over Chicago, and Autumn stretched with it, softened by the sun, loosened by laughter, open in a way she hadn't felt in years. With the kids still in Atlanta for a few more weeks, she and Amir made an unspoken pact: to soak in every drop of this peace. This softness. This rare, uninterrupted "just us" time before real life came knocking again.

They needed every moment to connect in ways never explored; to learn the shape of this new intimacy, built on the foundation of their old friendship.

The air at the Taste of Chicago was thick with hickory smoke and the sound of sizzling Polish sausage. Music pulsed from a nearby stage, but they were in their own bubble, blending right in with the sea of sundresses, tank tops, and open-toed sandals.

They weaved through the crowd, a team now, no longer just friends, sharing a single, greasy egg roll, their fingers brushing. They sipped from the same cup of frozen sangria, his mouth following hers on the straw. When he playfully fed her a strawberry, the simple, public act of intimacy felt so new, so *teenage-y*, it was like something straight out of a summertime montage.

When their hands softly collided as he passed her a napkin, the touch lingered. A slow, deliberate warmth that was no longer a question, but a statement.

Their laughter was easy and loud, the sound of two people finally, fully unfettered.

Amir grasped her fingers as they passed a stand serving elote and jerk tacos. "Let's get some, this is my favorite."

Autumn raised a brow. "You trying to burn my mouth off? You know I don't do well with hot stuff."

"I beg to differ on the hot stuff…" He flashed a fake pompous grin, put his hands on his hips, and did a slow, over-the-top belly roll, wiggling his eyebrows at her.

Autumn laughed into a snort, rolling her eyes. "Boy, if you don't get that old-ass Magic Mike routine outta here."

"Listen, I'm just trying to rebuild your spice tolerance, Hotlanta. You're a Chicagoan again now. Atlanta made you soft."

She smirked with exaggerated confidence as he lifted the taco to her mouth. "Soft? Never that."

Amir's free hand hovered beneath it to catch the inevitable mess, because no real street taco stays intact. As a challenge, he took a generous bite. Despite the taco's eight-out-of-ten heat ranking, he didn't even flinch. He chewed like a champ, then nodded with exaggerated approval

Autumn took the bait, biting down with feigned bravery, and immediately regretted every life decision that led her to this moment.

"*Ohmygod*, why would you do this to me?" she gasped, already reaching for the lemon ice like it was holy water.

Amir polished off a second taco, licking his fingers like it was a delicacy sent from heaven. "You didn't read the fine print?" he teased with a mouthful of meat and tortilla. "It's called 'El Diablo' for a reason."

She fanned her mouth with her napkin, eyes bulging from the burn. "My tongue is throbbing like it has a heartbeat. Why does it have a heartbeat?!"

"Because it just met a real one," his relentless teasing continued, thumping his chest.

Autumn groaned dramatically, slumping against his shoulder, laughing despite the tingling on her lips. "You wild, bruh." She sucked on the sweetened ice to soothe the fire on her tongue.

And in that moment, leaning against him, she realized her shoulders weren't tight. She wasn't performing. She wasn't walking on eggshells, anticipating the next wrong move. This effortless, ridiculous joy was so natural... it felt like the first deep, clean breath she'd taken in more than a decade.

They collapsed in the shade near Buckingham Fountain, knees brushing, fingertips grazing as they passed lemon ice back and forth. The breeze carried snippets of music and laughter, but it all felt distant, like they were the only two people in the park, floating in their own quiet orbit.

They spent the next afternoon supporting the launch of a Black-owned bookstore in Hyde Park, fingers touching as they trailed the spines of memorable indie titles.

Amir found a poetry collection and read an excerpt right there in the aisle. His voice was low and tender, a private, intimate concert meant only for her.

"You trying to seduce me in public with words?" Autumn teased as she eased closer to him, a finger trailing down his chest.

"If it works, it works." The husk in his voice, that smile, that familiar twinkle in his eyes—it was all beautifully disarming.

Their new rhythm was seamless.

Some mornings, he showed up at the coffeehouse without any specific plans: just to sit across from her while she reviewed invoices, or to help taste-test pastries. Most times, his eyes said things over the rim of his cup that had nothing to do with coffee.

Some days, she'd meet him at the center, watching him coach teens through drills, feeling a whole new kind of attraction that made her stomach flutter.

The nights were a different kind of heat. It was a fevered exploration, driven by an insatiable hunger. It was stolen kisses while she was at the stove, his hand finding the small of her back as they passed in the hallway—just a constant, simmering need. Every time they made love, it was a new discovery, the intimacy eclipsing each moment before it.

It had all become real. This was no longer a flame sparked by nostalgia. They were growing into something purposeful. Deliberate.

And then, *real* threw a curveball.

After a candlelit dinner at a restaurant tucked in the heart of River

North, they strolled back to the car with the easy intimacy of two people finally walking the same path. The city hummed around them: cars passing, indistinguishable chatter spilling from rooftop patios.

Autumn's arm was looped through Amir's as they laughed about the old couple who sat at the table next to them, and kept whispering and pointing, convinced they were celebrities.

"Must be my beard," Amir joked. "Got that Morris Chestnut meets Coach Prime thing going on."

"Man, if you don't saddown somewhere with that ego," Autumn laughed, tugging his arm.

They walked into the parking lot, still feeling the buzz from the Pinot, when they suddenly stopped as if someone hit pause on the night.

Moet stood beside Amir's Jeep, arms crossed tightly, her stance suggesting she had something on her mind. The light from the overhead street lamp revealed the hard glare in her eyes.

Autumn felt Amir's body stiffen, and a sudden wave of tension settled like a stone in her stomach. Her first instinct was to pull away, and she began to loosen her grip on his arm. But he moved faster, grabbing her hand and threading his fingers through hers, anchoring her.

Moet didn't speak or move as they continued their slow approach toward the car. She just stared.

Autumn didn't know if it was instinct or history, but something told her this wasn't just a run-in.

This was a reckoning.

WHEN THE LEVEE BREAKS

The atmosphere in the lot was cool and still, carrying the distant hum of the city: a passing bus on a nearby street, the faint wail of a siren miles away. A single street lamp casting a lonely, orange glow over the dark asphalt, making their shadows long and distorted.

What is happening?

Autumn barely registered the words in her own mind. They came more like static, a gut-level alarm she couldn't silence. Her eyes locked on Moet's stance: Arms taut. A plastic bag with a to-go carton clutched in one hand, her chin jutted *out.*

She remembered Amir's heartbreaking admission from that night by the lake.

"She told me she loved me... she wasn't surprised."

But Autumn didn't expect to see that heartbreak wearing lip gloss and standing by his Jeep weeks later.

So why was she here, looking like a storm with nowhere else to strike?

Autumn's heart gave a hard, sudden slam in her chest, and her pulse rate instantly tripled. It wasn't guilt that drove its pace; it was the unfamiliarity of the situation.

She had spent years bumping into women who'd shared time and secrets with Chris behind her back. Women who looked at her with pity, with smugness, with everything but remorse.

This was her first time being on the other side of the equation. The first time she was the one holding the man someone else had once imagined forever with.

And it didn't feel triumphant.

It felt tight. Cautious. Loaded.

Still, there was one steady thing: Amir.

His fingers remained threaded through hers, his thumb stroking the center of her palm in a slow, grounding circle. Like he knew she was seconds away from spiraling and wanted to comfort her without words.

It helped.

Not entirely.

But enough.

They stopped just inches from the car. For a few tense seconds, no one spoke.

Moet's gaze dropped to their joined hands. Her top lip curled just slightly, a flash of pure disgust, before it was smoothed away. She let out a dry chuckle that didn't reach her eyes.

"Well, damn," she said, her voice sharp. "So, this is really happening."

Amir let out a soft, heavy sigh. His voice was low, deep with his own sadness. "Moet. What are you doing?"

Her eyes narrowed to slits.

"I came to get takeout when I saw your car in the lot. I was just about to leave you a note, but then I see you two strolling and holding hands like you're the main characters in some corny-ass rom-com."

Amir shook his head, his grip tightening on Autumn's hand as if to reassure her while he addressed his ex. "I know this isn't easy. I get it. But I told you about me and Autumn."

"Oh, you told me," she retorted, her laugh sharp now. "You told me you had feelings for her. And I understood that. I even felt sorry for y'all. But, actually seeing you two..."

She looked away, her head giving a single, weary dip and sway, as if the image was a painful betrayal.

"Seeing you two together hits a lil different," she continued, her eyes moist and her voice thick. "I respected when you said it wasn't right to keep seeing me, Amir. You wanted to be honest." She shifted her eyes to Autumn. "But honesty and decency aren't the same thing, are they?"

The words were a direct hit, aimed not at Amir, but squarely at Autumn, who drew in a quick, hissing breath through her teeth.

Moet took a step closer, and the name she evoked sucked the air out of Autumn's lungs. "Asia was your best friend, right? Y'all grew up together. And now you're laying up with her man like it's cute?"

Autumn's shoulders tensed, but she forced herself to remember this was a woman in pain. "Look, I know you're hurt. And I'm sorry about that. But Asia died years ago..." her voice was clipped but calm.

"Girl, I call bullshit," Moet barked, her eyes growing wide. "Y'all must've had a thing even before she died. This don't just happen overnight. You probably wanted him all along."

Her words were cutting deep; not because they were based in fact, but because somewhere, a small voice in her head whispered, *what if she's right?*

Amir stepped forward, his voice firm. "Okay, that's enough. Moet, you're out of pocket."

She turned on him, her voice louder, brittle. "No, I'm not. You broke up with me to chase a fantasy from your past, and that's your business. But don't act like this is innocent. Don't stand here holding hands with your dead girlfriend's best friend like it's some damn fairytale. Y'all look foul."

The sudden rage in Autumn's gut blazed in her eyes. The empathy she felt moments before was slowly evaporating. She took a small step forward, her own chin lifting even as she continued to respect the other woman's pain. "First of all," her voice was laced with a fraying patience. "You don't know our history. You don't know anything about any of us."

Moet didn't blink, holding Autumn's gaze, her voice chilling.

"I don't need a history lesson to spot desperation. You're not in love, you're in denial. Look at you," she pointed to Autumn's face. "I can see the guilt all in your eyes... as it should be."

Amir physically inserted himself, stepping between them with his hands halfway up, like a human barrier. His voice was a low, tight command. "Moet, go. Please."

Autumn stepped around him, her voice low but icy. "I'm trying to be nice, but don't mistake this volume for virtue. Asia was my sister. This guilt?

It's been my shadow since she's been gone for reasons that have nothing, and everything, to do with Amir."

Moet stood firm. "Bitch, please. You're just messy. And to stand here and call that poor woman your sister when you're here with her man? I don't care how long she's been dead, you oughtta be ashamed of your damn self."

Amir tried and failed to quiet the storm, but the rage was beyond him. He pointed his keys at the car and unlocked it, then tried to take Autumn by the elbow.

She could feel it building, like steam in a pressure cooker. Her therapist would tell her to breathe, to walk away. But Moet's voice was the match in a room full of gasoline. And she was done being polite.

Autumn stepped forward, her jaw tight. Her voice was steady, but deadly. "I see what this is. You're standing here acting like you got some high moral compass, because you know you were just the woman Amir settled for after he couldn't have what he wanted."

Moet recoiled, the swift, jerky movement of her eyes showing a direct hit.

Autumn's pulse drummed in her ears.

Something deep, dark, and long-silenced erupted, a fuse that had been lit long before this night.

It sparked the day Asia died, when grief and survivor's guilt hollowed her out and left her walking through life like a cracked version of herself.

It burned hotter with every betrayal from Chris, every time she swallowed his lies and made herself smaller to keep the peace.

It flared brighter when she lost the career she'd poured everything into and was left discarded by a company she'd bled for.

And through it all, she carried the guilt of wanting Amir too soon, too much.

Then came Ekon, his words slicing through her like glass, accusing her of being the very thing she despised: a user.

And now, here was Moet, standing at the end of that fuse, unaware she'd just stepped into a minefield.

Autumn didn't let her voice rise. She kept it low. Controlled. Glacial.

"You don't get to decide how I heal. You don't get to show up and make this about you. You say I should have shame? Nah, sis. Shame is watching a man be in love with someone else and pretending you don't see it, just to keep your ego intact. You're mad at me because you were just the placeholder."

Autumn felt strangely distant from herself, the adrenaline making the scene feel blurry at the edges, her own voice sounding like it was coming from far away.

She wasn't erupting just at Moet.

She was finally answering every moment she'd gone silent.

Her eyes glazed over like stone. "You were never a real part of this story. You were just reading from the script that was written for me."

Moet lurched forward, but Amir stepped in the middle, his voice a sharp, desperate bark. "Enough dammit!" he shouted, holding a hand between them like a shield. "Autumn, let it go. Moet, go home!"

Autumn was still breathing hard, eyes locked with Moet's, daring her to speak.

Moet scoffed, the pain behind her glare sharper than anything she'd spoken. "I should've known y'all were a package deal the moment I saw you," she muttered, backing away. "Enjoy your fucked up fairytale."

She turned on her heel, stilettos cracking loudly across the pavement like a punctuation.

Autumn lunged forward, but Amir's arm wrapped gently around her waist. "Let her go," he said quietly into her ear, steadying her.

She stood there, trembling, the adrenaline suddenly gone, leaving her hollow and shaking. The sheer weight of the night, of the fight, of the truth crashed down on her all at once.

And then—

The dam of sixteen years shattered.

Amir pulled her into his arms, and her knees buckled. A raw, guttural sound ripped from her chest, filled with pure, agonizing release as she sobbed loudly. Her body shook with the force of every feeling she'd ever buried—for Asia, for him, for the woman she was struggling to become. He just held her, one hand cradling the back of her head, the other holding her tight, absorbing every tremor.

They stood there under the lonely hum of a street lamp, two survivors clinging to each other in the wreckage of love and grief's aftermath.

* * *

THE STREETLIGHTS BLURRED past in streaks. Inside the car, silence hummed louder than the engine.

Autumn sat rigid in the passenger seat, staring out the window like the answers to her unraveling were etched in the night sky.

Amir's grip on the wheel was loose, but his jaw flexed. The heat from the confrontation still hung in the air, like smoke in a kitchen after something burned.

After several blocks of wordless tension, he asked, his tone calm, but heavy, "You okay?"

Autumn let out a short, bitter breath. "Do I look okay?"

He didn't answer. He just kept driving, giving her space, even when it cut him open.

"I mean..." she continued, still staring straight ahead. "What if she's right?"

"About what?" his voice was steady, but it had an edge now.

She turned toward him, eyes red-rimmed. "That I'm betraying my best friend. Because I crossed a line I can never uncross."

"What, we're not allowed to be happy now?" he snapped back, his knuckles tightening on the steering wheel as the calm finally cracked. "We mourned, Autumn. For years. We didn't sneak. We didn't cheat. We grieved. We grew. And now we're trying to figure out if this thing between us is real. That's not betrayal. Shit, that's life."

Her lips parted, his sudden, raw emotion jarring her from her own spiral.

After a minute of silence, she exhaled, her voice softer. "I stepped out of myself tonight. I think I went off because she hit a damn nerve. Several of them..."

She turned to face him again. "What are we doing, Amir? Are we sure this is right? Or are we just being selfish?"

He gave a slow nod, processing her words. Then he asked, "Do you want to end this? If so, say that. But don't let Moet's rage rewrite our truth."

He met her eyes briefly before turning back to focus on the road. "Look. Asia was my girlfriend when I was a damn kid. But you are with the man I am now."

A sharp, hot sting blurred her vision, but she blinked hard, refusing to let the tears fall.

"You notice how she barely said anything to you?" she whispered. "She specifically came for me."

"I don't know what that was about," he muttered.

"I do," her voice cracked. "I'm supposed to know better. I was Asia's friend."

"And I was her boyfriend, Autumn!" he fired back, his hand slapping the steering wheel with a sharp crack, pain bleeding into his tone. "So, what does that say about me? I'm not accountable?"

Autumn ran a hand across her forehead, then chewed the inside of her cheek. "If we're both questioning our accountability... maybe we shouldn't be doing this."

The car stopped in front of Mia's house, hard and fast. The porch light flicked on as if it were waiting.

Amir cut the engine. "Listen. I loved Asia. I really did. But loving her back then doesn't mean I owe her ghost more than I owe my own life now."

She didn't respond.

"Let's go inside," he said, his voice calmer. "We need to finish talking—"

She unbuckled quickly. "No. I need space. To think."

He went rigid, his hands still on the wheel. He stared straight ahead, then nodded once, a muscle in his jaw jumping.

She exited the car, slamming the door harder than she meant to. Her heels hit the pavement like a metronome—sharp, rhythmic, angry.

He didn't wait. The engine revved, an angry crescendo on the quiet block as the car sped off, his taillights shrinking into the dark.

Autumn stood on the porch, keys in hand, her breath caught somewhere between fury and despair.

The only sound was the distant hum of the streetlight and the frantic, deafening beat of her own heart.

* * *

THE NEXT MORNING, the sound of kids laughing echoed through the house as Jordan and Layla burst through the front door, sun-kissed and full of more stories from Disney World and the summer spent with their dad in Atlanta.

Autumn plastered on her best 'mom' smile, arms wrapping tight around her babies, burying her face in their hair like she could inhale joy through them. She'd missed them terribly, and their return couldn't have come at a better time.

The next few days blurred into a flurry of back-to-school errands. She dove headfirst into organizing closets, checking off supply lists, and booking last-minute hair appointments at Mia's salon and the barbershop. Every store run felt like a mission. Every car ride was a buffer between her thoughts and her feelings.

Because thinking meant remembering.

And remembering meant reliving the fight with Moet.

The explosive anger in the car between her and Amir.

The silence between them was deafening. A full week passed. Her phone, once a source of easy, constant connection, remained stubbornly dark.

She'd check it at night out of pure, anxious muscle memory, her thumb hovering over his name, before tossing the useless thing across the bed like it had betrayed her.

Until the following Monday morning, when it buzzed, making her heart do a stupid, hopeful flip. And then she read the single, simple message.

AMIR

Can you register Jordan for junior basketball league? I'll cover the fee.

No "Good morning." No "How are you?" No "Can we talk?"

Just straight business.

And it made her heart ache.

She stared at it for a long time, unsure if she should reply with a quick "*Sure*" or say something more, something soft.

So, she just locked her phone and pressed it to her chest.

This was what space looked like. And it hurt like hell.

Hours later, Asia's Ember was closed. The chairs were stacked, and the lights dimmed to a soft glow above the counter. The hum of the refrigerator was the only sound.

Autumn sat at one of the small tables, her phone face down in her palm, like a dead weight.

At first, she'd welcomed the silence, convincing herself it was a necessary pause. A chance to think about what they were doing after the Moet fiasco.

But space had turned into absence.

And absence turned to ache.

The shop's quiet wasn't peaceful. It was loud, filled with the taunting void he'd left behind, all set to the soundtrack of Babyface's "And Our Feelings" playing low through the Bluetooth.

This wasn't just a complication.

A hot, sharp pressure built behind her eyes. She squeezed them shut, pressing the heels of her hands against them until she saw stars. But the truth was still there when she opened her eyes again, bright and undeniable.

This was heartbreak.

She missed her man.

Missed his steadiness, his laugh, the way he could say something ridiculous to make her smile. Missed his hand on the small of her back when they walked, like it belonged there.

She picked up the phone, her thumb hovering over his contact.

Should she call? Just text "Hey"?

Or just wait?

The problem was, she didn't know the rules. This wasn't a game she knew how to play.

She'd never asked for space before and actually meant it.

She'd never been in love like this.

This wasn't dysfunction, wasn't chaos, wasn't her chasing scraps of affection.

This was mature love. Mutual love.

And yet here she was, completely unprepared for the kind of silence that didn't come from anger, but from trying to do the right thing.

What was the protocol for this kind of limbo?

How long do you wait when someone loves you right, but you're still not sure if it should be right now?

She set the phone down. A single, hot tear escaped her right eye, tracking a slow, angry path down her cheek. She wiped it away, the frustration more potent than the sadness.

"Damn you, Amir..." she whispered into the silence. "Why does this have to be so damn hard?"

Outside, the street lamp flickered once, a lone light in the dark.

Inside, she sat in stillness, her heart full of love, her hands empty of the one person she wanted to hold, and her soul completely, terrifyingly, uncertain of what to do next.

WHEN YOUR HEART KNOWS HOME

*L*ate Saturday morning. Mia's salon was locked down like sacred ground, closed to the public, open only to the ritual of shared sisterhood.

She had shuttered the doors to host the monthly Bag Lady session as a Pamper-Me Day to acknowledge the end of summer fun. There were no walk-ins and no distractions. Just the Ladies, their truths, and support.

The hum of hair dryers layered over 90s R&B, Mary J reminding the room she's *Just Fine.* The beat was low, but the message rang clear. It was resilience wrapped in rhythm.

Brianna lounged in her fuzzy slippers, wearing purple hair clips, sipping a strawberry mimosa like she was front row at a concert during brunch.

Londyn flipped through a fashion magazine, offering commentary whenever the spirit moved her.

Josie sat cool beneath the dryer, while Ms. Jenkins sat in the corner and massaged Royal Crown hair grease into her own scalp, humming now and then like a Southern church lady.

Autumn sat in one of the styling chairs, her legs crossed, watching Mia part another member's thick curls into clean, even rows.

"I saw her eyes before I even heard her voice," Autumn said as she held a cup of tea. She shook her head slightly, the memory of the parking lot fight still a fresh, uncomfortable sting. "Moet wasn't surprised to see us. Sis was already boiling. All I did was light the match."

"Girl, she mad 'cause she lost a good man to a real one," Brianna quipped, not looking up from the drink she was nursing. "And you are not in the wrong. She lied and told Amir it was cool, but when she saw y'all together, that cool shit went out the window."

"She called me desperate," Autumn said flatly.

Brianna gasped dramatically, clutching imaginary pearls. "Desperate?! That's big talk from a woman who ain't even been with him that long and having emotions like they got real history together."

"She also said I was betraying Asia."

Mia's parting comb stopped mid-way. Brianna's mimosa froze halfway to her lips. The only sound left was the low hum of Josie's dryer as all eyes instinctively flickered toward Londyn.

Londyn let out a sharp "tch." She held up a single, manicured hand, not even looking up from the hair magazine.

"Nope. I'm lettin' y'all handle this one. My thoughts'll just start a fire."

And with that, she deliberately turned the page, the crisp sound of the paper a final, dismissive punctuation mark.

Josie, who had been watching Londyn's reaction with annoyance, let out a matching "tch" of her own. She shot a hand up, palm flat in Londyn's direction, before deliberately turning her focus back to Autumn.

She lifted the dryer hood from over her head and leaned forward. "Girl. People in pain say things they normally wouldn't. But it doesn't matter. Amir chose you, Autumn. Not Moet. And Asia is not here to speak for herself, but in a way, she already did."

Autumn blinked. "What do you mean?"

"That dream you told us about? Sounds like a blessing to me."

Brianna gave a knowing wag of her finger. "I keep tellin' you that, baby. That girl spoke to you from the grave."

"Mmm hmm," Ms. Jenkins hummed, her voice cozy as a quilt. "You've done enough second-guessing. What does your spirit say, baby?"

Autumn didn't answer right away. She sat back, chewing the inside of her cheek, the familiar doubt clouding her expression.

Josie leaned forward. "Listen, if I had a man look at me the way Amir looks at you, I'd be out here singing *If This World Were Mine* like SZA and Kendrick."

Mia looked up. "Um, you mean Luther and Cheryl," she corrected with an attitude. "Folk always giving credit to the remake. Point to the original baby."

"Whatever," Josie shot back with a middle finger.

The room erupted in laughter, the sudden, welcome noise shattering the heaviness in the atmosphere.

Even Autumn let out a real, unforced laugh, the knot in her shoulders loosening just a fraction. "Y'all are something else."

"Yeah, we are," Mia responded, braiding hair with ease. "But you know we got you. Listen, lil sister. We all carry guilt, okay. But don't let it keep blocking your joy." She tossed a knowing wink. "*None* of your joy, if ya know what I mean."

Brianna's nosy radar activated like a beacon. "Wait, what you mean?"

Autumn couldn't help but grin as Mia's eyes asked permission to share with the sisterhood. "Go ahead," she relented.

Mia broke into a wide, devilish smirk. "Boyfriend's a 'talker'."

The words landed like a delicious bomb.

Brianna screamed, fanning her face with her hands. "Shut the damn front door! For real?"

Josie, from under the dryer, just let out a low, appreciative "Oooooh, shit."

Several other women in the circle erupted with a chorus of knowing groans, a few of them physically leaning in, suddenly desperate for every detail. Ms. Jenkins, however, just tilted her head, looking utterly baffled.

"What's a talker?" Jasmine asked, having just walked in to lead today's group session.

"Hey Doc!" the women greeted lovingly.

"Hey, everyone. What's a talker?" she repeated, her curiosity piqued by the explosive reaction.

Brianna leaned forward, her eyes wide with a mix of mischief and pure, unadulterated envy. "Oh, Doc," she sighed, like she was remembering something delectable. "A 'talker' ain't just some dude making noise when y'all are gettin' busy. A talker..." she fanned herself again, "that's a man who is telling you exactly what he's gonna do, what he wants you to do, and what you're doing to him."

Mia chimed in, not looking up from her braiding, her voice low. "It's a whole other level of intimacy, Doc. He's not just in your body; he's in your head."

Brianna cosigned, finishing like they were giving a sermon. "And it will ruin you for every silent man you meet after. 'Cause baby, that kind of climax is otherworldly."

Jasmine nodded slowly, a thoughtful smile on her face. "So, it's not just about arousal," she clarified. "It's about verbal intimacy. Being guided. Affirmed."

Even Londyn, who had been silent, suddenly waved her manicured hand in the air. "Yes, Lawd! Tell the truth!"

"And Amir takes me all the way there," Autumn confessed, a small, involuntary shiver running up her spine as she thought of him. "It's like... he's narrating my own pleasure back to me. He doesn't even have to touch me..."

Ms. Jenkins licked her lips. "Chile, I bet his fine ass don't, over there narrating orgasms like Morgan Freeman."

The room exploded, a wave of shrieks and laughter so loud, even Mia had to stop braiding to catch her breath.

Josie fanned herself dramatically. "Honey, a man who knows how to use his words *and* his tongue like that? That's not just sex. That's a whole anointing. That's that 'searchin' for him in the daytime with a flashlight' kind of power."

The room buzzed, a fresh wave of laughter, knowing looks, and appreciative groans passing between the women.

Autumn looked at her support circle. A real, easy smile spread on her face, despite the heaviness in her heart.

She still didn't have all the answers.

But here, surrounded by all this wisdom and humor... she finally felt safe enough to ask the questions.

An hour later, the vibe in the salon had settled into the rhythm of the Bag Lady session.

Autumn sat with her knees tucked beneath her, the plush Fix Your Crown salon robe wrapped around her, soft and comforting. A mimosa was untouched beside her. Her gaze went distant, fixed on nothing, her whole body still as she gathered her words after Jasmine called on her to share.

"After my divorce, I focused on chasing success," she began, her voice soft but clear. "Before the layoff, everything was about the next goal, the next role, the next promotion. I was grinding so hard I didn't even realize I was burning out."

She shifted in the chair. "I didn't know who I was outside of that hustle. I thought if I just kept pushing, I'd finally feel worthy. Like, if I collected enough wins, it would override the shame of not being able to keep my husband to myself."

She laughed ruefully, her head shaking slowly. "Then that damn 15-minute calendar invite popped up, upending everything, and the silence after it for those first few weeks was so loud. I didn't know what to do with it. No meetings. No deadlines. Just... me. Staring at myself in the mirror. And I didn't even recognize the woman looking back. Just a shell built for achievement. But my soul was gone."

Mia, who had transitioned to working on Brianna, twisted a strand of her hair, slow and deliberate. The women held a respectful, supportive silence, giving her the space to unpack.

"After that," Autumn continued, "it wasn't about a career anymore. It became about soul-searching. Like... What makes me laugh? What makes me cry? What do I want that has nothing to do with proving myself to anyone?"

Josie nodded slowly. "Self-discovery is a job in itself, honey."

Autumn met her gaze with a thin smile. "Dating Ekon was my way of exploring freedom, and that was exciting. No strings, no real pressure. Just vibes and cute outfits."

A ripple of knowing chuckles swept through the room.

"I'd never done that before. I married Chris right out of college, and we were together the whole four years before that. There was no real dating, you know? Then the kids came, and my life became about them."

The ladies nodded.

"I had some fun when I first moved back to Chicago. It felt like I got to experience what the young me should have been doing back then. Even DeMonte was fun... until it wasn't."

A chorus of soft "Mmhmm's" and "I know that's right" went around the circle.

"For a while, I just wanted to flirt, sip cocktails, and get cute with no emotional responsibilities. But none of that fed my spirit. And now?" she paused, her voice dipping as she sighed. "I want to love again. But I want it right. Not rushed. Not forced. Just... real."

Her confession settled over the room, bringing a thoughtful, gentle silence.

Mia, twisting the final coil on Brianna's head, looked up from her work. "Sounds like you've already found it, sis."

"Amir's the one," Brianna said, snapping her fingers.

"Yes, ma'am," Ms. Jenkins hummed.

A collective agreement sounded off across the shop.

"You were never searching for a man, Autumn," she continued. "You were searching for yourself. Love just happened to be the bonus."

Tears blurred Autumn's vision, but she blinked them back, just nodding.

Because it all finally made sense.

The sun was slanting through the blinds now, casting golden lines across the salon floor as the session wound down, the women moving through the gentle rhythm of clean-up. Empty glasses clinked in the sink. The hum of a diffuser filled the space with the calming scent of lemongrass and sage.

Autumn swept a few stray hair clippings from the floor, her movements slower now, more thoughtful than task-driven.

She felt lighter, somehow.

Maybe the confrontation with Moet was necessary. Maybe that raw, uncomfortable moment cracked open the guilt she'd been carrying and split it wide enough for her to see past it finally.

Asia wasn't here. But Autumn didn't believe for a second that her spirit wanted her to suffer through the rest of her life as penance.

Asia was love.

And love didn't begrudge happiness.

Not hers. Not Amir's.

She could still hear his voice in the car that last night, low and full of ache. "*I loved Asia. I really did. But loving her back then doesn't mean I owe her ghost more than I owe my own life now.*"

He was right.

As she hung the broom on the hook near the back room, Ms. Jenkins walked up and pulled her into a soft embrace.

"When your heart knows where home is…" she murmured, "… don't second-guess it. Just make sure it's a place you're ready to live in."

The women gathered by the front, slipping on their shoes, touching up gloss, the room still crackling with the energy of all the laughter, tears, and truth that had been shared.

Josie grabbed Autumn's hand. "You good, sis?"

"Getting there," she sighed.

Just as she turned to grab her purse, Brianna popped her hip with a dramatic flick of her hand. "Good. 'Cause honey…" she declared, loud enough for the entire room to hear, "… you and Amir go together like Peaches and Herb."

Even Londyn co-signed. "Like Michelle and Barack."

Josie pitched in, "Like Ashford and Simpson!"

Ms. Jenkins added, "Like Donny and Marie."

The salon went silent for one stunned second before the women erupted in perfect, comedic unison:

"Donny and Marie?!"

The ladies burst into laughter as Ms. Jenkins shrugged and waved them off. "Y'all don't know nothin' bout nothin'," she declared as she put on her light jacket.

Mia raised her flatirons like she was holding court, each word a verbal clap. "Girl! Go. Get. Yo. Man."

Autumn looked at her sister, a slow, quiet smile spreading across her face.

It wasn't a fully thought-out plan. But that look said, without guilt or hesitation, *and will.*

37

REAL LOVE STICKS

*L*ate Tuesday morning. The sky above Ebondale was a dull, washed-out gray mist curling over the streets like the city was mourning summer's end. Rain drizzled like the weather couldn't make up its mind, tapping against Autumn's windshield with no real conviction.

She parked beside Amir's Jeep in the empty lot outside the youth center, the engine idling while she sat with her thoughts.

She'd just left the kids' school. It was their first day. Lunches had been packed, hugs exchanged. Her heart should've felt full, buzzing with the proud, bittersweet energy of a new adventure for them.

Instead, it was just... hollow. A muted space where the joy should have been.

Grabbing the manila folder off the passenger seat, she stepped out and hurried to the door, arms tight against the cold drizzle. The front handle didn't budge.

A colorful poster on the glass read, "We are closed for programming prep. The center will re-open next Monday."

She rang the bell, doing a little shimmy as the chilly air wrapped around her bare legs, making her wish she'd worn more appropriate clothing for this weather.

But maybe all her choices were intentional today...

After a few seconds, Amir's voice crackled through the intercom, flat and distant.

"How can I help you?"

She hesitated. "It's me—Autumn. I came to drop off Jordan's registration form for basketball camp."

There was silence. Not long, but long enough to sting.

Then finally: *buzz.* Followed by a loud click as the door unlocked.

Inside, the building was dim and unusually quiet, the fluorescent lights humming softly overhead. The sound of her damp sandals peeling on the tile was an echo that felt obscenely loud in the silence.

A "Welcome Back!" banner hung above the front hallway, but the cheer of it felt almost sarcastic against the gloomy air.

She followed the faint sound of music toward his office. When she recognized the song, she almost stopped.

Dru Hill. *These Are The Times.*

Damn. That was his "break in case of emergency" song. His "dismal headspace" anthem. He'd played it for a month straight after Asia died. He played it after his mom's funeral.

He didn't just listen to this song; he wallowed in it. And hearing it now made a cold dread settle in her stomach.

When she made it to his office, Amir was standing in the center of the room, clipboard in hand, counting bins of supplies stacked neatly against the wall.

He didn't turn when she tapped gently on the doorframe, and the non-reaction was a small, sharp prick. She had to clear her throat before speaking.

"Hey," she offered a small smile.

He didn't meet it. The frown on his face was deep, almost distorting his features. He grabbed the remote and lowered the volume. "Good morning. You can leave the forms on the desk."

The coldness in his voice wasn't harsh.

It was worse.

It was business. A smooth, polished wall of indifference, and she felt the chill of it seep into her bones.

She blinked, then stepped in fully, placing the folder on the desk. In the dead, heavy silence, the slap of the manila folder on the wood was as sharp as a gavel's crack.

She tried to find a familiar rhythm, anything to melt the ice. "So... you ready for your seventy-five kids next week?" she asked lightly, her eyes scanning his, desperate for a sign that the man she knew was still in there.

"Yeah," he replied flatly, eyes stayed on the clipboard. "We'll be ready."

Another stretch of silence settled between them, this one heavier and more awkward than the last.

"You here alone?"

He nodded without looking up.

More silence.

But she didn't leave.

Finally, he looked at her, and for a moment, his pen paused mid-air.

Her hair framed her face in perfect, voluminous curls that now hit the top of her shoulders. The deep side part gave her a timeless, sultry edge. Gloss shimmered on her lips, matching the rose gold on her toes. Even the way she stood, one hand loosely at her side, the other clutching the hem of her denim jacket, was a declaration.

Of effort. Of intention.

He swallowed visibly, then caught himself.

"You look pretty," he acknowledged like he was reporting on the weather, then quickly returned to his task.

The words were formal. Polite even. But devoid of the weight they used to carry.

She hated it. Hated this cold, stubborn silence that followed, seeping into the air just like the mist outside.

"Amir." She spoke his name softly, her voice small, almost pleading.

He kept counting and writing on the clipboard. "Yes?"

Her voice finally shattered, raw and trembling. "Dammit, look at me!"

He went rigid, his shoulders hiking up to his ears. He tossed the clipboard onto his desk, the plastic clattering loudly against the wood in the quiet building.

He straightened to his full height, his eyes locking on hers, and he exhaled a sharp, angry breath.

"Okay," he said, hands on his hips, chest rising. "I'm looking."

He paused.

"But what am I looking at?"

"What's that supposed to mean?" Her eyebrows shot together. "You're looking at me."

"Yeah, but which version of you? You keep switching it up on me."

He wasn't being cruel, that much, she was sure. Now that she could see him—really see him, without the barrier of business and formality—she expected to see anger. Judgment. But that's not what was there. He just looked... bruised and barely held together.

His eyes were weary. Dark circles had formed underneath. His lips were set in a straight line, like all the joy had been drained from him.

She opened her mouth, but nothing came out.

"You're looking at me, Amir," she protested finally, her voice softer.

He shook his head slowly and took a deliberate step back, a physical barrier rising between them.

"Nah. I'm looking at someone who runs hot and cold. Someone who kisses me like she's crazy about me, then ghosts me like I'm an afterthought when somebody pushes her buttons."

"That's not what I did," she defended, her tone a little edgier now. "And you could've reached out to me, you know."

His eyebrows shot up. "You told me you needed space! So, I gave it to you. But a whole week, Autumn? Without so much as a text?"

A hot, sharp pressure built in her throat. She stepped closer, her words gentle but jagged.

"I was scared."

"Of me?" His eyes widened in disbelief.

"Of us. Of getting it wrong. Of not knowing how to do this."

He crossed his arms, muscles twitching beneath the fabric of his long-sleeved tee. "Then say *that*," he demanded, his voice raw with frustration. "Don't leave me in the dark and call it *thinking*."

"I didn't mean to—"

He cut her off, his voice sharp with fracture.

"What the hell do you want from me, Autumn?"

Her heart gave a hard, painful jolt. She faltered, a dozen excuses dying on her tongue.

She could lie.

Deflect.

Blame everything on the guilt. Chris. Asia. Fear.

But she didn't.

Autumn inhaled, then released a long, slow breath as she met his bruised, questioning gaze with a sudden, sharp clarity of her own.

She lifted her chin, eyes glossy.

"You," she proclaimed with finality.

He didn't move. His expression remained hard, his jaw tight. "Why?" he challenged.

The single word wasn't a question. It was a barrier. He wasn't going to make this easy. He needed more.

She steadied herself, her breath coming out in a long, slow stream.

"Because you're my best friend. You are the only person in this entire world who sees me. Who truly knows me."

Amir's eyes narrowed. As much as he knew her, she was just as adept at reading him. That answer wasn't enough. Not after the distance. The silence. The sting of it even being an option.

She stepped closer.

"I love you, Amir. As my friend. As..." Her voice caught, but she swallowed and pushed through—"as my man."

His eyes scanned her face, as if he were searching for a crack in the truth, his expression guarded—afraid to hope.

"You don't act like it," he retorted, his voice flat, devoid of the warmth she was expecting. "You say you love me, but you ran out when it got uncomfortable. That must be that corporate kind of love, where you throw it away when shit hits the fan." A muscle worked along his cheek. "Real love sticks."

The last three words hit like an indictment.

She recoiled, her hand instinctively pressing against her sternum. The accusation stung, and the old defensiveness flared up instantly.

"That's not fair—"

He held up a hand.

"But it's real. Listen, our situation is unique. Ain't no doubt about it. But it's our reality. We either accept it as is or we let it go. Period."

His eyes softened.

"I play games on the court with these kids. But I don't play when it comes to love. And you—" he jabbed a finger in the air toward her, "you let Moet's bitterness steer our ship. You didn't trust us enough to stand in it."

There was no defense. It was the truth. Hot, weary tears finally spilled over, tracing silent paths down her cheeks. She had no fight left.

"I was scared, okay?" she repeated, her voice hollow. "Scared of losing what we've started. Scared that if I leaned in, and it blew up..." she swallowed, "I wouldn't survive it."

He squeezed his eyes shut, his whole face tight with pain.

When he opened them, they were damp.

"So, what are you saying now?" his voice was raspy but direct. "You ready to try... again?"

He took a step closer.

"But be honest. If the guilt shows back up, if Asia's memory taps you on the shoulder, are you gonna freeze... again?"

She wanted to scream *No*. She wanted to promise him she would be fearless this time. But the lie wouldn't form. All the emotions were still there, a cold, heavy reminder in her gut, and the silence that answered him was a betrayal she couldn't stop.

He nodded slowly, a single, devastating movement.

"As much as I love you," he said, his voice thick, breaking under the weight of his words, "and I do love you, Aut—I have for a long-ass time—I can't do this back-and-forth. This..." he gestured between them, "this has to be solid. Or it has to be over."

Autumn's words were thick, clogged with the tears she was trying to swallow.

"So, what are you saying? That you don't want us anymore?"

His gaze held hers, his expression firm as he measured his response.

"I want you, baby. More than I've wanted anything in my life. But what I don't want is drama. I went through that when I was young. We're too grown for that. I sure as hell will not go through drama with the woman I love."

He turned and walked to the window, his back stiff, hands at his waist.

His words didn't push her away. But inside? They cracked her wide open.

And in that new, raw space, one thought rose, clear and absolute: *I am not leaving without him.*

Not this time. Not when she finally knew, with certainty, where her heart lived.

To her, Amir was home.

Finding herself had meant losing pieces to the puzzle first.

Now, it meant putting them back. Carefully. Intentionally.

And he wasn't just a piece; he was the one who made all the others fit.

The way he loved: quiet, but absolute.

The way he saw her, even when she didn't see herself.

The way he never made her feel like she had to earn safety.

She was more in love with him now, in this very moment, than she was when she left the house this morning.

The thought was so clear, so potent, it stole her breath.

She moved toward him slowly, closing the gap between them.

"Amir." Her voice was barely above a whisper. "I'm not running anymore."

He didn't turn around.

"I'm standing right here," she continued, her voice growing stronger. "Not because it's convenient. Not because it's safe. But because I love you. No matter what."

He was still facing away, but his shoulders were trembling, a tiny, involuntary shudder, and she could hear the ragged, uneven hitch of his breath.

He was unraveling.

Holding on to the last thread of pride.

Clutching caution like a shield.

She took one more step until there was no more space between them, her chest touching his back.

Her hand brushed his, and when he didn't pull away, she turned him gently to face her.

Amir's eyes, red-rimmed and raw with a pain she could clearly see, searched hers, as if looking for the fear that would send her running again.

But all he saw was her. Real, raw, and finally unflinching.

"I love you," she repeated, her voice breaking with the weight of it. "And not just when it's easy. I'll love you when it's messy, maddening, and yes, when I start to feel guilt, warranted or not."

He swallowed hard, his throat working. But he stayed silent.

"Say something," she whispered.

He didn't.

So, she kissed him.

Softly.

He resisted: lips tense, his jaw locked like a final, stubborn wall.

Her tongue slowly traced his lips, like a silent plea.

A low, guttural groan vibrated from his chest—the sound of surrender.

His hands, as if with a mind of their own, betrayed his resolve. One found the small of her back, the other tangled in her curls.

And then... he kissed her back. Deeply. Passionately.

They finally broke apart, gasping for air, their bodies shaking, their foreheads pressed together. His voice was rough.

"Don't do this if you don't mean it."

"I do. I mean every single word."

He squeezed his eyes shut, but it was useless. A single, hot tear escaped, sliding down his cheek. Then another.

"No more running, Aut."

"I'm not going anywhere, baby."

He kissed her again. It was urgent. Full of meaning. Like he was making up for every missed moment, every lost chance, every wall that had been built between them.

Autumn melted into him like she'd been waiting her whole life to exhale.

They only pulled apart when their lungs demanded it.

Amir rested his forehead against hers again. Their breaths tangled, hearts pounding like fists behind thin walls.

His voice was low, hoarse with want and warning. "If we do this..."

She nodded, fingers curled into the fabric of his shirt, holding tight.

He searched her face one last time for doubt.

"We do it for real," he said. " No more running. No more disappearing."

Her answer came through trembling breaths. "I'm all in, Amir."

His hands caressed her arms, then slid around her waist, pulling her closer until there was no space between them. Just bodies, truth, and trust.

He kissed her again and didn't stop as he moved, walking her backward, until the back of her knees hit the edge of the couch.

She fell back onto the cushions, and he went with her, his mouth still fused to hers.

As their tongues danced, the world dissolved. Nothing existed but the hush of the rain against the windows, the warmth of his body on hers.

Autumn's hands slid to his shoulders, her palms pressing flat with a slight push.

He understood the assignment.

Breaking the kiss, he wrapped an arm around her waist. In one fluid, powerful motion, he rolled them both, shifting his weight and pulling her up with him until she was straddling his lap.

Her arms wrapped around his neck, her breathing ragged. His hands gripped her hips, fingers splayed wide. As his hardness grew, the thick fabric of his joggers was a stark, welcome pressure against the softness of her silk panties.

They rocked in rhythm, grinding like their lives depended on the friction. The motion was slow at first, sizzling. Then, as the pressure built, Autumn's movements increased.

"Amir," she moaned, forehead resting against his.

"Yeah, baby," he rasped, voice thick, his whole body seizing with each hard thrust. "You must be there."

Her eyes squeezed shut as his hands guided her hips, matching her rhythm, pressing down with each stroke.

She wasn't prepared.

The buildup was overwhelming. The touch she'd craved, the safety she'd missed, the love she'd buried... it all crested at once.

"Amir!"

Her back arched, a sharp, involuntary jerk as a loud cry ripped from her throat, a raw, guttural, shattering sound.

The force of her climax rocked through him, and his own body answered with a desperate, involuntary thrust against the fabric separating them.

A low groan tore from his throat, a sound of pure, agonized restraint as his hands gripped her hips to anchor himself.

His jaw clenched. "Shit!" he yelled out, eyes locked on her, his control hanging by a thread.

Autumn's chest heaved, her eyes still closed. When she finally looked at him, dazed, glowing, and wrecked in the most beautiful way, he just shook his head and whispered again—

"Shit."

Then, he lifted and lay her down on the couch cushions, following right after her to cover her body with his.

He kissed her, then braced his weight on his forearms, their noses inches apart.

"Damn, I love you."

Before she could respond, he eased back just enough for his hands to find the waistband of her panties, sliding them down her legs.

She returned the favor, her hands shaking slightly as she fumbled with the drawstring of his joggers, pushing them and his briefs down his hips until he could kick them free. He helped pull her dress over her head.

He settled back over her, and they lay skin to skin, their gazes locked. Then, he lifted just slightly.

"Keep looking at me," he breathed, a sensual command she readily obeyed as she took his hardness in her hand, stroking him with a slow, knowing pressure that made his body jerk from pleasure.

He took her hands and held them above her head. Then, he entered her slowly, the feel of him finally inside her making her whine. He pulled out just as fast, a brutal, teasing retreat. She cried out.

"Amir—"

"Shhh," he whispered.

He entered her again, this time sinking deep. He gave three slow, agonizing thrusts before pulling out.

When he entered the last time, their pace immediately quickened, driven by urgency and something deeper than lust. Their eyes remained locked.

Autumn gasped as her second climax crested, sending Amir past the point of no return. His hands gripped her ass, anchoring them both as they cried out in a loud, mutual release, meeting the moment together.

This wasn't sex.

This was soul-binding.

In the stillness that followed, they stayed wrapped around each other. Fingers tangled. Legs twisted. Hearts finally at peace.

Amir pressed soft kisses to her temple, her jaw, her collarbone.

Then he rested his head against hers.

"We got this," he whispered.

Autumn let her eyes drift closed, tears of pure relief sliding into her hair.

Her voice was choked, but sure.

"We've always had it."

3 8

THE HARVEST AFTER THE FALL

*N*ine months later...

Morning light spilled through the front windows of Asia's Ember in soft golden ribbons, warming the polished floors and dancing across the neatly stacked mugs on the counter. Autumn stood just behind it, hands wrapped around her favorite ceramic cup. The one Layla had made in pottery class, complete with a slightly crooked handle and the faint imprint of a crown on the base.

She took a slow sip of her signature roast. It was nutty, smooth, with a whisper of cinnamon. She let it linger on her tongue before swallowing.

Around her, the coffeehouse began to stir to life: the hum of the espresso machine, the soft shuffle of chairs being arranged by her team, the faint laughter of a regular customer seated near the front window, talking on the phone.

This was her sanctuary.

Her peace.

Nearly a year had passed since she gave birth to this dream.

Twelve months of early mornings and late-night inventory runs. Of sore feet, sticky counters, staff meetings, and handwritten notes from grateful customers tucked into tip jars.

Her eyes drifted toward the photo wall above the pastry case. Right in

338

the center: a candid shot of her from opening day. Her apron slightly askew, a wide smile stretched over her face as she leaned across the counter to hand a customer their first cup. Mia had taken it when she wasn't looking. Because of course she had.

Autumn smiled softly at the thought of her sister. She could still hear her voice during that Bag Ladies session, could still feel the weight of those words:

"You weren't searching for a man. You were searching for yourself… love was the bonus."

She hadn't fully believed it then.

She was completely bought in now.

Because love had found her.

Amir had always been both her calm and her fire; her quiet when she needed grounding, her strength when she needed support.

No dramatics. No guessing. Just consistency. Accountability.

Safety.

A man who showed up. For her. For the kids. For the community they both loved.

E Block was thriving. What started as a neighborhood haven had become a true pillar of the community, recently featured on the local news for its work with teen mentorship. There was now a waitlist to get in, and some nights, with his head resting in her lap, he'd whisper dreams of opening a second location.

"Just dreaming out loud," he'd said.

But Autumn had seen it in his eyes; he was already drawing up blueprints in his mind.

The kids were flourishing, too. Layla was in honors math and had plans to start a kids' fashion vlog with her friends. Jordan was tearing up the junior basketball league and had declared, very seriously, that he wanted to coach like Amir when he grew up. Or, be a "money genius" like his dad.

"And if none of that works out, Mama," he told her over oatmeal, "I'll just make fire brand names for people and stuff."

There were still sibling squabbles, of course. Layla, now officially a preteen, had perfected an eye roll for every occasion.

Jordan, still in his silly phase, seemed to live for the sole purpose of pushing her buttons, usually by loudly declaring, "You're being so extra right now!"

But underneath it all, there was laughter. Growth. Stability.

With the city just beginning to stir beyond the fogged windows and her coffee still warm in her hands, Autumn stood quietly for a moment longer.

She closed her eyes and breathed deeply.

This...

This peaceful, steady, uncomplicated thing...

This is what home feels like.

Later that evening, the soft scent of mango butter wrapped the living room in warmth, mingling with the faint lavender drifting from Mia's diffuser.

Autumn sat wide-legged on the couch, a thick pillow on the floor between her feet where Layla rested, head tilted slightly as her mother parted, combed, and twisted her curls with slow, practiced hands.

The rhythm was familiar: greased fingers, clips snapping, the occasional wince, and "ouch" when the comb hit a knot. Layla's tablet cast a soft blue light on her face; her attention was fully locked into a video about teen skincare.

Autumn smiled at the image of her baby with a growing sense of self. She loved watching her bloom. And quietly, she grieved the fading of her 'little girl.'

Mia sat nearby, curled into the corner of the couch in a t-shirt and leggings, sipping from her oversized "Asia's Ember" branded mug. She was scrolling on a tablet quietly until Autumn spoke.

"It's been two years."

Mia glanced up, her eyebrows lifted in curiosity.

"Two years since I came back to Ebondale," Autumn continued. "Two years of couch crashing, co-parenting with Chris long distance, trying to figure out who I am again."

Mia set the mug down and leaned forward. "Girl, please. You didn't just figure it out, you built a whole damn business and healed half the women in this zip code with that soul-mending coffee."

They both chuckled.

Autumn paused, her hands stilling in Layla's hair.

"I think it's time," she said quietly.

Mia's brows creased. "Time for what, sis?"

She looked at her sister, her voice confident. "To get my own place."

A quiet moment settled between them. Mia blinked, then slowly nodded as the announcement sank in.

"Yeah," she whispered. "Yeah, I figured that was coming."

The silence was comfortable, but heavy with the unspoken emotion of her next step.

"You mad?" Autumn asked, gently starting the next twist.

"No," Mia sighed, but her voice cracked at the edge. "It's just... man. I finally got my sister with me. We made up for a lot of time. We've built some really good memories over these last two years. Even the chaos was fun."

Autumn snickered. "Like the fruit snacks war?"

Mia threw her head back. "Giiiirl! They turned this place into Chuck E. Cheese on steroids."

"They were wildin'," Autumn said through laughter. "Throwing gummies like they were dodgeballs."

"Running around, talkin' about 'This our house now!' like they paid rent," Mia added with a smirk. "Had my nerves shot trying to get that gooey crap out my carpet."

They laughed until their stomach ached.

Then, Autumn scanned the room; her eyes caught on the worn throw pillows, the framed Bag Ladies photo from her first session, the scuffed-up toy bin in the corner, the diffuser's steam curling toward the ceiling.

This space held her healing.

But it wasn't hers.

"I wouldn't have made it without you," she murmured.

Mia reached over and placed a warm hand on her knee. "Nah. You had it in you all along. I just gave you a soft place to land."

Autumn swallowed past the knot in her throat, nodding slowly as her fingers twisted the final coil and clipped it gently with a pink butterfly barrette.

Layla was dozing now, her head bobbing slightly, breaths slow and steady.

Autumn ran her hand over her daughter's crown, braids neat and shining. She smiled, then looked up at Mia with a new clarity in her eyes.

"This chapter's ending," she said, more to herself than anyone else. "But this new one... It's about to be on."

Mia smiled, her own eyes glistening with pride and a little sadness. "You ready for it?"

Autumn glanced down at Layla's sleeping face.

"Yeah," she said. "I'm more than ready."

* * *

One week later...

The hum of live smooth jazz floated through the coffeehouse, weaving between tables dressed in white linen and sunflower-filled vases. Balloons bobbed along the ceiling in warm tones of amber and copper, catching the golden-hour light pouring through the oversized windows.

The air smelled of roasted espresso, cinnamon, and pastries fresh from the oven—scents of comfort and celebration all wrapped into one.

A corner table overflowed with handwritten cards and bouquets. She saw one from Kendra and two more that surprised her.

One was from Ekon, his message simple and sincere: "Congratulations on your success. Wishing you continued prosperity."

The other, which almost brought a tear, was from DeMonte. The simple note, "I always knew you were a star," was so beautifully him.

A quiet sense of peace settled in her chest. These were full-circle moments she hadn't even known she needed.

Asia's Ember Coffeehouse was alive tonight, buzzing with hugs, laughter, and the clinking of glassware as the community celebrated its first anniversary with Autumn.

Earlier, the line had wrapped around the block. Now, inside, Autumn moved like sunlight, glowing in a deep crimson dress that hugged every curve with elegance and intention. Her curls were pinned in a loose crown, soft tendrils brushing her jaw.

She radiated ownership, confidence, and joy.

Layla, her mini twin, wore a matching junior version of the dress and presided proudly over the dessert table like a little hostess-in-training. Jordan, all dimples and energy, passed out mini "Jordacious Mocha Vibes" shots to guests with charming intensity, like the future mogul (or coach) he was.

A looping slideshow played on a nearby screen, featuring images from the past year: the "Coming Soon" banner, Bag Ladies Night photos, coffee tastings, and community events.

One photo drew smiles from everyone who passed by. It was Amir standing behind Autumn, his arms casually around her waist, both of them laughing with flour on their cheeks.

Autumn stepped up to a mic stand, her fingers instinctively brushing against the cool brass of the engraved plaque near the register: *In loving memory of Asia. You are the ember that lit this flame.* She felt a familiar, sweet ache in her chest, a reminder that all this joy was built on a foundation of profound love and loss.

She cleared her throat, her smile soft but steady as the room quieted.

"One year ago today," she began, "I stood in this space, scared out of my mind. I was doing something completely new. Betting on myself. And doing it all in the name of someone I loved dearly."

She paused to glance at the plaque.

"As you all know, Asia was my best friend. And we lost her seventeen years ago." She paused, biting back the sudden, hot swell of emotion. "She has been a constant presence, not only in this community, with that beautiful park named after her. But also, in my heart and in my life."

Her eyes landed on Mia, who smiled and blew a soft kiss of encouragement.

"This coffeehouse isn't just a business," she continued. "It's my second beginning. It's where I found courage. Peace. My people. And somewhere along the way..." Her eyes searched the crowd; past her friends, past the regulars, past her family, until they landed on Amir, standing in the back. He looked at her as if she were the only person in the room, his expression a storm of pride and love. "I found love, too."

Applause swelled, with a few whoops from the back and the sound of someone sniffling loudly near the front.

"Thank you all for being here and celebrating with us. Now please, eat, and drink plenty of coffee."

The crowd applauded again. Before she could walk away, Amir called out as he stepped forward, clearing his throat.

"The kids and I would like to present Autumn with a gift," he said to the crowd, giving Jordan a small nod.

Autumn blinked, surprised, as he and the kids joined her. She placed the mic in his outstretched hand, her smile beaming.

"Woman, you are the hardest working person I know," he praised. "That, on top of being an excellent mother, you still find time to give back to the community. We want you to know it does not go unnoticed. So, the kids and I tried to figure out the most appropriate gift to show how much we appreciate you."

The crowd clapped and smiled, with 'awwww's echoing around her.

In the corner, Jordan gave a silent thumbs-up before ducking behind the counter and emerging with a large box.

Layla joined them and presented the beautifully wrapped present. Autumn took it, a laugh already bubbling up as she started tearing off the paper.

When she opened it, there was another wrapped box inside.

The crowd laughed as she cast a wry look at the kids and Amir. Then, she unwrapped it, only to find a smaller box.

"Okay, y'all, not this tired trick," she warned as she tore into it. But this one wasn't empty, revealing four cruise tickets.

Autumn's jaw dropped. Her hand flew to her mouth as the kids draped their arms around her waist. "Oh my god... You guys!" she exclaimed.

"This is huge, y'all," she said to the crowd, holding the tickets up. "I've been saying I want to take a cruise for the last few months, so I'm glad somebody was listening to me."

The room laughed with her. Autumn turned to Amir to thank him, but he was no longer by her side. Her brow furrowed in confusion. She swung around... and saw him.

Kneeling on one knee, his eyes locking with hers.

The laughter in the room dissolved, replaced by a single, sharp gasp of anticipation. Autumn's own breath caught high in her chest.

Her mind, usually a frantic buzz of lists and plans, went utterly still. There was only the sight of him, her Amir, her anchor, looking up at her like she hung the stars and the moon.

"Two years ago," he began, "we were both standing in the same space. Uncertain, both still grieving, and trying to rebuild ourselves. You didn't just come back to Ebondale; you came back and reminded this whole community what it means to build something real. You reminded me what it feels like to love wholly, unconditionally."

He paused, his eyes suddenly damp, and cleared his throat.

"You once said you was afraid of getting this wrong. But you, and these beautiful kids... You all are everything right in my life. We started this journey as two broken people trying to find our footing. And look at us now. Standing on a foundation of love we built together."

He motioned to Jordan, who fished a small, black velvet box out of his pocket, a massive grin on his face. Amir took the box, opening it with slow reverence. Nestled in the velvet was a single, breathtaking fire opal, cut to catch the light and shimmer with all the colors of a glowing ember.

"Autumn Elise Gardener... you've been my best friend, my second chance, and the love of my life. Now, will you do me the profound honor of being my wife?"

A few stifled gasps rippled through the room, but she heard none of it. Her hands flew to her mouth as hot, uncontrollable tears finally spilled over, blurring the sight of him.

She nodded, laughing and crying as she let her emotions flow. "Yes. Yes, baby, I will."

The entire coffeehouse exploded.

Layla shrieked, fingers and thumbs connecting in the air. "She said yesssss!"

Jordan bounced in place, chanting, "Let's goooo!"

Amir slipped the ring onto Autumn's trembling finger and stood, pulling her into his arms as applause and cheers washed over them.

Their kiss was soft, sure, and laced with every broken promise that had finally been mended, every "almost" that had led them right here. She pulled back, her hand on his cheek, and saw her whole future reflected in his eyes.

This wasn't just a milestone moment. It was the end of the search.

It was home.

* * *

THE COFFEEHOUSE WAS QUIET NOW, its earlier electricity fading into the hush of night. The last glass had been washed. The music had softened to a mellow instrumental hum. Outside, the "Closed for Private Event" sign swayed gently in the breeze, catching the light like a final bow.

Autumn stood at the front window, arms draped around Layla and Jordan, both tucked against her sides, their faces sticky-cheeked and frosting-smeared. Their laughter was finally traded for sleep-heavy eyes and contented sighs. They leaned into her like they knew something bigger than celebration had happened tonight.

Outside, Ebondale rested beneath a canopy of golden streetlight and peace. Familiar sidewalks, paved streets, and thriving small businesses lit like beacons, all pulsing with the steady rhythm of community.

Autumn breathed it in.

Behind her came soft footsteps, then warmth.

Amir's arms wrapped around all three of them, completing the circle, anchoring them in stillness. His chin rested on her shoulder, breath syncing to hers without effort.

This was *their* rhythm now.

Not rushed.

Not perfect.

But steady.

She closed her eyes, letting the fullness settle in her chest.

Two years ago, she was broken. Starting over with shattered dreams and a bag full of pain.

Tonight, she stood inside the life she thought she'd lost.

Only to realize…

She'd been building it all along.

Her children.

Her business.

Her man.

Her peace.

Her purpose.

Autumn opened her eyes to the glow of Ebondale. This once-flawed, beautiful place that raised her, broke her, and built her again.

Her gaze softened. For years, she had been in search of Autumn.

Now, she was no longer looking.

Because she was already home.

The End.

ACKNOWLEDGMENTS

Writing a novel is truly a journey, and it is one I could not have completed alone. I am filled with immense gratitude for the many people who supported me and helped bring this story to life.

To my dedicated Beta readers: Thank you for lending your time and expertise to the early drafts of this novel. Your keen insights, thoughtful feedback, and honest critiques were invaluable. This story is significantly stronger and more polished because of your contributions.

To my wonderful ARC Team: Thank you for your incredible enthusiasm and partnership. Your dedication to reading on a deadline, catching those final details, and your willingness to champion this story mean more to me than words can express.

To my beloved family and friends: Your endless love and encouragement have been my constant motivation. Thank you for listening to countless plot ideas, for uplifting me during moments of doubt, and for your unwavering patience and support through this entire process.

And finally, to my incredible husband. You are my rock. Thank you for your steadfast support, your endless patience through the late nights and early mornings, and for being my greatest cheerleader. I could not have done this without you. This journey, and all its rewards, belong to us.

ABOUT THE AUTHOR

I've often been called an accomplished woman with a story that's as remarkable as it is inspiring. I was born and raised on the south side of Chicago, where I faced relentless bullying as a child. In part, because of this, I was shy and withdrawn, but that experience also sparked my creative side. I found solace in the world of books and writing, where I could escape, explore and create new worlds.

In 1980, when I was just ten years old, I hand wrote a thirty-page novel on notebook paper and sent it to Harlequin Books. Along with it, I included a heartfelt letter about my dream of becoming an author to uplift my family from poverty. Although the submission was rejected, the personal response I received ignited a fire in me—a determination to one day see my name in print.

Life, however, had its own plans. Despite excelling in school, my home life was anything but easy. By the time I was 21, I was a single mother of three, living on welfare after dropping out of school to care for my children. But I refused to let my circumstances define me. I fought through the walls of depression and self-blame, working tirelessly to achieve economic self-sufficiency. Having accomplished that goal, at the age of 46, I fulfilled a promise to my late mother by earning a bachelor's degree in education, becoming the first in my immediate family to do so.

No matter my life's journey, my passion for writing never wavered. In 2006, I self-published my first novel, *Ain't Understandin' Mellow?* and followed it up in 2007 with a contribution to the anthology *The Shattered Glass Effect*. My memoir, *Ruby Slippers: Fairy Tales My Mother Told Me, Real Life Truths I Never Told Her,* was released in 2013, offering a deeply personal glimpse into my life. After a hiatus following the tragic loss of my younger brother in 2018, I'm back with my latest novel, *The Bag Ladies of Ebondale.*

Together with my husband, I founded ScribeRite Publishing LLC, a testament to my unwavering commitment to storytelling and my mission to inspire others through my words.

But my passion goes beyond the pages of my books. For 24 years, I worked in the social service field, helping low-income residents access essential services and developing programs that nurtured the esteem and creativity of at-risk youth. Among my proudest achievements were mock trials and short film productions that gave these young people a voice and a platform. I expanded my creative horizons by writing and co-producing a short film, *Roses Out of Concrete,* shot in the very Bronzeville community where I grew up.

After earning my degree in 2016, I made a bold career shift into corporate America, landing a role with one of the largest retailers in the world where I still use my voice to champion for the community.

When I'm not working or weaving stories, I love nothing more than spending time with my family and friends, especially my beloved grandchildren. My husband and I share a Pomeranian named Bruno Mars, who, much like his namesake, is always ready to steal the show.

I hope everyone who reads my journey sees it as a testament to resilience, creativity, and the unbreakable spirit that has turned life's challenges into stories that uplift and inspire.

Want to learn more? Follow me on social media!

www.michelledavisnewell.com

The BAG
LADIES
of Ebondale
INSECURITY
TRAUMA
ABUSE
SELF DOUBT
FIX YOUR CROWN
BOOK ONE IN THE EBONDALE COLLECTION
BY AWARD-WINNING AUTHOR
MICHELLE DAVIS-NEWELL